Also by Regina O'Melveny

Blue Wolves: Poems and Assemblages
Fireflies: Poems

The Book
of
Madness
and Cures

Regina O'Melveny

JOHN MURRAY

First published in Great Britain in 2012 by John Murray (Publishers)
An Hachette UK Company

First published in paperback in 2013

1

Lines from *Purgatorio* by Dante Aligheri, translated by W. S. Merwin, copyright © by
W. S. Merwin. Used by permission of Alfred A. Knopf, a division of Random House, Inc.

Lines from capitolo 24 by Veronica Franco in chapter 5, "The Courtesan in Exile," from *The
Honest Courtesan, Veronica Franco, Citizen and Writer in Sixteenth-Ventury Venice*, translated
by Margaret Rosenthal, © 1992. Used by permission from the University of Chicago Press.

Lines from Ovid's *Metamorphoses*, translated by A. D. Melville (1998), "The Doctrines of
Pythagorus," p.335, XV, Lines 103–105, used by permission of Oxford University Press.

Facsimile map from *The Mercator of Europe* © Walking Tree Press.
Reproduced with permission.

Inset map by G. W. Ward

A CIP catalogue record for this title is available from the British Library

B format ISBN 978-1-84854-707-0
Ebook ISBN 978-1-84854-708-7

Typeset in Bembo by Palimpsest Book Production Limited, Falkirk, Stirlingshire

Printed and bound by Clays Ltd, St Ives plc

John Murray policy is to use papers that are natural, renewable and recyclable
products and made from wood grown in sustainable forests. The logging and
manufacturing processes are expected to conform to the environmental
regulations of the country of origin.

John Murray (Publishers)
338 Euston Road
London NW1 3BH

www.johnmurray.co.uk

For Bill and Adrienne

Contents

CONTENTS

Nullaque iam tellus,
nullus mihi permanet aër,
Incola ceu nusquam,
sic sum peregrinus ubique.

No land now, no air
is constant for me.
Because I dwell nowhere,
I'm a pilgrim everywhere.

—*Petrarch*

Le aque sta via ani e mesi, e po' le
torna ai so paesi.

The waters vanish for months and
years and then return to their home.
—*Sixteenth-century Venetian*
proverb

That which wounds, shall heal.
—*Attributed to the oracle of Apollo*

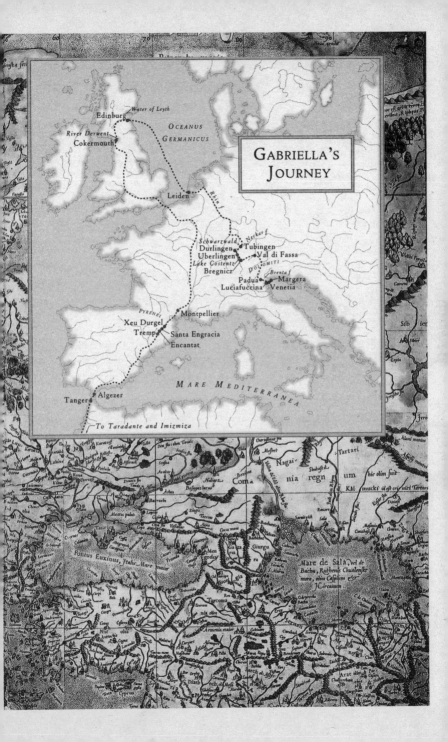

GABRIELLA'S
JOURNEY

Edinburg
Water of Leyth
River Derwent
Cokermouth
OCEANUS
GERMANICUS
Leiden
Rhil
Schwarzwald
Durlingen Tubingen
Uberlingen Val di Fassa
Lake Costentz
Bregnicz DOLOMITI
Brenta f
Padua Margera
Luciafuccina Venetia
Neckar f
PYRENEI
Montpellier
Xeu Durgel
Treemp
Santa Engracia
Encantat
MARE MEDITERRANEA
Tanger Algezer
To Taradante and Imizmiza

The Book
of
Madness
and Cures

Prologue

"I don't know where my own body begins or ends," said the young girl of Imizmiza. Her mother had summoned me, the only woman physician within hundreds of miles, to tend her twelve-year-old daughter, who suffered the grave consequences of corporeal confusion. The girl sat at a cedar table near a narrow window in the red earthen house. She told me, through a dark veil that flickered as she spoke, that she sensed the fear of entrapment that the tethered horse knew in the field. His visible breath pulsed in the cold air as he drew the rope taut, while the groom approached, currycomb in hand. She told me, "The man who strokes the horse with five different brushes in strict order of succession, the man with a head like the knot

1

at the end of a rope, he is smaller than my thumb—" And then she laughed suddenly, surprising me.

Before I could puzzle this out, her mother approached us and chided, "Come, Lalla, put on your riding skirts. You're taking the horse out today."

The girl stared at the plank table where her left arm lay with the grain, her right arm resting bent against it. She whispered, "I'm too heavy today, I can't move."

And though she made an effort, she couldn't budge.

When I placed my hand upon the wood lightly, as if touching the fuzzy scalp of an infant, she sighed and closed her eyes. When I removed my hand, she sensed it immediately. I tried to lift her arms from the table but she was rigid. Later, inclined by some inner urging, she separated herself and wandered as if in a trance, when at last her mother could direct her to her beloved horse or to her bed for an afternoon nap.

Wherever Lalla stopped, she became part of the thing she touched. When she rode her walleyed and snorting animal, she sweated like a horse. Froth gathered at her lips and neck. When she slept, she might not wake for days, for the bed itself was her motionless body. Meals were the most difficult. She refused whatever food she touched, confessing a horror of eating her own flesh. Though her mother fed her like a babe with a small wooden spoon, she grew thinner and thinner.

At length I suggested a slow cure. I would need the assistance of her mother and aunt—though the aunt, a large, choleric woman, obstinately insisted that Lalla was not in need of curing, and certainly (she glared, scrutinizing my face and my dress) not by a foreigner. The girl simply possessed a clairvoyant body, the aunt said, challenging me. "We mustn't take away the girl's talent."

2

"The girl doesn't have command of her own life! One must stand apart in order to truly know another," I said.

Lalla's mother, a small, dark mountain of a woman, also veiled, asked, "Will she be able to marry and bear children?"

"I don't know," I confessed.

The cure, then, consisted of words. I advised her mother to name her hand, to name the distaff upon the table, and the table itself. When I came to visit, I'd ask Lalla, "Where is your arm, your hand, your hip?" Sometimes she could answer and point to that part of her body. Other days she regarded me with a kind of panic, as if she didn't understand my question and feared terrifying penalties for this. I touched her hand, and then her mother or aunt would repeat the word for hand, to calm her. Gradually she responded with more and more movement until her ability to unfasten herself from her surroundings was accompanied by a kind of plaintive joy. For separation meant that she had changed and that the unknown surged forward to meet her.

I've since come to believe that the world is populated by multitudes of women sitting at windows, inseparable from their surroundings. I myself spent many hours at a window on the Zattere, waiting for my father's return, waiting for my life to appear like one of those great ships that came to harbor, broad sails filled with the wind of providence. I didn't know then that during those fugitive hours beneath the influence of the damp moon, I was already plotting my future in pursuit of the past. I'd grown transparent as the glass through which I peered, dangerously invisible even to myself. It was then I knew I must set my life in motion or I would disappear.

CHAPTER 1

❧

God's Work or the Devil's Machinations

Venetia, 1590

From the foreign marks and characters in diverse hands and languages upon the sheet of paper that enclosed it, I could see that my father's present letter had traveled, a lost communiqué, through many of the cities on his route. It had been nearly a year since I'd heard from him. All told, he'd been gone since August of 1580. Olmina, once my nursemaid and now my servant, had slipped the letter lightly on my desk that stifling July afternoon. She may as well have released a viper that gives no warning before it strikes.

"If my mother reads this, you know she'll twist it into some kind of offense, no matter what it contains," I warned, tapping the closed letter nervously on my palm as we stood in my shuttered room, the summer tides slopping noisily on the stones below my window, the warm stench of brine stinging the air. Poor Mamma. She'd always perceived the world to be against her. Happiness was never to be trusted. And yet, I thought vaguely, neither was sorrow. Didn't each come to season in the other? Sometimes our Venetia gleamed a miraculous city on the summer sea, and later during the winter *acqua alta,* she sank into cheerless facade. Then the floods engendered spring. Someday she might all be submerged, a dark siren whose lamplit eyes have gone out. Yet others might see beauty there where we walked in the place become water.

"Don't worry, Signorina Gabriella." Olmina pressed a fore-finger beside her broad peasant's nose, a sign that she knew how to keep a secret. Her pale blue eyes glinted in the dim light, though I'd seen those same lively eyes turn dull as slate when she was questioned by my needling mother.

"I don't think she's even missed him these ten years."

"Ah, signorina. She seems to yearn for the role of widow . . ."

"So true, dear Olmina. But even there she's unsuccessful. She'd have to give up her luxuries and frippery." Though I often sensed a sad futility under her frivolous pursuits. There was more to her, perhaps, than I knew. I'd often seen a fear without cause flickering across her face. If she were a widow, she could wear it more openly, even though the source was still obscure.

"Well, if you don't mind"—Olmina rolled her hands within her linen skirts, nodding, her gray hair poking out from under her pale, unraveling scarf—"I've a stack of dishes to wash in the scullery and my own luxury of a nap waiting for me at the end of that." She grinned and then stumped down the stairs, her short, formidable figure still strong in middle age.

As I stared at the unopened letter, I thought of the ways my life had shrunk since the departure of my father ten years ago. I didn't dream of many things anymore, of traveling to distant countries, even with the rare — though ever declining — freedom I could claim as a woman doctor. As we say in Venetia, the world comes to us to beg favor, and I consoled myself with this. Still I could see even now my father's kindly yet remote ash-brown eyes, his raven-and-carmine robes, and as I held his letter, a small voice that had long been silent within me spoke. *Let me accompany you, Papà. Don't leave me behind.*

His previous letter had arrived last year from Scotia, where he expressed his vague intention of traveling even farther north to collect the powdered horn of the unicorn fish, a cure against lethargy. Or perhaps south to the torrid clime of Mauritania or Barbaria, where he might find the rare bezoar stone that takes all sadness into its density and renders lunacy its wisdom. As with the arrival of all his letters over the years, I had marveled at these cures, at the riches his medicine chest must contain by now — and wished deeply to see them for myself, to acquire them for my own. But his words hid something I couldn't quite name, though they crept like sighs under my breath. Words like *lethargy, bezoar, sadness.*

I broke the red waxen seal of the letter, which clearly had already been opened several times, the Mondini crest obliterated and then reaffixed. I could make out the smudged name of Tübingen below it, though not in my father's hand. Was this the city of origin or had it been forwarded or returned there by mistake? How many strangers had read his letter? Looking for evidence of heresy? Surely they were disappointed. As I shook its contents out upon my desk, a single sheet of bone-white paper unfolded. My father's usual courtesies were absent and his scratchy handwriting appeared labored.

> *Gabriella,*
>
> *You may have denounced me or given me up for dead. I cannot justify what has happened any more than I can explain the friction that underlies the harmonious rotations of the spheres. It would be too simple to say, God's work or the devil's machinations. I will not be returning and it will be the better for you. I now entirely prefer my own company to that of others. The days perplex my will and yet I have become a perpetual traveler. Do not blame yourself, as you are wont to do. Above all do not send after me.*
>
> *December*
> *Your father, E. B. Mondini*

I let out a long breath.

Then a heat rose in me. Even though my blue room, lit by the slatted green window, gave cooler refuge than most other rooms in our villa on the canal, I felt that I was burning underwater.

After some time, when I folded the missive, I caught a faint whiff of rose attar, my mother's favored scent. Had she already read my father's words, or had this essential oil traveled all the way from Mauritania?

I stood up, withdrew from my bodice a chain that held a key warmed by my body, and moved to the foot of my bed.

The cassone (once meant for my dowry) now concealed the packets of my father's letters and could only be unlocked by this key. I turned it and the catch sprang open. The letters were organized in order of arrival rather than creation, because lately I couldn't tell when he'd penned them. The exact dates no longer appeared on the last few letters. They'd arrived close together but seemed to come from cities as distant from one another as Almodóvar and Edenburg. Had he simply forgotten to note the date? Sometimes the day and month were there, but not the year. Sometimes he wrote only, *Winter.* And because the letters were entrusted to different couriers, from the princes of Thurn and Taxis's messengers to traveling merchants, pilgrims, and doctors who'd undertaken scholarly journeys, their dates of arrival were useless in determining his whereabouts at that moment. His words described a meander through Europe that had finally — until today — vanished in silence. My father had become a voice out of time.

A quick, rustling footfall outside my half-open door alerted me to my mother. I slammed the cassone shut, briskly locked it, and fumbled the key back into my blouse.

My plump mother entered in some disarray, her violet red-lined dressing gown flapping about her shoulders, her long, pointed slippers down at the heel though fashionably slashed with many small cuts to reveal the blue beneath purple leather. She came and stood very close to me, setting her green eyes anxiously upon mine.

"So? What did he say?" Her yellow hair (a shocked white at the roots) fell about her face.

I stepped back. "What are you talking about?"

"The messenger left a letter with Olmina." She waved her

white hands. "I followed her and stood outside your door listening to a most charming conversation."

For the love of the Virgin . . . "I'm a thirty-year-old woman, a doctor who deserves some privacy and respect." I spoke calmly but clenched both fists at my sides. Though accustomed to my mother's petulance, I also felt slivers of panic driven under her words. She didn't want to be cast aside. Sometimes I forgot that my father had left both of us.

"What does he *say?* Is he returning home, that profligate husband of mine?" She grew more shrill.

"No," I said. "In fact, it seems he's never coming back."

She brought up a hand as if to strike me, or was it to protect herself? Then she let it fall to her side. For a moment her dejection clenched me. My mother, who'd always loomed large, shrank to a troubled child.

We stared at one another.

Olmina appeared on the landing behind her, hands still dripping with dishwater (for she'd rushed up to my room the minute she'd heard the commotion). She shook her head. "Come, Signora Alessandra," she murmured to calm my mother. Olmina touched her elbow but my mother stepped back, crying, "Your hands are wet!" as she pushed past her, descending the staircase in a tumult.

"We live on the water," I said after she'd gone, "and she fears a drop."

"Oh, we know it's not just the water." Olmina shrugged. "She can't bear the touch of the tide, any hint of change, you know. When one has known too much early on, then any change is a threat."

I nodded, recalling the swift rot and death of her father from the plague of 1575. Though a young woman of fifteen, I hadn't been permitted to say good-bye to my grandfather. My father and mother didn't want me to see him so disfigured (it was all right to view a patient but not one's kin), and so, oddly, he remained well in my mind, then gone. But my mother had witnessed his end and somehow she was never done with it. We didn't ever speak of him.

Olmina added, "I'm sorry, signorina. I didn't think your mother saw me when the messenger came." She dried her hands vigorously now on the stained brown topskirt that was folded up into her waistband.

"It's not your fault," I said. "Olmina, remember Signor Venerio lo Grato? Married to the same woman for fifty-one years. He wanted to mend her distrust, I suppose, with his kindness, though it never seemed to be enough. Then one day he took his slow stroll along the canal, and when he returned he stood at the bottom of their stairs shouting, '*Finito. Finito.* I'm done — do you understand?' And he left her. They say a spring returned to his step."

She smiled and said, "Yes — his unreasonably bitter wife now had something to be bitter about. I hear he went to live alone on one of the outer islands. Hmm, he was such a handsome youth, those fine calves and thighs . . ."

Then Olmina came over to hug me. "Don't mind her fits. She's as regular a squawker as the crows, as Lorenzo likes to say." Lorenzo was Olmina's husband, a man who usually kept such comments to himself. I laughed a little at his foolishness. I wished it were that simple.

~⚜~

When Olmina ushered the gentleman from the Physicians' Guild into our courtyard later that day, I'd just awoken to the bells of evening rebounding back and forth across Venetia. One belfry set up a clanging, then another started up slightly off pitch, and others followed until a resonant din shook the air and rang the grogginess from my head. My book of poetry by Veronica Franco lay open on the bench to the passage

> *Nor does virtue reside in bodily strength,*
> *but in the vigor of the soul and in the mind,*
> *through which all things are known.*

I sat up on the bench in the courtyard where I'd been napping, and parted the low branches of pomegranate. There he stood, Dottor Orazio di Zirondi. His ample paunch advertised his wealth. I noted the black robe, the chains of gold and silver, and his doughy hand laden with rings. I quickly gathered my thick hair back into the net from which it had fallen, though I still must have appeared untidy. Out of the corner of my eye I could see my mother sitting in the shade of the wall, fanning herself above the lacy leaves of rue. "Ah, there you are, Signorina Mondini." He bowed slightly in my direction, his round face like a poorly kneaded loaf.

"Come and sit over here, dear Dottor. Olmina will bring us some lemon water," my mother said. "You can join us, Gabriella."

"Thank you, signora. Very kind, but I have business with your daughter, a communiqué from the Guild of Physicians. Then I regret to say that I must be on my way."

My mother snapped her fan shut.

I stood up and faced the doctor. "What is it the good doctors wish to tell me?"

"Dear signorina—"

"You may call me Dottoressa Mondini."

"You cannot expect me to do that, my dear. The title belongs to your father."

"Ah." I was starting to suspect why they had sent Dottor Zirondi instead of my friend Dottor Camazarin. "I detect the reek of some scheme—"

"Gabriella! I never taught you this lack of civility," my mother said, stepping forward to touch his sleeve. "Please excuse her, Dottor Zirondi."

The man sighed and narrowed his eyes. His gaze flitted uncertainly between the two of us, trying to discern what ancient rivalry he'd interrupted. Then he went on. "Given that it's been a decade since the departure of your father from this serene city, and especially now that no one has heard a word from him for the past two years . . . the guild . . . the Council of the Guild of Physicians can no longer support your membership without the mentorship of your father. We have allowed this to go on too long. Women physicians, as you well know, are not permitted. I am sorry. The guild is sorry. But this is by order of the council." He gave a peremptory little bow, nodded meekly at my mother, and excused himself.

"Wait!" I cried. "What about the women, my patients?"

He gave me a cool glance. "The women will be looked after, signorina. Have you forgotten the many excellent doctors we have here in Venetia?"

Though the guild had restricted my practice to women after my father departed, then forbidden me to attend their

12

meetings, I didn't believe that they would expel me altogether. I thought about the young courtesan five months gone and spotting blood (who would tend her during her pregnancy without scorning her for her profession — as some male doctors were known to do?) or the old wife who suffered from chronic catarrh and a drunkard husband who refused to pay for her herbs. I tried to keep my voice level, to maintain my composure. "But they are men. And most women much prefer a woman. Surely, sir, you would want your wife to be looked after by a woman, rather than some prying man, professional though he may be?"

Zirondi sighed. "My wife is in excellent health and I would look after her myself."

"What about those women who have no doctor as husband, who are sometimes"— I paused —"examined overmuch, if you take my meaning?"

He shot me a look of disdain. "Signorina, you are insulting my colleagues. I'll listen to no more of this. Good day to you both." And he swiftly left the courtyard.

After a moment, my mother turned back to glare at me. "See?" she said quietly, snapping open her fan. "This is all the result of your insolence."

I couldn't bear to look at her or surely I'd say something I'd regret that would fuel our long-standing dispute over my decision to work as a doctor. How my mother loved the spice of quarrel! I had no wish to feed her anger. Instead I stalked into the kitchen and found Olmina at the table cutting an onion. She dropped her knife when she saw my face. "Walk with me," I said.

She quickly drew a shawl about her shoulders and took my

arm. We walked past my mother, still fanning herself in the courtyard, and left the house to pace the slippery, water-stained stones at the edge of the sea until night forced us indoors. When at last I returned to my room, I reread my father's letter repeatedly. *No*, I wanted to tell him, *it will not be the better for me if you don't return. I'll lose my vocation. And it will not be the better for you.* For I could detect in his words that something was off. *The days perplex my will and yet I have become a perpetual traveler . . . Above all do not send after me.* It barely seemed that my own father was speaking.

I will not send after you, my father, I decided that evening. *I will come myself.*

CHAPTER 2

❧

Salt and Sweet,
Tears and Milk

When I last saw my father, in my twentieth year, he was pacing uneasily near the tall open windows in his study. "I'm planning a journey north," he'd announced abruptly, his broad back to me as he pulled a book bound in red maroquin from the shelf of his voluminous library. "I'll be gone for some time." His black hair, speckled with gray, hung damply about his neck in the noonday heat. "I won't be able to take you with me."

He turned and peered at me with hard, indiscernible eyes through round black-rimmed spectacles, holding *The Book of Diseases* like a small shield and then setting it down upon his slanted desk. As I hesitated to respond, clutching my hands within the pale blue folds of my skirts, he moved closer to the window, his pointed slippers hissing on the smooth terrazzo floor. He removed his jerkin and tossed it on the windowsill, then leaned forward in his linen shirt and claret breeches as if to catch a cooling breeze from the lagoon. None was forthcoming.

I couldn't find my voice, though I nodded and stared at the reading wheel, which stood at least two meters high, opposite him on the other side of the window. The upright circular device resembled one of those pleasure wheels seen at fairs, hung with little seats (in this case, lecterns) that revolve with much shrieking from the children. It awaited completion by Agostino Ramelli, my father's friend and an architect of rare literary machines.

"Gabriella. Is that silence of yours . . . impudence or assent?" my father asked, clasping his hands resolutely behind his back. He would often carry his hands this way, in the manner of men who walk through the city, pondering the silent stones or the rumor of water that lies beneath them.

I shrugged. The air grew closer around us, and though I suffered the heat, I withdrew into a dry, cold temper. I moved toward the reading wheel, edgily tapping one of the larch spokes and setting it in lopsided motion. The oak axle creaked and three small lecterns swung to and fro. There would be eight when it was done.

My father glared at me briefly. Then he sighed, not unkindly, looking back to the sluggish sea. The wheel, motionless now, resembled a large clockwork arrested by neglect. As if the great hub of the sun, to which all other cycles were bound, had lapsed in the sky. The wheel anticipated my father's volumes on diseases. But his work had come to an unforeseen halt in the universal malaise of August.

"What about Ramelli's wheel, Papà?" I asked in a pinched voice. "Don't you want to see it finished? Won't you complete *The Book of Diseases*?"

He groaned. He'd been unwell lately and endured a bitter humor. For months I'd devoted time every day to copying his nearly illegible, rapidly scrawled notes on diseases and cures, occasionally taking liberties with those phrases I couldn't understand and inserting my own. He gently berated me on that account, though he was reluctant to take the time to clarify his intent. So I continued with my own interpretations and simply didn't show them to him, compiling my own parallel encyclopedia—a mute companion to my father's volume—which I kept in my chest.

Across the broad canal the gray-green island of the Giudecca shimmered dully in the heat. Thunderclouds lurched upward and sideways, lending their leaden color to the sea and their implausible dead weight to the air.

I spoke again. "You know that I'm your best nurse and scribe. Let me accompany you, Papà. I don't flinch from a wound; why would I fear a journey?" I placed my hand gently on his thick shoulder. It still conveyed some of the strength of his youth. At that moment one of the great trading vessels slid into view, its sails slack in the windless afternoon.

"I've no need for an assistant now. I'll simply be gathering more notes."

I removed my hand, leaving a faint, clammy print on his shirt. "But surely you'll be called upon as a doctor? Who will suture the wounds for you? You know I employ the finest stitch." It was true, though my hands were rather large and coarse for a woman of my class. What I left unsaid was the

17

fact that his hands were no longer as steady as they had once been. "And the strands of my hair provide the best thread."

My father once told me affectionately that my wiry red hairs were stronger than threads of linen.

But he shook his head now and placed both arms upon the marble sill, as if struggling to steady his resolve. We watched the mullet fishermen standing in black gondolas upon the water, heard the fletched sound of their arrows stinging the air. How I loved to stand by him in quiet observation of the world. He was my spyglass and magnifying lens, my kind instructor and stern doctor. We witnessed the mingling of cruelty and cure in disease, the loss that redeemed itself in healing and also the loss that never ended. My father possessed no other children and so he had always shared the gifts that were destined for a son with his daughter.

From this distance, the fishermen were almost stationary, planted on a solid gray surface, the tilting of their boats imperceptible. The black cormorants that surrounded them stood out with the certainty of inked type rising from the flat bed of the sea as if they were spelling out the letters of a word. The illusion of *I* (swallowing fish), *S* (at rest), *T* (wings outstretched to catch the sunlight). Was it *istante, istanza, istmo?* The illusion slipped away when the birds plunged into the water after a stricken fish. From time to time the fishermen struck at the cormorants with poles, oars, nets, or whatever was at hand. The rattle of oars against rowlocks and the cries of the birds disturbed me. My throat tightened suddenly, as if I would cry like a little girl.

"Daughter," my father finally said, "there will be no discussion on this matter." He didn't turn from the window and improbably addressed the air. "You must look after your mother. Your earnings will be hers as well, though I'm leaving ample gold behind to keep the two of you for years. My bags are packed. I need your assistance now in replenishing my medicine chest."

"I'm occupied this afternoon," I answered sharply, considering the irascible charge—my mother—being hefted on me. Would she appreciate me finally if I were her support? I doubted it. I clasped my hands upon my stomach. "I have to clean the lancets. We agreed to assist Dr. Torrigiano with a bloodletting while the moon is still in the second quarter, or have you forgotten?"

"You'll have to go in my place," muttered my father. "I must attend to the final details of my departure."

What caused this hasty decision? Or had change formed slowly in the alembic of his discontent?

> We were still beside the edge of the sea
> like people who are thinking about their journey
> who in their hearts go and their bodies stay

I murmured these lines from *Purgatorio* more to myself than to my father. Still I wanted him to answer me in the old comradely way, but when he just stood at the window in silence, I did not repeat myself.

The next morning my father slipped away while I slept, without any leave-taking. Though he rose early, he must have been exhausted from the quarrel with my mother the night before.

"Don't tell me what to do!" I'd heard his voice late at night, roaring through the house.

"Why would I try? You've never listened to me," she said glumly. "All that matters to you is that dusty volume of ailments. Yet you fail to cure your own foul temper!"

"You understand nothing, woman!" The floor shook above me as my father strode back and forth in their chamber.

"You understand less! I've tried to hold this household together for the sake of your profession and our little family. But you're a specter to me, always locked up in your study or out on your rounds. And now you're going to leave altogether?"

"If it weren't for my daughter and my peers, I'd have left long ago."

"She's my daughter too."

"She may be your flesh, but she isn't your daughter."

I couldn't hear my mother gasp, but I felt it from the vast intake of silence that sucked all the air from our house for an immeasurable length of time.

Now I began my preparations for my own journey. But my mother suspected that something was afoot. Though it was time to retire, she paced the corridor and after a few turns pushed open the door to my room without knocking. She swiftly took in the scene of my satchel and clothing spread out upon the bed, my medicine chest open, and papers scattered across my desk, and she understood.

"Oh," she said, her face reddening in the warm light of the candles. "You're going to abandon me. Just as your father did."

When I ignored her, she added, "Go ahead, waste your fortune, Gabriella. But don't expect a dowry when you return."

I stopped my packing, stung by her insinuation (my lack of marriage prospects). "Mamma," I finally said. "My dowry is here"—I held out my hands—"and here"—I tapped my forehead.

She walked over to my window and peered out past the shutter at the city's faint lights smoldering in windows, faltering on the water. "Oh, I see, yes—that will serve you well when you encounter a suitor. I can't wait to hear what he'll say." She turned back to face me in frustration. "Or rather what he won't say, when he disappears quick as a quenched flame." She pressed both hands to her heart. "I want you to be content, Gabriella. Bear children. Why not marry a good doctor? Why must you *be* one?" Tears started to her eyes, for we'd had this conversation many times before and I'd left the room. But this time I simply stared at her, fierce and speechless with hurt. We were on opposite sides of a deep channel, no bridge between us. The sea ran on in the dark. She dropped her eyes and began to pace again back and forth the full length of my floor, heels clicking marble and then going mute across the wide Ciprian carpet.

We heard a sputtering and both of us swung to the open doorway. My mother's gaunt young maidservant hovered nervously with a guttered candle, hooded by a large shadow in the corridor behind her. "Your bed is turned, my lady," ventured Milena. She fidgeted, rubbing her skeletal neck with her free hand, her long fingers strangely delicate.

I sighed and said, "I'm not abandoning you, Mamma. I will find your husband and make our family whole again."

I spoke with willful sincerity, as if I could claim the distant harmony from childhood, if I hadn't imagined it in the way a child will construct peace out of necessity. I pushed my extra skirts and blouses down into the leather satchel with my fists to make room for more clothing, to counter my mother's rancor.

She touched my shoulder. "Gabriella. Don't leave. I . . . I need you here."

I'd never heard my mother say those words. Without looking at her, I answered, "Mamma. My mind and heart are set on this."

My mother, for once, fell silent. Then she left me.

My mother also left me the day I became a woman. I was thirteen and undressing for bed with Olmina's help, under my mother's watchful gaze—a rare occasion. She'd been instructing me as to what gown I should wear for an upcoming wedding when Olmina cried out happily as she tugged my chemise over my head. The dark red streak on my garment announced the change. I hadn't even sensed it, though now I felt a vague thrill and confusion. She laid the chemise tenderly on the bed. I hugged my sleeping smock to my body, shivering. Tears sprang to Olmina's eyes—but my mother froze.

"You're no longer a girl!" she moaned, as if it were an unforeseen calamity. She must have observed my distress at her words, for then she said, "It's only the beginning of desires you'll never quell, my daughter. The end of simple pastimes." She must have been speaking of her own change, for had she forgotten that I assisted my father in his work and engaged in few simple pastimes? That I'd observed disease and death? But she didn't wish to hear of those things. She bit her lip and fled the room. My body had betrayed her dream of me and it could not be taken back. Salt water had seeped into the well. I no longer belonged to her, if ever I had.

Olmina, not my mother, taught me how to use the sea sponge, how to tie it up under my smock with a silk ribbon (once round my waist, between the legs, then fastened to the waistband) to catch the flow. My mother never spoke of it again.

Late the next afternoon, I continued packing, taking my father's letters and a small bottle full of ashes from the chest to pack in my satchel.

The previous November, I'd returned from tending an ailing friend to find the letters from my beloved Maurizio (twelve years dead of tertian fever) cast upon the grate, glowing packets of ash, with the string that bound them a hot and shrinking vein. I thought of the fine blue veins beneath his temples, which I'd liked to kiss. His cheek. The perfect cowrie of his ear.

"If you don't rid yourself of the past, you'll never possess a life in the present!" my mother had exclaimed as she stood near the charred letters. "I did it for you. Love wants a scorched field for the new seeds to take. Otherwise you'll never find a husband."

I'd clasped the fire shovel with such force that she stepped backward in fear and fell against the kitchen table, crying out for her maidservant. I could have struck her. But I turned away to scoop the ashes from the hearth. Later, when I was alone, I poured them gently through a parchment cone into a bottle that I keep in my medicine chest. What a small heap of ashes for so many letters! My lover's words weighed no more than a few breaths. My father's letters wouldn't follow such a fate. I planned to deliver all but a few into the hands of a dear friend, Dr. Cardano, for safekeeping on the first leg of my journey.

Soon, I heard a flamboyant voice from downstairs. It was Cousin Lavinia, who wanted to bid me farewell, for I'd sent her a message by way of Lorenzo.

"Come up to my chamber," I called out. My mother, not one to miss a conversation, followed her on the stairs.

Lavinia cut a messy figure in the streets of Venetia, for she loved drawing, and as a girl, she reveled with me in copying the various bones and skulls my father kept in his study. "What's this one, Dottor Mondini?" she'd cry out to him as he wrote at his desk. And though he'd feign annoyance, he usually answered her questions with a smile—questions that I was often too reticent to ask, preferring instead to consult the Vesalius *Epitome*. Often he'd put down his quill and watch us for a while, as if it gave him great joy. Lavinia studied the bones' forms for the art of beauty while I learned their names and contours for the art of physick. Thus we often kept each other company on long afternoons in our separate worship of bones.

"Gabriella, you're really leaving?" she asked. I recalled former visits, Lavinia with rolls of paper under her arm and charcoal stubs in her pockets, the dust smeared on her hands, arms, face, and clothing. Today she was merely out of breath, for—though I envied her ripe beauty—her ample body often slowed her down. My own body, neither full nor thin, seemed ordinary by comparison. She turned briefly to greet my mother, who chided, "My dear, I'd greatly appreciate it if you could resuscitate my daughter's reason."

"Ah, you should know better, Signora Mondini," Lavinia teased, "than to ask me to restore her senses, when you've often decried me as lacking my own!"

But my mother was in no humor to smile in reply. Instead she looked down, brooding, as if there beneath the floor in the shifting island mud there might be a god to answer her prayer, to bind a mother and daughter. But finding no answer, she clutched her skirts and left my room.

"So?" Lavinia kissed me on each cheek expectantly.

"Yes, it's true." We sat together on my bed. "I've resolved to find my father, to bring him back, and to help him complete his encyclopedia, *The Book of Diseases*."

"But won't it be dangerous?"

"Staying here may be more dangerous," I said, placing my pale hand over hers, with its habitually blackened nails, now also flecked with pigments. She'd been painting with egg tempera. "I'm slowly being smothered, by the guild, by Mamma . . ."

She nodded. "I'd heard from my mother that guild members condemned your use of certain herbs when the men were in my father's shop. These rumors stew when you have a gaggle of doctors waiting for their remedies to be measured by my father's fumbling apprentice."

"Why didn't you tell me?"

"I wanted to protect you. And I thought it idle complaint. After all this time, why would they sever your membership?"

"The reason given was that I lack a mentor."

"That's nonsense. There must be a dearth of new patients,

so they plucked a reason out of the ether that fills their poor brain-pans."

I laughed and said, "Well, now I can seek my way in the larger world. I'll visit those cities renowned for their universities of medicine and garner letters of recommendation — how will the guild refuse me then?"

"Yes, Gabriella. You'll practice your art." She set a brave face. "Just as I will practice mine. But what about other languages — how will you speak?"

"It will be small worry. Many speak our melodious tongue. And my French and English are fair, since I've had occasion over the years to practice with foreign physicians at our table."

"Where will you go?"

"Come, I'll show you." I led her to my desk. "There, and there." I moved my finger tentatively along one of many possible routes I planned on my Mercator map. The candle flame stood absolutely still in the evening torpor. She bent to watch me.

"See? Beyond Padua the great centers of medicine in Europe beckon: Leiden, Edenburg, Montpellier. And Tübingen, where my father's last letter was recently marked."

"But why not stay with Dr. Cardano and write to these other universities for news of your father? Otherwise aren't you striking out at great risk, into the unknown?"

I barely heard her and instead spoke the names of the cities again in a low voice. My breath quickened, my heart and mind leapt far ahead of me. I glanced toward the open door to the corridor and quickly stepped across my room to shut it. "Lavinia, I *want* the unknown." I touched the map, its paper softening to a kind of flesh in the hot, damp air.

She stared at me in astonishment and then flushed with the

pleasure of understanding. "I almost wish that I could go with you."

"Come, then!"

"No, I could never leave Venetia. I don't hunger for the journey as you do."

She hugged me impulsively and rushed from the room, her black hair loosening from her snood as it fell on the stairs, her coarse linen work dress rustling stiffly.

"Lavinia!" I cried, picking up the ecru snood. I ran to my window but barely glimpsed her form as she turned the corner near Campo Sant'Agnese. I held the snood for a moment with affection, then pressed it down among my things in the satchel.

The following morning I listened to Olmina knock her wooden clogs about the stones of the Zattere as she paced in irritation. Her singsong voice called up to my window from the narrow wharf. "How long must we wait, signorina?"

And then: "Dottoressa Gabriella, the gondolas are ready!"

Her impatience was born of reluctance. When I asked her and Lorenzo to accompany me on the journey, she'd pleaded, "Let us stay, Gabriella. The journey does not bode well. I smell a corpse in the future." But she was always casting *tarocchi* cards and predicting ruin, so I paid her no mind. She continued, "We should be patient and await your father's return. For sooner or later the city will pull him back to her embrace, no?" She didn't want to leave her city—the city that rose from the silt of salt marsh, the city that rocked upon the tides like a marvel run aground.

Olmina had ordered my life since birth. A few months before my arrival, her own child had been stillborn, its head wrapped with the caul (a sign of second sight, a talent never to be realized), and so she took me to her breast as a babe; I suckled both salt and sweet, tears and milk. Over the years, she'd protected me from my mother, who'd refused to nurse me, for as a young maiden of only fifteen, she was frightened, I suppose, of what had happened to her body. She didn't take to mothering easily. And her own mother, a lay healer falsely imprisoned on charges of witchcraft, wasn't there to tend her. Even now Mamma would tell me, "Oh, Gabriella, I wept when you were born! Your head emerged so misshapen, I thought I'd brought forth a changeling!"

There were a few early years when Mamma amused herself with me as one would with a doll. She dressed me up in uncomfortable frocks. She twisted my damp red hair into ringlets around her finger. She placed me on a cushion before one of the windows so that I could watch the ships on the canal, dusted my face with white powder, and told me not to move when her friends came over to talk and preen. But I remember a day shortly after my third birthday when I didn't listen. It had drizzled for weeks. Olmina gave me my own bowl of chestnut dough to form dumplings. I squatted on a rug on the kitchen floor (though mostly I just clenched the dough in my little fists with delight and squeezed out bits and pieces). My mother bent over me, firmly holding my arms as if she could fix me to the floor, and said, "Stay here, do you understand? Do not leave this rug, or monsters will come out of the cellar!" But if there were monsters in the cellar, I wasn't sure I wanted to stay in our house.

While Olmina rolled the dumplings on the thick table with her back to me, and my mother pulled up a chair and dozed before the cooking hearth, I slipped away, determined to explore the wharf before our house. I hastily put on my child's cape and woolen cap, and pushing open the door Lorenzo had left ajar when he went out that morning, I tumbled out into the day. The rain had paused, the ships rocked like houses afloat, and I squealed with joy at my freedom, running along the stones to the edge of the water. Merchants stared at me, two nuns asked me where my mother was, sailors sang loudly and waved, and a lady with her servingwoman reprimanded me harshly when I bumped into them. I found a cat with three legs under a bench. I tasted a bit of bread that had fallen on the stones, then spit it out again. I clutched the beautiful damask skirts of a woman in purple who laughed at me and asked me my name. The wind hurt my ears. All at once the dark cloud of my mother descended. "Don't you ever do this to me again!" she shouted as she yanked me along the stones, my feet flying off the Zattere at intervals. She locked me in her closet. "I'll confine you to this place from now on, do you hear?"

After sobbing quietly for a while, I fell asleep. Sometime later in the uncertain dusk of that place I awoke beneath a boned farthingale, as if within the rib cage of a great sea creature. In my dense imagining, my mother became a leviathan. I rocked back and forth beneath the ribs of the beast. She couldn't harm me there, because I was hiding within her. Or so I imagined when Olmina came jangling her ring of skeleton keys to fetch me for supper.

Olmina knew all the secrets of our household, which is why my mother refrained from throwing her out, lest she directly feed the ravenous ear of Venetia, which thrived upon the misfortunes of others. It was Olmina who later, when I attended university, urged me to hide my medical writings, which I promptly did, behind the lesser medical texts that my father rarely consulted. My mother seldom entered his study and had to ask for the key, as my father knew full well her jealous habit of stealing into his papers and shuffling the pages. "Materia medica is your mistress," she'd say when she was upset. He took the keys with him when he left, citing fears that his rivals might try to steal his writings or his books, though perhaps he was truly wrestling with the rivals within.

For months I suffered my father's absence twice over: the lack of his presence and the dearth of his written words. I became so disturbed by the locked room that I considered ways to break and enter, with the clandestine help of a locksmith (though I knew it wouldn't remain secret for long) or by breaking a window with a stone and enlisting the help of a glassmaker as an excuse to go inside using a ladder (though that would be very suspicious, and ridiculous too—bedecked woman doctor swaying upon ladder). Of course these schemes were only a distraction. Some essential part had been stricken from me. But in one of his early letters to me from Padua in the fall of 1580, he had a change of heart.

And in the hub of the reading wheel that we removed to your room before I left, you'll find a central round peg that, unlike its fellow on the other side, may easily be pulled out. In the small hollow there, you'll find an extra key to the study. Keep this key, then, for it was yours originally anyway, dear Gabriella. Under no circumstances lend it to anyone. Lock yourself in when you visit the study, so that no one may guess the room has been opened, and enter only with caution, when no one is at home.

I trust you'll continue your studies and writings on diseases, which I may join to my own when I return. Who knows but one day you will outstrip my own research and inquiries into the vast nature of the maladies that beset us. This is the duty you have to your elders, to complete what they cannot . . . even perhaps to complete the healing that they cannot or choose not to pursue.

I was glad to have access to the study, though after a while my joy carried a bitter aftertaste. As the years passed, my father's study stood in our home like a strange mausoleum to his absence. I entered from time to time to read and to wipe the shelves and tables, which accumulated dust that fell from I know not where (since the windows and doors were always closed), unless it was the brief dust of the world I brought in with me. I also spoke with his ghost—a peculiar thing to say, I know, when a man is still alive. But that is how it was. *Papà, where are you now? What cures are you working? I have a patient suffering languishment, and all the usual simples have failed to quicken her. What must I do?*

I never wrote there at his desk, though, because I didn't want to disturb his things. If I left everything as it had been when he went away, perhaps that unchanging order would hasten his return. But of course nothing was changeless. The ink curled and dried in its pot. Minuscule insects consumed the quills. Webs shrouded the books.

By contrast, I kept the windows of my own room open in nearly every weather. On this day of departure, I gazed across the small side canal at a winged lion of mottled stone with a lifted paw, dispassionate as a saint. He'd inhabited that outlook for my entire life. Sometimes cats slept beneath his mossy stone chest, multiplying his remote expression while the dim mirror of water below overturned him. In the Rialto Market they sold palm-size lions carved in jasper alleged to cure fever and dispel poison, and some carved in garnet, cure-alls and amulets against the dangers of travel. Though I barely believed in such things, I'd purchased one.

The narrow corridor below my third-story room was still pooled in shadow despite the advance of morning. I could see a thin ribbon of sea, the San Vio surging into the swash of the Canale della Giudecca, which joined in turn the Canal Grande di San Marco, then the tides of the lagoon, and finally the open Adriatic. When I breathed in the smell of sea from below my window, I could also detect the metallic scent of ice, the source. Rivers and mountains.

A muffled knock at my door.

I opened it to see Lorenzo, Olmina's short, wiry husband, who brought me back to matters at hand.

"Dottoressa, please, Olmina is pulling my beard! We must reach Padua by evening. All the leather bags and provisions are loaded, everything except your medicine chest."

Lorenzo had also joined our household when I was born, his eyes and skin the color of dark shellac, as if he were a man made of wood. He was born in Pinoa, and his mountain dialect gave him a halting speech and manner, like one of those exotic creatures merchants bring back from their travels: Numidians and their dromedaries, or listless Barbary apes. Lorenzo often complained about the moods of the Adriatic. "Just give me terra firma, Tirolia, instead of this city ruled by moon and mud, where our lives are as sloppy as the sea!"

Olmina always defended Venetia (this was the fray and habit of their marriage): "If it weren't for this city, La Serenissima, we would be griming about in some frozen hut, our feet wrapped in last year's straw, staring out at your beautiful mountains. That's firm land for you. Have you forgotten your toes?"

Three of Lorenzo's toes had gone char black from frostbite and had to be severed when he was a child. He always stuffed the right foot of his brown stockings with wads of wool to compensate for the gap, after plucking burrs from the rough fleece. "La Serenissima!" Lorenzo would repeat sulkily and spit into the sea. He was phlegmy and possessed of a cold, overmoist nature.

Now I closed and firmly latched the dark green shutters on my window for the last time. "Thank you, Lorenzo," I told him. "I'm coming. I was just leaving my devotions." Even as I excused myself in this way, I thought of the old proverb: *Where there are three physicians, there are two atheists.*

Lorenzo grinned, as if he'd overheard my thoughts.

I clasped the twin dolphin handles of my oak medicine chest, and refusing Lorenzo's help (I always carry it myself, wary of the influence of others upon the medicaments), I descended the cramped stairs.

"Mamma?" I called out.

I was greeted with silence. Lorenzo stepped back as I called out her name again, this time adding a farewell.

From the cool recesses of the house, her voice shot out through the corridors. "Now I will be free to enjoy my life!" Her bluster didn't fool me.

Again, I said, "Farewell!" I wanted to say, *Be well, Mamma.*

Be content, but my throat closed and my mouth tasted brackish. The old salt of grief was in it.

There was no reply. Silence dropped like a heavy plumb in my belly, which tightened against it. Against weeping. Despite having endured her swerves of mind and heart for years, I still wanted my mother's blessing.

Once I was outside, the sun's glare, multiplied by the water, struck me full on.

"Finalmente!" Olmina glowered in the bow of the pitching gondola.

I stepped into the stern, followed by Lorenzo, and was thrown unceremoniously forward as I flung the chest down with a thud in the center. I chose the seat facing backward, to see the house I was leaving. The faded ocher walls stood discolored by the sea, gray and green at the foundations as if the building itself were a decaying body. Bricks the hue of dried blood were exposed near the water where the plaster had fallen away. The weathered doors, toothed from rot at the bottom, remained closed. Was it possible that I hadn't noticed the decline of my family's home until just now?

Yet other houses were in decline too or crutched with scaffolding in restoration. As we slid through the calm water to the steady dip, pull, lift, drip of the oar, I watched the Zattere retreat, then San Marco appear beyond the other bell towers, steeples, canted roofs, the other quarters shabby, mossy, glorious, gleaming, prayerful, lively, sorrowful, muted, exuberant, fleshy, fabulous, then diminished—made one by distance, faint, flat, bluish white, thin as gauze I might use to wrap a wound.

The gondola swayed, and I lifted the satchel of my father's

letters to my lap. Though I knew I'd packed them earlier, I checked again—they were all inside, tied neatly in bundles.

I watched my home recede for the last time. Every faraway window was shuttered against the heat but one. No hand parted a curtain there. No visible face watched us go.

CHAPTER 3

~⚜~

Dr. Cardano's House

The fields on the road to Padua shimmered with ripening millet, and an army of cicadas steadily drilled the air. As a curious little girl I'd once brought my father a handful of perfectly split cicada husks and asked what happened to their bodies rent asunder at the highest pitch of summer. Did they turn into small scorched spirits? Did the spirits then chafe the air in heaven? My father had smiled at these questions. *Gabriella,* he teased, *they sing until they burst!*

We approached Margera in the gondola after little more than an hour, just as the midday bells began to ring out. My uncle Ubaldo awaited us on the small wooden dock and led us to the animals: five mules and his own horse, Orfeo, a fine black

Murgese. Orfeo gleamed darkly in the noonday sun and jostled the mules, which stood nearly as high as he did.

"Gabriella!" My uncle clasped my arm, and through my sleeve I could feel the calluses from ironmongery on his hand. "Aunt Cecilia is very disappointed that you're not stopping at our home. What's the hurry after all these years?"

"It's restlessness unbottled at last, dear Uncle. I don't want to linger at the outset of the journey, and I'm anxious to cross the mountains."

I leaned forward for a hasty farewell kiss, first on one cheek and then the other, as Lorenzo finished outfitting the mules with our supplies. How odd it was to say good-bye to the near image of the man for whom I was searching!

After riding sidesaddle for a short distance, I grew uncomfortable, and against Olmina's protests I unfurled my linen skirts and rode astride my horse (the way my uncle had taught me many summers before). What a relief! In future I vowed to wear breeches beneath my skirts in the style of Venetian courtesans. I'd packed just such a pair of fine women's breeches for relaxing when skirts felt too oppressive, and now I had another purpose for them. The luxury of damask would serve as riding garment.

Behind me the walls of Venetia — her palazzi, *scuole,* churches, and convents, her infinite exquisite and horrific prisons — blurred with the swampy sea. She was truly a strange theater. For as much as travelers glorified her beauty and wealth, the delicious, insubstantial semblances she put on, I knew her as substantial, weighted, and hard. Stones, bricks, pilings driven into the clay. She stood against the vaporous and mutable sea that was always trying to claim her, and the best she could do was to withstand it, to toy with it for a while. Venetia, a dense accretion of lives, announced the solidity of those lives in a broad villa or narrowing passageway. In stone lions, parapets, and empire. But the water was always there. Much has been made of the city and her looking glass. But sometimes I thought she was a flawed and dull glass (what is glass after all, but sand?) trying to reflect the water without much success. How could our edifices, how could we, in these poor, troubled bodies, cast light?

As we traveled farther away, the city dimmed even more. The men of the Physicians' Guild and their jealousies lost their edge. The tightening noose of their injunctions against my practice lost its threat. I began to feel free of them, able to work my skills upon whoever was in need of my help along our journey.

I'd already resolved to pursue notes on diseases completely unknown to those most esteemed doctors of the guild. My father would be glad of that. In a letter from Leiden in the spring of 1581, he wrote:

I grow frustrated with my notes at times and have failed to appreciate, perhaps, the good degree of your help in these matters. However did you unravel my thoughts, my girl? I think that maybe your unusual position as a woman in this profession allowed you a certain winding approach that, while appearing childish at the outset, proved more effective than my sharpened intelligence at times. I recall when you brushed the hair of the furry girl, drawing her out of her closet, rather than directly assessing the amount of hair on her body and its obstruction of her life. We were better able to suggest a situation for her, though her parents wouldn't hear of it. In short, I miss your sinuous logic. Together we make the finer doctor. But alas, the world does not welcome women to this role. Yet I keep you as muse, though you are distant, as you must be.

How many hundreds of miles would we have to travel? Every mile was a thousand steps, *mille,* according to the ancient Romans. Olmina sniffled softly as we rode, but Lorenzo was gleeful. "Stop that noise, woman, we are going to see the world!"

"There is no world outside of Venetia," she said.

"We will carry our world with us, dear Olmina," I reassured her.

"It seems that we *are,*" complained Lorenzo under his breath, annoyed at the necessity of three pack mules for our leather bags and provisions.

"Lontan da casa sua, vicino a qualche disgrazia," Olmina warned. *Far from home, closer to misfortune.*

"*O Dio mio,* we cannot live by fear alone!" Lorenzo said, and then he slapped the rump of his mule to escape us.

We both began to laugh at the odd sight of his ruffled thatch of gray hair and short, bony limbs and body jouncing down the dry road.

Later we were no longer amused when the dust settled upon us like grimy flour. *You're going to regret this journey, Gabriella, for it will only bring hardship!* my mother had warned. We'd only begun, and already my ungloved hands were swollen in the heat as I wiped the grit from my face with a small lace-fringed handkerchief and drew the veil down from my broad straw hat.

We were silent as we passed through the small village of Luciafuccina. No one was about. Undoubtedly they were eating the midday meal in the fields or within the cool of their houses, shuttered tightly against the heat and mosquitoes, which coagulated from the very air and attached themselves to us like floating head-pieces.

Lorenzo stood up ahead, swatting at the cloud that hung in a dark halo about his head as he watered his wayward mule at the edge of a line of poplars. Their branches teased us with silvery pieces of light, a treasure that never reached the earth.

Two more hours to Padua.

As we rode on, the flatlands gave way to lazy slopes where villas with ramshackle dovecotes clustered under the cool limbs of great oaks and chestnuts, overlooking orchards strung with grapevines. Stone-terraced or walled gardens of lettuces, radicchio, melons, and herbs checkered the land with an even geometry, as if a giant with a tremendous rake had grooved the curved earth into squares, lines running first one way and then perpendicular, so that the plots would surely appear woven if one were a hawk wheeling above them.

I was lulled by their pleasant aspect; when I felt I might fall asleep on Orfeo's back, I caught the refreshing smell of wet sand from the Brenta River. The grand gateway into the city of Padua—the pale stone Porta del Portello—was flanked by rows of gondolas and boats knocking against the stone steps. Boatmen loaded all manner of things for market or transport, from caskets of wine, baskets of fruits and vegetables, and lengths of wood to portly dignitaries. Some empty boats thudded with deep, hollow sounds against the stones of the city's thick bulwarks. The raucous boatmen were a spectacle, emboldened to comment on every passerby, taunting students, singing to women, and hooting even at nobility!

Of course I kept my gaze straight ahead as I rode out in front, though I was tempted to smile at the foolish lyrics they sang to my horse:

> Oh handsome black mount,
> bearing delight!
> I'd gladly swap burdens to give
> her *the gallop all night!*

Lorenzo, who rode at the end of our string of animals, raised his fist. Beside me, Olmina sat upright and impassive as an oar as her mule steadily plodded forward.

My friend Dr. Cardano's home was a dark red two-story villa, separated from others by walled gardens, overshadowed by a broad plane tree that rested one limb firmly on a corner of the red tile roof, like a workman resting an elbow on a wall, shrewdly observing the world. The villa appeared freshly plastered, like an old fop made up as a young dandy, for the windows and roof still sagged.

Dr. Cardano took some time to come to the door. When he opened it, I noted his muddled look and the sparse white hair gone astray around his face. He smiled and rubbed the top of his head briskly, as if to kindle his wits. The blue veins of his temples stood under translucent skin. "Dear Gabriella! I've been waiting for you."

"I'm so glad to see you, Dr. Cardano!"

I took his thin arm, and we passed into the cool interior of the house, the red tile floors underfoot still holding the cold of night. Olmina followed me. Lorenzo walked around to the back, where he could loose the animals to feed. I was glad to be in this household again, for it had once been a second home for me. I recalled when my father first brought me here as a girl of eight.

He had bragged to Dr. Cardano, "My daughter has a good eye for locating wild herbs, and you'll find her skillful at making a poultice. But most of all she's a fine observer."

"Hmm, we'll have to be careful what we say and do around her," joked Dr. Cardano as he bent to take my hand and peer into my face, while I stared at him boldly (a ploy to cover my fright).

"What a plucky child!"

From then on, I grew more and more into the spirited child he imagined me.

We entered a darkened room, where Olmina folded back the creaky green shutters. "How are you, dear girl?" Dr. Cardano turned to me. "You've grown into such a captivating woman."

"Ah, good Doctor, I see that you're not wasting any time," I teased.

He shrugged. "I'm old and have no time."

"Are you ill?" I grew alarmed.

"No, no. Old age is the illness." He grinned. "But I'm still lively enough."

The weariness of the road abruptly fell away as I recognized the room my father had habitually occupied when we'd come to stay. The room felt untouched and intimate as a closet left behind by someone who has died.

For a moment I couldn't bear it. Yet it was a spacious room with a large canopied bed in the center, a small bed niched in the wall, and a pleasant sitting area near the window. From there I could view the silvery orchards of olives and their lengthening shadows cast eastward toward Venetia. Orfeo and the mules grazed contentedly on grasses under the trees. An old woman in a black scarf and dress squatted near the far garden wall, resting her arms on her knees, her skirts fanned out around her.

"Oh, there's Gesuina, who refuses to use a chamber pot!" Dr. Cardano laughed.

The old woman wiped herself with a handful of leaves and stood, then shook out her skirts and looked up into an olive tree as if contemplating this year's harvest. Then she noticed us and stared. It was that fierce, uncompromising gaze one sees in widows, the constant reprimand against everyone and no one in particular, except perhaps God.

We didn't speak of my father that evening, for I was too fatigued after supper. When I retired to my room, Olmina already lay gently snoring in her sleeping niche in the wall.

I sat on the edge of my bed and opened the lid of my medicine chest. I looked upon Asclepius, the physician-god who heals through dreams, and his daughter Hygieia, goddess of sound mind, both painted there in splendid colors by Annibale Brancaccio. The bearded god, draped in a simple robe, stood facing me on the left; in the center was a wondrous staff, sprouting leaves at its tip and twined by the curative snake. On the other side the lovely Hygieia of the blue-green eyes, faintly revealed by her linen garment, stood in profile and gazed outward with a questioning look as she offered a small bowl of some mysterious substance to the snake.

Soon I closed my eyes and promptly fell asleep.

The next morning I sought out Dr. Cardano so that we could speak of my father, but he fumbled and made excuses, claiming he needed to carry out some professorial errands, among them returning books to a bedridden colleague who suffered from dropsy. I wondered why he was avoiding the conversation.

I spent most of the day in the orchard, pacing the rows of trees and sitting at the long wooden table with books on anatomy I'd selected from his superb library, feeling guilty (though not too much) that I'd brought them outside without asking him. I pored over the wonderful Vesalius, *De humani corporis fabrica* (*On the Fabric of the Human Body*), for Dr. Cardano owned a much finer and fuller edition than ours. We possessed the *Student Epitome* in Latin, which presented larger illustrations for studying (but fewer examples), printed on inferior paper.

This book had the ability to calm me, especially book one—the things that sustain and support the entire body, and what braces and attaches them all (the bones and the ligaments that interconnect them)—for I never ceased marveling at what lies within us, and even the manner in which the parts are named. For instance, Vesalius examines the origins of certain terms: *verticulum, vertebra, spondulos.* For us, the Latin *vertebra* means what *spondulos* meant to the Greeks: any bone of the back, which is also called *verticulum* by many, probably from the shape of the pivot or whorl (*verticula*) with which women weight their spindles. After reading this, I thought of the spindle whorls of the vertebrae that weight my spinal cord, the nerves spun from the distaff of the brain. Thought resembles the thread drawn out by a woman holding her distaff wrapped with raw wool, the thread lengthened and dropped to the plumb of the spindle and its weight. The heft of gravity, the body always pulling.

My thoughts unwound, tugged, and wound to another form. I'd never visited Dr. Cardano without my father, whose absence bore down on me like the ponderous day's heat. One would think that void would be a hollow thing, but no, it was an invisible burden, pervasive, atmospheric, and almost forgotten, until one was struck unexpectedly by its force. There before me, my father had stood under the flowering apples in another season. White petals shook loose around us. "One could almost dream of a different world here in this garden," he said sadly. "A place without plague or the other countless afflictions that we often bring on ourselves." We walked through the ancient orchard, where a few hollow, gnarled trunks still brimmed with walnuts the squirrels had stowed there in the fall. The unexpected reserves cheered us. Now I looked for them again. Yes, there they were in the storehouses of the old trunks. Nothing was wasted, not even emptiness.

Before the evening meal, Dr. Cardano and I sat together at the small table in the guest room. The windows were closed and shuttered against mosquitoes. Olmina was mending in the corner; we'd barely begun our journey and already I'd torn a hem. I stared at the small fire in the grate (for though the days were hot, the nights fell chill—one could feel the presence of distant mountains). I fidgeted with the green tassel at the corner of the tablecloth.

At last Dr. Cardano haltingly expressed his regret at my father's disappearance and how unusual it was that his letters ceased. He admitted he possessed no fresh news for me, as he hadn't received any letters for two years. Still he divulged something of my father's mood when he departed Padua for Tübingen that August ten years ago.

"He was in high spirits and eager for the journey, though he expressed remorse at leaving you behind. He wanted to protect you from the hardships of the road, my dear. Pardon me for saying this," Dr. Cardano ventured ruefully, "but I also believe he wanted to inhabit another life, and you would have reminded him of his duties."

"What other life?" I sat up on the red velvet cushion of my chair.

"The one imagined but never created, which doesn't succumb to fear. Who knows?"

"And what life is worth living if it shuns those who provide love and consolation?" I protested. I took a sip of the blood-orange grappa the doctor poured for me from a squat amber bottle and coughed, my throat burning from the spirits. Olmina glanced up sharply from her handiwork, frowned at me, then bent her head and resumed her stitches.

Dr. Cardano waited as we listened to the tiny rhythmic pops of her needle in the fabric, followed by the drag of the sliding thread. Then he responded, "The life of the false ascetic — if your father was ever shadowed by a sin, it was this. For he did not wish to turn toward God. He simply wanted no more of the world." The doctor stared at the pointed toes of his tawny leather slippers at the end of thin-as-a-plow-handle legs.

"My father loathed religion for its deceptions and indulgences." I spoke in a low voice, afraid of the inquisitor's ears even in the house of my father's friend. I was echoing the sentiments of heretic Lutherans. One never knew who was listening at the door.

"Which is why I call his leaning a sin—perhaps he wanted to flee into nothingness, without sanctity," he mused. "Like those wild woodsmen in Moravia who turn into animals and live on grubs, berries, roots, and any flesh they can scavenge!"

"Dr. Cardano. That's a legend, not a true account. Are you toying with me? My father turned into a lone beast? No, I believe something has happened to him, to confound his senses, some illness or mishap."

The quick rasp and snip of Olmina's scissors punctuated the air.

The doctor uncorked the bottle again with a dull plunk and poured himself another glass of grappa. "Might I see a few of his letters, if you would be so kind?"

"Certainly. In fact, I'd prefer to entrust most of them to you." I rose and withdrew a packet from my satchel.

"There was rumor of his suffering an unknown illness, from a colleague abroad."

My heart sank at his mention of this. "What colleague, where?"

"Dr. Fuchs in Tübingen wrote to tell me that your father acted most strangely while staying with him, was very withdrawn and secretive. He often spoke to himself while in his room with the door locked."

"Oh." I laughed uneasily. "He often did that at home, working out his ideas aloud. Though it troubled my mother, so that she put cotton wool in her ears. 'What decent man converses with the air?' she'd say. It never bothered me, because that is how I knew him. Maybe I thought all fathers did that. Didn't he speak to himself when he stayed with you?"

"Hmm, well, since my room's on the other side of the house, I suppose I didn't hear him. But he was never unsociable."

"Maybe he and Dr. Fuchs had a disagreement." I didn't want to believe that my father had gone austere or, worse, bereft of reason.

Dr. Cardano opened the top letter, one of the first ones I'd received, and began to read it aloud, as if to read it silently was a breach of privacy.

Dear Gabriella,

The decline of the body is certainly a sorrowful thing, as you mentioned in your last letter, especially in the elderly poor, for it is also the decline of the will. This may terrify me more than anything else, for I have found myself capable of bearing pain, but what if I were stranded without recourse to affect my condition? What if my family and means were taken by the plague? I have seen many a starving old wayfarer blank-faced with hunger, hunched in a ditch, hand stuck out like a stick of wood for alms. The eyes of such a person are no longer the eyes of a grandmother or a grandfather but rather the ravaged sockets of permanent grief or hard rage. I fear them, for it is beyond me to help, but for a small bit of bread. The beggar may be the god in disguise, as the Greeks once believed. If so, the gods are everywhere among us, gaunt and withering . . .

He went on, but I no longer heard the words. I'd read them often enough at home in my room, trying to evoke his company. The fire spent itself and the room grew dark. Outside, the sunlight bled from the red-tiled roofs and left them ashen.

". . . Tübingen, December twelfth, 1580." Dr. Cardano stopped reading. Olmina finished my hem.

"Gabriella?" the doctor asked.

"Yes?"

"Why take this trip to foreign cities to find your father after all these years?"

"If I could persuade him to return, things would greatly improve for us. My mother frets beyond reason. My life in Venetia is a prison. I can no longer practice medicine there, and my father's last letter proved a fine gadfly, stinging me to change things as they are."

"I'm an old fool, but I ask you, is this really the best course to follow?"

"Ah, you've been troubled by the worry in my father's letter. 'Of what use is grief ?' he used to ask in times of disquiet. 'It's for holding each other,' I said as a girl of ten. It can bring us to that calm when we know we're not alone, that affection that can even bind strangers."

"What do you mean?"

"I find solace in every stranger I help with my art of physick."

"Oh, Gabriella, that is dangerous."

"Why?"

"Because as you well know, there are those you can't help."

"But one must try."

"The doctor is not a sister of charity, but a scientist, and what you want—even if it's communion with another—is irrelevant."

"Not communion, Dr. Cardano, but recognition."

"Of what?"

"Of pain, brokenheartedness. The more we can openly bear, the more we can cure."

"I heartily disagree. We must keep the proper distance, my dear."

Olmina sighed loudly with disapproval.

"What is it, Olmina?"

"Well, I'm no doctor and no educated person." She shot Dr. Cardano a glance that verged on audacity, and I was glad the fire burned low. Maybe he didn't see it. Years ago, Dr. Cardano had reprimanded me for allowing—and even encouraging—my servants to speak freely. My father never seemed to care much about it, though he didn't interfere with his friend's reproach.

Olmina continued, "Sometimes you folk make too much of a thing that's simple."

"So what do you say, my smart maid?" asked Dr. Cardano.

"I'm no maid, to begin with." I held my breath at that statement, but Dr. Cardano only narrowed his eyes. Olmina continued, "Smart in what way, I'm not sure. But if you ask me what use is grief, I'd say it's got no use. There's no mincing of doctors or ranting of frocks at the pulpit that'll convince me otherwise. We don't know the use. And that's why, Gabriella, I think your father kept asking the question." She looked at me sadly. "It burdened him. I like the answer you gave as a young one best. We may as well hold each other." She hugged her belly for emphasis and stared back at the fire.

Dr. Cardano shrugged and raised an eyebrow in mild disapproval, though after all these years he was familiar with Olmina's homely wisdom.

"You may not like my methods, Dr. Cardano, but I must pursue my vocation as much as I pursue my father."

"You were always headstrong, Gabriella. Why should I think you altered now?" He smiled fondly, then lapsed back into his own thoughts, creasing his brow.

Lorenzo poked his head in the room a moment later. Noting our solemn faces, he said, "I don't want to disturb your cheer, but supper's on the table, and I for one am going to eat!"

CHAPTER 4

⚜

A Tether

After a week as Dr. Cardano's guest, I broached the subject of departure at midday dinner. When one has waited a long time, I reasoned, suddenly one can wait no longer. Even the small delays prove intolerable. Dr. Strozzi, a peer of my father's, joined us for dinner as well. I turned to address Dr. Cardano at the end of the long oak table. "Have you heard any news of snowmelt in the high passes?"

"Hmm." Dr. Cardano mulled the question over, frowning a little.

"Are the oxen drawing logs on the roads through Bressanone yet?" I persisted, for that is how they test for avalanches, and the treacherous snows had been heavy this year.

Dr. Cardano glanced at me sternly, holding a spoonful of pottage midair. "Surely you're not thinking of leaving already?"

I stared down at my bowl, at the peas and beans in their thick mess. "I must cross through the mountains within a few days, so we can reach Tübingen—one of my father's early stopovers, I believe—before the bitter weather comes. The sooner I leave, the sooner I'll find him."

Professor Strozzi stared at me from across the table, the scowl lines on either side of his down-turned mouth a permanent sign of disapproval, so that in fact it was difficult to tell what he really thought. I recalled that the first time I'd seen him (I was a child of only five or six) I'd dubbed him the Statue, for he resembled one of the formidable patrician busts that lined the corridors of the University of Padua.

To my amazement, he said, "But the moon is waxing, and we'll have to tie you to the quince tree like your father!"

Dr. Cardano shot him a look of such rebuke that it could've been a slap.

"Tied to *what?*" I was sure I'd misheard him.

"Nothing, my dear, nothing," muttered Dr. Cardano, swiftly turning toward the kitchen and exclaiming, "Ah, here's the next course—bread, wine, and company makes even fickle Fortune smile!" One of the servant girls carried in a fresh basket of bread, which saturated the air with rosemary, while the other girl brought an egg *erbolata* studded with parsley and flowers.

"Ah, celestial dish!" squealed Professor Strozzi, whose enthusiasm for astronomy was only surpassed by his gluttony. "A constellation worthy of Cassiopeia's table, though the queen thought a bit too much of herself!" he said, eying me across the table. "The last time I saw you, Gabriella, you were only a wisp of a girl at twelve, hanging on your father's every gesture!"

I ignored his gibe. "I'd like to know why he was tied to the quince. Was that some practical joke?"

"Oh no, no," the professor mumbled uncomfortably, shifting in his chair.

Dr. Cardano intervened. "Leave it alone, dear girl. The *limonia* chicken is here!"

"I just want—"

"Listen to Dr. Cardano," chided Professor Strozzi. A tiny bit of egg hung from his chin as he hunched forward.

"I just want a simple answer—why was my father tied to a tree?"

"The only thing that could subdue him," Professor Strozzi offered dryly. "He was on a tether, you know."

Dr. Cardano slammed both hands on the table. "The chicken grows cold and the boiled sturgeon is here. We'll not speak another word till we've enjoyed our food!"

"A *tether?*" I felt my voice rising incredulously.

The professor nodded and began sopping up the garlic sturgeon sauce with a small chunk of bread. Some of his teeth were missing and so he masticated very slowly, though with evident gusto. A distressed Dr. Cardano held the edge of the table as if it would leap away from him.

Uneasily I recalled my father's rages—especially the moods that erupted out of nowhere in the months before he left. There was also the rumor whispered by my mother, which I'd ignored for years, since she invented tales for her own amusement. Yet I began to question whether some truth shot through this rumor like a bright thread in monotonous silk. As a young girl I'd overheard her speaking in low tones to a friend near the open drawing room window. I played in the courtyard just below, out of sight, arranging a fleet of small wooden ships Lorenzo had carved for me on the sea of gravel.

"Well, it's no wonder his wits have gone astray. You know about my Cipriot mother-in-law? She told me in a letter that she hung silver spoons from the twisted tree in their courtyard against the evil eye. Against the moon. Her husband railed against her, for more often than not, the spoons would be gone in the morning."

"How could that be?" asked the friend.

"Oh, I guess the young men—including Bartolo, before he was my husband, of course—got a firm hold in the wall, climbed into the ancient mastic tree, and pocketed what they could reach. Later he broke nearly every window in the house, throwing pilfered spoons at the moon's reflection."

"But why did he do that?"

"I don't know, he was angry!"

"At what?"

"'Too many moons,' he said. Watching him. He was drowning. Can you imagine? He said that in recollection to me. And after that incident he made himself scarce. He caught a ship to Venetia and soon began his studies in Padua. My father arranged the marriage after he became a doctor. A young man of such promise . . . I thought him handsome even if fanciful. His foreignness, his strangeness, was attraction."

I'd always dismissed the family madness as colorful hearsay. But I was also troubled by another possibility hinted at by my mother. When does fancy become lunacy? And what of this tether? Had these men fabricated this story to harm my father out of jealousy?

Not Dr. Cardano, surely. Nor even Professor Strozzi, who lived solely for stars, planets, and supper. It was something else.

For the moment, I decided to bide my time, and like the astronomer, I ate with a kind of vengeance, as if food could sate my apprehension—tart chicken, sturgeon boiled in wine, followed by pungent fennel-and-onion salad. Dr. Cardano didn't pursue the subject of my journey or my father. I would speak to him alone later.

After we finished eating, I stood from the table as the gentlemen relaxed in postures of satiation. "I believe I'll take a walk in the famous garden of cures," I announced.

"The sun will overpower you," Dr. Cardano warned, "and most certainly bring on dyspepsia and an ill temper."

"I'm already feeling a little ill tempered."

Dr. Cardano rose. "Young woman, your father would not approve. You should be taking your repose like your sensible servants." He stood in the doorway that opened onto the inner courtyard, where the terra-cotta walls and paving bricks radiated heat. We could hear Olmina's cheese-grater snoring in the kitchen and Lorenzo's frightening gasps outside as he slept, stretched on a bench under the stout, gnarled quince tree.

"My father is not here," I reminded him plainly. "Besides, I have a great desire to see the garden again, to observe the medicinals in full leaf and bloom. And let's not forget, for those who are napping, that onions and garlic bring on nightmares."

Dr. Cardano patted my wrist with his brittle hand, a brief gesture of conciliation, and then lifted his palm to his mouth to suppress a small belch. "You must see the exotics that have arrived from the New World. The *patate,* the curious sunflowers, and the tomatoes." Here he paused for a few moments as if he had fallen into reflection. "If you lived here, Gabriella, the garden of cures would always be at your disposal."

Dr. Cardano hinted at his desire for marriage (a winter groom–spring bride affair, though I was swiftly approaching my summer) in nearly every letter he sent to me. "Ah, and if you hadn't guzzled wine, you'd know better than to suggest such a foolish thing to me again," I gently rebuffed him.

"I won't accompany you, then," he said contritely, his long face reminding me of some great flatfish. "Giannetta will attend you."

"Wait." I lowered my voice. "What's this about my father being tied to the quince tree?"

Dr. Cardano looked away. "Your father hid his strange moods from you well, Gabriella, although it wasn't so troubling early on. As he grew older it . . . worsened . . . and perhaps that is also part of the reason he left you."

I pulled him into the corridor, away from the prying eyes of the others. "So this is how you're trying to dissuade me from my search, by playing up my mother's gossip about the Mondinis in Ciprus? A clouded mind does not mean madness. Maybe it's some tangled grief. Or maybe my father suffers an undisciplined heart. We don't know." This last statement startled me.

"Oh, Gabriella, I know very little about your father's family and their history, for your father never wished to speak of it. And yes, I'd heard from your mother once that a certain branch of the family there tended toward madness, though she never divulged the manner of their affliction. But this I know," Dr. Cardano said. "Your father suffered intemperance of the moon. It . . ." He waved his hands as he searched for the right words.

"It *loosened* his mind as it grew full. Often he planned his visits here during that time. Can it be that you never noticed that his absences began with the increase of the hunchback moon? That is when we bound him to the tree, to prevent him doing violence to himself. Or others."

I gasped. "I don't believe you!"

The doctor blanched and promptly turned away, his head sunken upon his shoulders as he retreated down the marble corridor toward his sleeping quarters.

But I was unrepentant and could not bring myself to follow him. Instead I stepped out onto the hot cobbles of the street, striding toward the garden in the thick, humid light. I didn't wait for the servant girl Giannetta (ignoring the custom that a woman must never walk alone in the streets) but yanked my straw hat onto my head and hastily tied it under my chin.

In an empty corner of the Hortus Botanicus, beneath an ancient chestnut tree, I found a cool stone bench. Burdened with the heat, I closed my eyes and leaned back against the trunk. The geometer Daniele Barbaro had designed this garden with such perfection, circles within squares within circles, the whole earth and its four directions compassed, to mend the agitation and chaos of the world. I breathed in pennyroyal, dittany, rosemary, meadowsweet, mountain savory, and lemon balm—all excellent for calming the spirits.

Giannetta appeared after a short while, her flaxen hair pulled back in two long braids tied together at the middle of her back. She greeted me with a quick curtsy, then in the smallest voice asked permission to join me on the bench, which I granted. We were the only two in the garden. Though I doubted that she would divulge anything, I asked, "How did you find my father the last time you saw him, my dear?"

"Oh!" She turned the eyes of a startled animal toward me. "I can't say, signorina. I was so much younger and . . ."

"Don't be frightened. We'll keep it between you and me."

She stared down at the petit-point work she'd brought with her, colored silks on a linen book bag for one of Dr. Cardano's herbals. The half-completed embroidery showed a woman gathering herbs that towered above her all out of proportion—great trees of rosemary, fronds of anise, copses of basil. "I think he was a very sad man. I saw him pacing in his room one night when I brought him his tea, and he said that he longed for his own city. I didn't say anything because it's not my place, you understand, signorina, though I wondered why he'd leave it, then. That's when he also mentioned you."

"Oh?"

"He said, 'I once had a daughter who . . . ,' but then he didn't want to say any more, and he seemed upset. He gestured that I should leave him."

"Did he ever say more, to Dr. Cardano, perhaps?" My voice remained calm, though my stomach clenched.

"I'm not the sort who listens at doors. But sometimes I heard them speaking about things I didn't understand. Mercury and flasks and fire, I don't know."

"Don't worry, Giannetta, I'm not going to lay blame on you. If you think of anything else, you can tell me, yes?"

"Oh yes, signorina. You know, I never had a father, so I think you must be very lucky." And after that, as if embarrassed by saying so much, Giannetta fell silent and turned diligently to her sewing.

Lucky, I thought, cautiously turning the word around in my mind as if it were a barbed thing. The rhythmic clicks of her needle against the thimble, and the taut pull as it pierced the cloth, joined the sputtering fountain and the monotonous tick and whir of insects to lull me to sleep.

I stand at the edge of an island. The rushes hiss warnings, shhh, shhh, shhh. Venetia floats before me like a dead stickle fish, her spines become toppled bell towers, cathedrals, the pitched roofs of the Ospedale degli Incurabili; all these protrude at odd angles from her bloated form. I wade through sedge grass along the shore. The edges of my sopping gown trail me with small delayed ripples as I search for something in the dull green water.

Then a chest — a medicine chest — appears upon waves that move like lips in speech.

It rolls toward me. As the deep red box dips, I notice the crest of the Mondini family painted upon the lid, a double griffin with a snake in each claw.

The chest opens and spills loose vials upon the water. Hundreds of little bottles roll and gleam and drift apart like droplets of mercury. I try to gather them up in my skirts, but the current disperses them, clinking against each other, into the rushes. I can barely move from the weight of soaked skirts and the pull of mud on my slippered feet. The rushes sigh, shhh, shhh, shhh. The bottles ring out all over the marsh. Other things escape as the chest capsizes — lead boxes, glass bowls sealed with parchment lids, blue quetzal feathers from the New World, snake castings, light bones like wands spinning haplessly in the water. Then scissors, surgical knives and saws, lancets, clamps, forceps, and bleeding tools, mortars and pestles, which unaccountably float. Leeching cups, urine flasks, ear scoops, artificial noses and ears of wood that suggest submerged bodies.

All scatter inward toward the stagnant meanders of the marsh. I want to gather them up.

But I'm gripped by the mud.

I can reach the handle of the chest, however, and right it. But now it is larger and becomes the long skiff of a casket. Shhh, shhh, shhh —

I awoke with a jolt, sweating and adrift. Giannetta still sat next to me sewing (it seemed she must have been stitching an eternity). She took one more loop and left the needle in the cloth. She put her arm lightly around me and wiped my forehead with her handkerchief.

We sat a little longer, saying nothing, before we returned to the house.

That night in Dr. Cardano's study—he was kind enough to leave me alone at his tilted desk during the evenings—I began work upon my own notes for *The Book of Diseases*. I took a light supper, goat cheese with bread grilled upon the hearth, dried black olives, and wine. I liked to eat slowly, intermittently, while I formed my thoughts. A chewy crust of bread always anchored my words, while wine brought on certain deft phrases (which didn't always hold up to daylight).

These hours of candlelight, encircled by a studious darkness, drew me closer to my intent. The muted cries of owls and the sorrowful quavers of nightjars kept me company. Even when I wasn't putting words to page with the quill and indigo ink I preferred, I was more at peace than in the day.

I realized this was the solitude my father tasted and loved, which I also loved. Often, at home in Venetia, we would read or write in our separate chambers, though I might visit his study from time to time to ask a question about the healing properties of something such as aurum potabile, the gold suspended in spirits that purportedly could be sipped as a cure-all. He would pause, whatever he was doing, and answer me thoughtfully yet simply, as if sharing a piece of bread. "What is meant by gold? The thing in its purity or surrounded by other minerals? The gold of dreams? And then each temperament may react differently, just as elements respond to light, some trapping it, others magnifying it."

And I would leave his study content, even if the questions were unanswered and more questions lingered. I was comforted merely by the rise and fall of his room's reflected light upon the canal waters, which I could perceive from my window. Then the light would be extinguished, and this too was re-assuring, in the way that the rhythms of work mend the days. I was pleased to be the last one awake in the house, keeping my small vigil.

The light from his room still rose and fell for me, from the various cities of his visitations. I'd been rereading his letters, trying to surmise his route by his mind's tenor. In one letter from an unnamed place, yet with the date February 5, 1588, he wrote:

How I treasure the dark nights when my candle is the only one lit, perhaps, in the entire city. It may be that when no one else is about, I find greater entrance to my soul. It is not a simple matter of uninterrupted time. No, it is the darkened theater just after the play, the street after the festival, the emptiness that holds the semblances. There is something hallowed about the late hours that suspend one's life. To be apart, to be silent, to pace or lay down the heart's agitation. To find in words the plangent bell that calls one home. And if by chance I should move to the window and see another window, far down the street, lit for a scholar or a corpse vigil or even a midnight birth, we are instantly bound by the intimacy of our solitude.

And, I now wanted to add, the intimacy of things! For here in Dr. Cardano's study I was surrounded by the amiable calm of books, a few small boxes and majolica apothecary jars, which I resisted opening (not wishing to pry into the doctor's cures without permission), a celestial globe, a bronze armillary sphere, a pair of scissors, a slim knife for trimming quills, and a lonely silver key that hung upon a nail without its companion lock or chest anywhere in sight.

How agreeable to have such a quiet room at one's disposal. I was free of the interruptions that came at home from my mother, the servants, and the raucous din of ships in the Canale della Giudecca, unloading and loading, thudding, jarring, creaking, along with the loud gabble and shouts of sailors.

But sometimes in stillness, there is left still one's inner clamor. Perhaps this was the very thing my mother feared most, for she always surrounded herself with chattering friends and never sought a moment to herself. She couldn't bear that I spent hours alone, as if that solitude were a slight against her. Or perhaps she worried that the daughter bore signs of the father's obsessions.

Once, as a young girl of ten, I was sitting at the window, a book of hours open in my lap, though I wasn't reading it. I loved to watch the light unspooling on the water and the shadows climbing or descending the walls of the villas. If I could discern the patterns in this movement, then, I reasoned in my child's mind, other worlds would open to me. I'd see things that most people missed, not that I felt unusual in this. My young friends and I believed that most men and women missed half the world (except for my father, who'd mastered an uncanny field of vision and possessed the ability to detect whenever I crept into his study, even though his back was turned to me and he was deep in study).

That afternoon, guests of my mother had arrived and I'd chosen to remain upstairs, though she'd repeatedly called me down, ignoring my wishes. Finally she bustled into my room without knocking, and in a low, pinched voice so the guests below would not hear, she said, "I don't know what to do with you. Do you want us to donate you as others have given their daughters to the nunnery as tithe?"

"Yes, donate me," I said defiantly. Her face colored. "I'd be glad to leave!" I knew full well my father would never allow it, so it was an empty rebellion.

At last I relented and went downstairs, where two young women and an old dowager questioned me about my book of hours, my tutors, and my poetry. I'd shown the latter to no one. (My mother had discovered it while poking around my desk. Thief!)

I barely spoke, and later, when her friends left, my mother startled me by crying out, "I really don't know you at all, Gabriella!" *And you never will, Mamma.* My mother wanted a daughter to reflect her. Someone to share gossip, clothes, and the latest shape in beauty marks (black felt crescents were all the rage then, glued to a cheek or a shoulder). Someone to be her confidante. But I was a shadow she could never grasp, though she might call that grasping love. Yet I couldn't truly know her either. When she chastised me, there was always something behind it I couldn't name, as if she were slipping into a chasm and clutching at me at the same time. I didn't want to go down with her.

Sitting alone in Dr. Cardano's office, I shook my head. Here she was, in my thoughts again. I'd left her behind, and she'd still found a way to haunt me. Tonight I wrote with her living ghost there in the room, treading back and forth. How would I ever make peace with her? I set down my incomplete notes for a disease familiar to me on an unbound sheaf of paper.

MELANCHOLIA:

When One Is Weighed by a Leaden Sadness

Melancholia seeps into one's life like the metallic sand of an hour-glass. Despondency accrues. One suffers from inertia and wan complexion. My friend Messalina grew so disconsolate that no one could find a cure, not even my father. The use of plants with a moist nature, such as watercress, lovage, and water parsley, could not counter her dry, cold humor. It is said that the black bile of melancholia devours even stone with its terrible acid.

On a bone-aching afternoon of rain, I found Messalina seated by the casement of her room near Campo San Polo, a square of lace abandoned on her lap. She stared at a tiny insect, which crept along the sill. When I addressed her and took her limp hand, she didn't answer but continued to watch the insect until it wriggled into the miter of the window frame. Years passed like this in a cruel paralysis for Messalina. The women in her family insisted that she rise from bed to resist the dotage of her malady. They dressed her and led her to the casement, moving her like an enormous puppet, so empty of will were her limbs. Before my father left, he counseled her to keep her windows open so she could breathe the salubrious air of the sea and exhale her gloom.

Sometimes she recovered briefly and began to pace through every room, making lists of the most minute repairs that needed attention, much to her mother's chagrin. "A new hinge pin for the dowry chest, for this one is bent; new plaster for the corner of the attic kitchen, for this corner is crooked; a new pot of cochineal for the dressing table—look, the powder on top is darker than the powder underneath . . ."

And so on. But one dank January, she would not return to us. Every afternoon for a month I visited Messalina, spoke to her, touched her arm or hand, but she didn't respond. Once, in a moment of weakness, I confided to my friend an unforeseen yearning for other parts of the world. I confess that her silence encouraged me, and I began to work out my plans in the presence of her fixed demeanor. Other times I hoped that my schemes would draw her into her own imaginings or that my discontent would distract her from her own. But it became clear that I wasn't helping her to recover. She was always seated at the window, her chin resting upon one solemn fist, her eyes blankly measuring nothing.

At last I resolved to try the cure of the Terme of Montecatini, though I couldn't transport her there. I employed two men to travel to the springs and return with five barrels of sulfurous water. Messalina's aunt and mother and I set about collecting huge copper kettles and pots that the servants filled with the malodorous waters and hung upon iron hasps in the fireplace.

One by one, as the covered vessels boiled, the servants carried them upstairs to her room, where the windows were now shut. When all the pots were set about her, I signaled the servants to remove the lids. Her room filled with moiling vapors until she was nearly obscured at her window seat. As I waded through the steam, which reeked of damp plaster and volcanic minerals, her clammy face appeared above her loose smock and turned toward me like the slow revolution of a globe at the urging of one's hand. She was an unrecognizable continent, a Sargasso Sea. Glassy beads of sweat stippled her temples and upper lip. When her eyes found mine, her pupils widened as if she had flushed them with tincture of belladonna. Her gall-brown eyes dilated with a ferment that spilled from little wounds everywhere, invisibly issuing from the veins of our lives, from the wall joists and the dark timbers of the ceiling, from the spaces in the perfect square of white lace that her mother desperately continued to lay upon her lap, from the cracks in the gondolas drawn up to the steps in the canals, from the sea itself.

Without uttering a word, Messalina spoke with her eyes: *Go away from here, Gabriella, and save yourself! Find your father!* It was then I noticed the straight razor hidden in her sleeve and a small open notebook beneath the lace, filled with strange geometries like rhumb lines. I warily removed the razor and she didn't resist.

Her mother continued the sudorific cure at my suggestion, for it offered Messalina some relief for a few days. But later that February, even as she seemed to be improving, she leapt into the freezing sea and drowned. Now all the shutters on their house were always closed, summer and winter, whether to keep the ghost of Messalina from entering or to prevent her leaving, I could never be sure.

In the refuge of Dr. Cardano's study, I set down my quill, then closed and tied together the cover boards that protected the manuscript, just as the beeswax candle began to sputter, its warm, unguent scent urging me to sleep. My mother had gone.

CHAPTER 5

⁓❦⁓

One Must Be Kind to Beasts

When I bade farewell to Dr. Cardano, he startled me by weeping upon my collar as he held me. "So brief a stay after so long, my dear girl. I'll be here, even if you never find your father."

"You're very kind," I mumbled in embarrassment. For a moment a part of me balked, a bird hopping in its unbolted cage, terrified of space.

I restrained an odd impulse to stroke his polished skull as it met my cheek, for simple fondness might be read as invitation to pleasure. A woman must always be so prudent—though I hadn't longed for a man since the death of my beloved Maurizio. I was wedded to the work of physick, which now stood as my husband and keeper. One who wouldn't die and leave me bereft.

"Good-bye, then, Gabriella, and keep well upon the road." Dr. Cardano composed himself and leaned upon Giannetta's slender but strong arm. "Remember the salutary qualities of lemon balm for your spirits."

"I thank you for your kindness, dear sir." Without warning, my eyes welled with tears, for I suspected we might never meet again. The hardship of old age was not far from him, and an uncertain journey lay ahead for me.

After three days of climbing, our little company traversed Passo Rolle and descended between the mountain ranges toward Val di Fassa, our animals glutted on abundant grasses and wildflowers. I grew dizzy from the high mountain air and profusion of green, as if the succulent saxifrage, campanula, and yarrow were intoxicant. Lorenzo and Olmina rode before me and sang all the way up and then down the switchback path.

Sometimes I joined them in my dusky voice, in songs for mending nets, caulking boats, or stanching high tides (which I'd overheard on the Zattere), siren songs of boredom, songs for lulling babes, drawing lovers, or scorning those in high places. All this salty music high in the Dolomiti, as if we were rocking upon the sea instead of mule and horse haunches! What a pack of fools we must have looked, a commedia dell'arte. Olmina an earthy maidservant, Lorenzo a manservant of supreme alacrity—and how would I cast myself? Headstrong Isabella or shy Pedrolino, energetic observer of human follies? Or as la Dottoressa, pompous pedant, extemporizing at every moment, spouting great gobs of Latin? There was something of my father there, and something of me (though I winced to admit it).

At last we glimpsed a village below, really just a huddle of single-and two-story wooden houses with steep mossy roofs and crooked walls, balconies hung with ragged, faded old rugs, for fine weather meant a good day for rug beating. A young woman with heavy arms stood on a balcony with a flat wooden bat, her hips swinging to the right as her arm swatted left, and Lorenzo let out a shout: "Oh, wonderful town! I feel I've come home!"

"Looks like a bunch of rickety henhouses," Olmina teased good-naturedly.

"But what a farmyard, eh?" He waved his arm to include the lush green valley rimmed with jag-toothed mountains, the river ribboned with light, the forest that gave off a sweet resin scent in the waning heat of the day. "Just smell those woods, that meadow." He took a deep, noisy breath that made us laugh.

Olmina rode up next to him, and their mules jostled one another.

For a moment as I ambled up from behind, I could have taken them for young lovers, their knees barely touching. Lorenzo reached across to touch her hand upon the saddle. If I weren't there, perhaps they might have kissed, and this both astonished and delighted me. But he quickly withdrew his hand and the mules parted.

The sun slid like a coin behind the sleight-of-hand peaks before us, and we all joined in on a lullaby Olmina had murmured to me since I was young.

Fai la ninna bebé
che ora viene Papà
e ti porta din-don
fai la ninna bebé.

My father wandered somewhere ahead of me, a thousand miles or ten. Perhaps at this very moment he was returning. He could be rolling slowly upon his own barge of a horse, that black monster Stelvio. Though now that Stelvio was older, his manner might be softened, the edginess in his eyes gone docile, if indeed, poor creature, he was even alive. My father always warned, *Let him see you. Don't sneak up on him.* But I was afraid of that horse's stare, just as I feared the abrupt rebuke of my father's rage.

He could be approaching me now with his two attendants, if they still accompanied him. Though really I had no reason to question their loyalty. We'd always assumed they'd send word if something happened. But since they couldn't write (unless they enlisted the help of a scribe), they might've been unable to dispatch any news. And besides, messages are easily lost . . .

There were so many ways to disappear in this world, I mused: by land, in the sea, kidnapped by thieves, set upon by vagabonds, forced into battles or chained to galleys, vanquished by gambling. And of course, the one possibility I pushed furthest from my mind: disease of all sorts. For what good was a doctor who couldn't cure himself ?

As we continued on our way to Bregnicz, a week's ride or so from Val di Fassa, Venetian spice merchants headed to Piamonte warned us, "You can't go by the Costentz, its waters have swallowed the road!" In my determination (what Olmina calls my obstinacy), I refused to listen to them. Venetians are accustomed to the *acqua alta*. Indeed, my father, Dr. Cardano, and I had passed this way easily over a decade ago to visit an old friend. We were forewarned of submerged roads then too, but we waded through without mishap (other than muddied clothes) as the shallow waters receded.

Also, I was fighting a desire to return to my former patients, the women I'd only been able to notify of my absence by message. Who knew what course a new doctor would follow. Would he be undoing my cures?

My father had often noted the complement of a woman doctor in the room. "They speak to you more readily, Gabriella, and give you advantage in seeking a cure."

"I'm able to listen too, Papà. This art, not taught at university, is my greatest teacher."

"Not your father, then?" He smiled as he sat at the desk in his study.

"Ah, the one must precede the other. How could I learn from you without listening?"

"Though we all jump in too soon sometimes, don't you think?"

"I know, I know," I said, feeling a hot twinge of embarrassment. "At the beginning I was far too eager to give my opinion. It's not easy when I have to prove myself tenfold to be taken seriously as a young woman. Two faults in one. Yet every day now I remind myself to bow to the unknown cause."

"We worship at the same altar, my dear. Malady and death, the greatest teachers."

"And the patient herself," I couldn't resist adding.

Now, as we rode, I sometimes grew annoyed with my horse (though the hot weather also pricked my impatience). We'd entered the sullen dog days of August, month of fevers. Dog Star and sun together in the sky generated more heat (or so the ancients believed). My restless animal balked at the slightest crackle in the dry leaves or even at a thin rivulet threading the road. Lorenzo grumbled at me for my ill temper with Orfeo, but Olmina defended me. "Don't be harsh on the signorina. Horses aren't the only ones that catch a burr in the hoof !"

"But one must be kind to beasts," he muttered.

"I'll try," I promised him, and I sincerely meant it, though not long after, Orfeo halted and dug in his hooves, stricken by the mystifying vision of a curved stick in the middle of the road. "Boiled-Eggs-for-Brains!" I flung the words under my breath. The pack mules took advantage of the delay to wander off and enthusiastically crop grasses and blue gentian among the stones.

Lorenzo dismounted and kicked the offending stick aside. He wryly warned, "Don't forget that trouble rides a *fast* horse!"

A fast horse would have gotten us to Lake Costentz by now, I thought.

The high fields smelled of scythed barley and threshing, old apples, and Rhenish. Sheep stood unmoved in the middle of mountain paths when we rode up, and they turned their implacable dun faces toward us, bleating loudly and sticking their tongues out. Lorenzo sat up in the saddle, leaned forward, and commanded them in a quick, low tone to move their woolly rumps. The flocks miraculously parted. Sometimes, as we moved along, I noticed that the three rear pack mules abruptly picked up the pace, setting off a panicky crunch. Lorenzo would turn round with a long, "Ooooh, oooh," and slow them down. That they listened to him seemed no small marvel to me. After that, he'd sometimes pivot in his saddle and glance behind us.

"What are you looking at, Lorenzo?" I'd ask.

"Oh, nothing, signorina. Just keeping an eye on them."

But I noticed that he wasn't checking the mules as much as scanning behind them. Would wolves hunt us in broad daylight? Or was there a madman roaming the woods? For there were many folk three bricks shy of a load, as Lorenzo would say, turned loose like kittens dumped in a wild place, when they weren't thrown into the lake in a sack of stones. But Olmina used to say, *La paura è spesso maggiore del pericolo,* and if indeed the fear was worse than the danger, I should keep it to myself.

Still, the jitters of the mules often ran through the loose ropes connecting us like the twitching of nerves.

A week after we'd left Val di Fassa, we finally approached the swollen waters of Lake Costentz. The animals shied back, all six of them, with looks of terror on their long faces. Olmina spoke in a tone of dread. "Ah, Signorina Gabriella, look at the village there on the far shore, the poor drowned cottages."

I surveyed the flooded lake (none of us knew how to swim), and blunt misgivings rose up, but I hid them. "Those towns remind me of a collection of bones—like our bodies," I mused. "Remember the little Chapel of the Innocents, bones as lintels and stacked as posts, skulls and vertebrae as ornament?"

"Oh, but signorina, where will they live now, those inhabitants of the drowned villages? And by what path will we go?" Olmina cried, pushing her gray hair away from her face, tucking it back into the faded red scarf from which it had escaped.

"Maybe we can pick our way along the higher ground," I offered with more conviction than I felt, glancing up at the flanks of the mountains.

"We can walk the animals," Lorenzo asserted, and he gestured widely with his lean arm. "The water looks shallow."

"I don't like this one bit," muttered Olmina.

"At least it's not rising—you can see the old high-water marks there, a meter above the present level," I added, pointing to some rocks banded with mud.

But none of us moved as we stared at the pale gravel swath of the road where it slid beneath a wide finger of the lake. The reed beds lay sunken, in some places half-submerged, pointing their thin green fingers at the sky. Ducks and coots swam across the underwater track. The day was still warm, but a stiff wind came up from the other shore, raking the lake's surface into small, choppy furrows as it approached us.

"Well, let's get on with it, then," said Lorenzo, sighing.

He dismounted and cut a length of willow to sound the water's depth as he led the way. Olmina and I dismounted and tucked the hems of our skirts into our waistbands so the folded edges rose to our calves. We began to wade ankle-deep, sometimes knee-deep, through the edge of the lake, following the winding trace of the underwater road. My feet slid back and forth in the sloppy leather of my sodden shoes. Lorenzo's mild limp grew more pronounced; Olmina swayed side to side, swinging the table of her hips in a slow rhythm. We pulled the reluctant animals after us. As we sloshed through sheets of water that mirrored the mountains and fitful heavens, I said, "We're treading on the sky!" seeking a diversion. Olmina rolled her eyes at me, and Lorenzo said nothing as he probed the flood before him.

The cold lake rose through my skirts. I became a wick for all that was shapeless and heavy, things that skulked at the bottom of Lake Costentz. Though I prided myself on a certain mettle, I finally stood, shivering and unable to move. Orfeo shoved his sloppy, bristling lips against my ear and I held his anvil head to mine for a moment. Then I pushed through the water again.

As we shuffled around a small promontory, another village came into view close by. The black wrought-iron benches of the town promenade descended blindly down the slope until they plunged below the water. Alder leaves drifted on the surface, around the roofs of houses that now resembled strange shale-and-wood rafts. The water stuttered in the dark mouths of half-submerged windows. Part of the town was still visible above water, and a few stout men — solemnly smoking long clay pipes at the edge of a cobbled street that vanished into lake — watched us approach as if they were witnessing apparitions.

Large whitecaps clipped the lake. Orfeo snorted behind me. His hoof caught — suddenly he buckled forward, and I shouted, watching him go down, as a stirrup snagged my left foot and I flipped backward, stunned by cold water. He dragged me along a slippery bank, gasping. The horse labored underwater and we descended. He dealt me a dull blow to the chest and shoulder. I couldn't breathe. Muted shouts rang out above us. The shocked whites of his eyes flashed as he sank, his legs still toiling.

My dress coiled around me. Water forced my mouth and broke into my lungs. I flailed hard. The dark sealed my eyes.

⁓❦⁓

I woke up choking.

A barrel-chested man bent over me. He smelled of sausages and sotweed. I shook with cold, then retched and retched again, shutting my eyes against the stranger, ashamed.

"This lady should not be wandering with only servants on this dangerous route, even if she be a pilgrim, which clearly she is not!" His harsh voice boomed over me. "Where is her staff and scallop shell or other holy badge? In plain fact she shouldn't be on the road at all, which is not a road, now that the lake has claimed it!"

"Signorina Gabriella." Someone carefully wiped my mouth with a cloth. "Signorina . . ." It was Lorenzo.

Olmina moved her crooked hands upon my head. "*Madre di Dio,* come back to us, child!" Her fingers were twigs scraping my skin.

Two men carried me into a smoky half-timber house nearby that reeked of mildew and up several narrow stairs into a plain attic room. I trembled down to my bones as Olmina changed my wet clothes for dry, while I lay abed. Every few moments I gulped air. My chest burned. I thought, *What I truly need is a good infusion of coltsfoot with honey,* but before I could ask Olmina to brew it, my heart jolted and I sat up crying, "The medicine chest!"

Olmina drew me back down to the bed. "Orfeo sank, the chest went with him. But you are with us and that is the most important thing."

The medicine chest—the ashes of Maurizio's letters (a medicament for my own longing—the powder of his words, which I could actually touch), the herbs and metals that I'd collected over the years . . . If I could hold the jar of dried hyssop my father and I had gathered near the hills of Verona, then he would still be with me. Those tiny blue flowers caused bruises to disappear, according to Pliny. The bruises on my chest and shoulder . . . Where was I?

"What is this place?" I mumbled.

"You're in the house of Dr. Wassler, one of the men who pulled you from the lake," Olmina reassured me.

I scanned the room, disoriented. A thin, weedy woman stood in the corner wringing her hands. "Who is that?"

"Mrs. Wassler, who's preparing a woad-leaf plaster for your wound. Orfeo gave you quite a smart kick with his hoof, poor beast."

Orfeo! He was gone.

The woman squeezed damp leaves over a basin with bony hands. Her blue eyes focused intently on her task, though her thin mouth twitched. A woolen scarf covered her hair. Dr. Wassler stood behind her, frowning, though I couldn't make him out very well because the only light in the room came from the small fireplace. Were there no candles? When the fire flared for a moment, his freckled head shone, fringed with straw hair, bobbing and nodding as he spoke briskly to his wife. The wind rattled the shutters and droned down the chimney.

When Lorenzo came to stand beside my bed, I spoke in a whisper so Dr. Wassler couldn't hear. "Do you still have the maps and my notes for *The Book of Diseases*?"

"Yes, yes, signorina," he answered under his breath. "I have them in safekeeping in my satchel—don't you fret."

He patted my shoulder and I yelped. "Oh, I'm so sorry!" he cried.

"What is that fool doing?" barked Dr. Wassler in broken Italian. "Get out of here, peasant, and let me tend to the woman."

"No! I want him to stay!" I said.

The doctor pursed his lips.

I felt my sore chest and left shoulder with my right hand, palpating for fluid or solid swelling, but then a sharp pain shot under my breath. I wept, unable to tend myself. "Look at all the trouble I've caused. Are you all right, Olmina?" I moaned and clasped her hand where it rested near mine.

"I'm soaked." She sighed. "I'd love a hot bath right now in a fine porcelain tub. And that will happen when we return home," she declared. When she saw my face, she added, "With your father, may we find him soon, please God."

Lorenzo grunted assent and stared at the floor.

Dr. Wassler approached and spoke coolly, as if I weren't present, as if he were demonstrating the skills of dressing a wound to an unseen audience in an anatomy theater. "Nothing is broken here. The worst part may be the bruising or perhaps a torn ligament here in the shoulder." He spoke to the ceiling as he pressed my shoulder, and I gritted my teeth to keep from crying out.

The doctor's black eyes met mine. I was glad for his care, but not his disparaging look. His wife approached to apply the leaf plaster on my shoulder and tie it there with bandages of torn cloth.

"So, young woman," the doctor said, addressing me, "what is the purpose of your journey here in our parts?"

I closed my eyes and left Olmina to explain, for I trusted her to say just enough.

I ached for days, unable to sleep. The doctor's wife gave me chamomile, gentle flowers that often calmed me, though they had little effect now. Sometimes I dozed while scraps of dim conversation came and went.

"We must persuade her."

"You're right, Olmina, though I doubt even now, when her horse crops dirt, that she'll go back. Our little doctor is tenacious."

"Our little doctor is a fool!"

I slept.

One night after everyone else had fallen asleep, Dr. Wassler appeared in the dim light of my room in his nightshirt and groped his thick yellow fingers along my arms toward my chest. "What are you doing?" I called out loudly.

"Shhh, be quiet now. I'm observing your responses."

"In the middle of the night? Go away!"

He sat at the foot of my bed and stared at me. "Be quiet now, I won't hurt you."

"Olmina! Lorenzo!" I shouted, raising myself up to my right elbow.

"They're sleeping in the basement with the smoked hams. They can't hear you. You can't summon them unless you practice the black arts. And in that case I've a friend who knows how to deal with your kind. He works for the bishop!"

The stairs creaked and Mrs. Wassler rose through the opening in the floor. She was wrapped in a brown wool shawl, her loose black and gray hair rumpled and almost lovely. But she had a fierce look on her face that shocked me. "Come to bed," she said to her husband's back.

His face darkened and he shot me a look of pure hatred. "You don't command me!" He turned to face her. "But as it happens, I've finished my examination of the patient."

She stood aside and waited while he descended the stairs.

"Thank you," I murmured gratefully.

"I'm sorry for the ill conduct of my husband," she said. Then she descended the stairs, her face now slack with sadness.

After she left, I rose, aching all over, and clumsily pushed the small table over to the stairs, turned it over to cover the opening in the floor, and set a chair upon it. At least I'd hear him if he tried to enter again. I stirred the fire to bring up some light and pulled my map of Germania from the satchel, laying it out on the bed to plot the next part of our journey.

In the morning I confided to Olmina that we'd depart immediately. She didn't question me but commenced packing our things. Lorenzo purchased fresh provisions (ham, cheeses, bread, apples, and wine) and a mule, Fedele, from one of the villagers. This plodding animal moved like a barrow loaded with bricks. But chastened by the loss of my horse, I resolved to be grateful for my mule.

As we set out in the early afternoon, I turned to Dr. Wassler, who stood frowning next to the chalky walls and dark half timbers of his house. Nearby, the pine and cedar trees wheezed with the gusty wind that raked their branches. "Thank you, Doctor, for tending my health." I was glad to leave but vexed with pain. "And I want to express my gratitude to your kind wife."

He nodded, arms crossed on his tightly buttoned-up shirt and waistcoat. "You should not be traveling north, you know. There are those who would denounce you in our country. A woman doctor is near a witch!"

I recoiled at his words but said nothing. There were such

denouncements in Venetia; they were usually rare and aimed at the poor country midwives, like my grandmother. I had no desire to confront the doctor. Who knew how they dealt with such things in this place?

Dr. Wassler then said in a louder voice, "Return to Venetia! Your father, like any good man, would want you at home. No daughter of mine would be wandering the countryside."

"You have no daughter," said his wife at the door, bereft of any expression.

I bade her well and she lifted her hand before she turned to go inside.

CHAPTER 6

⟨❧⟩

Before the Sea of
Black Woods

We left the half-drowned village behind us, carefully skirting
the receding edge of Lake Costentz as the hours drained like
the waters of a wound. An odd assortment of things appeared
at the lip of the lake's descending wake, a line continuously
redrawn like those maps of the Old World and the New, where
the shapes of sea and land never remain constant from one year
to the next.

The dispossessed objects unsettled me: A crumpled lady's
ruff like the jellyfish that beach themselves at the edge of the
Venetian Lagoon. Mud-caked wooden drawers, their contents
churned and lost or astonishingly preserved in their little arks.
A thin baleen comb embedded in silt like a fossil from a cabinet

of wonder, an object of no consequence awaiting its turn, in hundreds, even thousands of years, to harden to stone, then be discovered and set upon a shelf to be admired. As a child I'd believed that spirits inhabited every tree, every stone. I'd said to my father, "Everything is alive!"

Olmina had laughed at me. We were at the table, about to dine on her minestrone. The soup made me happy. It had the fragrance of the garden and her hands and the hearth in it.

My father said, "Even the door?" He gestured to the half-open entry.

"All of them," I answered, pointing to the yawning cupboard, the window shutters, the little painted doors on the book cabinet, the medicine chest.

"Don't talk nonsense!" my mother said.

"How do you know they're alive?" asked my father.

"They speak, they say *come* or *go* or *stay.*"

"Ah, and what does the chest say?"

"Don't encourage her in this foolishness! Do you want a child possessed?"

"It says, *I'm a mouth. Put your ear to me and listen.*"

"That's enough! Eat your soup."

"No, you may speak, Gabi. Things do speak to us."

My mother glared at him and then left the table, stepping out into the courtyard. My father sighed and went after her.

I remained at the table and Olmina sat down to keep me company. "Sometimes we can't always say what we hear. Others don't understand." She smiled at me and patted my hand. "Eat your soup."

"The medicine chest says, *Everything is alive and everything has a secret.*"

She raised her eyebrows at me. "Lift that spoon before the soup gets cold."

I obeyed. I overheard my mother from the courtyard, saying, "The girl must be instructed in the ways of the world, not in these fantasies you create for her."

"But my dear, it's only a game."

"A serious game, don't you think? Given that you're half here and half there."

I wondered what she meant. There must have been a gesture too, perhaps her open palm to signify the world, and fingers at the temple to signify the mind.

In the end my father gentled her. "Recall when we first met and strolled arm in arm along the Zattere? With your mother, who taught me the uses of so many herbs? She encouraged your stories about the ships coming in to anchor, the origins of their cargo, the distant world beyond Venetia. She liked my stories too!"

"Ah, my poor mother, and look where it got her! But yes, you appeared to me from one of those ships, from Ciprus. How handsome you were, your ink-black hair almost blue, your eyes half-closed as if dreaming."

"And you, my dear, were a dazzling species of dove, preening there at the balcony."

"Now look what you've done—distracted me from Gabriella."

I sipped the last of my soup, tilting the bowl to my lips as I would never have been allowed to do if my parents were at the table.

"Have I? Come back to dinner, then."

"Scoundrel!" But there was affection in her voice.

∽✦∾

I also believed, in my child's heart, that the world truly wanted each one of us in some way. Now I felt how insignificant our little passage was upon this earth.

We rode late into the evening before coming upon another walled town hooded by thick forest. My head and shoulder ached, numbing my brain to anything other than maintaining an upright position on Fedele. In the sky near Cassiopeia, shooting stars fell like broken lances one after another, piercing the air with stubs of light, repeated on the lake's surface.

"Remember the Canto della Stella, when we once sang to the stars, signorina, in the Christmas procession near Lago di Garda?" Olmina asked, full of wonder. "You were only a tiny girl when you asked me about the frozen fires of the stars that burned upon the lake. Was the sky above the same as the sky below? Your father laughed at your curiosity and said, 'Everything above is reflected below. Even the darkness.'" She paused, then added, "An odd thing to say, if you ask me."

I nodded to please her but said nothing. My father respected the darkness, even sought it out at times, when he'd sit musing in a dim room or, during summer, in the courtyard lit only by stars. *The dark is not evil. Only men make it so. Just as foxglove is not an evil plant but becomes poisonous when misused in too great a dosage.* My father sat in the dark to think, because all creation begins in shadow.

We were alone upon the road.

We wound our way through the low hills covered with gray

orchards, ghostly fields of grain, and vines, the vast lake gleaming like dull metal to our left, the scythe moon having set long ago, and soon arrived at Überlingen.

Unfortunately the southeast gate was closed to us; the gate-keeper would not open despite our cries. So we turned round and viewed the dim hamlet that spread out from the moat enclosing the town. The faint light that glimmered here and there from houses scattered up the mountain unexpectedly comforted me. They were small, secretive beacons before the sea of black woods where the road led next. We could go no farther this night and would have to rely on one of the houses to take us in.

When we drew close to the half-timber house near the mill, I could make out a wooden sign painted with a crude bed and a bees' skep, hanging above the door. Lorenzo knocked, and a widow in all-black garb, bent as a latch, came to the door holding a candle. "What's your business?" she asked, clutching a thin shawl to her chest.

"We'd like a room and some food, please, dear madam," Lorenzo answered, since he spoke the best German. He hastily removed his rough woolen cap and held it in his hands, nodding to her in courtesy.

She lifted the candle and frowned. "It's late for travelers to arrive."

"Right you are, madam, but our journey's been slow and muddy. My mistress nearly drowned in the lake not so long ago, so we're riding with more care."

She scrutinized me. "That explains her piebald face."

I cringed, embarrassed.

"I thought you'd been set upon by robbers. Or maybe you're

vagabonds setting a trap." She inspected our faces once more. "Well, come in, then. I'm Widow Gudrun. Mind you, I can only offer a plain repast. Bread, cheese, onions, and beer."

Lorenzo perked up at this. "We're most grateful," I said.

"And how many days will you stay, then?"

"Perhaps a week. I need to rest in a peaceful place."

"Apart from the bees in the orchard and the boatbuilders hammering all day down the lane, you should be fine."

"Ah, I should feel right at home with that," I answered, thinking of the boatyard not far from our home. "We come from Venetia."

"Ah, hmm." She stopped and looked me up and down once more. Then she muttered, "Sea people, then. Well, come in. Lake people aren't so different. We both share the flux of the water, though we lake dwellers keep more to ourselves, I think. It's the knowing of a place bound by mountains. While your water seems without end."

CHAPTER 7

The Widow Gudrun

We slept well that night, Olmina and I sharing a bed, fragrant with mint, that wasn't infested with fleas and lice for once. Lorenzo slept outside with the mules, insisting that fresh hay would make the finest bed for him.

After our morning meal the next day, the widow squinted her hazel eyes at the bruises on my face, shoulder, and chest, then beckoned me into the adjoining room. By means of a half-frayed rope, she pulled down a ladder to the attic. She pressed a knobby finger to her lips to signal quiet as she disappeared up through the narrow opening. When she returned, she brought down dried ivy leaves (the same faint green color of my own lost supply) and let up the ladder. Then she pounded the leaves and added them to a bowl of hot water. She applied poultices to my bruises. "Signorina, tell no one about this, not even your servants," she cautioned. "The priest doesn't approve my medicines."

"No one will know," I reassured her, and then I hesitated before saying, "I'm a doctor myself, though I've lost my medicine chest." And with that small confession, I felt suddenly hollow and insubstantial.

"Keep quiet about that, if you know what's good for you," she said.

I spoke to her about the chest, its contents, and the theriacs of my father, but her eyes roamed and she fidgeted, so I kept the details about my notes for *The Book of Diseases* to myself. Instead, I told her that I hoped to visit Überlingen's famous hospital, Der Spital, where curative sulfur waters eased the heart and stomach. "My father and I are writing about cures and diseases—perhaps you can help me by sharing some of your remedies? I'd also like to observe their manner of treatment at the hospital."

The widow straightened up as much as her poor curved spine would allow and put her hand on my shoulder. "They don't take kindly to women doctors around here, no matter where you're from and who your father is. And you can't visit Der Spital. The well-heeled doctors there are afraid of us. We know things. And women who know things are dangerous."

"Women can be afraid of women too," I said wryly.

When my father presented me with the medicine chest at the dining table upon my sixteenth birthday, how my mother paled in dismay. But she already knew that her dream of a daughter as companion would be unfulfilled. I held the chest as if it were a newborn and hurried up to my room to be alone with the contents. Every jar, every bottle, shone more precious than any gem.

At sixteen I was unafraid of the future, and certain of my father's trust in me. Asclepius and Hygieia both greeted me from the inner lid of the chest every time I opened it. Sometimes I felt a small heat in each palm when I tended the sick alongside my father. When we were present at the bedsides of the incurable, he wisely refused to attempt a cure, though I often remained beside the dying after my father took his leave, for the warmth in my hands hadn't subsided. I could still give comfort, though I never spoke to him of this. Perhaps he thought I lingered with the patient out of womanly compassion. I did mention it once to Olmina in our small garden, when we were deadheading the basil to bring it back to leaf. She nodded, saying, "The mountain healers who sell barks and roots in the marketplace kindle these small flames in their palms too."

My mother had overheard us from her window. "Come up here, Gabriella!" she called.

Olmina glanced at me knowingly, raised her eyebrows, then bent her head and knelt closer to the basil.

I trudged up the stairs. "What is it, Mamma?"

"You must never discuss such foolishness with the servants, do you understand?"

"Yes, Mamma."

"And you could never possess such a talent. Only the saints embody such gifts. The mountain people are heretics!"

"Yes, Mamma. I'll never speak of it again."

She looked me over. "See that you don't," she said, plucking at loose threads on her lacy white cuff.

I returned to the garden and worked in silence next to Olmina, content just to be listening, for the green world spoke to me — the garrulous herbs, dense-throated trees, and fluted waterweeds, even the humming lichens and mosses that chinked our walls. Mushrooms breathed like small sleeping children. The whole landscape, then, sustained me in my art.

I suspected now that the Widow Gudrun also shared this green talent. As she tended to my bruises, I studied her hands. Her fingernails were stained brown from digging the earth.

I grew stronger in Widow Gudrun's care, and as the days passed, I went out riding with Lorenzo and Olmina. We went to the marketplace to collect new pouches and jars of medicinals to replace my lost stores.

Once, we encountered other travelers and a splendid black horse that had lost its footing, badly gashing its foreleg on a rock near the moat that slanted sharply away from the road. The rider, a Bavarian nobleman, appeared uninjured. He knelt, patting his horse, soothing it in the mysterious guttural syllables of his language, while his servants looked on. Though I'm not accustomed to working with animals, I paused — incautiously — and spoke. "Forgive my intrusion, sir, but I'd recommend wrapping a cold-water bandage with yarrow round that wound to stanch the bleeding. There's much growing freely in the nearby field."

Startled, he stood. "Dear lady, I greatly appreciate your advice," he said. "I'm fearful of the proudflesh that might form beneath the knee. If not tended well, the scar will mar his beauty. Since you appear to know about these things, won't you help?"

"My lord!" remonstrated one of his men, a rough, square-jawed fellow. "You don't know what sort of woman this is and you're asking her to look after your horse?" His own bay snorted and pranced restlessly to and fro.

Before I could stop him, Lorenzo retorted: "Don't you question this renowned doctor from Venetia!"

"Ah! Signora," the Bavarian nobleman said, bowing, "please forgive the discourtesy of my man there—he only intends to protect me. Lord Christof von Altenhaus at your service."

"Olmina—will you cut some yarrow for us?" I asked as I swung from my mule's back. "Let's not waste any more time. The poor animal is suffering." For while we were going through our niceties, the horse moaned where he lay, pawing the air as if to get up. I turned to the gentleman and asked, "Do you have any cotton or linen cloth?"

He shook his head. I bent over, lifted my damask skirt, and tore a large strip from my underskirt. The lord, his three manservants, and the gathering passersby watched in astonishment. I sidestepped carefully down the bank and dipped it in the cold water of the moat.

"Calm your animal!" I ordered when I returned and rinsed the horse's wound. Lord Altenhaus knelt and slowly stroked the horse's head and neck. Lorenzo jumped down next to him, placing one hand on the horse's head, speaking that monotone of soft words that no one understood but the animals.

I borrowed thread and needle from a laundrywoman in the small crowd and ran it carefully through the ferny yarrow leaf that Olmina brought me, attaching it to the horse's flesh as I sutured the wound. It was a hand's length long but fortunately not too deep. No tendons were harmed. We macerated the rest of the yarrow on a flat stone and placed it against the closed gash, then bound the cloth snugly around it.

"This will do until you find a proper horse doctor," I reassured Lord Altenhaus.

His pale green slippers, stockings, and striped doublet were soiled with horse blood and the filth of the road. His soft-brimmed hat was the only article of clothing left untouched. The horse whinnied, struggled to rise again, and at last succeeded. With a rowdy mix of hurrahs from a few youths, the crowd dispersed. Lord Altenhaus offered to pay me, but I refused. I owed a debt to another horse that I'd never be able to repay.

When we left them at the side of the road, I looked back. What a strange and consoling sight, I thought, to see an elegant man kneeling in the mud over his frightened beast. For some reason he entered my mind for days afterward, the green plume in his hat a valiant pennant fluttering from the tower of a besieged city. He reminded me of a young Venetian nobleman my father once treated, Signor Valdaccio, ornately handsome but haughty with his paramours. Lavinia had once succumbed to his tangy beauty, though she too had been scorned. He could be kind, but only at his own whim when it pleased him to play the radiant benefactor. Yet Signor Valdaccio weathered a terrible fever that left him stripped of frivolity, for in sickbed isolation he'd grasped that his influence, like Venetia, was illusion, but disease unites us all. *Le malattie ci dicono quel che siamo.*

I spent many days at the inn reading over maladies my father and I had struggled to comprehend. As I continued to heal, I wanted to know cause and cure more fully.

HORN OF THE UNICORN:

For Loss of Desire

The pulverized horn, very rare and unstable in the light, must be retained in a dark bottle and used sparingly. While I question the origins of the so-called horn of the unicorn (who has ever seen such a creature?), I do not question its efficacy.

When preparing to administer the powder, you must avoid disturbing the contents with any sound such as speech or with any motion such as jiggling the bottle, for it will alter the pitch of the desires considerably. Remove the fine grains with a small spoon and sprinkle over the scalp or the palms of the hands and gently massage into the skin, taking care to wear gloves or else the physician may become inflamed. The patient must choose an object such as a small portrait of the once beloved, or even an emblem of work, such as a chisel, if the person wishes to rekindle a passion for a vocation.

One caution: If too much powder is given, the patient may dwell upon the very thing itself rather than what it signifies, like that king who fell in love with the ring rather than the woman and couldn't release her even after she died (for the ring lay under her tongue). At last the bishop withdrew it from her cold mouth, but then the king fell in love with the bishop. The cleric wisely tossed the ring into Lake Costentz, and the king, poor man, sat in a small boat for the rest of his days, lovesick over the water.

The powder should be given in the evening, for sleep is advisable thereafter. The course of the dreams will indicate success or failure. The object of desire will appear along with those hidden imperatives that dreams offer us. Hunting scenes and cardoons promise success. The appearance of scissors grinders and women with black teeth warn against intemperance.

My wounds knitted and my bruises faded to a pale mold green. Days flared orange and yellow with autumn trees fore-warning winter, rousing me again. I didn't want to be delayed by an early snow, when Tübingen, a city promising news of my father, lay but a few days' ride ahead of us. But before we departed, I decided to stroll the rocky northern edge of Lake Costentz, for though I'd nearly drowned in its waters, I liked to safely lean close to its lisp and whisper, cupping my ear. Here was a wordless language, good counsel for the journey.

Picking up a dead willow branch, I idly struck the thickets along the shore as I walked. Lorenzo, following along behind, laughed a little. This irritated me until I saw myself as he did — an unruly woman whipping the wind, while unbe-knownst to her she dragged the flotsam her skirts collected: broken minnow jaws that caught the hem, a scraggly bit of rope stuck with thistle heads, a dark scrap of paper.

"Now all I need is a saucepot on my head to be Mad Meg," I said, laughing with him.

I sat upon a log to disentangle my unintended spoils. When I plucked up the bit of paper, I saw that it came from a crude *tarocchi* woodcut: L'Amore. But the usual image — a pair of lovers beneath a round green wedding canopy with a little lapdog at their feet — was gone. Instead my hem had snagged the piece with the blindfolded Cupid, a quiver in one hand and an arrow in the other. Such an innocent little god as destroyer. What would Olmina make of this?

The afternoon light faltered. There was nothing I liked so

much as this late harvest season, when shadows lengthened and the world began to retreat from itself. I left Lorenzo to rest on a large, flat rock, glad to be walking alone for a bit. The lake lapped at its shore, a sound like the tides sloshing in the canals back home, but the smell here was tamer. Suddenly I wanted brine. I wanted that large view of sea too, scattered with islands. This curious nostalgia for home did not include people or even buildings, but smells, stones, the way sounds tunneled through Venetian passageways.

As I gazed on Lake Costentz I thought against all reason that it looked pitifully small, even though it was an enormous lake. Was this what my father felt in Venetia? The pitiful lagoon? As if a bodice with iron busks were too tightly laced around his soul?

I walked until I came upon a rank smell and followed it into low-lying bushes. A couple of bustards squawked and flew up. I quickly pressed a crumpled handkerchief to my nose and mouth, choking with the stink. I saw now what they'd been feeding upon. A dead horse, boiling with maggots. Orfeo's face (for surely it was him), drawn back in a grimace, eyes voided, throatlatch protruding, yellow teeth glowing in the oily flesh. Strands of black ants spilled from his openings. Someone had rifled the saddlebags of their contents.

And of course the medicine chest was gone.

I stumbled back. "Lorenzo, Lorenzo!"

But he couldn't hear me. I flung my arms out, signaling him till my sleeves came undone from their lacings. At last he noticed and half ran, half hobbled toward me. When he saw what I'd found, he commanded, "Don't look at him, signorina, please turn away . . ."

But I couldn't. Even as a child, I was riveted by the whole messy thing of life—from afterbirth to dissolution. Always fluids, water, blood, urine. Seepage. My father's sweat standing out in little globules on his forehead in the anatomy theater, in the birthing or dying rooms, in the kitchen over pottage. Once, he hurled the medicine chest across the room in a fury, and the little bottles chattered and broke. Spillage. Mercury, anodyne, infusion, distillation, tincture.

Lorenzo and I knelt a few feet from the horse in the loose thicket, as if in some wordless prayer. Then abruptly Lorenzo removed the bridle from the collapsed flesh and we salvaged the saddle and the leather bags.

"Strange that they took the medicine chest but not the tack," he muttered.

"Maybe they'll come back for it," I suggested. The hem of my dress inadvertently swept across a black kidney in the open back of the horse. I stumbled to the lake's edge to scrub it. A taste of bile rose to my mouth. Lorenzo meanwhile dowsed the bags and halter in the water. "It'll be hard to wash the death out of things," he said matter-of-factly.

"Salt and rosemary cleanse rot," Olmina used to say when Papà arrived home smelling of corpse.

"You don't have to be a doctor to stink of doom. Soldiers, butchers, kings . . ." And he gave a cynical little laugh. "Or a cardinal, if you'll pardon my saying so."

Then he touched Orfeo's hoof and his face fell into grief. "Only the animals understand us, signorina. I don't think San Francesco preached to them. I think he listened."

At last, lugging the wet tack, we left Orfeo to the beaks, teeth, and mandibles that would have him. I placed my hand upon Lorenzo's shoulder as we walked, startled by its boniness beneath the doublet. What if the reason for my father's silence were as plain as the silence of this dead horse? Perhaps he had drowned in a swollen river and washed up on a bank far from any habitation. Or robbers had slit his throat and left him in a ditch beneath the blackberry canes. Or he had stridden into a lake wearing iron shoes.

But these doubts subsided when I remembered his final letter. In the end, he chose isolation. *I will not be returning and it will be the better for you . . .*

That evening, I searched for my father's letter from the autumn of 1584, as someone might turn to a book of hours for solace. There was some phrase: "our rib cages hives for wild bees . . ." I was troubled by the death of my horse. My stunned detachment and revulsion broke into a flood of sadness. Though I'd been impatient with Orfeo, I'd grown to really like the horse, whose fine senses made a closer connection to the world than my own. He had carried me. He was powerful and lithe. Blame edged up to me, and I felt the weight of his death.

Nothing comes about as one hopes; nothing is as it seems. Today on the road we were seized by ermine-cloaked noblemen who took all our stores and money after falsely greeting us with kindness. One of the noblemen tossed my medicine chest on the ground, squatted to examine its contents, opened some of the bottles, and dumped them on the ground after sniffing each one. Fortunately some of the more valuable cures lay in a hidden drawer that he didn't notice. His cloak swung open to reveal a burly man in peasant breeches. These were no noblemen. My two men hung their heads, useless as usual, though to be fair we were outnumbered. The five thieves then demanded I prepare a stew of two hares they'd caught. They enjoyed consigning me to the work, while my men stood by, fidgeting awkwardly. The main thief poked me with his riding crop. "Doctors are nothing more than scullery maids anyway, concocting brews, isn't that so? Let's see if the good doctor can make us right!" And so I did, with a stew containing sage, garlic, barley, and all-heal (the latter, of course, putting them promptly to sleep). And since the fools didn't think to share with us, we were alert. We made off with all our stores and most of theirs, as well as some very fine bottles of wine. We took their mules too. I suppose I don't consider it thievery to steal from thieves, though I wouldn't recommend it. My conscience still smarted a little, along with the pleasure of imagining their reactions when they awoke. We weren't far from Edenburg, where my colleague Dr. Urquhart helped us to try to find the owners of the mules (unsuccessfully—thirty men turned up to claim them, so we simply sold them for a pittance) and was glad to share the wine with us. Thus ended my brief career as a thief. Of course we just as easily could have fared otherwise. There could have been a Scotsman with my medicines calling himself doctor, traveling the countryside, wreaking harm, while we lay staring up at the oak canopy forever, our mouths loam, our rib cages hives for wild bees. Now I am ever on the lookout for an ermine-cloaked nobleman or, for that matter, a priest or a ragman. Someone will pursue me and I won't know who he is, friend or foe.

CHAPTER 8

~&~

Fires That Never Burn

The next morning, before we departed, I showed Olmina the fragment of L'Amore with only the blindfolded Cupid printed on it. "I guess there are no lovers in my future," I observed.

Olmina peered at it and rubbed the paper with her thumb. "No lovers that you suspect," she corrected me with a smile. Hope was a plain thing for her, common as bread. But I couldn't hold it after Maurizio's death.

When he fell ill, I didn't doubt he would recover, for he was a spirited young man. We'd met in the university cloister of Padua, first by shadowy glances, then by introduction through Papà, for Mauro was his student and I was ever at my father's side. Mauro had persisted with me in spite of my father's disapproval (though even then at eighteen I was beyond the common marrying age of sixteen). Odd to consider that the father who had once wanted to keep me so close could then abandon me a few years later to my own wits. But Mauro finally won him over with his natural intelligence and his confidence, which hid his own yearning for a father he'd never known. For a while, Papà relented and mentored us both.

Mauro and I also taught one another, in a shared scientific passion for the anatomical mysteries of the body, which soon enough led us to explore what could never be taught. I learned the contours of his sorrows there in his slightly bent shoulders, though surely he could draw himself up in pride for his work. His lucent green eyes always sought me out, not only for supple curve and softness, but also for places I couldn't see in myself. He gave them to me, gifts of blind sight regained, as if he were a mirror before and behind me—the grace I didn't know I had, the impatience I'd disowned. I too presented him with invisible impressions. "How well you know me, Gabriella!" he'd say, startled as a wild buck in the woods, when I glimpsed a hidden ferocity or brilliance. And the words! We could use the Latin from Vesalius in ways I am sure no professor ever intended. *Arteria magna, ex sinistro cordis sinu oriens, et vitalem spiritum toti corpori deferens . . .* For it was beautiful upon our tongues and we traced all the lines to the heart.

In illness his pulse jumped to my listening ear upon his chest. Though he shook terribly from the fever, he came through the first day glistening, purged. I gave him a tea of holy basil and black pepper. Even after the second bout, two days later, he rebounded. He held my hand with his damp one, those long, pale fingers adept at the vocation of surgery. But the fever wrung him out like a rag. His black hair clumped with sweat and his eyes shone dense as silt. His mother, an elderly woman who'd borne him late in her childbearing life, had a small bed made up for me next to his so that I could remain with him.

"He'll recover more quickly with love at his side," she said, and she pressed her papery palm to my cheek.

One morning after a week I awoke and opened the curtain to his bed. He lay still, staring at his blue canopy, rigid mouth open, emptied of breath, his bedsheets drenched as if he'd been lifted from a river and laid upon his bed. I held his cold hand with both my hands, thinking, *I must warm him*. But death stole the heat.

The world was wrong. The lack was everywhere. His great heart gone and mine gone silent.

My palms went numb for months, though I told no one of this but Olmina, and she said, "The little flames will return, you'll see, signorina." Yes, they returned, like scalds from a pot handle. The skin grew slick and pale as scars there. When my father saw my hands, he shook his head. "Grief speaks in strange ways, my daughter."

Now I tucked the remnant of L'Amore into the pocket of my skirt. Then we took leave of Widow Gudrun at her door. I'd grown fond of her crotchety ways and storytelling in the evenings.

"We're setting off for Tübingen, to find Dr. Rainer Fuchs, a friendly rival of my father," I told her. I leaned forward and said quietly, "Dr. Fuchs, like you, employs the curative powers of plants."

The old woman looked as if she'd been struck. I realized my mistake too late and tried to amend it. "I meant to say that like you, he *believes* in plant remedies. My father informed me in a letter that Dr. Fuchs is writing a materia medica that he aims to complete before my father finishes his *Book of Diseases.*"

She frowned at me and crossed her thin arms across her chest.

Of course she couldn't read, and books mattered naught to her. And here I was prattling on. I blushed. "If you need to send any letters along, we'll be moving on to Leiden after that. Many thanks for the good meals and fine bed!" I touched my left cheek and shoulder as if to reassure myself that the pain had left too, though a deep ache persisted in my shoulder and chest above my heart. "I appreciate the herbs, and the honey for our journey. My bruises have nearly vanished."

She looked down. "I only took care of a traveler's wounds as any good country dweller would."

"Widow Gudrun." I moved as if to gently touch her arm.

But she shrank away, seemingly in a great rush to go back inside her house. "The bees need tending," she explained. But then she paused and seemed to have a change of heart, as one might after having for a long while hidden something that finally can't be ignored. She leaned forward to confide, "I heard of a Venetian doctor traveling through here a few years ago—I wasn't going to tell you, didn't want to worry you. His cures were ineffective and many people grew sicker. If I were you, I wouldn't ever say I was a Venetian or a doctor. Some are still angry." Then she gave us a curt wave and disappeared into the dark entry of her house, black skirts flaring behind her.

"A strange woman," commented Olmina as we headed north, the mules picking up a good pace.

I couldn't speak for a moment, for if I'd stunned Gudrun by mentioning her art, she'd flung it back at me in warning—though that doctor didn't sound like my father, for Papà was competent and trustworthy. But how many Venetian doctors were traveling the countryside?

"She's fearful," I said, regretting that I'd mentioned her plant cures aloud.

"Ah, the crone's just used to her own thoughts and none others'," Lorenzo declared. "Didn't you notice that we were the only lodgers for the whole two weeks?"

"Yes," Olmina said, "and I also noticed that she was always going up to her attic late at night too, for who knows what reason!"

"Maybe that's the only place she can find any peace," I said, still trying to make up for my slip, though what good it would do now I wasn't sure. None of us would report her to the bishop anyway.

We veered away from Lake Costentz, riding into the black woods above the Rhine. The pines, beech, and fir closed around us like a heavy mantle, thinning the sunlight. The mules nodded as they slipped into a steady pace, swinging their heads neither right nor left. Though Olmina grew apprehensive, Lorenzo was lighthearted to be among the trees.

He began to recount stories of this wood, the Schwarzwald, that his father had told him. "Beech will lead the way—the old ones live in those trees, and it aids the gout. Some say it tempers those who are quick to quarrel. And pine, that sweetest of woods, eases the heart. Firs foretell the storm before a cloud appears in the sky, when their cones open."

"And blackthorn?" I asked. "I've heard about the benefits of its oil."

"Ah, he's a dangerous one, you know—the thorns and the thicket. All I know is blackthorn tells us winter is coming. Contrary as he is, his fruit ripens when all others die."

Olmina spoke up. "I prefer the elms. What do you say, old man, about them?" She hadn't ventured a word since we'd entered the woods over an hour earlier.

"Elms belong to the lady and make a fine cordage if you need it," Lorenzo explained, proud of his lore.

"I like the stands of larch," I added, "blazing with color. They are fires that never burn."

A thin wind brushed the uppermost branches above us, like skirts trailing across an immense Persian carpet. At the top of a hill we paused before a small wooden shrine, a box with canted shingles of bark on top that had been nailed to a stout pine trunk. Moss surrounded the crudely carved and painted *madonnina* within, clad in a faded blue robe with stars. One hand held a lily, and the other palm was open, upturned, whether in supplication or solace I couldn't tell. Small tapers had been lit and burnt down. "Who would light a candle here?" I mused. "There's no one for miles around."

"Pilgrims or thieves, one never knows," Lorenzo said. "Even curmudgeons pray in these out-of-the-way places."

I dismounted and opened my saddlebag, removed a small bottle of rose water from my silk bag of powders and scents, and sprinkled some at the feet of the little Virgin. I prayed that we might find my father safe in Tübingen (where one of his letters originated) or that some sign of his whereabouts might come to us. Her face was streaked with a yellow-green fungus, the same luminous growth that mottled the bark and limbs of the trees.

She offered a plainer intercession with God in this remote place, if he happened to be listening. Or perhaps wood was wood, and nobody was listening but the devil in the shadows. *Il diavolo si nasconde dietro la croce,* they say.

Olmina prayed, while Lorenzo observed the rooks that gathered on the ridge above us.

We met no other fellow travelers in the forest, so when late in the day we saw an elderly peasant couple approach, bent under loads of wood, we were alert.

They looked upon us with equal alarm. I wanted to avoid the suspicions we encountered in the lake villages with Dr. Wassler and the servants of Lord Altenhaus, so I offered them bread and Friuli wine.

"Oh, many thanks, my lady, we'll take a small sip," said the portly old man, who appeared hollow, but not sunken eyed, as if only recently deprived of food. His wife, a hunchbacked old woman possessed of a jaundiced complexion, drew Olmina aside and whispered something in an urgent voice.

"Signorina Gabriella," Olmina began in an anxious tone, "these good people say that we won't reach the nearest town, Offenburg, before nightfall. They've respectfully offered us their own shelter so that we don't have to sleep out in the wood."

I stared up the road, enfolded now in a brooding gray haze. In truth, I'd wished to be in Tübingen by now.

I considered the peasants. Did they mean to rob us? I could

almost hear my father's voice: *Be shrewd, my girl, no matter what you do. In an unknown place, trust no one.*

I called Olmina over out of earshot of the old ones. "What makes you think we can believe them?"

"They're straightforward, signorina, and very frightened. I can smell the fear in them. I don't think thieves would be so afraid. We're alone, unarmed."

"And pray tell, what does fear smell like?"

"It's pungent, like animal musk, and sets me on edge too."

"All right," I answered reluctantly. "But we must be wary."

"Lorenzo and I could take turns keeping awake."

"Well, we'll see." I urged my mule back toward the couple and asked, "How far to your shelter?"

"Close by." The old man waved a hairy, freckled hand.

"All right, then, thank you for the kind offer."

They brightened and picked up their step. As we turned off the road onto an invisible track, Olmina and Lorenzo walked ahead with the peasants and struck up friendly conversations just out of my hearing. I didn't mind, for I knew they'd inform me of anything important. It was better this way, for the peasants would feel more comfortable speaking away from my presence.

The old ones, Gerta and Josef, lived deep in the black wood (not so close as Josef first suggested), their dwelling hidden by hawthorn thickets. I was uneasy until we entered the hut and the dry scent of rosemary, mint, and caraway filled our senses. The woman, despite her sallow skin (which should've signaled a slow temperament), grew energetic and lit a fire, putting on an iron pot of wild leek soup. The man cut a sausage down from the three that hung from the ceiling. We added our raveled bread, the last of the pickled Venetian sardines, goat cheese, and wine to their rough table and began to eat with great savor.

Afterward we drew near the fire, all sitting together contentedly on a single thick bench. But when they heard we were going to Tübingen, Josef proclaimed, "You won't be able to travel there looking like that, in skirts!"

Seeing my puzzled face, Gerta spoke up. "The women are *gone*. They've been taken for witches, the little daughters too."

Josef hunched forward, coarse gray hair poking like hog bristles from his wrinkled neck. "The bishop of Wirtenberg . . . ," he mumbled. "His men took them all away from Durlingen, our town. We hid in an old root cellar, or my Gerta would have been taken."

The old woman laid a knotted hand on his shoulder.

I stared into the cinders that flaked apart on the hearth. "What happened to them?"

"Don't know, exactly. They never came back. There are towns around here with no women at all."

So that was why the old ones were living alone here, hidden in the forest.

There had been witch trials in Venetia too for many decades. It was worst during the plagues. Widows suspected of consorting with the devil were buried with bricks thrust into their mouths. They were tossed into the trenches dug for the thousands of plague dead on the island of Lazzaretto Vecchio. This was said to prevent them from returning to feed upon living children.

My mother had cried, "What witchcraft? What a scandal!

To throw a poor old woman into the common grave, silenced by a brick." Then, in a low voice, she said to Olmina as I listened nearby, "The inquisitor needs a brick to the head—that's what I think." And for once I agreed with her.

Her own mother had been a widow, condemned during the panic of 1575 but luckily absolved by the influence of family friends. And now I thought, *Oh, my mother is a kind of widow.* There were the straw widows, those discarded mistresses. But what could I say of a wife who didn't know where her husband was? Married to want. A lack widow.

Most of the time a woman accused of witchery in Venetia was a midwife who would be imprisoned, but children were never blamed. *The little daughters,* Gerta had said. Olmina slipped her arm through mine as we huddled there before the sputtering flames.

"How could this happen?" I asked, greatly troubled.

Josef explained: "At first the bishop sent his inquisition to Durlingen and got the help of the village priest, for there was rumor in town of a widow at the edge of the village being a witch. She'd always acted sullen and was ill treated by her husband. But after he died, she said whatever she wanted to, even if it meant that she cursed the landowner who raised her rent, or refused the priest entry to her hovel. I understood her anger, but a woman must bite her tongue, especially a woman alone."

"All her children had died or gone somewhere else, like ours." Gerta spoke more faintly and looked down at her hands as if silently counting her offspring—the dead, the ones gone to sea, the ones gone to other lands for a better life, whom she would never see again.

"I'm glad, you know"—her voice grew hoarse, as if she were about to weep—"that our daughters have left and been spared the fate of others in our village."

Josef put his arm around her.

She continued, "The widow. When a neighbor wouldn't allow her goat to graze in his pasture, as he'd always done for her husband, she told him he'd shrivel up. Well, as it turned out, he did, and he never fathered any more children. She also grew an amazing garden of herbs and medicinals that some say came from cuttings she stole from the rectory plot. I wouldn't begrudge her that, even if she did. Some said that she called down the moon. Sometimes she'd stand by her gate and fling abuse at the passersby . . ."

"We didn't mind—she was amusing," added Josef. "She once called the burgher a sausage head, meaning his sausage was displaced, if you take my meaning."

The two of them laughed at that, as did Lorenzo. Olmina just shook her head.

"But then they took her away. Later they took more women away. We thought it was for questioning. The husbands and sons didn't interfere," said Gerta.

"Maybe they thought that the more they went along with it," Josef continued ruefully, "the sooner they'd get their women back."

"But only the bishop and his men came back," Gerta said, "and the bishop announced he would make an example of village women who consorted with demons. Especially the weather witches, who'd brought severe cold to the land and ruined the crops. He would purge the village of all the whore witches. That's what he said."

"That's when we left," Josef declared. "We know this forest well. I'm a woodcutter. But we have to keep moving, keep hiding. Don't know when it will end." He sighed. "A few days ago there was a lot of smoke coming from the village."

"And that's why you must stay away from Durlingen!" warned Gerta.

"We'll go by another way to Tübingen," I agreed.

"Can't," Lorenzo said brusquely. "We need stores."

"There's no other way, then," Josef spoke flatly. "Go in men's clothing."

I protested. "I don't have any men's clothing. And if we get caught? How can we do this?"

"I think we must," Olmina admitted.

Lorenzo didn't say a word but stared uneasily at us.

"We must say that we come from Luciafuccina, not Venetia." (I avoided saying "that glittering whore of the Adriatic," but I knew it was what foreigners liked to call her.) I smiled at Olmina to reassure her. "From now on, we're countryfolk."

"I never was a Venetian," objected Lorenzo. "Let me do all the talking."

"Oh, now we're done for!" Olmina said. "Why don't we pass Tübingen?"

"No!" I said sharply. Then I softened my tone. "What if my father is there? I have to be sure."

"Sure! And sure as the grave!" She stood up and paced the small dirt floor.

"Oh, little wife," Lorenzo said softly, "we could just as soon find death here as in the city."

"You won't find your grave here, I can tell you that," said Gerta in a hurt tone, crossing herself.

"I meant no offense," mumbled Lorenzo. Olmina rolled her eyes.

"We'll go as men, we'll travel quickly." I set down the plan as if I were confident, though my stomach clenched. Olmina moaned and sat back down next to me on the end of the bench. Owls started up in hushed hoot and echo, the sentinels of night, and we huddled in silence for a long while until it was time to sleep.

Later I awoke, unable to fall back asleep.

I sat up (I was closest to the wall and so could do this without disturbing anyone) and withdrew quill, ink, and paper from my bag. Still disturbed by the story of the bishop-protector turned tyrant, I began to write in the dim light. The others snored in dreadful discord.

THE MALADY OF MIRRORS:

A Rare Disease about Whose Origins Little Is Known

The sickness is cast in two forms. In the first, a person intends a movement, a look, or a word and carries out its opposite. A woman extends her right hand to caress the hard stubble on her lover's down-turned chin and pummels his forehead with her left fist. Or a man dealing in pears switches from a plain chant, "Pears, ripe pears!" to a smothered whisper: "Don't expect to get any pears from me, you villains!"

In the second form, the person sees the true expression of his movements, desires, and thoughts only within a mirror. A priest (or even a bishop), for instance, intends a pious smile and sees instead the vulgar frown of sanctimony.

Father Arcibaldo, a clergyman of noble origins, was afflicted with this peculiarity, and he carried a small oval mirror with him everywhere. Set in onyx and bound to his wrist with a silken cord and tassel, the mirror dangled and flashed from the folds of his robes. He could often be seen walking in the Citadella, gazing obliquely at the mirror he held in the palm of his hand, at his face, grotesque and angry, or twisted into a strange smile. Those who wished to divine his true mind often tried to steal a glance in the mirror. He then took to the habit of carrying a heavy stick in his other hand, for smacking those who weren't swift or subtle enough in their purpose. Some called for him to be defrocked, while others called his disease a hoax embellished by the nobility and clergy alike to excuse his cruel actions and words. Father Arcibaldo himself simply said, "A priest is a different kind of man and therefore must be respected absolutely! No commoner may question him!"

In the first case, a cure is worked by arming those around the sufferer with mirrors to be fastened upon vests, bodices, hats, and gloves and even upon the brow with a silver ribbon. In the second, the victim must relinquish all his mirrors, thus defeating his singularity. He must look to others for his reflection, the thing perhaps most abhorrent to him.

As I settled into sleep, I also thought of my mother, who had always wanted me to be the mirror tied to her wrist.

Early the next morning, Olmina became Goodman Olmo (in Lorenzo's clothes), and I reluctantly became Gabriele Silvano Mondini (in the woodcutter's clothes). Gerta cut Olmo's stiff gray hair to just below her ears with a sharp pair of scissors.

My dear companion sat motionless as a wooden saint on the bench, her eyes closed, hands clasped in her lap. Then Gerta turned to me. She stroked my long auburn hair with hands that resembled roots unearthed from an old furrow. "I should cut this, signorina. I don't think you can hide it."

"Let me try," I insisted, and I stepped outside. I sat on an old stump near the hut and worked the comb through my hair. So many knots! And my neck tense as a rope. But little by little I worked it loose. I brought my hair forward over my shoulder, parted it in three, and plaited it snugly. Pine limbs lifted and fell above me in an uncertain wind.

I wound the dense braid around my head and tied it beneath a broad hat with flaps that Josef gave me, then shook my head vigorously. The braid stayed firm. Olmo patted the hat, tugged at it all around to make sure it was secure, and pulled the flaps down even farther. She understood how important it was for me to keep my hair. For on nights when I combed out the braid, I cleared my thoughts. Snarls and angers, knots and sorrows, tangles and perplexities. And sometimes little things fell out, like millet or bits of quill. Clenched brown spiders, the black pips of an apple, tiny shells or stones. And once a small animal tooth. When Olmina combed my hair when I was a child, she would lightly rap the comb on the side of my head. "Where do all these things come from, Gabriella? Your hair has a life of its own!"

I handed over my brocade skirts, bodices, and silk underdresses to the old woman and kept two plain linen smocks (one of which was Olmo's) — gifts for my sisters, I would say, if we were searched or questioned. Olmo gave up her only other dress and underskirts. I hid my small adornments (the filigreed earrings from my Cipriot grandmother, the simple gold ring from my father) in a handkerchief rolled up inside a leather pouch, the so-called codpiece in my hose, under the front of my rustic shirt and doublet.

I strode back and forth before Josef and Lorenzo, who turned their heads away, embarrassed by the sight of my legs in woolen hose. I liked the feeling of ease without bodice and skirts. I could breathe and stride freely.

"Pardon my saying, signorina, but it makes a good manly impression, if you know what I mean." Olmo was trying to cheer me, and perhaps herself too, for I must have worn an anxious face after I'd handed over my dresses to Gerta. She'd fingered the rich cloth and nodded at her unexpected good fortune, even as Josef looked sulky at the loss of one of his two sets of clothes.

Then Gerta pulled a small cluster of three oak nuts from her pocket. "From the Holy Oak at the center of the wood. The grandmother tree. They'll give you strength when you're broken."

As we rode away, I turned in my saddle to bid the old ones farewell, but they'd vanished, their cottage—and my exquisite dresses—already taken back by the shadowy forest.

"Coraggio!" I said, more to myself than to anyone else, persisting in such bravado, though I knew it was a poor defense against the days to come. Durlingen, empty of women and girls, lay ahead.

After riding most of the day under the shifting trees and gray sky awash with a thin gruel of clouds, we entered the town. A few chimneys gave off strands of smoke. Everything was shut up tight. Not even a scrawny dog trotted out to nip at our heels.

We reached the Marketplatz, where dead spikes of loosestrife stood askew. A single sorrowful oak at the center of the square was singed and brown. The stone chapel was closed. A dingy midday drizzle began to fall and the moistened dirt stung our nostrils with a seared odor.

The wet, burnt smell reminded me of the charred ship that once drifted toward the Venetian Lagoon in a similar grim rain. I was thirteen. My father and his friend Paolo Benvenuti the joiner took me (against my mother's vehement protests) out to the Cavallino in the late afternoon, where our gondola worked against the tide, one among a black flock of gondolas that had come out to see the ship.

The edge of the storm swept on toward Venetia and ceased briefly above us while more rain advanced from the east, downpours that resembled dark mourning swags hung over the sea. The rudderless Portuguese caravel drifted near one of the mouths of the lagoon, its lateen sails reduced to sooty gauze, its partly burnt hull, masts, and long yards a black skeleton. The planking had warped away from the frame in places from the spasms of the ship's fire. On the bow, though, the eyes, painted one on each side by the ship-wrights, remained, blistered and peeling, those eyes that Portuguese sailors declare will always see the way. Even so, the ship heaved blindly toward us.

"It's a plague ship!" someone shouted in a panic. "They burned it to purge the pestilence!"

"Or a fire ship!"

"What's that?" I asked my father.

"A ship deliberately set ablaze and abandoned to drift toward the enemy fleet."

"What's it doing all the way up here in our Adriatic groin?" asked a coarser voice.

"Fools!" my father grumbled. "The ship's crew was gutted by scurvy or carelessness, more than likely."

"Unless it's one of those vessels cursed by Sant'Elmo and his bloody windlass," muttered Paolo Benvenuti.

"You've got it wrong," my father reprimanded him. "Sant'Elmo and his fires at the masthead *protect* the sailors. They invoke him against seasickness and troubled bowels."

"You believe that, do you? Well, he didn't do much good here, now, did he?"

"What about you, Gabriella?" My father turned to me. "What do you think?"

With all the sincerity of my young age, I answered, "The saints forget us sometimes."

My father smiled. The caravel broke up on a sandbar, and now we saw its unintended cargo. The burnt dead spilled from the spongy timbers of its belly, a few tangled in the sail stays. But these were not as fearsome as the fat white dog that swam from the wreckage, eyes blunted with hardship, conveying both indifference and hatred as it struggled toward one of the gondolas. The gondolier struck at it with his oar, and the dog swerved toward us. To my amazement, my father stayed the arm of our gondolier and knelt to pull the thrashing animal over the bow, rocking the gondola wildly.

The beast tore at his glove. But when he spoke to it in a low growl, it dropped to a crouch, snarling and shaking with cold. The sky and sea were lead black now as the pale corpses dispersed around us, giving off a cold, thin light of their own. My father ordered the gondolier to row us home.

"What shall we name this mongrel, then?" he asked.

"Cerberus!" I piped up, for I'd been reading stories of the Greek underworld.

"But he doesn't have three heads."

I considered this. "Not that we can see," I said.

"Very well, then." My father attempted to pat the creature's head, though the dog recoiled. "May you protect us, Cerberus, as well as you protect that other realm."

I sat still beneath the curved wooden canopy in the center of the gondola, opposite my father and Paolo Benvenuti, silently watching the dog and the small ocher lights of the living that glowed from the windows of Venetia, across the black water. I wanted to forget the dead floating around me.

Now in Durlingen, just as on that night long ago, the dead occupied the air around me.

"Lorenzo, what is that smell?" I asked, still disbelieving, as we circled the scorched tree, for there was more in it than burnt wood.

"Oh, signorina—*signor*, I can't say. I can't say. The fire seems but a few days old."

"How can you tell?"

"The sap bleeding from the tree is new."

Perhaps that was why there were no people in the square. It was too crowded with the invisible ones, the women, the little daughters. "We have to leave this place!"

"Not in a hurry." Lorenzo spoke in a low, restrained voice. "We don't want to provoke suspicion. Let's get our supplies."

Olmo looked at him in dismay, but I knew he was right.

Two men moved beneath a coarse hemp canopy at the corner of the Marketplatz, a young, thickset peddler with a rough table of bread and peppered hams, and a gaunt woodsman selling rope and firewood. They were in the middle of packing up their goods, as there were no other buyers and perhaps had not been any the whole day. They stopped their work and stared at us.

"You're not from here, are you?" the stocky man inquired. His grin was slightly contorted by a pink sickle-shaped scar on the left side.

Lorenzo greeted them and dismounted, while Olmo and I drew our mules beneath the deep eaves of the town hall for shelter from the drizzle. As Lorenzo muttered that we must gain Tübingen by the end of the week and needed supplies, I glanced around the silent town. No curtains were drawn by a curious hand. Not a single child appeared.

"Not many co-come through here since the—the burnings," stammered the gaunt one.

"What burnings would those be, my good man?" asked Lorenzo plainly.

"Evil ones. The—witches, you know, soured the milk, ca-called down the hail, ruined the crops, raised the plague, stole the new-borns, shriveled our manhood!" He spoke in a grotesque singsong as if reciting a nursery rhyme. "Kissed the devil, danced in the woods, strangled the lambs in their sleep. Laid curses on those as refused 'em alms!" The man's face convulsed, his jaw drawn back, his broken teeth bared.

Lorenzo stared at him and then away. He stroked the long forehead of his mule and then turned back to the first man. "Do you have any apples to sell?"

"No, no, apples are finished. But I've got that perry wine. Sure you won't come and drink with us?" The man was insistent, fixing his stare upon my smooth ungloved hands.

121

"Sorry, we must be on our way," Lorenzo answered flatly. He purchased three loaves of rough brown bread and a small smoked ham, stowing them in his saddlebags.

"We're not good enough then for you folk, are we, you foreigners and your high-flown manners!" The man curled his lip. Then in a throttled voice he said, "Do you think I wanted to give up my child?"

For an astounding moment, I thought he would burst into sobs.

But as we turned our mules, he cried out, regaining his harsh tone, "I'm onto you fine gentleman with your milksop hands, don't think I don't know what you are!"

The tall, gaunt one yelled, "Whoremongers, despoilers!"

I kicked Fedele's stout sides to a quick trot. Without warning, a black-haired cleric scuttled from the building next to the church. Suddenly I felt the long rope of my auburn braid drop to the middle of my back. The cleric opened his mouth as if to shout, and I dug my heels hard into Fedele's belly. With Lorenzo and Olmo and our threesome of mules following close behind, I bolted through the streets, Fedele's hoofs clanging stones like hammers against iron. The frightful clamor spurred him on even more toward the edge of firs beyond the town.

I thought I would never be warm again.

I thought I would never sleep.

Sometimes we dozed by daylight, lined up like dead pike on a clutch of leaves, unwilling to risk a fire. We covered ourselves with our blankets and fir needles and left the animals tied to our ankles. We traveled at night through the dismal wood and avoided other villages altogether.

Durlingen—with its burnt square, shut church, priest, scarred peddler, and woodsman—haunted us.

Olmo severed my braid with her cooking knife the first night after Durlingen and it fell heavily to the ground like a viper. I buried it in the prickly loam and Lorenzo helped me to set a heavy stone on top so that no animal would dig it up. For a moment I pictured a starving wolf dragging my red braid through the forest and those vile men filling his body with arrows. I imagined the bishop and his men ransacking the countryside for the mistress of the braid.

When I did sleep, I saw mounds, hundreds of such braids, thin blond, glossy black, thick gray, wispy brown, coppery, curly, short, long, looped together, and tied at the ends. Ribboned. The braids of little girls, maids, mothers, nuns, and crones.

I imagined the townsmen, stricken before the bishop and his inquisitors like those countrymen made to hobble their dogs while the nobility hunted deer through their fields, trampling their crops. I could see the dry branches loosely bound in stacks and set upon one another as firewood.

When I woke at dusk, I could almost smell the bishop's malevolence in the very air around us, like the smoke of burnt hair.

That's when I would write a little to keep spirit and senses honed.

INVIDIA:

An Invisible Worm That Consumes the Heart

In the countryside they say this disease lies dormant for many

years in the bowels of wild boar and has its origins in the
uneasy corpses they grub in the winter woods when acorns
are scarce and there is nothing else to eat. The bodies have not
been properly laid to rest. They are the murdered or the lost,
the starving or the mad who thrashed their way into the thickets
of death and couldn't be recovered. The unwanted children
cast aside in the forest. The prostitutes grown withered. The
lepers and their foul rags. The ambassadors from foreign countries and their entire entourages strangled in their sleep. The
witches who preferred the wolf to the bishop. The earth gobblers
who couldn't withstand their hunger. The men who grew
leaden. The failed miller poisoned by nightshade. The Gypsies
who savored the wrong mushroom on their midday outing.
The tired saltimbanques. The frantic mothers of blue-lipped
soldiers. The lost fathers. The astronomer who swallowed his
books in small bites every night to avoid the tribunals. The
miller's daughter. The noblewoman unable to discern day from
night, city from wilderness. The suicides. The little girl who
ran away. The veneer artist whose crippled hands froze shut in
the gray curls of his dead wife. The bubonics. The victims of
falling sickness who walked into the woods alone. Survivors of
char and blaze who preferred death. The slow of mind and the
infirm of body. The lost fathers. The boar snuffle and gobble
this half-frozen and decayed flesh. But rancor doesn't dissolve
in the powerful swine stomachs. Instead it lies in the folds of
sausages-to-be. The pork-bowel casings in the duke's cupboard
or the peasant's larder are filled with an envy of the living,
which cannot be sated.

One treatment is preventive. As my father cautioned, do not
eat pork, or you'll be eating the undead. The other treatment

upon the advice of the Benandanti, the green witches, has been said to work well among those mountain people. The infected person must walk in an unfriendly wood and converse with the abandoned dead. The visits should include certain gifts for the dead, who must be neither kin nor friend. The person must address someone she doesn't know, ask him what he wants, and honor his request. It seems that sometimes one of the dead may stand for all that are troubling the bowels of the afflicted. Yet the irascible dead may ask for something impossible, like the ears of a former rival or the fingers of one who has wronged them. In the first case, a substitute may suffice, such as a sketch of the rival's ears or perhaps an earring. But in the second case, there may be no amends, unless it be truth telling, like a rosary repeated over and over again.

The cure is difficult to effect, however, for it may take many years, and often persons stricken with *invidia* are not willing to persist. Some prolong their conversations with the dead and thwart the cure by delaying their requests. Others prefer the ferocity of *invidia* to the difficulties of their own lives. Like the bishop of Wirtenberg, who surely envies the women their wisdom, the envious love their disease too fervently and would blight the joy they cannot own.

CHAPTER 9

⟨≈⟩

Dr. Rainer Fuchs, Professor of Botany

After four days, we emerged pale and drawn from the woods and came upon a region of brown hills covered with leafless pear, apple, and chestnut trees and withered vineyards. A young peasant, her face pocked and red, worked upon one of the vines with a rusty pruning hook.

Lorenzo halted his mule and hailed her. "Good day, dear woman. Excellent old vines under your care, eh?"

She barely glanced at us and didn't miss a cut.

"We're traveling to Tübingen. Is this the right way?"

She lifted her arm toward a large hill to the northeast. "There it is, Castle Hohentübingen, and if you smart gentlefolk walk blind down this road, it will smack you on the head!"

She gave a short, dry laugh and turned back to the gnarled crown of her vine.

The road followed the swift, flat Neckar River, its surface streaked by gusts of wind. It was the end of September. As we neared Tübingen, we could hear the punt boats tied up at the bank as they struck each other with dull knocking sounds. They reminded me of gondolas tapping out the tides. My mother's fingers absently tapping the kitchen table when she was caught in some reverie. As a child I would place my hand atop hers, to stop the tapping and bring her back.

I almost wished for my mother to be here with us, instead of remaining a kind of prisoner in Venetia, even if it was an island bejeweled with flashing prows, water-soaked stones, mosaic-flecked churches, glistening eyes of love and conspiracy. Underneath it all, we knew we were nostalgic for a place that didn't exist. Perhaps that was the source of my mother's tapping—restless illusion.

Once, she'd waited for ships carrying rare cargo from other countries. Then my father arrived, their emissary. I wondered if she'd really wanted to go to those places, into the shifting haze, something other than the island. But hadn't that been my desire all along, because I feared becoming trapped like my mother? Now I wanted to rescue her from afar (though she wasn't asking to be rescued). I smiled. And bring her to this bitterly cold road? Meanwhile the hot winds from Barbaria could be blasting the cool passageways of Venetia even as we shivered in this northern place. Most likely my mother would be soaking in a cool cistern-water bath for relief from the heat. How I took pleasure in that clean, mossy smell! Now I longed to be home, seeking refuge from heat, rather than biting the wind.

Peasants with cartloads of wood and merchants with wagons stacked with wine kegs passed us, drawing their cloaks about them, staring at our clothes and mules with mild suspicion; no one greeted us. How very different from Venetia, I thought, where we always greeted a stranger, not always out of friendliness perhaps, but at least out of curiosity.

As we entered the city, pausing near the stone walls, a large wooden hoop bounded down the narrow dirt street directly toward us. My mule balked, backing into the other animals, and brayed with alarm. The hoop struck him lightly in the chest and sprang to the left, wobbling and finally settling on its side.

A little girl of ten or eleven in a soiled blue woolen tunic ran down the hill, stick in hand, and curtsied awkwardly to us, mumbling a shy apology. A small group of her friends laughed and pointed from the top of the hill.

After days of not glimpsing a child, we stared at her with relief. The flaxen braids that escaped her red cap were tied behind her with a blue string, and her dark eyes glinted with play. Her flushed cheeks were smudged with dirt.

Embarrassed by our oddly silent attention, she tried again and again in vain to right the hoop. Finally I dismounted and came to her aid, lightly striking the stick with a forgotten kind of joy against the hoop. I walked with her up the hill to the half-timber house that she pointed out as her own, though she didn't speak a word. Her friends hung back and gawked at us. Then I asked her in my broken German—reminding myself to lower my voice (and how strange it felt, this first time speaking aloud as a man!)—if she could direct us to the university buildings.

"Yes, thank you, sir, this way, sir," she said. She skipped ahead with her hoop whirring alongside.

We led our animals into the numbingly cold alleys, which, it seemed, hadn't received sunlight in months. We pushed through a group of beer-swigging men who sneered at us. One of them, a sallow burgher with a head like a bludgeon, growled harshly at the girl. "I'll birch you proper when I get home, girl!" He struck the back of her neck as she passed. She half stumbled, then fled ahead of us, clutching her hoop and crying. Without thinking, I spun round to confront the man, perhaps her father or uncle, but Lorenzo's coal-black eyes warned me to keep going. I lurched forward as the man spat insults that I couldn't understand at my back.

After we'd left them behind, Lorenzo admonished me, "We're foreigners, never forget it! And peasants as well. The girl's not allowed to speak to us, though the drunken father's the one that should be flogged, if you ask me!"

As we picked our way up the hill, the mules' hooves clanged and crackled the crust of light ice that sheeted the muddy passageway. The girl, hugging the hoop to her body, disappeared down a side alley.

"Wait!" I cried out, for I wanted to give her a coin for her trouble.

But she didn't turn.

I could see the parish church now and the Alte Aula, the central university building, where a few gentlemen in fur-lined cloaks and tall hats gathered at the entrance. I approached one of them and inquired where I might find Dr. Rainer Fuchs, professor of botany. Again I spoke hoarsely to disguise the feminine timbre of my voice.

At first the gentleman didn't answer and scrutinized us carefully. I could smell the lavender perfume upon his cuffed gloves as he stroked his mustache. Maurizio had worn that scent sometimes to cover the smell of cadaver when he joined me after the anatomy lecture at the university. We often skirted the edge of that other world in the name of science, and it added an unexpected tang to our love, for we thought we knew more than others about brevity. A strange sort of arrogance to breed such deep affection. Yet there was more. In Mauro's perfume his soul mingled yearning and fear, along with his own body's warm scent of refuge. Lavender was less mask than entry.

Once more, I addressed the gentleman. "Forgive me for neglecting to introduce myself—Gabriele Silvano Mondini, doctor of medicine from the University of Padua. We were forced to assume these plain traveling clothes when we came upon some trouble in the Schwarzwald."

The gentleman nodded and extended a dark, thickly sleeved arm toward a row of houses to indicate where the professors resided. The inner silk of his sleeve flashed red. He accompanied us and knocked upon a thick oak door with a heavy black ring in the center. A wizened man, sharp at every angle, answered. He tilted his head, assessing our presence, as he rolled his crooked hands in the soiled apron at his waist.

"Is Master Fuchs at home?" our gentleman inquired.

"Yes, yes," croaked the man, "but he's at work and doesn't allow interruptions, mind you."

"Please inform him that Dr. Mondini has traveled a long way to pay him a visit and would like to know when it would be convenient to return," I said.

The spiky little man scowled and closed the door. Several minutes later I could hear Dr. Fuchs's full-bodied bellow: "Let them in, then, Hans, show them in!"

I thanked the gentleman who had led us here, and he bowed as he pulled his dusky cloak about him. The manservant opened the door, and a young boy leapt out to take care of the animals. He stared at us boldly, his scrubbed face a moon, his hair the color of damp barley. Lorenzo grinned at him and said, "Where to, young man? You lead the way!"

The boy took his time, shifting his fresh look from one to the other of us, breaking into a smirk as he stared at my smooth skin and delicate features. I noticed the soft fuzz of a mustache on his upper lip and felt the lack on my own. Then he clasped the reins from Olmo and me and snicked to the two mules, leaving the others to Lorenzo.

"This way, old man, if you"—his voice broke and shrilled—"can keep up!"

Gangly Hans led us inside. I sighed with relief when we crossed the threshold and he shut out the world behind us. He directed Olmo to the kitchen as he walked ahead with knees that never straightened, guiding me into the dim study, where all the windows were shuttered against the chill but one, the window above the sloping desk of Dr. Fuchs. A feeble light surrounded the doctor, who stood facing away from me, his blue-white hair spread out upon his collar like a whisk. He stared at something in his hand and swung around to speak, thinking no doubt that I was my father. "Well, Mondini, I'm surprised you've returned—though I've something of yours here!"

His hand extended a small boxwood case.

Then he froze, spying my face.

The case, however, sprang open with a smart click, for he'd inadvertently touched the tiny brass latch upon its back. The inner maroon velvet held two pairs of spectacles, one with baleen frames, the other with iron frames wrapped in green silk at the inner rim.

"Yes, those would be my father's," I responded to the consternation in his slate-gray eyes.

He abruptly snapped the spectacle case shut and dropped it into a half-open drawer. I turned to close the study door and was about to explain when Dr. Fuchs walked over to me, frowning.

"You, sir, are an impostor! Dr. Mondini has no son, only a daughter in Venetia."

I removed my broad-brimmed hat, allowing him to see my face and my coppery hair, which fell to a crudely chopped length around my ears. "I am that daughter, sir, in disguise. The woods south of here aren't kind to a woman." My voice rose in tone again. I bowed my head. "Now you see Dr. Gabriella Silvana Mondini. If you need further proof—the spectacle case—I can describe it perfectly. The exterior is carved with two sirens, one on each side of the hinge. A wind curls from their mouths and ends with a flourish of fish. They are women in head and torso only; their arms are fins, and their lower bodies, dolphins. Inside the case are the words, 'Do not be seduced by false visions. Death lives in every maiden.' Though I would add that death lives equally in every man as well."

A long moment lapsed. Bells started up outside the room, severe and stony in their ringing. A spent fire hissed on the hearth to the left and I noticed the carved mantel, wondrously decorated with various leaf shapes.

"Lift your head, then, dear lady, let me observe you," Dr. Fuchs instructed me.

I lifted my head and noticed that dried plants—rue, mint, vervain—hung from the ceiling, and mugwort was tied in a bundle above the niche where a bed lay, its down quilts mounded like winter drifts. All around the walls were shelves, cabinets, niches of books.

"Hmm, yes. I do see the doctor in you." Dr. Fuchs turned back to his desk and again withdrew the spectacle case from the drawer. "I owe you an apology. Please forgive my hasty judgment. Here, you must keep these for your father. I think he missed you a good deal, for he was troubled and wouldn't speak but a few words about you, and those caused him pain, for he called you his helpmate and colleague. He was a man who could focus to a pinpoint of knowledge for days to the exclusion of all else. He greatly admired my herbals, you know. I remember once he spent days examining drawings and speci-mens of burdock, claiming some cure he'd learned from your mother's mother for old women's troubles. I only knew about its efficacy with tumors. I wasn't clear about why he was so keen on it. But when I questioned him, he said there wasn't enough attention given to women and those ailments of the moon."

I felt my heart quicken, and despite myself, my words rushed out: "My father and I were working on a complete book of diseases, to include those often overlooked by good doctors, namely the maladies of women. That is, until our work was interrupted by his departure." Inwardly I was rather astounded that I'd said, "My father and I . . . our work . . ."

"Ah, very ambitious, I'm sure!"

"I hope to rejoin him when I discover his whereabouts. Have you received any word from him?"

"No, not for a year or more."

My breath sank, as if weighted with stones.

Then the professor of botany continued, slightly irritated: "That letter bore no indication of its origin, with his thoughts running scattershot. I'd asked him to collect unusual plants for me, to add to my collection, but he was not forthcoming with the eloquent descriptions of place as was previously his habit. For as single-minded as he could be, he could also be diffuse."

"I'd very much like to read the letter, if you'd permit me," I requested. "Perhaps it will yield some bit of information for my search, for it seems that my father has disappeared."

"Oh! That is disturbing news." Dr. Fuchs raised his eyebrows, then turned back to his desk, opened a small drawer, and pulled out a single folded sheet of paper from a bundle of many. "Peculiar, isn't it, that your father, who customarily wrote several pages, sent me this single sheet and a pressed bulb, which he failed to identify?"

A small sliced cross section of a bulb with spidery roots stuck to the paper. Surely Dr. Fuchs recognized the hyacinth, whose fresh bulb was poisonous, though it was styptic and diuretic when dry and powdered. What message was here? The hyacinth could also be made into a bookbinding glue. Was this a challenge or a good-natured jibe at Dr. Fuchs: among the two men, whose book would be published first? I sensed there was something he wasn't telling me.

I perused the letter quickly and then handed it back to him. A couple of sentences stood out from the others. *I would like to study the world like a solitary in a tree and remain there for the rest of my days, but still I travel, aimlessly . . . I have based my life upon the ordering and naming of things, and now I wish to be nameless.*

I touched his spectacle case in my pocket with a sudden recognition. Without his eyeglasses, he could not see things clearly.

I had only to close my left eye to grasp this, for my right eye was marred by the same poor vision that also troubled my father. The room lost definition and gained shadow. Then I opened both eyes. The room sprang forward into clarity again. For a moment I imagined my father squinting toward the shape of the world, though I was sure by now he would've had new eyeglasses ground. Yet as I gathered from this dispatch, there was another kind of vision eluding him.

Dr. Fuchs leveled his gaze at me with keen curiosity. "You must have a well-stocked medicine chest. When you've rested I'd like very much to take a look at it."

I stared into the dying fire. "My medicine chest was lost in Lake Costentz, along with my horse. I must procure new stores of herbs and remedies." I shivered involuntarily. "The loss was great—several theriacs came from my father's own recipes."

The doctor sighed, disappointed. Then he called out, "Hans, Hans! Fetch the logs, stir the fire, the lady is cold!"

"Please! Dr. Fuchs, don't call me 'lady'!" Suddenly I recalled the stinging glance the Widow Gudrun had given me when I blurted out her secret—now I fully understood it. "I want to remain a man for a while longer. I still don't feel safe, for the bishop's men may have followed us here. I beg you to protect my disguise."

"As you wish," answered the professor, tipping his head back slightly to inspect me once more, pressing his lips together in a slit, and protruding his paunch. "Though the bishop's reach does not extend here." Then, in a low voice, he added, "Hans is nearly deaf. I doubt that he heard me."

He took my hand, staring at my strong fingers, and then led me from the room. "I'll show you to your sleeping quarters. Please return when you are refreshed and we'll take a light supper together. My sister has a son who is rather slight. I think his doublet and breeches will suit you. Let's try to find some clothes more befitting a wo—" He smiled. "Forgive me, a *man* of your class!"

The room I was given was well appointed but drafty.

I rose and moved about to warm myself and added an oak log to the fire. I pulled a coarse sweater over my nightshirt and drawers. Then I began one of those pointless tasks that sometimes comforts one: making a list. I removed all my garments from the walnut trunk and drawers to consider what I might need for the next part of the journey. The oak log finally spit and flared among the embers, lighting up the narrow chamber. How odd to see all my things empty of me. I turned to my clothing as one would turn to scraps of a geography that must be pasted to a sphere. Even the regions that were missing, the lost things, should be noted.

A pair of lady's leather slippers tied with latchets from Padua
A lace collar from Burano
My hand mirror
The medicine chest

All lost in Lake Costentz.

A skirt soiled by horse blood discarded in Überlingen
Two brocade dresses abandoned in the Schwarzwald
My vocation

I missed the rounds of patient visitations, the practice of
cures. For hadn't I put on the profession of my father? Now
vanished, he occupied the whole globe. Still. In his letters he'd
brought me to the places he traveled. He'd tried to give reason
for leaving me behind. There was the letter from Scotia:

March 1585

Dear Gabriella,
May this letter find you in good health and able vocation. I trust
all your wants are being met, and remember, you may always
request help from Dottor Cardano if you are in need of a man's
advice with financial or professional matters. I know the guild
members in Venetia resented your presence even when I was there
and so may cause you some chagrin. Hold firm to the purpose
of physick, to your work. Dear Daughter, I do miss your help
with the copying and arrangement of my notes for The Book
of Diseases, *for sometimes I can't even read my own writing*
(this is not from feeble vision, only the terrible recurrence of
untamed thoughts). I'm reminded, however, that it is best that
you remained there in Venetia, at least for now, as I met with
an instance of the dangerous jail fever here in Scotia. I must
confess shame at my own cowardice, because I could do no more
than flee after being called to treat a gentleman recently released

from prison (by all reports innocent). I recognized, from accounts I've read, the dreaded fever that just a few years ago devastated so many in Oxford, the Black Assize, when tainted prisoners fatally infected the court itself and then many hundreds beyond its purview. Of course I noted the symptoms at once, the fever and red wheals upon the chest, back, and arms, some stinking of gangrene. The words of Foscatero blazed in my mind, defining contagion that "passes from one thing to another, and is originally caused by infection of the imperceptible particles." I could not touch him. My fear that the imperceptible could leap from the suffering man to my own person overcame my most honorable desires as a physician. As in the plague of 1575, when our city was besieged by invisible particles, I took flight without thinking, How can I alleviate this horror? I don't feel absolved now by the apparent truth that nothing could be done. I only feel absolved in the case of that long-ago Venetian plague by the fact that in escaping to the cottage on my brother's land in Padua, I saved your life and that of your mother. How does one do no harm? You and I, Daughter, have discussed this many times, housebound by pelting rainstorms when sky merged with sea and we couldn't tend our patients. What is the least harm? This question is ever before me, a trembling needle that never quite rests on its compass face. Therefore, to answer the disquiet of your last letter, I do not abandon you. I protect you.

Your father, even in distance,
Dottor Ernesto Bartolomeo Mondini

Despite the fire beside me, my chilled body felt as though it barely belonged to me. Would I find myself only when I found my father? I'd lived a good many years without him, but I now saw those years in some way adrift. Even when I wasn't thinking of my father, I was always waiting for him to return.

The following morning the shutters on my windows shook with bursts of brisk wind, hung silent, then rattled again. Something dropped from the roof, knocking first against a ledge, then thudding to the street below, a loosened roof tile, a gable hinge, or one of those pulleys used to lift foodstuffs to the upper floors. The whole town, in fact, was losing bits of itself as the raw winter wind buffeted the houses, though it was still only October.

I dressed and sat at the window seat overlooking the soiled banks of snow dully lit by a gray afternoon. The dangerous weather would prevent us from traveling any farther. How long would we be delayed?

I heard a firm knock at the door.

"Come in," I murmured.

Dr. Fuchs lumbered in, Olmina behind him with a tray of fragrant mint tea, which she placed on a small marquetry table inlaid with light wood vining through dark.

"I have a letter for you, dear lady," he announced, and he examined the room as if to discover something about me by the arrangement of my things. Or maybe he was hoping that I'd lied about the medicine chest out of proprietary intent and he'd find it here. He moved with a kind of ceremony, setting the letter carefully on the thick sill with two hands. I recognized my mother's handwriting at once.

"I beg your pardon, Dr. Fuchs. I'd like to read this alone," I said, excusing myself, and then when I saw his expectant features fall, I added, "I'll come down later, and if you'd be so kind, we can peruse your marvelous herbarium and discuss the medicinal qualities of the plants."

"Yes, of course, the herbarium." His brow lightened somewhat. "I have a great many labels to pen. There are still so many plants in the presses from summer efflorescence that must be removed. The garden always grows far ahead of me, I'm afraid. My collections will certainly outlive me!" he exclaimed good-naturedly, shrugging his shoulders. I smiled to notice that, in fact, a crumpled alder leaf lay stuck to his woolen shirt.

As soon as he clunked down the stairs, I opened the letter, at the top of which Dr. Cardano had written, "Signorina Gabriella, I've forwarded this letter at your mother's request. May it find you in good humor. Your friend (under full moon and new), Dr. Cardano." That was a troublesome reference at the end, meaning, I suppose, "In ill health and good, whether mad or sound of mind."

I turned to my mother's tight cursive, vexed that Dr. Cardano had probably read her words. Her lengthy sentences ran all the way to the edges of the page and allowed no margins for one to breathe.

Dear Gabriella,

My most difficult daughter, yes, you are disobliging, as you sign your letter. But do you forget? Your father charged you to remain in Venetia. To care for me and, I might add, to care for yourself. But you were ever running away to explore — the garden, where a large black bee careened (you grasped it and were stung), the wharf (you might have been stolen), the marketplace (you were lost for half the day). But the more I held you, the more you squirmed to get away. I have never understood. And now, you believe you can be independent like a man and go wandering in search of your father, facing so many dangers. Come home, my girl. Your father has only bequeathed you a void—if he wanted to return, he would have. What's the use of chasing after him? His servants would have sent word if something had happened to him. This mania of yours, which I also believe has been brought on by those books you are constantly reading, which are not fit for a young woman (the parts of the body!), has erased your good sense. I've seen this obsession before in your father, and it led him to reject all things that didn't serve his studies. While this may be more seemly in a man, it is only unfortunate in a woman. I have always had to contend with your father's indulgence of you, and now see the result—a daughter who doesn't know her place in the world! I must speak my mind more openly: I've had a dream whose import I do not doubt. Your father was spellbound by a young linden in the form of a woman. Her skin shone green as moss and he strode into the woods with her. I cried out for him but he never turned. Your father is not lost or ill. He abandoned us under pretense of this book. Many years ago he was lulled by the women who were born with the caul, those cunning witches in the mountains who believe their healings to be true. Now his mania may have taken him farther afield, though he has always been leaving us. But Daughter, I have always had you. Please forget him and come home.

9 September 1590
Your ill-fated mother,
Signora Alessandra Serena Mondini

He was *always leaving.* I clenched the letter in my hand. My mother could twist the truth while still conserving some part of it. She knew him in a way I did not. Had their early affection been marred by some bluster (on his part, on hers)? Maybe neither of them could overcome the rash words that provoked old sorrow.

"Il vento impetuoso accende il fuoco oppure lo spegne, signorina," Olmina cautioned. *The impetuous wind can ignite the fire or put it out.* She was well acquainted with the grievances in the letter. Their repetition oddly sustained my mother, even as they wore down the people around her. She must have felt powerless. The recitation of grievances was strange balm. I too had felt it. But I never shared my grating sadness with her. Olmina rose from her chair to console me, but I waved her away.

I'd heard that story of the Benandanti many times, how my mother believed my father was seduced by one of the green witches with their herbal decoctions and willow staffs. Only a few years after he'd left, she'd begun her life anew in the glittering drawing rooms of Venetia. She often lay abed till midday, and then after hours of preparation (the white powder on the face and bosom, eye kohl, shrewdly placed beauty spot, and lip and cheek color, the jewels forbidden by the sumptuary laws — nonetheless she had secret pockets sewn into her skirt so that she could remove a pearl necklace or faceted ruby earrings at will), with poor Milena, her maid-servant, in tow, my mother clattered down the stairs in her cioppini. She'd engaged a gondola to a friend's house for an afternoon and evening of gilded chatter and piquant rumor: who forked whom, who knifed whom, what the priest said in the confessional, what the Council of Ten confided to the little courtesan of Thessalonica, and how she parlayed that confidence.

These were my mother's concerns, interrupted only by lute playing and supper. Perhaps she no longer cared for my father, or perhaps she hid herself, a frightened girl, beneath all the frippery and sharp-tongued scorn. I didn't know.

Still, her letter burned in my mind. I considered, what if my father had truly disavowed us? He was always leaving us. Then this final disappearance was only a continuation of what had come before. No. I couldn't believe it.

We'd extended our stay in Tübingen with Dr. Fuchs because of the harsh weather. After a week, I rarely ventured out into the streets of the city, for even as a man without voluminous hems to worry about, I hated the stinging cold and foul mud that spattered everything. The wind swept the acrid stenches of tannery, slaughterhouse, and dung from the lower town up toward the university and the castle and drenched us all in its ill vapors. At times I took refuge in the parish church; its steep Protestant arches seemed a vaulted stone forest. The quiet appeased me and I liked the plain sounds of the Protestant bells, distinct from Catholic bells in their ringing.

Once, I was accosted by a rough Swabian student who, not knowing I was a woman but having overheard my Venetian accent at the door, took me for some kind of intruder. "Halt there, foreigner! This is a sacred place for Protestants, not the trough at which Catholics feed!" (Why he'd assume that every stranger was a Catholic, I've no idea.) He shoved my shoulder and pushed me beneath an archway near the entrance.

I said nothing. The smell of frozen stone pricked my breath keenly as a blade. Other students gathered behind him, leering.

"Leave him be, he doesn't understand you," said another student.

I couldn't see this new voice well in the dim light but only detected a black hat that spilled yellow curls from beneath its rim.

"He shouldn't be here," grumbled the Swabian, his nose flat as a spatula.

"Sorry, didn't mean to offend," I blurted in broken German. "This church—very beautiful. Not a Catholic, not a Catholic," I lied, waving my hands before me in remonstration. Suddenly Olmo burst forth, fresh from the Marketplatz, bread basket in arm, loaves poking out, and pulled me out of the corner so quickly the others were too startled to respond.

"That's very fine!" shouted the Swabian after us. "You have to be rescued by your manservant, eh?" I shot a glance back over my shoulder. They all laughed—except for the one with yellow curls.

I noticed him later, following us back to Dr. Fuchs's house. He knocked on the door several minutes after we returned, and Hans opened it, grumbling.

"I'd like to speak to the young man who just returned with his manservant," said the tall man, his bright hair gathering the dry snow that began to fall heavily and steadily around him. I stood upstairs, watching him through the window. "You remember me—one of Dr. Fuchs's students, Wilhelm Lochner."

The breath of his words hung visibly in puffs before the jutting face of Hans.

"Can't see them, they're indisposed now," Hans replied. "You know these foreign ladies—the doctor and her maidservant can't take much of our cold weather, ha!" he spouted. I nearly gasped. Then, realizing his mistake, Hans thrust the door shut without a word.

The young man, Wilhelm Lochner, looked confused. He stared upward toward the wavy panes of leaded glass and the thick velvet curtain that hid me from view. As I peered down at him, he appeared to be underwater, eyes blue-silver as coin, the snow churning around him like whitewater at the rudder of a ship. I studied his black cloak, black and yellow striped breeches, and yellow hose, which revealed supple calves. Wilhelm stood there for a while, staring at one window and another, and then at the brisk little stream, channeled from the Neckar, that ran at the edge of the street behind him. He waited for so long that when he left, a dark hollow of earth remained where he had stood in the dull broadloom of snow.

After he'd gone, the snowfall filled in the hollow, opening one within me. Here was a man, I realized, who had sensed me through my disguise. I spoke quietly to the closed window and the submerged world beyond the imperfect glass: "Wilhelm Lochner, come in."

CHAPTER 10

❦

Where the Root Is in the House, the Devil Can Do No Harm

The next morning, Olmina shook my shoulders abruptly to wake me. "You have a visitor. Or shall I say a patient?"

"Olmina?" I stared at her, for now she wore women's clothing for the first time in many days.

"Ah, well, I suspect that all of Tübingen knows now who is staying at the house of Dr. Fuchs, thanks to Hans. For one servant speaks to another, and one student speaks to many! That one with the yellow hair, who knows what he's said. Anyway, I'm weary of men's garments. I like the feel of more cloth around me."

"But what's this you say about a patient?"

"It's that fellow who stood at the door yesterday. And mind you, signorina, I don't like this. Be careful."

Wilhelm Lochner had returned and requested a consultation with the foreign doctor. Dr. Fuchs thought it odd, and then he considered that it might be rather edifying, or so he told me later. Hence, to my frustration, he agreed without asking my consent.

After a short while (I didn't take long to dress, for unlike Olmina, I liked the ease of dressing as a man, even if everyone knew I was a woman now), I descended the stairs and entered the study, where the two men were seated before a boisterous fire. "Have you ever visited a woman doctor, then, Mr. Lochner?" I asked, skipping the usual courtesies and coming straight to the point.

Both men gaped at me rather foolishly, though both had already seen me in male garb. No doubt my legs were provocative in chestnut breeches. Men rarely perceived even an ankle, unless it belonged to a mistress or wife.

Wilhelm Lochner stood and bowed. "No, I've never had the distinct privilege of meeting a lady of this profession before you." He was brilliant as an equatorial bird, with stockings striped in three kinds of blue, indigo velvet breeches, a purple doublet, and red gloves that matched his deep red boots. "But how did you come by my name, dear lady?"

"I overheard you yesterday at the door." I paused, then continued rather coolly, "So what is troubling you?" I didn't want Mr. Lochner to know that his concern at the church had attracted me.

"Gabriella," Dr. Fuchs broke in, "Wilhelm was acquainted with your father."

"Ah." I now regarded him more carefully. That was sly of Dr. Fuchs.

"What do you recall of my father?" I asked, not feeling so hasty now, sitting down in a chair opposite the two men. I felt a little distracted myself by my exposed legs, stretched out before me, flickering with firelight.

"Your father," replied Mr. Lochner, "was a very intelligent doctor who soothed an ulcer upon my leg, though Dr. Fuchs did not approve of his cure." He cast a mock-challenging glance at his professor and then returned to me. "Now I'm suffering this skin ulcer again and wish to hear your recommendation."

"I'll have to view the offending ulcer first, if you'll permit me."

He appeared surprised at my request. Perhaps he expected me to either confirm my father's cure or inquire after Dr. Fuchs's suggestion, like those philosophical doctors who pay little heed to what is before their own eyes when prescribing a cure. Either way, he didn't tell me what was used. He was testing me, then.

"I'll step out of the room and return when you're ready," I proposed, and I left him to partly undress.

A few minutes later I was summoned to view Mr. Lochner, who stood with his back to me, his breeches scrunched up, his left stocking rolled down to reveal the back of his taut thigh, where a small, round ulcer wept. I examined it carefully, touching the skin around it, at which Mr. Lochner winced in pain. "I no longer have my medicines at hand, Mr. Lochner," I said, breaking the disconcerting silence in the room. "But I'd recommend a poultice of hemlock for this kind of stubborn lesion."

He glanced over his shoulder at me with a slightly bemused

smile, while Dr. Fuchs shook his head and said, "Your father suggested comfrey, which frankly I find to be ineffective in these sores."

"Ah, he did," I mused. "I'd say that would be an excellent thing for a fresh suppuration in the skin. But since you told me you've had the ulcer a long while, albeit of recurring habit, something more potent is needed."

Dr. Fuchs spoke up: "But hemlock, my dear! It's dangerous and the devil's herb besides!"

"Yet didn't I spy the poison parsley in your medicine chest in the herbarium? I've heard it said, 'Where the root is in the house, the devil can do no harm,' and further, 'If anyone should carry the plant about on his person, no venomous beast can harm him.' A bit of the devil repels the devil, then!"

Dr. Fuchs reddened, whether from embarrassment or irritation I wasn't sure.

"You may roll up the stocking, Lochner," he said brusquely. "And as for your interpretation, Gabriella, those adages come from ignorant midwives, not doctors."

So it was irritation, then. Since I trusted the experience of midwives, my own anger rose in their defense, though I said evenly, "There is more than one path to healing, Dr. Fuchs."

"And we've seen that here today in this very room, have we not?" interjected his student, still standing with one stocking up, one stocking down. He smiled at me.

I began to laugh a little, in spite of myself, and even Dr. Fuchs smiled now at the gaudy young man who stumbled toward me with a sort of bow. "Thank you, Dr. Mondini," Wilhelm said. "I see that the daughter is just as wise as the father."

My neck tingled pleasantly when he called me Dr. Mondini. Perhaps I was not just a novelty to him, a "dear lady" doctor.

Then he turned to Dr. Fuchs. "Could you have your man prepare the hemlock for me? I'll pay you well, master."

Dr. Fuchs grumbled as he left the room, and I followed him to help assemble the cure. A short time later, after having soaked a strip of linen in the hemlock decoction, I returned and wound the compress around the leg (which I noted was quite firm), covering the ulcer.

Mr. Lochner flinched and wobbled, at one point inadvertently resting his hand on my head while regaining his balance. Then he stroked my hair once furtively before facing away to draw up his stocking and fasten his garter. In that moment the firm back of his thigh, those muscular lineaments, usually unseen, possessed a crude power to move me.

I rose and observed him struggling with the garter. When he turned to thank me, his clear blue eyes were chagrined by his fumbling.

I looked away. "Mr. Lochner, if this doesn't prove to be efficacious, you must consider the maggot cure. For they will debride the flesh that clings and doesn't heal."

"I'd rather not take that cure till the grave!"

"But surely you've studied its great benefits? The worms consume only dead flesh, so you should have no qualms about it."

He bent close and murmured, "I would gladly be debrided if it afforded me more time in your company."

I stepped back (though some yearning in me invisibly sprang forward) and extended my hand. "Good day, then, Mr. Lochner. We must meet again here in a week so that I can reexamine the ulcer. Remember to have your servant change the dressing at least twice a day."

He smiled secretively and pressed my hand. "Thank you, Dr. Mondini. I'll send word regarding a time we may meet and speak of your father. I'd like to hear more about the Paduan philosophy of medicine. I know a quiet inn that women may attend for refreshment, though you must dress as a woman then. If you were found out to be masquerading as a man, you'd be severely punished. Surely Dr. Fuchs has warned you that women may be put to death in Germania for such an offense?"

Dr. Fuchs spoke in a low voice. "I didn't wish to frighten her. And besides"—he smirked—"the lady is very obstinate."

"You're right, of course." I nodded. "Though it doesn't seem fair, does it, that men wear the more generous clothing, and we the more constrained."

"What would the world come to if women wore the same garb as men!" cried Dr. Fuchs, throwing up his knobby hands.

"Then men would have to seek something other than a cunning sleeve or elaborate bodice," said Mr. Lochner, and I laughed aloud. Then he said, "Good day, Dr. Mondini," as he donned a broad ocher hat and longcoat and departed with a kind of foolish strut, whether intended self-mockery or simply good spirits I couldn't tell.

I hadn't laughed so easily in months.

Olmina watched all this from the doorway with narrowed eyes, arms crossed upon her chest.

CHAPTER 11

༺ঞ༻

Manifestations of
Solar Madness

"Good to see you once again, Dr. Mondini." A shadow hidden at the base of one of the watchtowers detached itself from the wall and stepped forward. "May I walk with you?"

"Of course, Mr. Lochner!" I answered, startled and pleased. It was a chill afternoon, a few days after I had addressed his ulcer. Olmina and I were walking near the silt-brown Neckar River, where the last ocher leaves of fall now huddled under snow along the dark banks. Both of us were back in our proper clothing, but my cloak and skirts barely kept me warm as fitful gusts wheezed through the trees.

Wilhelm Lochner was cloaked in gray, no longer displaying his colors.

Olmina grunted and held fast to my arm as Mr. Lochner offered me his. I didn't take it.

"How is the leg?" I inquired.

"Healing slowly, but the edges are shrinking."

"The hemlock's doing its work. You're not dizzy, are you?"

"No, no, I've had no unpleasant symptoms." His woolen coat brushed against mine as he drew closer. "I'm glad to see you before our next meeting at Dr. Fuchs's house."

Olmina sighed in forbearance.

I ignored her and (willing to be a fool) responded, "I'm glad to see you as well."

He laughed a little nervously and then asked, "Would you ladies like to join me for a cup of hot brandy? There's a wonderful inn not far from here where the alewife also serves wine—with a lump of sugar if you prefer. But of course you know the medicinal benefits of our excellent brandy, eh?"

"That would be very kind of you. I could use a little medicine for the melancholia."

Even Olmina—who enjoyed a sip now and then—brightened and nodded.

We quickened our pace, and as we turned a corner and neared the dense, leafless willows at the base of a pitted battlement, I noticed a place where it formed an angled stone seam, a hidden, sheltered place for lovers. *What if Olmina weren't here, would I let . . . , or better still, would I draw Mr. Lochner against the wall and pull his long-coat around me, would I spark desire like flint against the cold?*

As we headed up one of the steep streets toward the inn, I noticed that he appeared younger than I, perhaps twenty-two or twenty-three. I wasn't old, yet suddenly the daydream fled.

My reddish-brown hair hung ragged and short beneath my hat, and my lips felt chapped as I licked them in the bitter air.

A scattered snowfall flew here and there, uneven white flakes like bits of charred paper. Night didn't fall; rather, day leached from the air and dark caulked the spaces left behind. Gratefully we came at last to the Inn of the Blue Knight, its faded sign (a noble on a white horse with blue livery) wagging crookedly with each snowy gust. We entered a low-ceilinged drinking room that hummed with conversation and muted laughter. We found a snug wooden table near the fire, Olmina sitting next to me on the bench and Mr. Lochner opposite.

I noticed other women in twos and threes with half-covered baskets from the marketplace, round loaves of bread still steamy and filling the air with the simplest sort of pleasure—the scent of barley bread. Many of the customers ate their fresh loaves on the spot, with a bit of honey and a white cheese called *quarg*. Mr. Lochner ordered some for us from the thin-as-a-punt-pole alewife, along with our brandies.

So this was the drinking place for maids, wives, and widows after they'd gone to market. There were a few men here too, tucked into the corners, who seemed strange interlopers, spectators among a roomful of women. The plain creamy cheese, bread, and drink were the finest feast we could have desired at that moment. Soon my throat warmed with brandy. "Truly, Mr. Lochner, I had no idea such places existed for women. In Venetia we savor our wine at home or at the homes of friends."

He gave me a warm, appraising look and said, "Please call me Wilhelm. May I call you Gabriella?"

"I rather like 'Dr. Mondini,' but of course, call me by my given name."

"And you may call me Lady Olmina," announced my companion (having quaffed her brandy rather quickly), muffling a guffaw.

I turned to look at her in mild shock, for I'd rarely seen her intoxicated—or even ironic. But her humor pleased me. Wilhelm laughed and asked her, "A bit more brandy for the lady?"

"Oh no!"

"Oh yes!" he said, smiling, as he motioned at the pale alewife to fill our pewter cups a second time.

"Mr. Lochner," I blurted out, "would you tell us more of my father, for as you may know, he's become lost to us."

"Your father was very preoccupied with his book. And you know, he had a sort of rivalry with Dr. Fuchs."

I'd suspected as much but said nothing.

"There was some question of a cure that Dr. Fuchs felt your father had stolen from him, to redound to your father's credit in *The Book of Diseases*. Your father insisted that cures should be available to all and not remain the property of this or that herbalist. But Dr. Fuchs wanted to be a coauthor, for he'd been working on a book of simples. Your father left with some ill feeling, I'm sorry to say. I found pages of his book, which I'm sure he didn't intend to leave behind, in Dr. Fuchs's study."

I sat up, surprised. "Do you still have those pages?"

"No, I came across them, but I didn't dare remove them! I'd be banished from university if Dr. Fuchs found out. He's my guardian-mentor."

"I wonder how he obtained those pages. My father is very protective of his manuscript . . ."

"It would've been the last day, when he was departing, so he wouldn't have missed them."

"What did they contain?"

"I didn't read through the whole section—it comprised maybe twenty pages—because I could hear Dr. Fuchs shuffling back to his study. He sometimes let me read his books and write my annotations there . . . but what I perused had the title 'Manifestations of Solar Madness, Correlative to Lunacy.' It explored common and curious diseases, from fevers to solar bedevilment, where a man considers himself to be the very fire in the sky and wanders naked, shedding his light. Or so he believes."

I lowered my voice. "Where are the pages kept?"

Olmina came out of her happy stupor to chastise me in a loud voice. "What are you thinking?"

"*Shhh!*" both Wilhelm and I exhorted her.

Then he continued, "Dear Gabriella, I don't think I should reveal that. It might bring you trouble."

"I would like to add them to my own pages of notes."

"Ah, you are writing a book, then, too?" He sat up straight and set down the brandy he'd been cradling with both hands. His eyes darkened with interest.

"I was assisting my father."

"Ooh," groaned Olmina. She poked me under the table. "You're saying too much to this stranger."

"He's no stranger."

"Oh yes, he is. You know nothing about him!"

"We know nothing about Dr. Fuchs, really, either," I declared.

"And you know nothing about me!" She began to get weepy.

I turned to her, chuckling. "Olmina, eat some bread. You'll feel better. What don't I know about you?"

She leaned into me and asserted, "I know how to read, for one thing. I taught myself and read your father's books in the middle of the night when you were all asleep." She put her head down on her arms on the table.

I stared at her, amazed. "*That's* why you know so much when we treat the patients. I thought you learned by observing my father and me! What a dullard I've been." I should have been upset, I suppose, but I couldn't muster it.

"Well, well," observed Wilhelm, "there are three doctors at this table—one true, one student, and one hidden! To all the doctors here!" He raised his glass, and Olmina and I did the same, all three of us united, conspiratorial now, and grinning.

"Please don't tell anyone," Olmina mumbled. "Lorenzo doesn't know—he'd be angry at me for endangering our standing with you."

I hugged her and promised my silence. She knew how to read, my servingwoman. I was proud, astonished. What else didn't I know? More and more I saw those closest to me as vast villas with secret quarters, whole wings, perhaps, that were hidden to me.

"My word, to never tell," announced Wilhelm, with a flourish that signified the brandy had now warmed his brain as well. "And dear Gabriella, beware that your host doesn't steal your words too. Are your notes safe?"

"Yes, I believe so, but I'll be wary."

"We should go," Olmina said. "It's getting late. Lorenzo will worry."

And so, unsteady threesome that we were, we swung back through the deepening cold and darkness to Dr. Fuchs's house, Wilhelm in the middle, Olmina holding his left arm while I held the right. Somehow we managed to keep one another afloat in this blundering symmetry, chattering and sometimes hooting, until we reached the door. The young servant boy, grinning insolently, let us in before we even knocked. There in the dark entryway, Wilhelm pulled my glove slowly from my fingers and kissed my wintry palm rather than the back of my hand, as I thought he meant to do. The press of his mouth felt hot as a brand.

After rising late the next day, I found myself of two minds. Wilhelm intrigued and delighted me, but already I doubted his intentions. Was he simply curious, or an agent of Dr. Fuchs, seeking information about my father?

In any event, I wanted to recover my father's papers.

Dr. Fuchs would deny that he had them, so I didn't bother to ask. Instead I persuaded him that I required the kind use of his library. Unfortunately he remained there in the room with me, writing at his own slanted desk for more than two hours while I pored over his voluminous herbals. All the while, I observed in detail the contents of his study, the dark wood bookshelves, the drawers—in particular the desk drawer where he kept his papers under ornate brass lock and key.

A couple of days passed like this. Outside, winter yielded a little and the enlivening sun returned. I'd learned as much as I could here from Dr. Fuchs and decided, after studying my maps and recalling one of my father's letters, in which he had fervently mentioned Leiden ("a city of intellectual fires even in deadest of winter"), that Leiden would be our next destination. I sent a letter ahead to Professor Otterspeer, a colleague and friend of my father (who'd stayed with him in Leiden), to ask him to procure us lodging. Then I informed Dr. Fuchs of my plans to leave. He didn't attempt to dissuade me, and I grew anxious about obtaining my father's papers. Finally, the evening before we were to depart, I requested a last opportunity with the books.

"Of course, of course, my dear," Dr. Fuchs consented. "And I should like to read some of your work this evening too, before you continue your journey."

"Perhaps we could share notes, if you would privilege me with a glance at your volume."

"That would be impossible." The doctor looked at me askance. "I show no one my work until it is finished."

I nodded in assent, although privately I was annoyed at his refusal.

That evening, Olmina joined us in the study. Dr. Fuchs unlocked his desk, pulling out his folio of papers. Then Olmina gently touched his elbow. "Would you like me to prepare some herbal decoction for you, sir? Signorina Gabriella here can vouch for my skill."

He pivoted heavily on his chair to face her, his moist eyes fixed gently on hers. "Yes, perhaps something to ease my stomach. I'm feeling dyspeptic tonight."

"Would you like to choose your own herbs, then?" Olmina cannily suggested.

"Ah yes, that would be an excellent idea."

Olmina extended her arm and shoulder to him, for he was very arthritic and, like many gentlemen of advanced age, suffered from stiff joints. He stared at his feet and leaned into her as they moved toward the door. She glanced at me over her shoulder, indicating the open drawer with her eyes. "We'll return shortly, signorina."

As soon as they left, I quickly examined the contents of the drawer, various loose pages of writings and some botanical drawings. There, beneath a folio containing watercolors of tubers, I glimpsed my father's unsteady script, a writing that seemed scrawled on the surface of moving water.

Quickly I clasped the papers in their plain folio and tucked them into my skirt band, then hurried upstairs to hide them. When I returned, Olmina and Dr. Fuchs still hadn't come back. I assumed my place by the fire once more and read about the nature of kohlrabi (*Brassica raposa*) and its purifying benefits.

When they returned, Dr. Fuchs didn't sit at his desk but instead settled heavily in the chair opposite me, where he motioned for Olmina to draw up a seat too. He sipped his hot tea slowly, slurping loudly.

"Gabriella, there is something I must tell you." He paused. "I've hesitated to say this earlier, but . . . your father was no great friend of mine. He copied some of the notes from my materia medica and then refused to acknowledge it." He watched my face to gauge my reaction. I remained calm, but his dyspepsia got the better of him, for he muttered crossly, "If you ask me, your father is the worst sort of scholar, a thief ! When he left, *furtively,* one of the copies of my materia medica was missing. It was no coincidence, understand? If you find him, you *must* return it to me!"

I looked down at the engraving of a monstrous cabbage.

"Well, what do you say to that?" he asked, perturbed by my silence.

"If my father committed any offense, I'll make sure that your work is returned to you, though I can't believe he would pilfer the work of others." I spoke boldly, even as I felt a tense knot of doubt forming in my gut.

Dr. Fuchs frowned, then yawned widely, showing his worn molars and three holes in the gums where teeth had been pulled. His eyelids drooped heavily and he rose clumsily with Olmina's help. Then, to my horror, he shuffled back over to his desk. *What if he notices that I've tampered with his papers?* I thought.

He shifted them about and paused as if inspecting something. "You may think he'd never steal," he said, turning to me, "but we never really know the ones close to us." Now the doctor spoke thickly. "Don't resume to know your father—uh, er, presume, I mean." He gathered his papers, stopped again, and tapped his fingers upon the desk. *What if, in a strange reversal, he decides to return my father's pages to me?*

But he put his own work in the folio, tucking it away in the drawer, then fumbled with the key in its tiny lock.

"I'm very tired, must ask you to excuse me." He struggled for speech, then staggered toward his bed in its niche and plopped facedown upon the mattress. Olmina smiled at me; she'd mixed a sleeping draft for him. Together we rolled him onto his side toward the wall beneath a hanging clump of mugwort, thought to bring pleasant dreams. Within a few minutes he was grating and gasping. Olmina pushed a pillow under his head, removed his slippers, and drew up the quilt, and then his snores subsided a little. She pulled the bed-curtains.

After we left the doctor and began to climb the stairs to our room, she whispered, eyes gleaming with a certain mischief, "Do you have the pages?"

"Yes, they're in my satchel. Thank you, Olmina."

"Good! I'll just go say goodnight to Lorenzo."

And there he was, in fact, watching us keenly from the door to the kitchen.

Dr. Fuchs groggily sent us on our way early the next morning, our mules well laden with stores—hams, blood sausages, cheeses, and flatbreads—thanks to Lorenzo's shrewd bargaining at the market-place.

My good man stood close by and helped me to mount Fedele. The botanist watched us for a moment, red faced in the prickling cold, and then lumbered back into his house. My mind kept wandering to Wilhelm—striding the nearby streets, or bent to a book at the university library, cheering the place with his vivid colors. The night I'd held his arm, the damp wool serge of his cape smelled like home. I wanted to say good-bye to that gentle man. My palm burned. I wanted to rest my hand on his face, his neck, feel the coarse bristles of unshaven beard. To laugh at his bright clumsiness.

Lorenzo smacked the rump of my mule. "Are we ready to leave, then, Signorina Mondini? Want to hold the reins?" For I'd let them fall and now he handed them back to me.

Hans alone remained to see us off. Briefly I considered leaving word for Wilhelm with the manservant but decided against it. He had already proved himself indiscreet.

I was anxious now to be on our way. I didn't want to be in the vicinity when Dr. Fuchs discovered that I'd reclaimed my father's writings.

Hans mumbled some words I couldn't understand. I thought he might be offering some sort of apology, perhaps for his earlier lack of prudence, but then he chuckled. Later, Lorenzo told me that the rascal had said, "Good luck to you travelers, for you'll never be seen round here again, I'll wager, with this winter at your heels!"

And so it seemed that we were trying to outrun the knifing cold for the whole next leg of our journey. We rode just ahead of a heavy storm front for two days to Bade and then boarded a sailing barge on the Rhin to finish the journey to Leiden.

CHAPTER 12

Lost Governance
of the Whole

Some travelers like to read about the places they visit in the fine or fantastic accounts of their fellows on the road. Others like to read the work of great persons who've resided in those towns or cities they'll attain. Still others revel in the local tales shared at taverns and inns. I read and reread my father's letters to find out how the road or the town ahead might reveal him.

Dear Gabriella,
    I have secluded myself in the Hollant winter. Dr. Otterspeer, meaning well, strives to draw me out to dinners and dissections, to small conversations and erudite ones, but I don't have the

164

heart for it. Especially after my stay with Dr. Fuchs, who vented his distasteful suspicions upon me. Something is slipping away . . . Colleagues are not the friends they once were. We are all grown bitter. Even my mild servants exasperate me with their ordinary questions: What fish would you like from the market, sir, what cheese, what ale? What, what, what. Make your own damnable choices, I thunder at them, and leave me alone! Ah, I don't doubt you've known these moods, daughter. These are the days I work up a fury at myself, like a dog tearing at its fur . . . Best to end this letter now and stop my growling. Better yet, to not even send this letter!

Your father,
Dottor Ernesto Bartolomeo Mondini

But he'd sent it anyway, this letter that followed his investigations of solar madness in Tübingen.

Nightly I slept with my father's pages beneath me to prevent Olmina from reading them. Sometimes she idly asked about the notes. "What do they say, your father's pages? Do they bring you comfort, signorina?"

"Oh, he's simply expounding on certain ailments brought about by excessive sun."

"Ah," she said with a sigh, nudging a place next to me on the deck, where we sat on a crate of half-frozen cheese. "It must be a consolation, then, with all this freezing weather. Though it would be beautiful land, wouldn't it, if it weren't for the fact that we're in it."

"You're right about that," Lorenzo said as he groomed one of the mules to pass the time. "Does this river ever end?"

"Now, where's your sense of adventure?" I teased.

"I lost that in the lake, I think."

"Ah, so did I." I stared at the black water thickening to ice near the banks.

"Oh, let's think of something to banish the gloom," Olmina cried. "Would you read to us a little to pass the time? Let's hear about those that mislaid their brains on account of the sun."

"No, actually my father's notes are rather dry and uninteresting in the end," I answered in a surly tone. For the truth was, I was disturbed by the strange orbits of his thoughts.

NOTES TOWARD MANIFESTATIONS OF SOLAR MADNESS, CORRELATIVE TO LUNACY

Instances of sun fevers, unnatural indolence, and solar bedevilment. The sufferer believes himself to be kin to the fire in the sky and wanders naked, shedding his light! The deluded man then sees himself as a god who moves slowly, generates his own heat, emanates excessive sanguinity, believes others are circling him like the sun compassed by six planets in Copernicus's *De revolutionibus orbium coelestium*. Or is this the kindling of suicide? Why, he must wonder in cooler moments, does he suffer this grandeur? The man afflicted with sun stands in opposition to a man troubled by that other celestial body, the moon, which quickens and slows, disappears in paltry reflection of the larger orb or in shadow of the earth . . . I disappear. How might I find relief? For I've lost governance of the whole . . . If the sun could somehow be employed to counterbalance the effects of lunar increase, then the unease, the disease of the lesser body, might subside . . . I must look into this with others of like intolerance. The circular nature of the madness, a mockery of the sacred, condemns a man to wandering.

What did it mean—*lost governance of the whole?* I worried about the rambling nature of these notes: I didn't want anyone, not even Olmina, to know about this.

Olmina frowned and looked away. How much did she really understand about my father's possible illness? No, she couldn't know. He'd hidden it so well. Unless my mother had confided in her. Or did we all really know and hide it from ourselves, calling it a quirk or volatility? When truly his mind may have loosened every month. Olmina hooked her elbow through mine as if she understood, and we leaned against one another, sharing our warmth.

"I can tell you about a different kind of light that addles brains up in the mountains," said Lorenzo, sitting on a bale next to Fedele. He waved his leather currycomb in the air, indicating the Dolomiti.

"What sort of light is that?" I asked, curious.

"The ghost trees." Lorenzo paused, pulling hairs clotted with dirt out of the comb. "I was only a boy, and I had to bring the wood in for the fire. But the midsummer sun had gone down . . ."

"Go on, now," urged Olmina, to my surprise. Usually she'd huff at such tales.

"The woodpile was finished, so my father told me to go into the woods, where sometimes a wolf flashed between the trees. I was frightened, but I knew a place where a great tree had fallen in the wind and broken many branches on the way down. I meant to gather them by the light of the half-moon. But when I got to the place, it was lit up and not by the moon. The tree gave off its own light."

"How could that be?" murmured Olmina, rapt as a child.

"It was the ghost of it, wrapped round it like a veil or a shroud. It sort of rippled, and I felt it was friendly to me. As I gathered some branches, I touched it."

"Did it feel like anything?" I asked.

"Like sticking your hand in a slow, cold stream. Then I thought it coveted me and would take me. I ran all the way back to our hut, dropping branches along the way. My father, who I thought was going to whip me, instead clutched me to him. '*Figlio mio,*' he said, 'don't ever go out there again unless I'm with you. Tomorrow we'll take the ax and cut it up.' 'Oh no, you don't,' said my mother fiercely. 'You'll be stricken with the shadows!' "

"What's that?" asked Olmina.

"You can't ever get them out of your vision—branches sawing at the edge of your sight. Look left and they stretch left. Look down and they fall. Look up and they lift their rough fingers. Men go mad after a while, axing the air to try to clear the thickets from their eyes."

We were silent then, each in our own thoughts, observing the smoke rising from hamlets along the shore, mute with cold. Seagulls on sandbars huddled in the snow of their bodies. Only the river spoke.

Later that night after Olmina fell asleep, I began writing in response to my mother's last letter, loath as I was to prod her vexation and receive another earful.

My dear mamma,

You may admonish me for thinking my father ill or lost, and you mention his mania for the book, for wandering. But I wonder now if there is something else that you couldn't tell me all these years. I'm asking about madness in the family, my father's Cipriot branch. I'd like to know what you've heard and whether my father ever crossed over, ever descended into that terrible place where the true world disappears. This may have bearing on whether I return, so you would do well to be forthcoming with me. I'm sorry I'm not the daughter you wished, nor are you the mother for whom I longed even though in the end that longing would be better directed to spirit or to Olmina. I wish you no ill. So there is a sad balance between our sorrows. Candor could give us a fulcrum toward change, if you wished it.

1 November 1590
Your daughter, Gabriella

As we drifted past the snow-heaped walls and terraces of Worms, we lost one of the mules to a freeze. The poor creatures had stood roped together on deck under blankets at night, pressed into one another, facing into wind or snow. Lorenzo spoke to them, brushed them down, fed them, and took them ashore to relieve themselves on the longer stopovers. But one mule on the outside of the group refused to eat, and that morning we found him seemingly asleep but gone stiff, showing his teeth in the final grimace.

"Well," muttered Lorenzo, "he's gone home to a far better clime."

"Oh, Lorenzo, how can we keep the others safe?" I cried as I knelt and stroked the dead mule's neck (so rigid under my hand), aware of the futility of my gesture, stung with shame for my part in his death. I'd been wrong about the weather, though it had improved over the past few days. November had arrived gnashing with ice and blizzard. We should have stayed longer with Dr. Fuchs.

"Give them our blankets," he answered without pause.

So we did. We also convinced the captain of the river barge to stack goods around our remaining five mules to create a makeshift stall. Now we all wore every bit of clothing we owned, and ate and slept in our many layers. Whenever I sat up on deck, watching the other sailing barges and ships, the shoreline and towns, pass by, I found a place near the mules and stroked them.

Olmina sang to them.

Lorenzo tended them.

I thought of Wilhelm and then pushed him out of my mind. I couldn't afford affection. I had to keep moving toward my father.

After twelve days, the grisaille fields and icy canals of Hollant appeared at last. We had arrived at Leiden.

We disembarked gratefully, barely knowing how to walk on land again, though the mules frisked and kicked up their hooves with joy after Lorenzo managed to half lead, half heave them down the gangplank. We asked directions to the Hortus Botanicus, where my father's colleague Professor Otterspeer's home was located—the helpful, bundled-up passersby viewed us with curious smiles, and I felt welcomed—and soon we found our way there.

When we called upon Professor Otterspeer, we were informed he had unexpectedly departed to visit an ailing sister for a week. Before this news could disturb us, the caretaker, a stout middle-aged man, informed me the professor had kindly obtained a place for us to stay. He led us to a small two-story wood-and-brick cottage just outside the Hortus Botanicus walls.

As we settled into our new lodging, I observed the view outside: you'd barely have known we were staying by a famous garden. Some valiant twigs poked through the snow; a few small evergreen yew trees in large pots suggested a pathway, while the pergola at the very center marked the demise of summer in its hood of snow.

As Olmina prepared our dinner, peeling and chopping, I pulled a chair up to the fire and turned to my notes, for it always lifted my spirits to touch the book once more.

MITHRIDATUM AGAINST POISON

The Greek physician Galen has stated that this famous recipe contains fifty-four ingredients. Others claim that the antidote (devised by King Mithradates in Pontus during the first century) contains no more than thirty-six. Whatever the number, the king was defeated by his own antidote, a cautionary tale for whoever wishes to take it in daily dosage. For Mithradates became immune to poison, and when he desired to kill himself honorably in the face of his enemy the Roman general Pompey, the king could not die by poison. He was forced to beg his servant to slay him. Therefore my recommendation is to give in small sips only when the cause under suspicion is poison. Be sure of the signs (and surely this requires another volume for all the varieties of poison). Another danger of daily use is illustrated in the tales of the poison damsels, girls fostered upon small doses of venom from an early age. The slightest kiss from such a girl grown into a woman would be fatal, and so she would be shunned by all men.

CHAPTER 13

❧

What Was Lost Was Returned

Over the next few days, I became intimately acquainted with the sound of the wind. It advanced windmill by windmill and then passed over us, setting up a slow shudder that could be felt in the very floorboards. Surely everyone in that moment stopped what they were doing and noted the change before they turned back to curing herring, planing clogs, or weighing the Edam. The Hollanters constructed their lives up against the encroachment of water, for the windmills emptied the marshes and the storm tides reclaimed them.

I'd barely regained my footing after days of rocking on the Rhin ship, only to arrive in a place where one never forgot that land was temporary.

~~❦~~

"Signorina Gabriella, haven't you heard me calling you?" Olmina was clearly annoyed, having been drawn away from bread making. I looked up from my notes to see her hands gloved in dough, her brow dusted with flour, like some poorly applied face powder. I smiled at her.

"Oh, I forgot, you're in that other world." She raised her eye-brows, then repeated, "A gentleman from Piamonte is at the door on some important errand. He will speak only to you about it."

I drew on my slippers and glanced for a moment in the small wavy mirror hanging in a blue frame on the wall. I suppose the gardener who'd occupied this cottage didn't need to see much of himself; the mirror only reflected half a face at a sensible distance. But now that I was more freely a woman again, I longed for a larger mirror. I could see that my feathery hair sprang like the pluckings of a pheasant around my face, in a length too long for a man now, but too short and unruly for a woman. I struggled to push it into Cousin Lavinia's snood, which ill served the purpose of containing it. She would have been amused. I could almost hear her back in Venetia saying, *Just throw away the snood, Gabriella. Let your hair wander.*

At the door, I saw a man with lively, close-set eyes and a fine auburn beard woven with gray. He presented himself as Signor Vincenzo Gradenigo, a merchant of dry goods. His two young servants stood behind, clearly bored. They held mules with bolts of cloth poking out, no doubt cambrics, fine silks, damasks, and brocades, and probably also unseen scissors, needles, and threads of different weights.

A ring hung on a yellow cord around Signor Gradenigo's neck, signifying Jewish descent, and his accent conveyed a cultivated tone. My ear was delighted by the slant of familiar sound, for Jewish physicians and scholars had often attended our midday table at home. The strict edicts of the Council of Ten forced them to return to the quarter built near the old foundry, the Ghetto, at night—though even this nocturnal exile within our city was not harsh enough for certain brittle minds, who wanted to banish Jews altogether.

"Signorina Mondini." Signor Gradenigo removed his broad red hat and smiled at me in a friendly manner, and then he bowed, exposing the swarthy orb of his bald head as he bent forward. "I have the honor of your acquaintance several times removed. First through the good offices of the fine Widow Gudrun, at whose inn you stayed in Überlingen. Then through a certain student of botany in Tübingen, Wilhelm Lochner." Here Signor Gradenigo paused and rose out of the bow to which he'd slowly descended. An involuntary jolt shot through me at the mention of Wilhelm. I struggled to keep a bland expression, though I doubt I'd fooled the merchant. At his full height, Signor Gradenigo examined my face, looking up slightly as he continued to speak. He was a little shorter than I, so I gained the rare advantage of a downward perspective toward a man.

His nose was narrow and handsome. His upper lip lay hidden beneath his mustache, while the lower lip formed around his words with great vigor. His brows joined in the center, and the veins were clearly written upon his temples. He drew back a little, and then I noticed that in fact his shoulders slumped (a habit of cloaked despondency, perhaps?) beneath the sumptuous broadcloth of his black shoulder cape.

He frowned slightly. He must have sensed that I wasn't fully listening to him. I brought myself back in time to hear him say, "According to the instructions of Widow Gudrun, then, I have your medicine chest in my possession and have come to return it to you."

"Oh!" I cried out in joy.

Signor Gradenigo extended his arm toward the mules, like a conjurer. I leapt forward and startled the poor man by clasping his shoulders in my elation. "Come in, then, dear gentleman!" I cried. "I'm truly indebted to you and would grant you a reward! At the very least you must take dinner with us." I turned around. "Lorenzo, Lorenzo! Come and take care of the gentlemen's mules!"

He appeared at once, as if he'd been waiting just behind the door.

"I'd be glad to accept your hospitality," Signor Gradenigo said, nodding. "But first I must settle us in our lodgings. Perhaps the signorina would like to renew her acquaintance with the inestimable chest, which I'm sure has its own story to recommend. There are certain things that contain more than their own history."

"Certain things too that erase history," I responded without thinking, and then, sensing my color rise, I quickly thanked him again.

The gentleman nodded graciously and delivered the medicine chest into my arms, with a slight pressure of his hand against mine as he released it.

I couldn't wait to take an inventory of the chest's contents. I instructed Olmina to leave me undisturbed for the rest of the day. I carried the chest to my room and touched the lid gently, in the way one would welcome an old friend, as I examined the brass hinges and handles, read the nicks and scratches that formed an account of its passage.

I say "read," but the chest was also largely illegible to me. I was shaken by the sense that it was no longer entirely mine. In truth it had become a foreign object, smelling of foreign goods. Woolen carpets, cinnamon, and oranges . . . perhaps rose water? And something sour I couldn't identify.

It had been my intention this very week to commission a new chest here in Leiden. I'd delayed so long, refrained from purchasing a plain chest, because nothing could replace the old one, and now the Venetian chest was back in my possession! What was lost was returned, but I could see immediately the contents had been viewed and handled by strangers. I realized this would also be an inventory of the lost, the stolen, and the damaged. Though a few things were reduced (the mercury one-fourth its original amount) and other things were missing (someone had broken a bottle of black salsify water and spilled chamomile powder all over the bottom of the chest), the actual losses were few. (Had the lake, the widow, or the merchant spirited away the rare and expensive Spanish oil? I wouldn't begrudge anyone this if it were so . . .) The Widow Gudrun had appeared sympathetic while we stayed at her inn, but perhaps she'd already discovered and hoarded the chest? It may have been close by, in the attic, where she'd ascended each night.

Gudrun (or Signor Gradenigo?) had taken out all the drawers and trays, all the pewter- and parchment-capped bottles — round, square, triangular, and rectangular — and examined them.

Someone had manipulated the bowls, scales, and small brass weights, marble mortar with agate pestle, pewter boxes, brushes, lancets, and needles and put everything back in the wrong order, though clearly some attempt had been made to arrange them, and this attempt was more disconcerting to me than a random shuffle. Someone had insinuated herself or himself into the scheme of things. Someone had stroked the wood with uncomprehending hands and scribbled words at the edges of the drawers, words whose meaning I'd have to inquire of Professor Otterspeer later.

The chest had suffered from the cold. The oak had tightened and warped against the brass corners and hinges. One night, I imagined, the widow must have understood she couldn't keep it, as her brittle hands wavered across the dolphin handles and the cartouches of a woman's head mounted upon them. Perhaps she looked upon the inner lid, the god Asclepius and his daughter Hygieia staring back at her as if they would ask, *Would you take what isn't yours?* and she became frightened. So Gudrun gave up the chest to one of her guests, the cloth merchant who was also on his way north, among his destinations Tübingen and Leiden. If this was all so, then I was glad that she chose her courier well. Another might have been sorely tempted to sell its valuable contents.

Though these intrusions into my medicine chest unsettled me, I was more surprised by what had been *added*. I soon found a needle, like an amulet or hex slipped into a person's clothing, the thin silver spike driven into the drawer groove in such a way that I couldn't easily remove it. A short length of red thread ran through the eye. Was this the widow's way of protecting herself against bad luck? Or was it the merchant's needle and thread?

I would have to find out.

Through the window shutters I could hear voices clamoring in the lane below. I cracked open the shutter, and the chill evening crept in. Stars pricked the sky like dull tacks, and a thin membrane of ice shone dimly on part of the canal below. To my amazement, the insubstantial had grown solid: the whole canal was covered with a frozen skin webbed with pale capillaries, cracks that formed as it wavered slightly from the motion of the water beneath. The canals in Venetia rarely froze, and I'm sure my father would've liked to see this. Perhaps he had seen it.

Why—I suddenly questioned myself—did I always wish to see things companioned by his eyes?

In a letter from Hispania in the summer of 1587, my father had written:

Remember when Avicenna noted, "The eye is like a mirror, and the visible object is like the thing reflected in the mirror." The orb of the earth, like an eye, collects the light from the sun, passing it through a crystalline atmospheric lens to retinal purpose, envisioning us. Maybe that's all we are, the little figures at the back of the vitreous humor of night, moving, gesturing, dying. Upside down like the creatures reflected on a spoon. And we think we are so large! We are so important! But we are socketed in our illusions. I am large to you, dear Daughter, and you are large to me. But we only flicker like insignificant sparks upon this earth.

That evening, though I knew well enough it was foolish for a woman to go out alone, I yearned to breathe fresh air, if only for a little while. So I dressed in warm stockings and breeches—I'd kept the men's clothing I'd purchased in Tübingen—and crept downstairs. No one in the cottage awakened. My companions (truthfully, after all that we'd been through, I could no longer simply call them my servants) lay snug in their bed upstairs. Lorenzo's snores reassured me.

I put on my boots and went out.

Frost on the ground crackled underfoot as I strode briskly along the canal. I liked being outside alone in a city of sleepers. Feeling myself a sort of ghost, I slipped through the town gate, which had been neglectfully left unlocked, and found myself outside Leiden's walls on the south bank of the Rhin.

Such a relentlessly horizontal country, the Netherlands! My life would thin out here. Rarefy. Where was the night watchman? The river was black and loud now, and though ice had begun to sheet at the edges, the currents carved away at it.

I stood there motionless for a long time.

When I turned my eyes back to the shadowy gateposts, two men moved there. One slid open the side of a lantern and lifted it toward me. The watchman. I also recognized Lorenzo's voice. He'd followed me.

"Signora!" he called out. "There you are . . ." He was breathless as he approached me. "Where . . . where are you going?" Lorenzo kept an eye on me far beyond call of duty, as if I were the daughter he'd lost so long ago, the baby with the caul who'd lived barely a day.

I couldn't find the words to explain why I had left. All at once I was very cold. I took his arm in silence as he led me to the gateposts.

As we walked back toward the house, I was astonished to see the whole aspect of the town altered from solitary to festive.

How long had I been gone? No more than an hour, surely! But here and there along the canals, bonfires had been kindled. Bundled children looking like animate loaves tested the ice with long sticks and tossed stones that either punctured the surface or skipped across the white rind like mice. One boy taunted his fearful younger brother, pushing him down the bank onto the congealed crust. The younger boy, red eyed and puffy faced, lay sprawled and motionless, while the older boy strode back and forth across the ice-covered canal, bragging, "I can go anywhere I want, I can walk on water!"

I stood near one of the bonfires with Lorenzo, my arm hooked through his, as we watched the little spectacles play out up and down the canal. Someone passed us small mugs of aquavit, pungent with caraway and pepper. How odd I felt, warmed by a sudden affection for Lorenzo. How upended my life had become! I was at the bottom of Fortuna's wheel now, hanging on by my ankles. And yet fatherless, was I not also free?

The bells sounded—it was six o'clock in the morning.

We had been outside for hours.

The next morning I determined to find Signor Gradenigo, to reward him and inquire about the red thread. Was the intent gift or guile?

When Lorenzo located his lodgings, he left my invitation to a simple supper at the cottage, though later I thought it foolish of me. What if they enforced a curfew on the Jews in the city? But when I located the caretaker, who was raking pruned twigs in the winter garden, he assured me, "No such law exists for Jews here in Hollant."

"Ah, that's fortunate," I said, explaining to him the edict of the Jews in Venetia. "They must be careful, or they'll be locked out of the Ghetto and into the dungeon."

"Deplorable!"

"I don't understand it myself," I agreed. "The council, you know, must draft its edicts, must convert all the little fears into dictates, or God knows"—I threw up my hands theatrically, delighted to speak so openly—"chaos will surely envelop us all!"

"Houses will collapse!" added Lorenzo, who'd been listening nearby as he filled a bucket at the well.

"Families will go hungry!" said the caretaker, joining in the spirit.

"Women will sprout tusks!" joked Olmina at the door. Then she looked to me to finish the game.

"Men will crawl about on all fours!" I said, imagining the guild and the council in that position, and—remembering their censure of my work, which had first sent me on this journey—it was not without some pleasure that I reveled in this vision.

When Signor Gradenigo arrived at the door that evening in his black coat and broad hat, he carried a small wooden box. It gave off a faint scent of cedar and something else I couldn't identify, although I could call it moldering, ancient leaves. Lorenzo welcomed him into the entry adjoining our humble kitchen and dining corner, and asked, "What's in the box, my good man?"

The merchant's eyes shone as he waved us away from it. "This is a surprise for all of you, but we'll not enjoy it until after the meal. I've had excellent profits today and I'm glad to share my good fortune with you." He set it upon a wooden shelf in the kitchen near the cobalt-blue jar of flour.

"Is it some kind of rare sweet?" asked Olmina, her interest piqued. She stood near the little iron stove, stirring the soup in a black pot.

"Loukum!" guessed Lorenzo, for he loved the chewy Ciprian sweet of honeyed nuts and oranges that we sometimes savored in Venetia.

"Oh no, unfortunately not. But that would be delectable, wouldn't it?" Signor Gradenigo laughed. "I regret to say I always devour my store of that delight long before I travel this far north." He removed his coat, hung it on a bent nail by the door, and patted his rotund belly beneath a rich brocaded doublet.

"And in spite of our longings, it doesn't smell sweet," I added. "But please have a seat at our plain table, Signor Gradenigo."

He nodded his head. "Call me Vincenzo, and I hope you don't mind my calling you Dottoressa Mondini, for I do hear that you are well versed in medicines and the humors."

I smiled. "Thanks to you, signor, I have my means of treatment back now. Though there is something unusual in my medicine chest—"

"Thanks be to the saints, supper is ready!" Olmina interrupted. She set bowls of soup and a board of spiced herring upon the wooden table laid with a dun linen cloth, along with a basket of fresh bread. The turnip and onion pottage smelled pungent with thyme and marjoram.

As I sat down next to her on the bench opposite the men, I asked, "Where did you find the lovely herbs?"

"Ah, in the Hortus under the snow, tender and fine as you please, once revived in warm water," she answered.

"And wouldn't that be theft of the cooking garden?" I prodded her.

She shrugged. "Who's out in this cold to catch me?"

"No one, apparently, and we are the lucky beneficiaries!" said Vincenzo as he dove into the soup with a large pewter spoon.

The room steamed with the fragrance of Olmina's soup, as if she'd infused it with the last ripening days of autumn. For a long while our conversation yielded to her talent. After we'd finished the meal, Vincenzo rose with mock ceremony and brought his box to the table, where he undid the brass clasp and lifted the lid. We were greeted by the most delicate smell, suggestive of old light and the faint scent of water in a still pool.

"Here we have the uncommon Yunnan tea that the Dutch nobles enjoy for over a hundred silver ducats a pound!" He circled his hand smartly. Inside, dark leaves were compressed into small round cakes. He passed the box to Olmina, who sat directly across from him.

Olmina set her sharp eyes upon him. "And why would you bring this tea to us, if you don't mind my asking?"

The merchant gave us a distant smile, though his eyes remained somber, as if he were thinking of some other place, a tea drinker's pavilion, perhaps, in a more temperate clime. He said, "Because it's a melancholy thing to drink tea alone. I'd rather share my tea with good company."

Olmina's face softened as she sniffed the rare cakes.

"Thank you, dear sir," I said. I closed my eyes when the box came to me. Yes, it was the smell of leaves, light, and water. They suggested something sweet and, even though shadowy and rich, still luminous, like a tree at the edge of water, reflected and reflecting. "This is the kind of tea that could help someone find a lost memory," I said, and I opened my eyes. I didn't want to let go of the scent and reluctantly passed the box along to Lorenzo.

"Mmm," he murmured as he stuck his nose into a tea cake.

Olmina set an iron kettle on the stove. When the water rolled to a boil, the merchant got up and moved the kettle to the back of the stove, lifted the lid, and carefully flaked a tea cake straight into the hot water, then quickly set the lid on again.

"I've heard that it's excellent for a clear mind and heart," he announced, obviously enjoying the simple preparation. He poured the tea into our mugs and we cupped our hands around the brew, enjoying leaves from the mountains of China. Outside, it began to snow, and we sat quietly for a while, alone and yet companioned in our thoughts, as if the tea's gift were not just its glorious scent but also this silence in common.

"Mens sana in corpore sano," I said, recalling Juvenal.

"And to 'Sound mind, sound body' I might add 'sound heart,'" said Vincenzo, smiling slightly.

"Ah, sound heart," I repeated. The snow fell harder now, making a muffled pelting sound on the roof. "I'm curious, to return to my medicine chest, about the needle and red thread. Do you know where it came from?"

"Hmm, yes, I noticed that after Tübingen." Vincenzo hesitated. "For I confess, Dr. Mondini, that I examined the chest a few times. It was of utmost interest to me, for though I'm not a doctor, the study of cures has been my avocation."

"And did you write upon the drawers, then?"

"Yes, I identified some of the medicaments in German. For I thought I might not find you . . . I hope you'll forgive me." He looked down into his tea.

I sighed at my own foolish indignation, letting it go as quickly as it came. "Well, it's no matter," I said. "So . . . the thread?"

"I can only guess, Dottoressa. When I reached Tübingen, I asked about you, and my innkeeper referred me to a student lodger down the way from the inn. I met the gentleman, Wilhelm Lochner, and we shared supper for several nights, getting on quite well. One evening I invited him to my room to see the medicine chest—it is rather a marvel, as you well know. I lent it to Wilhelm for a few hours, as he wanted to make a list of the remedies within, being the avid student. I stayed there in the room with him, recording my transactions for the day in my account book."

I clenched my mug, nodded, and sipped, but said nothing.

"I didn't see him slip anything into the chest, but I wasn't watching the whole time either. I must tell you that it was his express intention to follow you. I believe, Dr. Mondini, that he thought very highly of you and your cure, for his leg was no longer marred by the ulcer."

Everyone stared at me now, anticipating some kind of response, but I wasn't sure what to make of this. Did I want to see him? Yes, a little. But no, I didn't want to become entangled. "I'm not certain I wish to see him," I said carefully at last. "If you should encounter him here, I'd appreciate your discretion."

"You shall have it, but I must say the red thread may be a binding charm such as you can find sometimes from the traveling Romani. Maybe he meant it as a kind of message?" Vincenzo suggested.

Lorenzo snorted at this. "Why wouldn't he come right out and speak his mind?"

"The signorina left without seeing him," Olmina said. "How could he?"

"The Greeks say Atropos, the Fate who cannot be turned, snips the thread," I mused.

"And some Gypsies do come from the lands of Macedonia and Thrace," the merchant said.

"Then it may be a curse," I said uneasily.

"Or a charm, especially for a doctor, don't you think? For one must always bow to the goddess of necessity," the merchant said. "The Fates alone spin, measure, and sever our red vigor. Perhaps your little needle and thread is a reminder of this."

"But none of the Fates holds a needle—the *doctor's* art is in sewing, drawing things together again, closing the wound."

"If you can," Vincenzo said, in a solemn tone. "Some wounds, like some wrongs, can never be righted."

Olmina rose to clear the dishes and said quietly, "No doubt it's a love charm from Wilhelm, if you ask me."

I glared at her. "We need speak no more of this."

Vincenzo glanced away to spare me embarrassment.

"But I have another question for you," I said.

He turned his sharp brown eyes to mine.

"In all your travels, have you ever encountered another Dr. Mondini, my father?"

"Not exactly. That is, I didn't meet him myself, though I overheard a gentleman in Edenburg speak of his book . . . something about a vast taxonomy of diseases, though . . ."

"Though what?"

"I don't like to repeat rumors."

"Go ahead. I'll accept it as such."

"He said it was a very sorry thing when such a doctor had compiled a work of great breadth and excellence and yet was secretly unbound himself. Forgive me, but those were his words."

"And if that were true, how could that man create such a fine encyclopedia of diseases?" I asked rather heatedly.

"We often flirt with the very thing we create, don't you think? I myself create an appetite for beautiful bolts of cloth, which I may also be prone to love too much." He unbuttoned his doublet and patted an elegant violet and silver-wrought waistcoat.

"Ah, it's wonderful!" cried Olmina with admiration, for she understood quality cloth far more than I did, since she'd worked it into so many garments for our household.

"And you, Dr. Mondini, what edge do you play?"

"I am single-minded to a fault, perhaps, in my need to heal others, to heal my father, to find him."

"And your own ailment?"

I laughed a little. "I'm overly stubborn. I don't know."

"Not stubborn, oh no, Gabriella," said Olmina. "Unrelenting, hooked as a fish on a line!"

"Really? I'm not sure I like the sound of that. Hooked on what?"

"On your father, other doctors, the universities. What about your own instincts?"

"I know my own talents, don't worry. And I'm bringing them to the tasks at hand."

Lorenzo spoke up. "Of course you are. Olmina misspoke, didn't you, my dear?"

She folded her hands on her lap. "Yes, yes, I did. I just wish . . ."

"What?"

"I want to go home." She began to cry.

I put my arm around her. "Forgive me for dragging you on this journey. I am so grateful. And I too grow weary with the insubstantial traces of my father. But I must exhaust every lead, every place."

"Of course you must." She bent her head to my shoulder.

Vincenzo stood up. "And I must be on my way if I'm not to lose it in this snowy night. A wonderful repast, dear ladies and gentleman." He wrapped himself up tightly in his coat and pulled his hat down snugly upon his balding head.

"Just a moment," I said, and I quickly ran upstairs. I descended with a small purse of florins. "This is for your trouble, Vincenzo. Thank you for the chest and the message."

He pressed my hand kindly and nodded, saying, "I wish you good fortune in your journey, Dr. Mondini. May you find what you are seeking."

Lorenzo opened the door to the thick and darkening night.

Vincenzo raised his hand. "Good night to you all," he said. Then he turned and immediately vanished into the snowfall, even with his conspicuous black coat, as Lorenzo held up the lantern.

The next morning, Professor Otterspeer finally sent along a message with his servant, saying that he'd returned to Leiden and that he would come to collect me so that we might attend a dissection.

A few hours later, I watched him approach from between the half-open shutters of my room. I recognized him from the frontispiece engraving to his volume on anatomy, which my father possessed in Venetia, for the artist had rendered a fine likeness. He trudged through the snow along the canal and knocked loudly upon the door. From my second-story vantage, his black scholar's cap bobbed outlandishly above the frothy lace of his collar, like an overturned bowl on a river.

I gave a last tug to arrange my own ruffed collar, attached to a bit of silk covering my chest. Olmina brought me my new indigo woolen cape with a hood trimmed in ermine. What a luxury! I'd ordered it from a tailor off the Rapenburg Canal the second day after we'd arrived, to stave off the cold. Olmina requested a skirt the color of butter and was much pleased with the finished garment. The Dutch are truly master weavers, I marveled now. Tailor Zander, an uncommonly tall man, had stooped with great flourishes to present the serges from the coarsest thickness to the lightest nap, in tones of red, yellow, blue, brown, cream, and black. I was distracted by his fingers, surely the longest and deftest I'd ever witnessed. He kept a silver thimble on his third finger, even though he wasn't sewing at the time, and a row of straight pins in his waistcoat.

The anatomy theater would be quite cold, so I hurriedly grabbed my gloves from the windowsill, where I'd thoughtlessly laid them the previous night. The lambskin was crisp, but the wool inside quickly gained warmth from my hands. I stepped out of my room and descended the narrow flight of stairs.

Lorenzo was nodding in an amused fashion at Professor

Otterspeer, who stood just inside the door and spoke an Italian in which he fancied himself fluent. When the professor saw me, he smiled imperiously, red cheeked with rosacea, which blossomed like a map upon his face.

"Signorina Mondini, my dear lady! A pleasure to meet you at last, in person," he declared. "Please forgive my inconvenient delay."

"Don't trouble yourself about it, dear Professor," I replied. "It's good to meet you as well. I must thank you for procuring our lodging. If you don't mind, I prefer to be called Dr. Mondini."

He raised both shaggy eyebrows then as he took stock of me. I was about to step outside, but he stopped me, holding my arm as he lifted up a small cloth sack I hadn't noticed, and announced, "I have something here that your father left behind."

I opened it and peered inside to find a pair of gored black shoes, slightly worn, smelling of neglect. Olmina took them from me quickly, saying, "Go now with the professor. You can ponder these later." She glanced at Lorenzo with a knowing look, as if to say, *The father is growing ever more distracted,* or was it me of whom she was thinking?

"Go on," said Lorenzo, giving me a little push toward the professor, who'd already stepped outside.

Was my father leaving parts of himself behind, like bread crumbs in the old tales, to tell the path? First the glasses, now these shoes.

"I trust you have viewed an anatomy before?" the professor queried me, somewhat condescendingly, as we began to walk along the canal.

"Yes," I said, "I've observed a corpse cutting several times in Padua with my father"—that last word stung—"but I look forward to witnessing the Dutch manner of dissection, if indeed it's distinct from the Italian." I added mechanically, "I appreciate your kind invitation," taking small, hesitant steps on the icy ground.

"Your father would have wished it, though I don't know if it is kind or not," he said, "since this morning is thick as unshorn wool." We proceeded to tunnel through the fog, which hung so densely now it remained open behind us like a corridor that slowly folded in upon itself.

"Professor," I said, measuring out my concern in small words, "can you tell me more about my father and his stay here?"

"There is nothing much to tell," he said curtly, squinting ahead into the dim wall of white. "Your father lodged here for several months in the very cottage you're renting."

"Really?" I'd imagined my father in finer receiving quarters.

"Yet he remained a very closed man. It is dangerous to be so closed. He would lock himself up for days at a time. Now, while I'm respectful of the solitary sort, if you're not a hermit pressed into the discipline of prayer—and maybe even if you are a hermit—the mind can become an extravagant thing, lose its bearings or, contrariwise, become so bent upon a certain object that all manner of balance is lost. Especially for one who is not accustomed to our winters."

A few other people, spectral, moved past us as we spoke, though we could scarcely see them. It seemed we were alone in a pale room of indeterminate dimensions.

"Did he behave strangely otherwise or say anything untoward?"

"Once, he said he was studying the edifying effects of the

grave and needed to be left alone." My companion shook his head.

"Do you remember any pattern to his moods?"

"What do you mean?"

"Certain days, certain times . . . ?"

"Ah, I see what you mean." He stopped, looked up, and appeared to be searching the air. "No, I can't really say that I took note, for I lost patience with him a bit and gave him what he wanted—a self-imposed isolation. I informed him that he could be edified all he wanted, but to let me know when he wished to discuss medicine again, like the good doctor he was. I was somewhat offended, you see, by what I perceived as a lapse in collegiality."

"Did he ever come round?"

"Yes, the day he left. Your father seemed genial enough then, apologized for his abruptness. He attributed his attitude to the cold and the perpetual dusk of the Rhinlandt winter. He explained that he must further his studies in Edenburg—"

"Ah," I said quietly, considering my next destination. I had thought we'd go to London, but I decided to go on to Edenburg.

The professor didn't seem to notice. He continued, "And so graciously, upon departure in the early spring, he embraced me and I forgave him, for I'm affected by the winters myself, and they've grown worse and worse these past years."

The professor stared down toward the canal, which lay solidly frozen, where small boats sat like so many shoes stuck in ice. Occasional objects studded the surface—a barrel, a rasping log, the odd coil of rope, a broken wooden skate.

One question nagged at me, but I didn't speak it aloud: *Why did he leave his shoes behind?*

When we crossed the bridge toward the Beguinage, I shuddered at a bloated gray piglet that stared blankly at the sky, half its body lodged beneath the ice, two legs stuck out like the tines of a pitchfork.

"What a waste of good sausage," gibed Professor Otterspeer.

I drew my hood close about my face with an involuntary shiver, thinking of the pigs I'd observed as a child, hung from the stable eaves when they were to be butchered, near my great-aunt's house in Fossatello. Their trussed bodies twisted like the pupae I plucked from bark when I wandered in the woods. The pigs shrieked in the blue morning hour as the butcher and his wife held buckets beneath the brisk red streams issuing from their stuck throats. Even now I couldn't touch roast pig. Wise Ovid was not altogether wrong when he wrote:

> *Peace filled the world — until some futile brain*
> *Envied the lions' diet and gulped down*
> *A feast of flesh to fill his greedy guts.*

When at last we reached the anatomy theater, the professor paid our admittance, as was customary, and we entered the hall. We were among the first to arrive, part of an audience that he assured me would be mostly students, some wealthy burghers, a small number of their wives, and other curious townspeople willing to pay the fee. The corpse lay outstretched on the dissection slab, his body beneath a coarse linen sheet.

"And who is the unfortunate youth?" I asked.

"I believe he was some vagrant, probably searching for work in the mills. He was found on one of the back roads, naked and rigid as a block of wood in the ditch next to his bony mule. Someone had stolen his clothes and boots," Professor Otterspeer informed me. "The wretch lay unclaimed for several days. An ignorant foreigner, no doubt."

His comment upset me, but I said nothing.

We approached the subject and the professor lifted the cloth.

"He appears nearly intact," I observed, avoiding the man's face, "unlike those cadavers removed from the gibbet, which have been scavenged by wild dogs and ravens."

He lowered the cloth with a peculiar tenderness. "I'm surprised that you can view the corpse so candidly, Signorina Mondini. Most women keep their distance. As perhaps they should, don't you think?" There was a slight gleam in his eye, which led me to believe he didn't speak seriously, though he wasn't entirely in jest either.

I ignored the fact that he would not address me as Dottoressa. I asked, "So you haven't brought your wife to attend an anatomy, then?"

"Oh no, my wife would never come, though she has no trouble chopping the head off a pullet and yanking out its entrails! I've actually tried to persuade her to visit, for I believe the demonstration to be most enlightening. But she sees no point in it, calls it an unsightly spectacle. But there are other wives here I could introduce you to." Professor Otterspeer sniffed slightly and withdrew a petit-point handkerchief for his florid nose.

"That won't be necessary," I replied. I wanted to be alone with my thoughts. I didn't ask how they came by permission to dissect the body. Even though unclaimed, such a corpse in Italy would be buried in a pauper's grave. In Padua, where for the most part the bodies of criminals were used, dissection was considered the worst possible punishment, inflicted in addition to the death sentence. Some people believed that when the dead were resurrected on Judgment Day, the dissected corpse would wander about searching for its lost parts.

"Well, my dear, your father has certainly raised you with the independence of a good son. I'll leave you, then, to view our fine collection of skeletons. If you'll excuse me, I must speak to some of my students." He bowed and retreated.

When he spoke the word "father"—in fact, every time he'd spoken the word—I felt a numbing cut at the center of me. Now, in this setting, I missed my father more than ever.

I looked once more upon the cadaver, foreshortened from a distance, the head closest, the legs pointing straight away from me. Professor Otterspeer hadn't replaced the cloth all the way, and the face lay partly exposed. The dark yellow stubble of the dead man's beard stood out on his chin like random bits of chaff, and his stringy blond hair fell away from his broad brow.

I felt the vague shock I always felt in the presence of the dead, the unsettling sense of defilement, which usually passed like a brief nausea. The man's life, after all, was gone. He was no more than a carcass of days, but one that would yield up its secret structures, the marvels of the inner body, even in death apparent. I couldn't allow myself, though, to imagine the color of his eyes, nor what they had sought out in life. The plump young woman, perhaps, who would caress his face, the impoverished family he'd left behind. Or the joy afforded by his mule's hot breath upon his frostbitten fingers. Nor did I wish to know his name.

Still, the nausea didn't pass.

I turned away and surveyed the room. I remembered my

father's caution from the very first occasion I viewed a dissection. "If you fear the corpse," he'd said gently, "be sure not to look at the face or the hands, Gabriella, for they are the most human." What if my father was such a corpse now, mistaken for a vagrant, his parts cut open and identified, then tossed away in some foreign land as victuals for dogs, rats, and vultures? But I pushed this thought violently from my mind and continued to look around the wooden amphitheater.

Skeletons were arranged in various postures, the human ones holding banners with Latin phrases such as PULVIS ET UMBRA SUMUS and HOMO BULLA. The skeletons didn't sadden me but felt familiar and faintly ridiculous, one with a plumed helmet, seated upon a fleshless nag, crossbow in hand, and one in the corner casually leaning on a shovel.

All around me, men with slit pantaloons and doublets, and a small number of women, some with many short slashes in their sleeves and bodices, according to the current fashion, gathered and conversed, their vivid colors alone making the chamber warmer now. I glanced out the long windows on either side of the room but could see nothing of the frozen garden. The fog had orphaned us from the rest of the world.

I walked around the amphitheater and examined the animal skeletons. The wolf, singularly designed for the hunt, seemed almost friendly to me, in that it so resembled a dog. On impulse I stroked the chalky, smooth slope between the eyes. How benign was bone that once was threatening. The weasel presented a sleek form and egg-shaped skull, as if the meal it so relished corresponded to the form of its thoughts. The still deer relayed the quickness of its bones.

But I was most drawn to certain animal skeletons that I

hadn't observed before, such as the elegant swan, emblem of poets. The skeleton was no less pure than the creature. The swan, by virtue of its very size, exhibited mythical bones. Yet along with its beauty there was a kind of monstrosity, especially in the serpentine neck, which seemed inordinately long and curved, surmounted by the skull, which resembled a leper clapper, while the heavier skeletal body and great wings hung behind with a contrary force. The pinions, broad as they were, could mirror those of a seraph. If swans were as fierce as geese, though, then they would be demon and angel in a single creature.

"Signorina?"

The professor had returned. He led me to one of the privileged benches near the front, clasping my elbow through my sleeve most firmly, as if I might fall without his support.

Most of the amphitheater afforded standing room only, between narrow wooden aisles and railings. The demonstrating physician—"a doctor, not a barber-surgeon, like those at the Royal College of Physicians in London," whispered Professor Otterspeer—made his entrance with his two assistants, along with three musicians, who would be accompanying the event on viol, lute, and viola da gamba.

Dr. Zuyderduin, a man of middle age, robust figure, and copper hair, began with a small introduction and courtesies in Dutch, very little of which I understood. He began incising the skin evenly in each region, drawing from a remarkable assortment of flaying knives, scissors, scalpels, forceps, needles, spatulas, and grossing tools. He was assisted by the two students, one with sponge and bowl to sop up blood and fluids, and one who held back portions of skin or tissue when necessary, tacking the muscles on a wooden block, tying up or arranging segments of flesh.

The musicians behind them, meanwhile, bowed and plucked away at their instruments as if we were seated in a pleasant chamber among friends. The viol player sawed rather dreadfully, the viola da gamba man performed well enough, but the lutenist lingered with the notes as if he found their melancholy resonance in the corpse, sheep-gut strings companioning the man's ligaments. His plucked notes came with an almost imperceptible delay born of deep courtesy. He watched the dissection as he played, while the others, perhaps repulsed, gazed toward the audience and the skeletons at the top of the amphitheater.

As Dr. Zuyderduin worked, he swayed when the lutenist played alone.

I never ceased my amazement at the calm demeanor of such doctors who, while fishing about in the soupy viscera, could pull out the definitive organ and expound upon its position in the body. The soul seated within the liver, the heart, and the brain or (some have argued) within the ephemeral pineal gland. How the body yielded itself, both capacious and densely pressed, like the thick pages of a foreign text that we must translate.

The doctor droned on in mingled Latin and Dutch now, as he disrobed the cadaver down to its pink bones. The audience murmured with the revelation of each new part as the commonplace body gave way to the secret body. The Dutch were more respectful in this regard. The audience in Padua often grew rowdy with discourse and raillery, which on occasion required a few sturdy men to push back the crowd and restore order or to remove some jeering youth from the balcony while the doctor waited, scowling, with his finger on a crucial tendon.

I glanced at the half-hidden face that I'd avoided, as if to test myself. From this angle I could see that the chin was unimposing and the lips generously curved even in their rigid state.

Wielding the scalpel with great precision, Dr. Zuyderduin proceeded, after finishing with the abdomen (as the viscera were the most susceptible to putrefaction) and the torso (displaying the lungs and heart), on to the head (sinking his hand deeply between the lobes of the brain, searching for the pineal gland, which corrupts so rapidly, though he didn't find it) and then approached the sinewy arm.

As the demonstration progressed, the effluvium of the cadaver caused us to press handkerchiefs and sleeves to our faces. The sprigs of rosemary cast about the floor did little to help, for the organs reeked with an acidic, musky, almost palpable stench. Fortunately the good doctor motioned for his assistants to remove the entrails in a bucket provided for that purpose. He turned down the flaps of skin to cover the abdomen and drew the linen sheet up around the cadaver's chest.

He began to dissect the arm and the hand, which lay half-open, loosened from its previous state of rigor mortis, in a manner that seemed to invite a handclasp.

Let my death, then, be your gain. Let the touch that wounds, heal; the incision, instruct. These words, unbidden, seemed to come from my father, though I couldn't recall the exact occasion on which he had spoken them—but some other presence that was not my father burdened me too. I struggled to push it out of mind.

Under my breath I recited the Latin names along with the

doctor as he described the flexor muscles and their insertions into tendon. This calmed me. The corpse-fingers curled as he lifted the muscles. My father once told me that the great Vesalius and his fellows blindfolded one another and fingered bones from the charnel house outside Paris in order to memorize every one by touch.

In my lap, my left hand lay within the right, and I felt the fasciae, muscles, ligaments, and tendons as Dr. Zuyderduin communicated their placement and sectioned each part, turning back one palmar muscle and then another until the hand fairly bloomed upon the table among the scissors, pins, and clamps. How odd to be the subject of one's own inquiry, as if the hand had an existence of its own, like a small, clever animal that carried out my wishes or clenched itself against me. According to Galen, the hand truly exemplified the whole. From the hand of God to the hand of flesh . . .

Professor Otterspeer touched my arm. The demonstration was over. The doctor, his assistants, and the viol and viola da gamba players were leaving. Only the lutenist remained, staring up at me.

My body trembled. Something was wrong.

"What is it, my dear?"

I quickly stepped down to the table, to the left side of the corpse, and noted his hair tied back with a thin red thread. I turned him on his side before anyone could stop me and felt him open in front, unexamined parts slipping out.

"What are you doing?" cried Professor Otterspeer.

There it was on the left leg. The small puckered mouth of the healed ulcer. I pressed my palm over the scar, scarcely able to breathe as I spoke: "I know this man."

The professor pulled me away from the table. "How could you possibly? You're overheated, my dear. Come outside, the brisk air will do you good."

"No, I'm certain. He was no vagrant!"

"You're mistaken, my dear. Come, I will take you home—"

"I *know* him, he is Wilhelm Lochner!" I cried, feeling sick. "That is his name!"

The men and women in the lingering crowd gawked at me. I stumbled ahead, refusing the professor's dark blue sleeve, with its many small slits flashing russet cloth beneath. For the first time, I saw in that fashion a mockery of dissection.

I too owned such a blouse, and as I stumbled outside, gasping to draw in the cold air and clear my head, I vowed I would never wear it again.

CHAPTER 14

⚜

The Patient Owns the Remedy

Olmina put her arm around my shoulders as I sat shivering on the bed. "Are you ill, signorina?"

"No!" I said angrily, and I wept. "Wilhelm was on the slab, it was him they cut."

"Oh no!" She put both hands to her face. "My dear. Are you sure?"

I turned my fierce face to hers. "I have no doubt."

"Such a lively young man!"

"If it weren't for my abrupt departure . . ."

"What are you talking about?"

"He must have followed me here. Remember what Signor Gradenigo said?"

It was her turn to be fierce. "You've got nothing to do with it."

"I don't know. I carry bad luck, like one of those plague women who survive while others die around them."

"We don't know what they carry . . . Maybe it's a blessing so that they may help others."

"Oh? And what about my father? He has fled me. Maybe he too has died."

"Now your wits have gone astray, signorina. You're no maidenbane. No one holds the threads that tie us to this life. Not even God, if you ask me."

"The Fates, then?"

"Maybe, yes—the Spinner, the Measurer, the Cutter."

"But I feel my father now like a small ghost, as if he lived in the medicine chest in a bottle. What does it mean, if not that he's gone?"

"It means you're bereft of your reason, grieving for a living man. Let's give Wilhelm his due and let the living be." She lit a small candle, placed it in the window, and murmured a prayer for the young man of extravagant colors. Then she said, "You should sleep now, Gabriella."

But I barely dozed that night. The next morning, I decided there was no longer anything to keep me in Leiden, for Dr. Otterspeer was the only one who'd truly communicated with my father during his stay. And I now found the closeness of Wilhelm's body unbearable, for he couldn't even be laid to rest in a pauper's grave. The ground was frozen solid. His corpse would be slumped in the icy cellar of a university building near our cottage, waiting for spring, when he would be buried, along with the other dismembered dead from the anatomy theater, outside the town walls.

"That winter of your father's solitude," Dr. Otterspeer told me a few days later, "there was more to it, dear child, than I first told you." He glanced at Olmina and she discreetly left us alone in the kitchen. Lorenzo had gone to the marketplace.

"Once, early on in his stay, when I brought him some supper, he answered the door fully clothed but discalced." He lifted his eye-brows and opened his gray eyes wide, reliving the moment. "He said that he was effecting a new cure for his own malady. Understand—it was December—the stone floors were cold as ice."

"What sort of cure?" I asked.

"He said that he meant to draw strength from the earth and shoes were an impediment. They blocked the elementals. I replied that he stood upon stone paving—was that not an obstacle? Then he marched through the frozen garden in his bare feet!"

The peculiar spectacle of my father deliberately striding in full dress but discalced upon the crackling white paths of the botanical garden reminded me of the solar man, in lesser measure. "But when he departed, was he wearing shoes?"

"Boots, boots for the journey, he said. But no more interfer-ence from soles when he was residing in a place! 'If the monks can walk without shoes in observance of spirit, then I can walk without shoes in observance of cure and vigor,' he explained."

I envisioned my father pressing dark footprints between the rows of sleeping plants. If only he'd left such prints for me to follow.

"I didn't understand what he was doing," said Dr. Otterspeer. "But he was so convinced of his rarefied logic that he almost persuaded me that his experiment — if that's what it was — might be of benefit. That is, until he became so solitary he was unapproachable."

I penned a brief note to notify Dr. Fuchs of Wilhelm Lochner's death, though I delayed sending it. Most likely he would blame me for a double theft, the death of his student and the spiriting away of my father's papers. Though worse by far would be the loss of his excellent student, for a good mentor like Dr. Fuchs often doubled as a father to his several scholar-sons. At last I sent the letter with a desolate heart. Even though Wilhelm hadn't been, nor would be, lover, I thought of him as friend. And that word lay like a hand on my heart. *Friend.* I might have corresponded with him or simply recalled his wonderful, gaudy presence. Now he was butchered, an instrument of science. And I was more alone in the world than before.

Olmina and I began packing while the fog curled and uncurled around us, appearing and disappearing through the gate to the frozen garden. I packed my father's things in a small satchel within my larger one. Shoes, glasses, notes.

As she packed, Olmina complained, "Signorina, it's the middle of December. Can't we wait until March? You're courting your death with this blind will of yours!"

"What did you say?" I asked, turning away from the window where I stood.

She began moving about my room in a sudden burst of activity, opening drawers and pulling out clothes from the depths of the armoire. Then she spoke again. "You want to force your father out of the thicket! You want the world to yield to you, but you're no princess or queen! And even queens sometimes hang by their ankles!" Olmina went red and then abruptly thrust her face into her blue apron and ran out of the room, weeping.

I opened the window and stuck my face into the cold air. Shingles of ice slid from the roofs, heated by the chimneys. Icicles shattered like glass or thudded upon the snow. Passersby with miserable faces slogged through the cold slush and mud of the street below. Olmina was right.

Truly it was odd to be gripped by urgency to find my father now, when he'd been gone for so many years. What difference did waiting a month or even a year make? I felt my father to be in some form of danger from a rambling mind, but was I perhaps the one in danger from the opposite? A mind clenched, fixed upon this search?

We should wait until spring and then make our way to Edenburg in Scotia.

I'd almost set my mind to this course of action, when Lorenzo returned from trading words with a few sailors as he gathered our supplies. They'd warned *against* waiting till March, when the winds gust fiercely in the German Sea.

In the end we compromised: we waited a week to obtain ship's passage to Edenburg.

In the meantime I wrote a letter to Dr. Hamish Urquhart, professor of natural philosophy in that city, requesting his help with lodging. My father had recommended him highly.

I spent my remaining time in Leiden writing, for the contemplation of disease, I'm reluctant to admit, gave me strange solace.

THE PLAGUE OF BLACK TEARS:

A Lachrymose Infection of the Tear Ducts, of Causes Unknown

Some midwives say the onset of a foul wind steals words from a person's lips and causes this plague. Sometimes it afflicts nuns or monks of those orders who take a vow of silence. Prisoners who are forbidden to speak, people who lose their voices out of grief, children who are always ordered to be silent, may all succumb. I've observed a certain kind of dream that many of the sufferers have in common, the vision of a city where the inhabitants are forbidden to weep. Their tears must be clandestine, under bridges at night, or as one patient related, "Be sorrow's vessel, don't give it away."

The person is usually not aware of the infection until she reaches the final stages when her tears thicken and turn black. Blindness and death may result. The plague is contagious and will even spread through shared dreams. Strangely this disease is also passed on by women who sew alone at their embroidery frames and cry from the unformed words that populate their loneliness, or by fishermen who are mute as they mend their nets, lost in morose humors that only the sea can bring on. When the women and the men weep, they unwittingly pass tears along the skeins of thread or filaments of net, which travel on to the next person who touches the line. They may also contract the plague if they kiss each other's eyelids. The sick person may not know about the malady for months, even though she awakens in the morning with dark stains upon the pillow. She may assume the smudges come from her penciled eyelids or brows. But in the advanced state she can't fail to notice the ink-dark tears that flow from her eyes.

My father often told me, "The patient owns the remedy." In this wise I followed the cure of a young woman, Annabella, who saved her black tears in inkpots and then wrote with them until over time they clarified. Though the cure was long, the plague thinned and subsided at last. Several victims who didn't know how to write were still comforted, though I can't say exactly why, by the little jet-black bottles that they accumulated on their shelves. The only difficulty I encountered, especially in Venetia—a city where they will try to sell you anything—was the connivance of two or three disreputable fools who tried to hawk their own tears. Of course, for a while certain aristocrats coveted these inks that leaked from the intimate sorrows of others, but they soon discovered that their own tears darkened. No one was immune.

CHAPTER 15

❧

The Vanishing Bend
in the Path

After a rough three-day sea journey from Leiden — we survived solely by chewing dried ginger (promoting heat in the body and alleviating the sea nausea) and by clutching the deck railings while the German Sea heaved itself upon the bow — we neared the port of Leyth, below the hills of Edenburg. Lorenzo fairly leapt to the coign of the crescent-shaped seawall to help the crew tie the lines. I felt dazed and scoured by the journey. Our poor animals, suffering from the voyage, set up a raucous braying in their excitement to regain the land.

Dr. Hamish Urquhart — I guessed it was him, for no one else resembled a professor there on the waterfront — approached the ship, leaning into the offshore wind like a dark snag to meet us. The professor almost immediately lost his flat cap as a gust picked it up and tossed it into the water, exposing a crop of red hair that flared like a torch. His narrow beard, a darker red, outlined his strongly contoured chin. Dr. Urquhart was a disconcertingly handsome man, and surely, I thought, there would be attendant arrogance, in spite of what my father wrote of his amiability.

I stood and attempted to straighten my coat and skirts, while the wind defiantly whipped everything into disarray again. I must have appeared ragged and unsightly, dark circles under my eyes from the sleepless nights at sea, and I couldn't have smelled very pretty either. So much the better, then; let it work for me in my need of solitude.

Lorenzo meanwhile disembarked and walked up to the man without any qualms. He introduced himself and gestured toward Olmina and me on the ship. Once the mules had safely come ashore with our supplies, Lorenzo held my hand firmly and led me with unadorned courtesy down the gangplank, which dipped and rose with the frequency of breath.

The Scotsman moved with barely concealed enthusiasm to take my arm when I wavered on the stone pier, though I swiftly warned him away with my eyes. "I'll be all right," I said simply.

"Dr. Mondini, please be . . . after a long sea journey, one must . . ."

He spoke in incomplete sentences, as if his thoughts were elsewhere. "Oh, pardon me . . . Dr. Urquhart, at your . . . service."

A handsome gentleman without guile. I'd have to be doubly wary.

"I've obtained a carriage," he offered.

"I'd like to walk a little and see the city as we approach. Is it far?"

"Not at all. We'll pass along the Water of Leyth and be there within an hour."

Olmina came up beside us and spoke frankly. "I'll take advantage of the ride, sir, for I'm sure I'll have plenty of time to acquaint myself with your fine city." Then she added pointedly, "And so will you, signorina."

"I can't get in a carriage right now. I need the still ground beneath me."

"I'll accompany her," Lorenzo offered as he reluctantly turned over the reins of the rowdy bunch of roped mules to the professor's manservant. Lorenzo gave the youth a few clipped instructions. "Hold 'em firmly, but let the rope play out a bit—they've been cooped up aboard ship. Let 'em have at some grass too."

The professor appraised our animals with admiration. "If you ever decide . . . to sell one of your fine beasts . . ."

"Why would we sell 'em?" interrupted Lorenzo, narrowing his eyes.

"Oh, I only meant . . . I have a good man, kind to animals. Didn't mean . . ." The professor grew flustered.

"Don't worry," I said, smiling a little. "We are perhaps more attached to our beasts than some. They've come far with us."

"Ah, yes . . . of course." He nodded and helped Olmina into the modest black carriage drawn by two small, stout roan horses. "Cowgate Wynd, then," he directed the driver. We watched the carriage set off in spurts up the hill, jockeyed between the steady pull of the horses and the push of five spirited mules.

"I hope they get there," muttered Lorenzo, pulling his rough green woolen cap down over his ears.

As we passed from the small port and walked along the damp footpath near the Water of Leyth, the landscape began to settle me after the days of rocking at sea. Lorenzo became like a young boy, cheerfully whipping the hedges with a willow shoot he'd picked up. Small clumps of leafless willows, alders, and aspen trees lined the banks and were studded with great numbers of tawny, rose-breasted birds that swung out over the soggy gold stubble of winter fields as we approached.

"Oh, what are those wonderful little birds?"

We paused, watching the flocks lift and fall in sinuous, then spherical clouds, their songs vibrating the air.

"Mostly linnets, a few buntings," the professor said. "They love to sweep through . . ."

"Yes?"

" . . . the barley fields. Hmm, for seeds."

"Are they tasty, then?" asked Lorenzo, probably thinking of spitted wrens for Santo Stefano's day, after Christmas. It was a custom I'd never been able to bear.

"No, no. I can't say." Dr. Urquhart extended his hand as if to ward off the thought. "I don't savor the little birds."

I was grateful to hear him say it.

"What's the difference between songbirds and, say, a nice, plump roasted goose?" Lorenzo shook his head. "You're killing them all the same."

"Yes, but the birds, they're part of . . . some larger"—he paused—"spirit that must not be touched, something we don't . . ."

"Understand, perhaps?" I completed his sentence. "If I killed the bird, I'd miss its song, its dazzling flight. A bright thing in the dark world would be lost."

"Well spoken, Dr. Mondini."

"Well, I like bird chatter too," grumbled Lorenzo. "But I don't think you've ever been hungry, signorina. It gives you a different outlook on the world."

"Yes, you're right, Lorenzo. Beauty comes to us more readily on a full belly."

We continued walking silently for a while. Then I said quietly to Dr. Urquhart, "As you may have gained from my letter, I'm tracing my father's journey to find out what I can that would lead me to his present whereabouts."

"Ah yes, your father . . ." He frowned and looked away from me.

"Any news?"

"No, nothing since he left . . . though . . . we could ask Dr. Baldino, who often discussed the past with him."

"Ah." I sank into weariness. But then I thought, *I must get to know this man a bit, before he takes me into his confidence. There may be something in his discomfort worth the telling.*

Bushes and trees I couldn't name gave off rich, pungent scents, sometimes reminding me of a steamy kitchen strung with herbs, other times of a garden mulched and abandoned to its season. I noticed the professor's smell too, a pleasant, earthy smell of animal heat suffusing wool. The sun came and went, lowering like a snuffed coal, as we reached the edge of Edenburg and proceeded to Cowgate below the Castle.

As Dr. Urquhart took leave of us at the lodgings he'd secured, he said, "You may recall, Dr. Mondini, that we're on the Julian, not the Gregorian, calendar here, so you've just traveled back . . . in time. It's ten days earlier than when you were on the Continent, so reckon accordingly. You have a chance to relive those days." He smiled broadly with some mischief in his blue-green eyes.

Our rooms were adequate, though small, the beds niched in the wall like cupboards with wooden doors that we could shut at night. The dun stone buildings all around were close and tall, but from our rooms on the uppermost floor I would be able to see a sliver of the Firth.

On that first night, questions I'd hidden within me since Leiden raked my mind like an anchor scoring the bottom of the sea as I tried to sleep in my cupboard, like a mouse in a narrow larder. Had Wilhelm Lochner really followed me to Hollant? His pale body on the dissection slab haunted me. Over and over his cut form repeated itself in the blue light of the anatomy theater.

Sometimes in the dream, Maurizio or my father lay cold, with eyes upturned to a dim ceiling. What did Dr. Urquhart mean by "Ah yes, your father . . ."? The anatomy theater loomed thick with night. I wanted to flee its dark, blood-muddied chambers, but I could not. Sometimes in sleeplessness I'd read one of my father's letters written in an ordinary rather than extravagant voice, to settle myself.

Dear Gabriella,

You have kindly asked about my book, and I can say quite frankly that the work progresses, though it becomes overwhelming at times. There are so many diseases that I don't know how I will fit them all in one volume. Perhaps I shall only include the ones with cures, for how desperate should we all feel as physicians to know so many that are incurable? Yet it is humbling, it is right, that we acknowledge them. It may be that some new medicine will come to light, from an old midwife or mother, or from some clever experimentalist locked in his alchemical cellar amid flasks, retorts, and furnaces. There is a clever man, Dr. Urquhart, a natural philosopher here who has made my days more companionable with his curiosity and pursuits of astronomy and metallurgy, from the melting of copper (that green dragon of the moon) to the larger schemes of matter, space, and time. I cannot pretend I understand everything he describes, but I find the conversation invigorating and amusing, though he sometimes becomes lost in the branching forks of his own thoughts and his Aristotelian studies. I recall a phrase I've read somewhere: "Where the natural philosopher finishes, there begins the physician." For we must come to earth, to our patient with the swollen ankles or the sorry wound, though we may rely sometimes upon the natural philosopher's theories and experiments. But now, my daughter, forgive me, for I must leave you. The practical gods have reminded me of their dominion. My lamp is out of oil.

Edenburg
Your father

A few days after we'd arrived, Professor Urquhart came round to collect Olmina and me for a midday meal at the home of his friend Dr. Baldino, who, he informed us, was in his ninth decade, a professor whose passion continued to be the study of memory and recollecting. He had also known my father.

This gentleman, Professor Baldino from Salerno, greeted us at the door of his four-story stone house. He appeared short and bowed like a hunchback, though he didn't truly possess that infirmity. His insubstantial white hair and beard wafted about him like smoke, though he fastened his dark brown eyes upon us with an iron focus. I like this impropriety in the elderly, who sometimes stare more fiercely at this world even as they glimpse the next.

"Welcome to my northern home, Dr. Mondini. Come in, come to the kitchen and tell me about your journey." He pressed my hand with crimped fingers that seemed white parchment stretched across the joints, hardened into a single brittle claw. He smiled at Olmina and Dr. Urquhart, displaying no more than four or five teeth, three on top, one or two (I couldn't quite tell) on the bottom.

He led us through the entry, past a cold, unlit room that appeared to be stacked with books and furniture, and up a crooked staircase alongside plain walls of dark oiled wood to the second floor, mastering each step one ponderous breath at a time as he clasped the railing. I felt my own inhalation slow to a stretch of years, as if I might be old myself when we finally reached the top.

"We'll dine here where it's warm. Isabella will prepare our repast and bring it to the table," Dr. Baldino announced, lisping through his gums.

A large woman with a gray braid that ran down her back in an ever tighter weave, until there was only a wisp of three or four hairs at her waist, stood busily trimming pale green and brown vegetables at the stone counter. The hearth roared loudly with the strength of a six- or seven-hour fire that had been constantly stoked and now heated a large black pot of soup. The kitchen radiated the heat of a long summer day. We seated ourselves gratefully, women on one side and men on the other, at the oaken table set with plain brown linens and pewter bowls and spoons, and began to sweat, gradually casting off the clothes we could respectably shed.

As we waited for our soup, I addressed Dr. Baldino. "As you may know, I'm seeking my father, who spent some time here several years ago, according to his letters, but he's unaccountably vanished. He hasn't written. I'd like to know if you can tell me anything about his stay or if you know where he is at present."

Professor Baldino folded his frail hands upon the table and regarded me with impenetrable sadness. "I haven't heard from him since he left Edenburg some years ago. He became a man of fulminant humors."

I grew restless at this lack of news and stood up, startling myself and the others no doubt with my sudden distress. I paced over to the window, where I could see only a blur of rooftops, since it was steamed up from the pottage. Olmina came and stood beside me, laying her hand on my arm.

Dr. Urquhart must have pitied me, for he jumped in with his jerky speech. "Your father's whereabouts . . . hmm—I can reveal nothing really, but . . . the distressing occasion of his lapse, six years ago. He suffered a commotion . . . of the mind, couldn't understand the orderly passage of time. He kept very late hours in his quarters at my house, then . . . slept all day, sometimes the next night, barely emerging when I knocked loudly . . . his door. Only one of his servants remained, for the other . . . had fled with his purse."

"That scoundrel!" I exclaimed, returning to the table. Olmina sat beside me.

Dr. Baldino watched me with heavy, kindly eyes.

"Fortunately he kept most of his money hidden . . . in his chest, or so . . . he told me—in confidence."

"Money and medicine in the same chest? That seems unlike him."

"I once observed your father through the half-open door, fully dressed in his doctor's red robe, black skullcap . . . at his desk, staring . . . out the window, tapping his quill but writing nothing upon the page. In the end he . . . needed to raise money and was forced to sell . . . most of his books."

His treasures! My heart sank. "Did the collection include a copy of the materia medica from Wirtenberg?" I despaired of the answer. "Yes, it did. Your father," answered the philosopher, glancing to the side as if seeing the book there, "yes, mentioned it was a gift . . . from a Dr. Fuchs?"

My face must have fallen, for he looked concerned. "What?"

"Nothing, nothing." I wavered.

"I would say he forgot himself," opined Dr. Baldino at last in slow, measured tones. "Even though that rhetorician of Bologna, Boncompagno da Signa, tells us that men of melancholy temperament have the best memory, for they retain the impressions of things, owing to their hard, dry constitutions." He went on with labored breath, "For I met your father many years ago in Padua, and I must say"—he paused to compose his words—"that in comparison to that period, the man appeared greatly altered. He could barely hold a conversation. His mind continually drifted and his eyes would fix upon a window, any window. If I had to say, it was almost"—he halted briefly, holding my eyes—"as though he'd lost track of time and only wanted to go into the fields and lose himself. Roam the land. I observed him more than once on the road to the Pentland Hills there." He waved his arm to the south. "I saw him on nights flooded by moon after midnight. I too suffer insomnia. It brings me solace to sit and watch the country there, as if I were an old sentry of history. But he sometimes appeared to be walking on all fours, barefoot."

After this astounding statement, I was dumbstruck. Dr. Urquhart interceded. "I don't know if you really saw him . . . now, or one of our highland foxes, lengthened by his shadow . . ."

"It was a man, and I knew no one else out at that hour."

"I can't believe such a thing," I said, even as my doubts grew.

"I once mistook a goat for a woman from afar, when it stood up against an olive trunk to pull at the olives," declared Olmina.

Dr. Baldino frowned at her.

"The oddest thing, to return to your father," said Dr. Urquhart, "was that after a brief stay, only six weeks in Edenburg, he'd . . . gone without even a leave-taking. May have suffered from severe nostalgia, a desire to go back to Venetia and . . ."

My head began to ache. "But I received letters from my father *after* that time," I said, trying to remember all the letters, "from France and the Kingdom of Spain, and he never expressed such an intention."

Dr. Baldino placed his hand on mine across the table. "It may be that I'm mistaken. Nothing is certain. But it's true that your father wandered the land at night, wrestling with something unknown in himself."

Isabella served our pottage. There was much silence over mushy colewort, parsnips, cabbage, beans, and dreadful oatcakes. We also had stringy pullets, which were oversalted and overcooked. I realized with embarrassment that the meal was prepared for the nearly toothless Dr. Baldino, and I had no cause for complaint, having all but four of my teeth still in my mouth.

As I chewed, a sentence I didn't speak aloud came to my mind. Not *My father has disappeared,* or *My father is lost,* but *I've lost my father.* As if he were a fallen coin I could find by dropping to all fours and patting the floor with my hands. *I've lost my father.*

Owing to harsh weather, we decided to remain the winter in Edenburg. Finally, Olmina proclaimed, I'd come to my senses.

One afternoon before Christmas I observed Hamish in the square in front of the church when he didn't know that anyone was watching, for there was a considerable crowd milling about. A few merrymakers flouted the recent Presbyterian rules that banned the old celebrations, electing a lord of misrule and parading him through the square on their shoulders with a pot upside down on his head (and ample ale in his belly, no doubt). Some lively carol singers (also at their peril from the church, whose special officers were luckily nowhere to be seen at this moment) imitated the joyous sounds of the animals at the birth of the Holy Child—the ox lowing, the ass braying, the calf bellowing, the cock crowing, and the goat bleating (the latter so pitiful that everyone began to laugh).

Hamish stood alone to one side of the western doors of High Kirk, just below the line of sunlight as Olmina and I strolled by. He was absorbed in a book, and his reddish hair stood about his head as if he'd run his fingers through it many times. He chewed on his nails thoughtfully, seeming to taste words that were impossible to place upon the tongue, as he leaned back against the wall, with one knee bent, oblivious to the revelry around him. I managed to discern the title—Aristotle's *De divinatione per somnum*—and recalled one intriguing passage:

> The most skilful interpreter of dreams is he who has the faculty of observing resemblances. Any one may interpret dreams which are vivid and plain. But, speaking of "resemblances," I mean that dream presentations are analogous to the forms reflected in water . . . In the latter case, if the motion in the water be great, the reflexion has no resemblance to its original, nor do the forms resemble the real objects. Skilful, indeed, would he be in interpreting such reflexions who could rapidly discern, and at a glance comprehend, the scattered and distorted fragments of such forms, so as to perceive that one of them represents a man, or a horse, or anything whatever.

So Hamish mulled upon the nature of dreams. I wanted to steer us away quickly, before he noticed me, but he peered up from his book—"Gabriella!"—and I was caught. I flushed like an aching girl.

Olmina tugged at my arm and said, "We must return to the house. The signorina is not well."

"I'm fine," I insisted, and I disengaged my arm from hers. Without any preface I asked, "So do you believe in divination by dreams as foretelling, simply tokens, or coincidences?"

He stared at me with curiosity. "It depends on what manner of dream we're interpreting. A night dream, a daydream. A consequence of tough pullets," he said smiling, "or some nocturnal form of Nature's sacred design. Or even the grace of a lovely woman."

It was the first time I'd heard him speak in complete, uninterrupted sentences. The narrow white gathers of the tight linen collar at his neck flickered ever so slightly with his pulse and breath.

"I believe," I said, "there may be resemblances to events in the future, or even anticipations of malady or healing. For once I dreamt that all the remedies and instruments from my medicine chest were scattered in the Venetian Lagoon, and I did lose that chest in Lake Costentz. Yet even after the chest was recovered, I found the medicines mislaid. Maybe the dream points to the cures written in my father's *Book of Diseases,* lost when he disappeared."

"Ah"—his eyebrows rose in keen interest—"I'd like to know more about it." He closed his book and slipped a slender finger from the page he'd been holding.

"Perhaps we can speak further the next time we meet," I murmured, not really sure how much I wanted to tell him. A damp breeze kicked up the air. I put my hand near my face to protect myself from the cold.

He clasped my upraised hand and pressed it between both of his warm palms, brushing my face with the back of his hand, and then he bowed. "Farewell, then. I look forward to our renewed conversation."

"Yes, soon."

I pulled my hand away, then turned, hooking my arm through

Olmina's soft, heavy arm once more, and strode away at a rapid pace, pulling her along with me, until she tugged back to slow me down.

"He's a handsome one, that man," she commented, "a bit rash, but the face of a seraph."

Ah, I thought, smiling, *so even Olmina has been moved by him.*

After that meeting, I found his tall, lank frame a singular source of disruption whenever he appeared. He differed greatly from my father, who entered a room and immediately established a presence with others. I knew where I stood in a room with my father, even with his sporadic ill tempers, for he was, at least at one time, an almost predictable class of planet.

But whenever Hamish advanced, I was unsure of my ground. I found myself leaning too close to him at times. I remembered the *pavana venetiana, the pavana ferrarese,* the exquisite dances of my youth, accompanied by the lute, an instrument considered too sensual for women to play. The evenings at the Villa Barberini, lit by long rectangles of late sun falling from the windows as we passed in and out of the circles of honey-scented candles. Back then, my mother looked expectantly upon my unflagging joy in the music. She thought of suitors; I thought of gestures. She'd never savored that kind of freedom, for she'd married my father at fifteen and hadn't known another before him. Sometimes when I danced, I imagined a homunculus, a little man dancing within at the center of me. (Is this what it felt like to be full with child?) I never tired of the saltarellos, the pivas, the *spingardi.* Until the death of Maurizio.

My notes for *The Book of Diseases* occupied me well as Edenburg's dark days of winter progressed, but I began to cherish the occasions when I would meet Hamish, and fret when I did not.

Christmas in Edenburg was a solemn affair. The inhabitants were forbidden by the Presbyterian elders to bake yuletide bread in their homes, and even the poor bakers themselves were interrogated about those who might order any such cake or bun. To cheer me, Hamish had agreed to escort me on another walk along the Water of Leyth the following day. Lorenzo joined us.

After we passed through the town gates, we followed the footpath that ran along the banks of the water, southward this time, toward its source in the Pentland Hills. Dark red coppices of willow stood dripping in the fog. Gorse and withered grasses lay sodden beyond the trees. "I warned you that you won't see much of the countryside today," said Hamish, amused that I'd insisted on going out anyway.

"Yes, but we can sense the fields and hills, the scent of winter earth. Maybe we'll even hear a few birds," I answered, pulling my red Hollant cloak about me. Naturally I couldn't admit to Hamish that I had just wanted to see *him*.

Lorenzo piped up from behind us. "This cold could split a stone! Still, it's better than coal smoke and gloomy houses."

"You're right, this is just the thing for a dry temperament, though I suppose we could do without the bilious cold," I agreed.

"And so, do you organize your book by the humors, then?" asked Hamish.

"I'm not sure thus far of the classes of malady and cure. My father hadn't yet suggested categories, so I lack his guidance."

We walked briskly as we spoke, to warm ourselves, and Lorenzo dropped behind.

"Wouldn't it be more useful to gather them under the elements of place rather than humors? For those of us who live in wet regions would be able to turn to 'Diseases Engendered by Rivers and Lakes,' 'Diseases Wrought by Swamps,' and so on."

I was delighted by this suggestion. "There is a great appeal to the Hippocratic Corpus," I admitted, "the three environs of Airs, Waters, and Places. But the places aren't entirely fitting for this work, though I'm drawn to the category of waters. When a person is porous, he is healthy. We may judge disease by the motions of water, how the urine flows, its color and quality, likewise the sweat, saliva, and tears. But the humors are more compelling for me. A melancholic can turn to her inclination and immediately find ways to restore balance." As I spoke, I warmed to his presence beside me. No man had talked so freely with me about medicine since my father.

The path curved with the water, which grew narrower in its channel. Hamish turned intently toward me. "Why don't you complete *The Book of Diseases* here in Edenburg? I'll gain permission for you to use the library. We have an abundance of medical volumes here!"

I was astonished by his offer. I stood mulling it over, rather guiltily. For shouldn't I want to continue the search for my father? "Are you sure that your peers will allow a woman in their sanctum?"

"They will if I insist."

All at once a flock of screeching jackdaws approached invisibly and then miraculously appeared one after another out of the white vapor with their wet black bodies, gray necks, and pale blue eyes, moving in uneven synchrony. Their haunting caws increased, and though we couldn't see them all, there must have been hundreds circling and creating the din. Hamish touched my woolen-gloved fingers. I didn't withdraw my hand but lowered my head and observed the sodden pointed toes of my shoes. As he moved nearer, I noticed a smell of binding glue, the sort that emanates from books. I looked behind to where Lorenzo should have been, but couldn't see him beyond the vanishing bend in the path. Hamish pulled me close while the raucous birds spun around us.

Then Lorenzo's loud voice cut through the fog. "Have you ever heard such an uproar?" We quickly separated, as yearning and shame flared through me.

We continued to walk, holding our separate silences like live coals. I involuntarily brought my hands to rest below my chest, as if to contain it, the way a pregnant woman will place her hands upon her swollen belly. Incongruously I thought of a strange tale my father had related to me about a seed bone. I mentioned this to break the silence.

"Tell me," said Hamish immediately, "what is a seed bone?"

"It re-creates the whole body. When my father first told me the story when I was a child, I wanted to plant every bone I could find in the sandy earth of our courtyard to see if it would make the magic. If the chicken knuckle would generate the chicken, the prickly ribs reconstitute the fish. Or if the tiny sacral bone I secretly obtained would grow into a skeleton or even a man. I'd stolen it from the charnel house on the island of San Michele, when we buried my great-aunt Tiziana. I wandered in the green cemetery, tapping gravestones with a long stick I found, while the rest of the families gathered beneath a black cypress, the tree of sudden death, Olmina once told me. That is why they are planted in cemeteries. Since then, I refuse to stand anywhere near one."

Close behind me, Lorenzo scoffed. "The only reason cypress mark the fields of the dead is that their roots are long and deep. They won't upend the coffins."

"And just how did you steal that bone?" asked Hamish incredulously.

"When I came to the charnel house, I reached through the grate on impulse, grabbed the little vertebra, and pocketed it. Two Capuchins, their gray hoods covering their faces, strode nearby but didn't observe me. Later, on the gondola returning to Venetia, I felt the bone jump in my skirt and I clutched it in my fist to keep it quiet. That night I secretly planted it beneath the pine in our small courtyard, but nothing ever sprouted. Even the vertebra disappeared, for when I tried to dig it up I couldn't find it."

"What a daring thing to do!"

I smiled. "I don't know. It seems I've always wanted to make fragments whole, whether it involves a bone, a book, or a patient."

He regarded me seriously with sharp blue eyes.

I stopped to catch my breath. The fog had turned to a wan rain. "I guess we should turn around."

"I'll agree to that, signorina. You don't want to come down with the ague," Lorenzo said, slapping his arms to warm up. I noticed both pockets of his woolen breeches bulging with small, thick branches, so that he resembled a sort of walking pollard.

"Well, I see you've found something to carve, then."

"Ah yes, signorina. I like alderwood for the sweet, smoky smell. Easy to work and doesn't feather."

"What will you carve?" asked Hamish.

"Hmm, maybe a little crèche for Epiphany."

"Careful, then," Hamish said. "Don't forget you're in Protestant country now, and Nativities are forbidden. Best to keep it in the house."

"How sad!" I exclaimed. I certainly wasn't a devout Catholic, but as a child I'd always enjoyed playing with the little figures Lorenzo had whittled.

Lorenzo shook his head and trundled ahead of us.

Then Hamish opened his great green coat and put his arm out toward me. "Cold?"

I moved closer so he could put it around my shoulder.

Lorenzo looked back and caught my eye as if to ask, *Are you all right with this man?*

And cautiously, I smiled.

We walked back down the path, gathering warmth from each other. Before he left us at our rooms, I said quietly, "Hamish, I'd like to come to the library, then."

The beauty of the countryside, and of Hamish, loosened my thoughts and my orderly plans. I began to consider that maybe I could settle in Edenburg, a city crowded upon three hills above an estuary. Wouldn't I find comfort in the penetrating damp, the salt fog out of the east like an old childhood friend? A sea like beaten tin. Tall ships ticking across the horizon like the ornate hands of a wondrous clock. For like Venetia, Edenburg conversed with a sea to the east and withstood mountain winds from the Highlands in the north. This correspondence of geography pleased me — the familiar and the foreign in lively accord.

I began to consider more deeply my desire to find my father. How well did I really know him? Perhaps that was why I carried the letters and read them with all the devoted habit a woman might apply to reading the hours. More often than not, he was my Compline, the last of the hours, when one contemplates the small death of sleep. My night prayer. *There, my father, you do exist. I have your words, even though you're not here.* I'd read them in different orders through the years, following chronology or place and now, on this journey, his nature. For it seemed another organizing principle cycled through his correspondence, like lunar phases, wheels of mysterious mood and reflection that weren't entirely clear to me, though I could feel their inner workings. There was that unusual letter from Montpellier in 1586 — unusual because he employed a rare tone of contentment.

My dear Gabriella,

I spend my days walking this strange half-abandoned city because I can no longer sit indoors. The season is spring, though the weather is still cool. A very fine fellow here, an old paper-maker from Alby, has proved to be my best companion. He doesn't ask me questions about my profession. He doesn't spar with my theories. And he couldn't care less about the Book of Diseases, *except that he's delighted that I've promised to request his paper through the Aldine Press in Venetia. He's shown himself to be a marvelous artisan even as he works here at the mill of a friend who's lent him a pulping hammer, vat, and screen. You would enjoy watching him, as you were always so engaged by how things are made, the beautiful mechanics. The other afternoon I sat for a while observing him working the hempen rags into paper. After previously soaking and boiling the fibers, he gently sieved them evenly onto a copper screen and pulled a sheet of paper out of the vat on that very screen. Then he couched it onto felt, where he pressed out the excess water. The old papermaker patted it all over (testing for uneven dampness) with unimaginable tenderness, as if he loved the paper. Then he left it to dry on a rack. I actually envied him his craft, the feel of it. The consequence of good work that he could hold in his hands. While our vocation may yield a healthy man, woman, or child, surely a happy outcome, it may just as well yield suffering or death. I wonder sometimes if that fires my passion to finish this book. To create something that I may hold in my hand, the very thing of it making me content. I know how it pleases you too, my daughter. May we one day find ourselves together at the Aldine Press, holding the book that offers help and knowledge to others, after it sustained us well in the making.*

Would a book satisfy my passion? Or was there something—or someone—else I should hold?

True to his promise, Hamish obtained permission for me to study in the library. He appeared there almost every day at the hour I arrived, no matter when I rose or went out. He must have set someone on watch—or perhaps he'd agreed to be my escort there, unbeknownst to me.

It was the only place I went. Lorenzo, who also accompanied me each day, waited outside the hall on a bench, for they didn't permit him to enter. Sometimes he whittled, always diligent about pocketing his shavings, much to Olmina's vexation when she washed his clothes. He guarded his pieces from inquisitive eyes as much as he could, though once a gentleman asked him, "What are you carving there, my good man?"

"Oh, barnyard animals for my granddaughter at home. This here's one of your furry Highland cattle." The man smiled then and left him in peace.

"I wish you did have a granddaughter," I said spontaneously, and immediately I regretted it.

"Mmh," he grunted, and he frowned down at the wooden animals, his whole body clenched against the past. He placed them in a worn handkerchief that he folded up and tucked into his jacket pocket.

I struggled to apologize. We'd never spoken of their baby that died, nor of the others that never came. But then he turned to me and said, "Maybe you'll have a girl of your own one day, and I can count her as granddaughter."

I didn't say a word. I'd thoughtlessly opened old sorrow for him, and in turn he stung me with hope. Somewhere within me, a vision sprang forth of that little girl from Tübingen, her curious expression, curls, and wayward hoop. I did want a child, and this unexpected longing flung me open, like a room of windows unlatched by wind.

I stood at the tall table fronting the literature shelves, with one foot up on the footrest, beginning to read from Petrarch's *Epistolae familiares,* a selection I'd come to by randomly opening the book. It was a letter describing his ascent of Mount Ventosum. *So many men have written on this subject,* I thought.

And so few women have penned a perspective. Hadn't Olmina and I traversed Passo Rolle and the Dolomiti? What about the shepherdesses there tending flocks high in the shimmering air of those mountains? But no woman, perhaps, had climbed deliberately to a peak. Someday I wanted to ascend and descend with purpose, just for the sake of the mountain. And so I returned to Petrarch. I liked the ending of his Mount Ventosum letter, not so much for the edification as for the arrival by moonlight.

How earnestly should we strive, not to stand on mountain-tops, but to trample beneath us those appetites which spring from earthly impulses.

With no consciousness of the difficulties of the way, amidst these preoccupations which I have so frankly revealed, we came, long after dark, but with the full moon lending us its friendly light, to the little inn which we had left that morning before dawn.

The friendly light, the little inn. The moon lending. They shone somewhere in my mind. So I wasn't particularly present when Hamish came up behind me and asked, "How are you, dear lady?" He pointed to the manuscript as if he were discussing Petrarch, so as to avoid rumors from his fellows, of whom there were several in the library at that moment, reading, discussing topics among themselves. A couple of them were watching us.

He looked over my shoulder and recited:

To-day I made the ascent of the highest mountain in this region, which is not improperly called Ventosum. My only motive was the wish to see what so great an elevation had to offer. I have had the expedition in mind for many years; for, as you know, I have lived in this region from infancy, having been cast here by that fate which determines the affairs of men. Consequently the mountain, which is visible from a great distance, was ever before my eyes, and I conceived the plan of some time doing what I have at last accomplished to-day.

"Thank you," I said simply. The sound of Hamish's rich voice anchored me, a welcome weight even as he read about a light, windy mountain.

A tall, austere young gentleman came up beside us. He pulled Petrarch's *Sonnets* from the shelf, tugging the book on its rope as far away from us as he could go, presumably to give us some privacy. Or was it repugnance at being close to a woman? I received my answer when he glanced at me derisively.

The young man, who clearly resented my presence, occupied far more than his space with the pressure of unspoken warning. He tapped slowly, loudly, on the slanted table as he read aloud. I could see no good of confronting him, though I felt the urge building in Hamish. So I linked my arm through his and said, "I'm ready to leave."

He smiled down at me, fierce and yet willingly calmed.

Strolling away from the library between the two men, Lorenzo and Hamish, on a rare sunny noon, I felt content. If indeed my father had disappeared, and *The Book of Diseases* had vanished with him, then I would dedicate myself to the book's completion. Though I lacked his full experience, I knew I could make up for it in time — with the added vision of a woman.

AROMATIC WATER OF RUE:

For Augury

Though rue may be employed internally as a remedy for many ailments, among them headache, colic, and women's lunar pains, and externally for gout, chilblains, and bruises, the water of rue is marvelous for sight and second sight. Writers, engravers, and artists relish the fresh herb with watercress and brown bread. Dabble the water around the eyes to settle murky vision and to summon foreknowledge in all things. The herb of sorrow is thus also the herb of grace, for the future already repents its errors. Some also claim that rue repels plague, biting chiggers, and curses. The evil eye squints from the scent of rue.

CHAPTER 16

❧

To Make Way for the New

"I'm your firstfooter!" hooted Hamish on New Year's Eve.

He had invited us to join a few friends at the table of Dr. Baldino just after midnight. But when he came by to collect us, he stood at our threshold, his eyes darting from one to the other of us with some hidden foolery.

"Won't you come in a moment?" Olmina asked as we took some time to gather our cloaks and hats.

That's when he made his announcement and stepped ceremoniously into our sitting room. He was handsomely attired in deep red velvet breeches, jerkin, and doublet, verdant hose, and a coat, and his maroon hat was adorned with a sleek black feather. "The first one to enter your home brings good luck all year," he announced. Then he produced a bottle of sweet wine, which Lorenzo gladly uncorked and emptied into four thick blue glasses that Olmina brought from the kitchen, for us to toast all round.

"To the New Year, then, the year of our Lord 1591!" I cried, delighted to be celebrating after the somber affair that was Christmas. I'd yearned for the lively colors of Venetia, and now Hamish had brought revelry to our door.

"Ah, so it would be on the Continent! But here in Scotland we're still in 1590, according to the Anglican Church. It won't be the New Year's Day till March 25, the Feast of the Annunciation of Mary. But I see no reason we still can't celebrate!"

"To our signorina, then, and her father," called out Olmina.

"To my dear Olmina and Lorenzo," I answered back, and then I added, "To Dr. Hamish Urquhart and his many gifts!"

The wine tasted of abundant, melodious happiness, and it sustained us after we left our rooms and walked slowly arm in arm, so as not to tumble into the slick streets. Hamish and I, and Lorenzo and Olmina, maneuvered our way through a light snow to Dr. Baldino's house. Many others were out as well, dancing and singing raucously.

"The church will have a hard time arresting so many people," Hamish said, laughing, as a man cavorted by us, stuffing his face with a forbidden holiday bun, full of currants, almonds, spices, and whiskey.

When we neared Dr. Baldino's home, the stone building stood transformed, flickering with warm amber candles in all the windows. "They are lit for strangers to find a way through the night," explained Hamish. He looked down at me warmly. "For travelers."

The pungent scent of yew greens and holly freshened the door as we entered, and the cold room we'd passed by on our first visit now blazed with a boisterous fire. The large house thrummed with lute music and affable voices coming from the sitting room on the first floor. It pulsed with conversations and laughter, and hummed with Dr. Baldino's steady, drawn-out words, as he held forth on some subject while leaning back in a broad gold-brocaded chair. A young manservant, his beardless face marked by a stray eye that scanned the entire scene as well as the individual, carried our coats away to a side closet and drew Olmina and Lorenzo upstairs to sit in the warm kitchen.

Hamish and I had barely begun to navigate our way through introductions and toward Dr. Baldino when Isabella of the long braid, now wound in a silver plait at her nape for the occasion, glided through the rooms with a small bell calling us to supper on the second floor. She wore a black gown with a high bodice and fine ruff and a sheer linen cap, giving her fully the appearance of a lady of the house. She and I were among a handful of women present, though I felt entirely comfortable there in the rooms thick with books, globes, maps, and various cabinets of curiosities. It seemed that along with his study of memory, Dr. Baldino possessed a passion for collecting the things of this world, whether they were natural or human crafted, perhaps so as not to forget the varieties of encounters that could be organized in the great theater of the mind. Chimerical fish and animals (those rogue taxidermies that delight many a collector—who knew if they were real or concocted?), catalogues, libraries, and clusters of things like bones, pressed leaves, shells, and minerals abounded, and

Hamish had to pull me along out of the room of shells to come to dinner.

Kind Dr. Baldino sat at the head of the table, frothy white hair combed into some semblance of style. He motioned for me to sit next to him at the long improvised table that spanned one dark red room, made an L-turn, and entered another great room, so that guests were both visible and invisible, the latter's conversations chiming from the other room like disembodied voices from the past. It wasn't until a little later that I recognized Lorenzo's quick remarks and Olmina's throaty laughter and realized that the other room held the servants, with Isabella presiding (for so Olmina informed me later).

I was glad to be seated between Hamish and Dr. Baldino.

"Tell us, Dr. Mondini, what do you do in your fair city of Venetia to bring in the New Year?" asked the latter, his eyes weepy with contentment.

"Ah." I thought for a moment, looking down and noticing Hamish's hand touching a fold of my yellow velvet skirt, which fell over the edge of the chair. "There is always wonderful feasting, but what I most recall are the bonfires and the music." I glanced from Dr. Baldino to Hamish and back again. "Even if snow and the *tramontano* winds fall upon the city, muffled men and women bring out their old goods—tables broken beyond repair, rotten curtains, broken cioppini, split wooden ladles, old love letters, though never books! We love our books too dearly, even if they're brittle and smudged with mold." It was hard to watch Hamish now, the dusky light kindling in his eyes. "Then we set fire to the old to make way for the new, in all the *campi* of our city. The fires are cast back by the mirrors of the canals, though I admit sometimes in wilder weather they sputter out. Still, it's a wonderful sight, fire multiplied by water. Often people shout and throw things out the window and you have to watch your head."

"Ah yes, I remember!" Dr. Baldino began to laugh. "It's been many years, but I remember people tossing odds and ends out the window in Salerno. Things crashing down all night long! Once, my brother, Giacomo, flung a marvelous pack of cards out the window on New Year's, accusing me of cheating because he was losing to me, as he often did. For I could keep the images of the cards he showed clearly in my mind for a long time—laid out as if upon a table. I was furious and ran down to collect as many as I could, before the bonfire consumed them."

"That must be the original source of enthusiasm for your field of study," joked Hamish.

"You're right, dear fellow. It was the university or the gaming tables, and I believe I made the proper choice, don't you think?"

"Ha, I don't think so, Orazio," cried a Spanish gentleman across the table, who'd introduced himself as Melchor de Ecija Zayas, a merchant of fine olive oil. "I wish you'd chosen the tables and come to Genoa with me, or Venetia, your fortunate city, Dr. Mondini." He nodded at me with a large smile.

I frowned, feigning disapproval in good sport.

Dr. Baldino replied, "Then I might not have made it to ninety-three, eh, Melchor? Someone might have abducted me for my talent or slit my throat at the earliest opportunity. Still, I wouldn't mind a card game of thirty-one after dinner tonight, if you are prepared to lose."

"I'd be happy to offer charity to an old man," Melchor replied, and he rapped the table with his knuckles, imitating the call to lay down cards in the game.

"Oh, and you believe seventy is young?"

"In your distinguished company." Melchor grinned mischievously, his eyes glinting from the creases of his plump lids.

Dr. Baldino gave a dry chuckle, then turned back to me once more, saying, "The music then, Dr. Mondini, tell us about the music."

"Sometimes the Fabrianis—have you heard of them?—sing out to one another from rooftops all across Venetia, making a harmonic instrument of the whole city, playing its corridors and muted canals with echoes that ring through open doors and windows, then vibrate in our bodies. The candles multiplied by glass and tides, the scents of Constantinopolis and Mytilene, the platters of fried squid and fish—all were infused with music. I enjoyed nocturnal walks with my servants and friends then, at the turning of the year, viewing the scenes of lit casements and the inhabitants within, listening to the diverse instruments and clear voices."

I turned my head toward the other room, where, invisible to me, Lorenzo and Olmina, those two who were most dear to me now, conversed with boisterous joy. He laughed and the whole table trembled. She joined in and the sea shook far off in its bed.

"By contrast, Edenburg is a hushed place, wouldn't you say, gentlemen?" Hamish declared. "No other cities mingle in its air, unless you count the sweets shop managed by the woman from Provins. I must take you there, Gabriella." He regarded me expectantly.

The two elderly men stared at me, as if suddenly trying to discern the nature of our connection. Was it friendship, collegiality, or something more? I wasn't sure myself. But I replied in an even tone, "Yes, I'd like that. We could bring back some honeyed fruit or *pignolet* for the good doctor here."

"Delightful suggestion," squealed Dr. Baldino, a small child for a moment. Then he commented, "Dr. Mondini, I also hear that you're making good use of our library, compiling a wonderful encyclopedia begun by your father."

"Yes, thank you, by the generosity of the university and, of course, my friend Hamish."

"I hope that we may see some of the pages before you depart our city?"

"Yes, as long as you promise," I teased, "not to submit them to your art of memory and claim them as your own."

"Ah, my dear, I no longer write, and the theater of mnemonics has faded for me now. It is only the rooms of the present I wish to inhabit. In fact there are days when I feel my collections have reached their limit, their linkages burdened to the point of rupture. Sometimes I wish I could wake up to an empty house."

"That's when you'll be dead." Melchor laughed, obviously a close enough friend to say such a thing.

"Ha! Or completely happy," Dr. Baldino said with a sigh.

Our conversation soon subsided as plates of boiled salmon, maced conger eels, oysters, periwinkles, mussels boiled with claret and cinnamon, special wheaten bread, and burdock root salad with dried herbs filled our table. Isabella served Dr. Baldino separately, his food mashed or cut into many tiny pieces. Her tender restraint seemed to me the perfect manner of a doctor. *There,* I thought, *that woman has a gift and no one knows it.* But then I believed Dr. Baldino did know, for he watched her leave the room with a kind of reverence.

Later, after a dessert of ginger rice pudding and sweet malmsey wine, and more good conversation, we walked toward home, all four of us hanging on to one another, dazed with the night's merriment. We paused for a moment to look upward. The snowfall had stopped. The clouds broke and offered us a glimpse of night sky bristling with keen bright stars.

By February, I frequented the library only two or three times a week, since I'd acquired patients through the goodwill of Hamish and Dr. Baldino, who referred Scottish ladies to my care. I was glad to earn our keep. I had my rounds back, in a small way. The company of women also provided another window into the life here. One lady in particular kept a garden of medicinals, and though her plants lay dormant, I was glad to discuss the properties of the simples with her, though I spoke to no one of this, cautious and fearful of the witch hunts that cast a disquieting torpor on the winter city. I didn't want to provoke suspicion in my pursuits of the art of physick.

More than anything, I found I distrusted happiness, besieged as I was by the memory of the curses my mother flung at me when she fell into her lowest moments: "Your father was too fond of you—that's why he left!" Or "Your father was jealous of you! Now he's fled in the name of this so-called"—and here she spat out the words—"*Book of Diseases,* and I'm left with no husband. You were meant to be his helper, not his peer." At this distance from my mother, I wished I'd done something other than walk away from her. But I was too shocked and hurt. What else could I have done? Perhaps say, *I am sorry that you don't have a husband.* She was cornered by old expectations in that great, sumptuous island prison. She was alone. I hadn't thought much about it then. And I unwittingly goaded her loneliness.

Still, the words stung as they returned to me at the end of February in the library, where I settled among rare books of anatomy, astronomy, philosophy, the splendid books of the hours, and the materia medicas, which I pored over with a kind of passion. How studious the other doctors thought me, yet there were times I read the same passage over and over until the words moved upon the page like insects. Perhaps I needed the cure Theodorus Priscianus recommended for painful thoughts: "If a loadstone be held upon the head it will draw out hidden pain, and the same effect may be obtained by rubbing over the forehead a swallow's nest thoroughly mixed with vinegar."

Draw out the pain. I had come to accept that I was driven away from Venetia as much as I was driven toward my father. I had presented myself in every city with such admirable aims: to follow his journey and discover his whereabouts. Did I wish to surpass my father in the art of physick, while lacking the full breadth of his skills? Was I truly a fraud without him? No, I was less experienced and yet I had within me a kind of observation and instinct that failed in him.

Here in the academy I remained a shadow, consoled by the long, polished tables, podiums, great chairs, and benches that harked back to the library of Padua. This was where it all began, the sanctuary of my father. Perhaps the only way I'd ever really know him would be through words and their spent heat. For it was my father who had taught me to love books for themselves, the smell of the vellum and paper, the rare authority of the pages. *Here, do you see this marvelous book? The skins of one hundred and eighty-two sheep!* he once pronounced, as he slapped his hand down on the stamped leather cover boards. *The book is a flock, a jewel, a cemetery, a lantern, a garden, a piss pot! Pigments ground of precious minerals, charred bone, lamp soot, rare plants and insects, pigments formed of the corrosion of copper plates suspended above urine.*

One afternoon, Hamish interrupted my reading of a gem-like book of hours, a page where I often lingered, San Geronimo in the Wilderness, his psalms compiled for the sick and the infirm. "I've worried for you." Hamish lightly clasped my left shoulder. "Worried that the shadow of the father also lay upon the daughter. I sent a note a week ago inviting you to walk with me but never received an answer."

His hand pressed gently through several layers of wool, my cape and sweaters, a linen blouse. A heat rose in my shoulder to his hand as if to a warming brick. There was no one else in the library, and the darkly paneled walls seemed to draw nearer like the sides of a wooden box; the precious volumes also conspired, like heads nodding closer, to overhear our words.

I turned upon the bench and saw only the curved lips in his beard, then felt the rimmed moisture of his mouth upon my forehead, then my lips. He sank next to me and fumbled with my bodice.

I held Hamish's face between my hands. I sought out his blue eyes. I could paint him now, so carefully did I see his face: his complexion pink as the saint's in the illumination, the carmine flush of his chest where the shirt flap opened, dangling its careless string. The light saffron hairs. I laid my ear to his chest and he held me. I wanted to know his music. The lute, the sound box, the fretted ribs.

Some women think of love as a rising thing, but I'd always

known it as a descent where I might lose myself or my beloved. A sweetness and then a severance greater than original solitude. And so, I feared joy. Yet there in the library, Hamish and I climbed the bright ladder of the body, as if it were sky and we a deafening, twisting flock of birds that could never fall to earth.

CHAPTER 17

❦

Sorrow Be Banished

Olmina planted herself directly in front of me. "If you're going to pace the room all day, you may as well come to the market with me and cover some distance." She thrust a basket at me.

I shook my head. "I'm not going out in that bone-chilling mud. Does it ever stop raining? Oh, Olmina, I don't know what to do!" I sat down hard, ballooning my skirts on a chair before the fire.

Lorenzo grunted as he whittled there in the opposite chair.

Olmina sighed. "Let me tell you something. At the New Year's dinner, Isabella said . . . 'I don't know if this will help, but please tell your mistress that her father, before he departed

Edenburg, insisted that he must find the bezoar stone *in the desert.*' "

I repeated these words in amazement. "Olmina, why have you waited over two months to tell me this? I've been swerved from my journey, but if Isabella said—"

"Oh, signorina, pardon my saying it, but what Isabella said proves nothing! She also called him 'a man of two minds, fleeing and returning, who thought a stone would help him to find peace'! If we are to go anywhere, our best course is home."

"There is a doctor with whom my father exchanged letters in Montpellier, and he is an expert on the correspondences of stones, the indigestible sorrows. I should write to him, or perhaps we should take up the journey again . . ."

Olmina took my hand and said, "Maybe you'd rather stay here and choose some small happiness? That Hamish is too handsome for my liking, but he stares at you as if he would devour you. Not many northerners are given to that kind of want and devotion."

Devotion. The word seemed unattainable. The memory of the afternoon in the library crackled within me like the atmosphere of approaching thunderstorm, distant and very near at once. I was mute, deafened. Hamish had called upon me afterward and we were dazed, couldn't speak of it, yet knew that it seared and united us. We were hungry for each other. But how to make a life out of this? Had my own mother and father known one another this way? If they had, was their life together afterward one of rancor and long mourning for what was lost?

I wondered how to come to devotion. The devotions. Habit,

prayer, observance of the other. I thought of Mauro. What good was the fidelity of touch and attention? He was gone. I sank into sadness and could see no way around it. I wouldn't admit that I lacked the plainest kind of courage. Instead I leapt into my habit of a different form of bravery (daring the journey again). We would leave in a fortnight for Montpellier. I didn't tell Hamish but left him a letter of farewell, explaining that we'd found a new clue to my father's whereabouts, the bezoar. And all around this truth, he must have felt the blatant untruth, for he didn't accept what I wrote.

We set off in the gray uncertainty of morning, with the Water of Leyth to the west. There were no flocks of jackdaws or linnets. They must have been sheltering in a sturdy oak—or at least that's how I wanted to see them. I felt the oak nuts that Gerta had given me, pressing against my leg in my pocket, and fingered them like lumpy prayer beads. The *tarocchi* card was there as well. *Am I doing the right thing?* I asked myself. *Should I turn back?*

We spoke little and rode through one winding river valley after another to the southwest. Most of the hills remained moth-brown, though it was early March. The trees were our constant silent witnesses, for no one but cider or ale fools would've been out and about in the raw, knuckling weather. *Am I a fool or a madwoman?*

After over a week of trudging through mud and dismal weather, sleeping in earthen houses with turf roofs and nothing more than hides for doors, we stopped near the river Derwent close to Cockermouth. We planned to rest for a week or two to recover our strength in the blue stone house of a baron, a lodging recommended by a solitary farmer who passed us on his way to town.

The lady of the house was pleased to have us, for this was not the season when they usually welcomed wayfarers. The men had all gone hunting with the baron, and the women remained scattered and apart in their stone houses. As I spent my time writing, she quickly learned to leave me be, though she did send little things up to my room to cheer me: pungent heather or the broken cups of wild birds' eggs. She pressed me to accompany her on excursions to meet the baron for a day or two at the stones of Long Meg and Her Daughters, or Wast Water, a black lake to the south, but I refused her invitations. Her life forced me to consider another way I might have lived, where a deep and varied music moved between a woman and her husband. I recalled my conversations with Hamish, his fervent body, and regretted everything I couldn't keep.

Lorenzo and Olmina, on the other hand, amused themselves with chores, songs, and games. They visited the markets on Wednesday and Saturday mornings to buy supplies and sample the ale that everyone seemed to drink morning, noon, and night. I meanwhile remained behind, dull as a stone, feeling heavy and tired. But I wrote.

LANA USÉE DE FLEUR:

A Vernal Disease That Causes One to Lose Appetite and Withdraw into the Darkest Closet of Her House

Every year when spring splits the world open with fragrance and color, many unfortunates suffer this ailment. Winter still holds them even as seedtime pulls them. My mother once mentioned an aunt Taddea, whom I scarcely remember, who endured *la nausée de fleur* every year. She couldn't pursue her work in the binding shop when her body revolted against spring. The guild, however, allowed her to assist her husband in the craft from her shuttered bedroom for the duration of the illness. Taddea directed helpers from the dark, and they brought the boards and paper presses, various papers and glues, and brushes and clamps she needed. She could not even bear to gaze upon a flower design, so the assistants avoided papers decorated with rosettes, trefoils, lilies, or leaves. Taddea worked more by feel than by sight in the continual candlelit dusk of her room. All went well unless the assistants or women in the family forgot to scrub off any scent they'd applied before they visited or delivered her food. She winced at their approach, coughing dryly, as she complained that scent attached itself more readily to women, that one sympathetic vapor would mingle with another. Red poppies, jasmine, orange blossoms, and all manner of wildflowers distressed her greatly.

I never understood her suffering until I treated a young Scotswoman, Emily, who, upon first spying drifts of narcissus in the fields, took to her bed and refused to taste any food. When I entered her room and observed the gauzy canopy of her bed delicately painted with violets, I immediately ordered it to be removed. Likewise the nightdress she wore, which was embroidered with yellow primroses. She showed marked improvement but still couldn't go near her window without catching the scent of narcissus. If she even distractedly glanced at them, she was unsettled for days. "The flowers are fatal and

251

no one else knows," she would whisper in a panic. "They pull you down into their poison."

I calmed her as best I could and began administering simple broths of violets, briar, and gentian, even narcissus from which the petals were strained. Like cures like. Flowers cure the unwitting maiden. The household lay under a strict order of silence regarding the true ingredients of the broth. Little by little, Emily improved, her wan face gaining color again, her limbs gaining strength. We knew she was well when she craved dandelions and threw her casement wide open.

Spring arrived, and one Sunday afternoon Lorenzo and Olmina insisted we all go to the village fair. I accompanied them, but while they danced in the village common to the barrel organ, bagpipe, and tabor, I felt thumped by dull clubs. My skin ached. Lorenzo and Olmina amused the English with their lively Friuli dances, Lorenzo kicking up his heels like a gangly grasshopper and Olmina spinning like a peg top. Not to be outdone, the English also danced by hops, frisks, and leaps as they made their circles round and round with clasped hands.

"Signorina, come and join us!" Olmina cajoled me. "You're so marvelous a dancer, you could show us the *contrappasso!*"

She held my hand and pulled a little.

I shook my head and sat back on the wooden chair brought me by a kindly old vendor woman. "My feet are too leaden just now, but I'll watch," I said, trying to appease her, keeping in mind the awkward circumstance of my presence among the countryfolk—I didn't want to become an object of speculation or mischief.

I was sitting near the cheese stall at the end of many food stalls lined up on the west side of the common, their gaudy awnings billowing in waves at the slight breeze that brought the first scent of the warming fields. The vendor hollered out her wares, some of which she patted with her stubby hand, as if coaxing them to further ripen.

Lorenzo tried to jolt me by bringing an aqua vitae. "Drink up, dear Dottoressa. Here's the medicine! Time to banish your troubles and follow the dance!" he cried, his eyes bleary with cheap ale.

"I'll drink and dance the day you sew a wound!"

"Come along." Olmina tugged his arm. "Mustn't get too forward with our lady."

Embarrassed, he bowed low, doffed his woolen cap. "I meant no harm, signorina." And then because he'd bowed so low, he kept going and fell over, finding himself embracing the dirt common, much to the amusement of all who witnessed him, including me.

"Oh, Lorenzo, I'm not angry." I smiled at his long face as he lay squinting up at me. "I'm just not a dancer anymore." After I said this, I felt I'd gone suddenly old.

At that moment a Fool strutted up with exaggerated, dangling sleeves trimmed in bells trailing the ground. He wore only stockings full of holes, no shoes or breeches, and a raggedy bicolored tunic of russet and white split vertically down the middle. His cap hung crookedly to one side, with three floppy horns tipped with bells. He put his hands on his hips and surveyed me with audacity, then grimaced at Lorenzo.

"That's no way to treat a lady, now. No falling at the feet, man. Kiss her hand, that's what they like!"

As he moved toward me, Olmina landed a good swift kick in his shin.

"Aaaah, aaaah!" He bawled like a babe and clutched his leg, playing it to the fullest. The small crowd that had gathered clapped and laughed, and the bagpiper sped up his tune. The Fool now hopped on one foot toward the center of the dancing. He let go of his leg and clutched a morris dancer in women's garb, who'd appeared, jingling bells at his knees, swaying a large farthingale back and forth in imitation of abundant hips. Unfortunately one of his stuffed breasts fell, though the Fool was quick to help him push it back up, at which moment the faux lady released a hearty fart. The nearby dancers hooted and groaned, giving her wide berth.

The stench drifted over to where I sat—unless it was some other reveler stinking up the air, for there were plenty of them vomiting and relieving themselves under the poplar trees that grew near the road. I'd witnessed a few rustic fairs in the Italian countryside (and courtly festivities as well), where taking one's pleasure meant dance and drink and bodily evacuations of all sorts.

Lorenzo managed to sit up, grinning, while Olmina helped him rise the rest of the way.

Against all better judgment, I allowed myself a little sip of the aqua vitae he'd left on the stool next to me. It was enough to warm me to the fair. I watched the children beyond the alehouse clustered in games of blindman's buff, leapfrog, and bowls. Runlets of ale and ivy beer spilled upon the earth. Pretzels and goat pies steamed upon the tables. Carter's bread and butter. And bowls of a foul-smelling porridge with lumps of sodden meat, probably a tough mutton.

Olmina offered me a flower of marchpane, knowing my fondness for almonds, and I nibbled it slowly, feeling my hunger for sweets return. Ring o' roses, somersaults, and trundling hoops. The children didn't care if their parents pulled their hair or swatted them with ladles or the flat side of a hand. It was fair day!

Churlish men strode about on stilts and whooped, some using a stilt to lift a skirt, others stalking up to the alehouse and purposefully bonking their foreheads on the crossbeams of the doors, just to make the children laugh. I found myself laughing, then quietly crying with an empty glass in hand. Olmina and Lorenzo were nowhere in sight. Mortified, I decided to slip away and walk back to the stone house alone, for it wasn't far from the town. When I stood up, the white-haired vendor came over and slipped a small cheese in my pocket. When I fumbled through coins I emptied onto my palm from a clever purse tied to my skirt, she picked a small one (which I didn't think was enough) and refused any more. Then she hugged me. "So, even ladies must weep in this life, eh?"

"No help for it. Thank you for the cheese, Grandmother."

"Oh, I'm not a grandmother anymore. Lost 'em to the pestilence two years ago." She stared off into the budding trees as if she might find them there.

Now it was my turn to hug her.

Halfway back to the manor, a few men near a twisted oak leered at me. I walked a little faster. One gadder dressed in green presented me a nosegay that I kept for fear of offending and later tossed in the hedgerow. Every now and then I heard a snuffling behind me, as if a man mimicking a wolf was stalking me. When I abruptly turned at the top of the hill to confront the one behind me, I saw the Fool, who promptly bowed widely and said, "Just looking after ye, milady." A plump little pig was beside him, dressed in a ruff collar. The pig trotted up to me and grunted. The Fool struck a staff that resembled a long femur on the ground three times. "May the cause of yer sorrow be banished!" Then he turned, somersaulted, and ran back to the dancing, the little pig scampering after him as fast as it could.

If my father was dead, I would have his grave. I would have his ghost if I believed in such things. We'd been traveling for eight months, and all my inquiries had led nowhere. One by one I was ticking off the places empty of my father. Though I now possessed his glasses, his shoes, and the description of a man unraveling in Edenburg. Perhaps I was the one unraveling? I had rested enough. I turned to my notes for comfort before urging our departure for Montpellier, where three of my father's letters had originated. Each time I touched the book, I regained the center of things. I found purpose in text and taxonomy.

PORPHYRIA:

An Abhorrence of Light That Causes One to Suffer Cankers and Grow the Fur of a Beast

From the time she was a very young girl, a woman in Lucca cringed at the light of the sun, the moon, even candle glow. Her hair began to grow in such thick waves from her face and body that from a distance, Irmina was sometimes mistaken for a small costumed bear escaped from the traveling carnival. Her poor, terrified mother begged a family friend, my father's cousin Signor Giovanni Albani, to send for a doctor. I accompanied my father to Lucca and met the young woman as she cowered in her mother's wooden closet. As she spoke to us through her pelt, I got the impression that Irmina was an anchoress deprived of solitude. She spoke in short, broken whispers. "I want to go away from people!" I remembered a deer I sensed one morning as the animal stood hidden in a thicket, its attention directed toward me, its stillness an opening in the landscape that led to some refuge.

Irmina's fur resembled brown water pouring, bending across stones until it reached the top of her loose chemise. I asked her if I could brush it, to gain her confidence, and she nodded. She closed her eyes as I drew the brush through her fur in careful strokes. I almost thought she would purr. After a little while my father steered me back to our purpose. He recommended that we examine her urine and saliva, and then we would suggest a course of remedy. I touched what I believed to be her shoulder and explained that we wished to help her. She shrank from my hand and pleaded with us to convey her to a cave. A small leather-bound Psalter lay near the toes of her red slippers, which protruded from a bristly layer of darker fur on the tops of her feet beneath the hem of her dress.

I thought of Santa Caterina of Siena in her white robes and black cloak, praying in her underground stone chapel at night, while in the hospital rooms of Santa Maria della Scala above her, the ill and the mad suffered in their beds. How did she bear it in the half dark, kneeling before the Man of Sorrows after spending all day tending the wounds, the gangrenes, and the invisible festerings? I once visited the little windowless cave of her chapel and unexpectedly found its half light to be like a hand laid upon the heart. Only a candle, a prie-dieu, and two small paintings, the Christ and the Magdalena completely covered in her own hair, occupied the room. But more than anything it was the odor of inevitability in the stone that strangely lifted my heart. One escaped doubt in the tomb. Here the saint found respite, silence, a recess from the sounds of pain, and acceptance.

After my father pronounced Irmina's waters barren of happiness, he requested a sample of her spit. When he saw it, he shook his head. "The nine disappointments here originate in her father's bloodline—discontent in love, in ambition, in beauty, absence of dreams, of wit, of friends, paucity of courage, of perseverance, of spirit. We can't cure her, my daughter. One of the most important things you'll learn in the art of physick is the recognition of God's puzzles or, as some might call them, devil's knots. He has created someone here who loves animal darkness. We can't cure her."

When my father spoke in this manner, I always felt uneasy and feared that the council might hear of his words. But I also sensed some wisdom turning in him like a wobbly wooden wheel. It rolled along but always seemed about to throw a rim and leave us waylaid. We consoled the parents, and as they were a family of some means, my father suggested that they could acquire land near Bagnoregio, a region reputed to contain many caves. The father received our proposal very badly and shouted at us, "My daughter will never leave this house, do you hear! Leave us alone if you can't cure her! Charlatans!" The mother wept. As we left I glimpsed Irmina at the window, the curtain of her hair separating at the sill where her yellow sleeve and hand appeared, a clenched paw cuffed with lace.

CHAPTER 18

꧁ꕥ꧂

The Sap That Slows
the World

The night before we reached Montpellier, I turned to this letter in unspoken appeal. *Give me a hint in correspondence, give me some fresh direction, Papà.*

My dear Gabriella,
My friend the papermaker has departed Montpellier and now I'm mostly alone. The majority of the professors have also left the city for want of students. After the full moon when I am better (for I've been keeping to my room for many days now, gnashing upon my own bitterness and illness, my loss of single-mindedness), I shall also leave for the mountains, which they say have benefits far beyond their waters. The ascent, I hope, will

prove salutary. Now I have a chance to test my desire for the solitary life, and yet while alone in my bare room, all I can think about is the fresh loaf of bread, salted butter, and wine that the woman here brings me once a day. Imagine! Not that I expected panoplies of angels, but perhaps some insight into melancholia, the discomfiting routine of folding suffering into a day, the way one folds a very letter. I write and expand upon my notes for The Book of Diseases*. Maybe that's all there is in the end. Papers on a desk. Papers in a volume. Pages turning in the mind, one after another, or scattered by the wind of moths. I think of those great black emperor moths with crescents marked upon their wings, emblems of night. My mother always said when she spied a moth in the house, "Someone is going to die!" My father would answer, "Someone is always going to die!" And if you can imagine, we laughed. Now, what am I saying, my dear? That one must laugh at melancholia?*

14 October 1588
Your humble father

We approached the town in the late afternoon, glimpsing the roofs and towers near the coast, though we couldn't see the Gallic Sea. It was a place that appeared lit not only by sun, but by some dull refraction of light through water, maybe the long, unseen fingers of salt marsh to the south, for I could smell its languid tang. We saw egrets standing on the backs of white horses in a luminous green field, and as we rode closer, four gulls rested motionless, one upon each corner of the clock tower that pointed skyward, along with the steeples of Notre Dame des Tables, Les Généraux, and Saint Denis. My father would've delighted in the symmetry of the birds. And Hamish, like me, might have wished to see them lift from the tower, then light on their corners again, lift and alight.

We passed by walled orchards and lush vineyards, through the archway of the eastern stone gate, and on to the quarter of Saint Firmin the Constant, where the small gray stonework buildings of the university of medicine stood, abandoned.

We knocked at the heavy wooden door of Dr. Joubert's address, a plain stone abode. A young man in his thirties emerged and greeted us with enthusiasm, like one who hasn't conversed with peers in a long while. He wore a mustache rather than a beard and appeared to be in excellent health, of sanguine temperament.

"Welcome, Dr. Mondini, splendid to meet you and your companions!" he proclaimed. He bowed to me and Olmina, then nodded to Lorenzo and stepped out into the street. "I have the keys here, there are two—this large iron key is for the front door, and the smaller brass ones are for your rooms. I don't intend to frighten you, but you'll want to lock the doors at night for safety. You never know when the Huguenots might come round again, seeking to denounce or detain anyone they think is a Catholic." He looked right and left in the street, though it was completely empty.

"Thank you, sir, we'll follow your good advice. As strangers we're unaccustomed to the ways of your town. But tell me, why do the streets appear so vacant at this early hour?"

"Ah yes. This quarter once housed over three thousand students, and now, since the university was ransacked"—he paused here, looking down out of deference and then back up at us—"there are fewer than a hundred left. Most of the university's books and furniture were destroyed by the Huguenots, you know, the French Calvinists, during the religious wars."

I'd heard about this but didn't realize the extent of the ruin.

"I'm so sorry to hear of it."

"Well, best not to speak of it any more," Dr. Joubert said in a low voice. "You never know who's listening. And since I myself converted, I must forget the old life." He hastily changed demeanor, moving with a quick, light step as we approached our lodging in one of several pale gray two-story buildings with dark slate roofs, just down the street. He knocked at a worn wooden door, and a young widow with flaxen hair opened and smiled at us shyly. She had a remarkably fresh complexion and lively blue eyes that contradicted her black mourning dress.

"Good evening, Widow Certeau. These are the guests I mentioned, Dr. Mondini and her servants. Will you show them their rooms, please? I'm sure they'll be more tranquil lodgers than that last group, the Hollanters bound for the New World."

"Yes, thank you, sir." She nodded and blushed.

"I bid you good repose, then." He turned to us and bowed slightly. "Send me word when you'd like to meet again." He strode back to his house at a strong, confident pace, seeming less an academic and more nearly a captain of the guard.

A young boy of eight or nine, probably Widow Certeau's son, for he possessed her creamy complexion and almond-shaped blue eyes, peeked out from behind her skirts.

"Show this good man where he can stable the mules, Dreux," she told him firmly, "and don't wander!"

He skipped out from her skirts and stared at Lorenzo with curiosity. When my man handed him the reins so he could lead Fedele, the boy smiled broadly. The two headed down the cobbled street, pulling the mules to one side to avoid the central gutter, where a runnel of dirty water backed up behind refuse clogging the drainage hole.

The widow directed us inside. "Come and I'll show you good people your rooms." As she walked briskly down a badly lit corridor, then up an even dimmer set of stairs, the keys tied to her skirt strings swung and jangled brightly.

"I see that you have another set of keys," I observed.

"Yes, my lady, in case a guest should breathe his last in the room, you know, we must have a way of getting him out."

Olmina balked at her frankness and asked, "Has anyone expired lately?"

"Oh no, this last bunch, they were lively as larks! But we did have one a few winters ago. An old papermaker who'd been coming for years to sell his wares to the university folk."

"Oh! And did he keep company with an Italian doctor, an older man?"

"Why, yes, now that you mention it. A Dr. Mondiale or something like that. They were often together. Is he your friend?"

"Yes," I said thoughtfully, without correcting the name, "he is my friend. How did he look? Was he in good health?"

"Well, honestly I never paid much mind, but he seemed well enough, though he paced a good deal in his room and was always shifting the little bit of furniture around." She ran her words together, all in a rush, the way shy people do sometimes. "Mind you, there's only a bed, chest, desk, and chair in a tiny space, so I'm not sure what he was arranging." She paused for breath and smiled. "Has it been long since you've seen him?"

"Yes, it's been long," I said.

"Well, the poor papermaker was not in good health. Poor fellow hadn't heard how badly the medicine school had been gutted. I think he was heartbroken at all the books that had been burned. But he never locked his door, so I didn't need the extra key. Here you are," she said, and she pushed open each narrow, creaky door in succession, three in a row. "You'll have to buy your own candles. When the warm days come, we keep the shutters closed and the rooms stay cool. Oh, and if you like, you can take your meals downstairs in the common room. Mainly pottages, bread, and wine."

"Yes, that would be fine."

She turned and left as quickly as she had come, hurrying on to other tasks.

Our rooms resembled the cells of ascetics with their floors and walls of squared gray stones. Still, we were content to each have a bed, a chest, a chamber pot, a ewer, and a basin. The rugless floors would be a shock at night and in the morning, to bare or even stockinged feet. The only fireplaces were downstairs in the kitchen and common room. I was grateful that it was May rather than December. These cold buildings of the living seemed more deathly than those of the cemetery on the hill as the evening light dropped.

In my dreams that night I glimpsed candles lit by mourners, flickering there as if in an ancient, faraway city. The houses of the dead appeared alive. *La morte guarisce tutti i mali,* my father would say in serious jest. *Death is a remedy for all ills.* Except in dream.

Wilhelm lies faceup on the slab in the blue light of the anatomy theater. I can't tell where the light originates, but it doesn't fall from the windows. It seems a kind of light from stage torches. I try to order my cutting tools on a small table, for I must find something in his body, though I'm not sure what it is. I'm terrified before his clean, uncut flesh, for it's like a huge blank piece of paper. My scalpel becomes a quill. I don't know where to cut. I don't know what to write there.

The next morning a light breeze brought us the salt trace of the sea as we walked to meet Dr. Joubert. Since the day was fine, he offered to show us the Jardin des Plantes near the Cathedral of Saint Pierre, for it was the pride of Montpellier and still under cultivation. As we approached the grounds-keeper's brick house, flanked by crenellated walls outside the city, I also mentioned my desire to see the octagonal anatomy theater designed by the illustrious Guillaume Rondelet.

"Oh, but that is shut up and surrounded by a garden of neglect. Wild grasses overrun the medicinals, though the fennel continues to thrive."

By contrast the Jardin des Plantes appeared a well-fortified garden.

"The Huguenots," he went on, "had also attempted to despoil this royal garden, for King Henry IV was their sworn enemy, but thank God, they weren't successful."

"How sad, to assault the poor plants of Languedoc and the herbs that would heal Papists and Protestants alike," I said. "The flowers don't discriminate. Only men with their superior reason."

He smiled a little, putting me at ease.

"The excellent doctor and botanist in the king's employ, Monsieur Richer de Belleval, whose work found its highest achievement here, has given us a great gift—a living compendium of plants!" exclaimed Dr. Joubert as he extended his left hand toward the walls.

Lorenzo and Olmina strolled behind us, arms linked as they admired the outlook of low hills and fields, pines, oaks, and sweet chestnuts and of woolly clouds drawn thin as if carded by the invisible combs of the wind.

"My father must have enjoyed this garden, though he made no mention in his letters. Have you heard any news of him, then?" I inquired.

"No, I was only an acquaintance." He stroked his waxen black mustache with thumb and forefinger. "The professor who knew him well—because he corresponded regularly with doctors in Padua, Salerno, and Bononia—left but a year ago." He shook his head regretfully, and as he did so, his round wide-brimmed hat suddenly lifted from his thick, straight hair with a gust of wind. He ran after it with surprising alacrity, black round cape flapping above red breeches and striped hose. After he retrieved it from the wayside brambles, he grinned at me boyishly, his face flushed, then quickly returned to his former posture of authority.

I couldn't resist laughing and marveling at how foolish we all were, poor, scrambling creatures with but a thin veneer of dignity. I retied my own straw hat more tightly.

Now he held on to his own as he launched into another subject. "Dr. Mondini, you must join the first class to be initiated again in a long time at the university. Perhaps as a guest professor? You can tell us about the book you're compiling. Don't be concerned that you're a woman. Who will protest, since I'm the only remaining faculty? As far as the students are concerned, I'll vouch for you."

I continued to walk on the gravel path beside him, considering his kind offer. "And when does instruction begin?"

"October eighteenth, the feast day of Saint Luc, physician and artist, patron of painters, sculptors, goldsmiths, notaries, surgeons, and doctors, as you undoubtedly know. The bells will call us to study at six o'clock, and there will be no classes Sunday or Wednesday, the day dedicated to Hippocrates."

"Thank you, but no, I must press on. It's only May and I can't delay my search for so many months."

Dr. Joubert looked crestfallen.

Then Olmina piped up close behind us. "Or perhaps the good signorina will soon tire of this journey altogether and take us back to Venetia."

"Ah, you've been wishing us back to Venetia ever since the day we departed." I stopped and turned round to smile at her.

But she wasn't smiling, only scolding me with her watery blue eyes. Lorenzo said nothing and simply stared off toward the hills, though he held on to her arm and patted it.

For a moment I let in the sinking possibility of a return without my father. "We won't be staying long in Montpellier," I said, turning back to Dr. Joubert. "It's true that I've grown weary of this journey." I lowered my eyes toward the hard-packed gravel, then looked back at the gentleman. "When does a wise adventure become a foolish one? When does daughterly devotion become untoward obsession?" These questions had risen and fallen under my thoughts yet startled me as I asked them openly.

"I would wish for such a daughter as you." He paused to knock at the groundskeeper's thick oaken door, where we now stood. "But I am a bachelor and know nothing of these things."

My spirits were dampened, since it seemed I'd obtain scant news of my father here. Still, I walked where he had walked. I traced his atmosphere like a hound on a scent. But now I was eager to see the contents of the garden for my own purposes.

The young steward, a man in grass-stained clothing, let us in. He held a rusted pair of shears in hand. We walked through the brick corridor to the other side, where the courtyard and its arcade overlooked one of the most remarkable gardens I'd ever observed. A triangular mountain of earth was terraced into six levels and supported at regular intervals a variety of vegetables, herbs, and trees, as well as the plants of Languedoc.

We descended the pathway that had been excavated around the small mountain. Other raised beds stood to the south, and all presented the solace of order. The crenellated wall enclosed the entire design, so that one also had the sense that we were in a garden of walls. How distinct from the round open gardens of Padua! One could feel the atmosphere of siege here and the bulwark of science raised against it.

After a long silence beneath the mounting heat of the midday sun, I asked the doctor, "If I knew the name and form, the habits of any flower, *Papaver somniferum,* for instance, could I alter events or even stop a war?" I motioned to the pods of those white poppies whose sap slows the world for those who taste it.

"No plant can stop a war, though many have started one. Think of the spices that are so precious to us. How many have died in their procurement. Saffron, cinnamon, mace, cardamom! Still, if any herb or flower could stop us, perhaps this one could. They say that those under the influence of its unripe pods are cured of overexcited nerves. Though others suffer paralysis."

"Whole armies could be fed forgetting, forgetting all sense of offense and defense, and then they might return to their families whole." I was not unmindful of my father's choleric humor dormant in me.

"Forgetting, though, is a dangerous thing, don't you think, Signorina Mondini? Would you have us all be docile cattle, our minds a series of stomachs?"

As Dr. Joubert and I spoke, Lorenzo and Olmina followed close behind, admiring the flowers, yet attentive to what we were saying.

"No, no." I laughed, picturing my companion on all fours engrossed in vetch. "But I've seen too much of quarrel and abandonment."

I walked on to view the singular harebells, mostly gone to seed, except for a few five-petaled bells hanging from delicate stems in a patch of shade. Unlike varieties I'd observed before, these were a stronger blue, chips of sky.

"They're old man's bells. Said to belong to the devil and to be coveted by witches for their fey qualities," he cautioned.

"Those witches who turn into hares and shake the flowers?" I smiled. "All I know is that the roots make an excellent compress for healing wounds. I've used them many times myself."

He glanced at me suspiciously. "Be very careful, signorina, very careful. I've never practiced the art of medicine myself, though as a professor I have the knowledge to do so. I believe in a fidelity to books and antiquity, no midwives' remedies for me." Then with a tinge of sadness he added, "Perhaps I envy you your experience," and he bent to the harebells for a closer look at the hidden interior.

"No need," I replied. "I'm not content, though I'm glad of my vocation. There is an abundance of sorrow in this profession."

"Still, you have firsthand experience of infirmity and death. Does it not bring you some wisdom among the days of despair?"

"I'm benumbed now and don't know what has happened to my wisdom."

"Now, signorina," interrupted Lorenzo, "I'm no educated man, but I've seen you do much good in our city and along the way here on our travels. And you too, my lively wife. You've picked up quite a few things here from our doctor, haven't you?"

For a brief instant, Olmina shared a nervous glance with me, fearing that she'd been found out, but because his tone was gentle, she simply said, "I have, haven't I?"

"Are you thinking of turning toward home, then?" Dr. Joubert asked.

"I don't know." I regarded Olmina and saw weariness that mirrored my own. "I haven't yet exhausted the geography of my father. One of his letters came from Hispania and another from Barbaria. We must depart to the west."

She sighed, for this wasn't what she'd wanted to hear.

CHAPTER 19

⟡

The Mountains Are Full of Wonderful Creatures

My dear Gabriella,

If a man could be cured by holding council with the very thing that wounds him, then this would be the place. For in this desert, where the night reigns above me like a mantle of fear become awe, all my worst fears—losing myself, the physical infirmities of age, even death—lessen with the knowledge of my utter insignificance. I know it must sound odd, but I am reassured. All my ambitions—my vocation as doctor, The Book of Diseases, that vast encyclopedia that was to be my magnum opus—these things are thin under the firmament. I have never seen stars as I have seen here. The spheres rasp against one another and we can see the sparks! The desert people understand.

Stars fly into our faces. I am small, I am small, and I do not care. And then the moon . . .

Oh, my father, I thought when I reread this undated letter from an unnamed place. *When you declare your fears, there is no mention of a daughter or the ones you love. You have left that for me to carry. I always wanted to believe you were going through a difficult time and were making your way back to us. This letter only a kind of elaborate fancy. Perhaps I have deceived myself. Perhaps I will go on deceiving myself for a while.*

We departed Montpellier for Santa Engracia. In spite of Olmina's disappointment that we weren't traveling east toward Venetia, she was cheered by the fragrance of yellow broom, sweet marjoram, and pungent grasses that flared yellow at the end of the day in the late May light. As we wound our way higher and higher into the mountains, with the peaks of the Pyrenei before us, my breath grew larger. The sweet pine- and fir-scented winds, clean light, and twisting waters cleansed this world and offered something that couldn't be imagined at lower elevations. The humors found their balance. No wonder the holy ones sought out the high places.

From time to time the face of Hamish arose in the early morning as I awoke, and I could almost hold his round chin, dimpled like the star at the base of an apple. I imagined a life in Edenburg, as the wife of a scholar, with children. But when I glanced in my hand-held glass each day, I saw a fuller face, for the journey had kindled my appetite, and a further dimming of youth. I had memorized Hamish as I had memorized my father, but the scent of his hair was the only resemblance the two men shared. A strain of pinewoods, smoky inks, stifling libraries, vellum books—yes, books. He was the story I hadn't fully read, the book that held a secret.

We often heard the distant bells of small towns clanging the hours, but especially dawn, midday, and evening, for these were the longest tolling. Some nights we slept in plain stone inns for pilgrims; a few nights when we didn't reach villages by nightfall, we slept out in the open, in shelters that ranged from a ring of old beeches with a fire going all night to keep the wolves at bay, to a tall circular stone enclosure broken on one side and entirely lacking a roof. When I questioned Lorenzo about this curious abandoned structure, he told me it was probably meant to protect the hives from bears. And indeed we found broken skeps inside, but no honey. It proved to be a fine shelter, canopied by the stars at night.

As we rode, steadily zigzagging up the steep mountains, the air cooled. No one worked these slopes for crops, and the shepherds who brought their herds out of the valleys for summer grazing had not yet reached the mountains. Here the soil was pale and spare, the stones reflective, unlike the darker loam of the lowlands, which held the sun. In order to stay warm and capture the best light, I chose the midday hours after dinner to write.

On one particularly gusty afternoon, we came upon two jumbled outcrops of boulders that inclined together near a rocky stream and formed a cunning hollow there, completely sheltered from the wind. The little basin of dark earth, formed by snowmelt that had already evaporated, seemed a warm sod cloak laid down beneath us, like wool to the touch. New grasses (which the mules happily cropped) clumped and needled up around the edges. We sat upon our cloaks, cupped by stone, warmed by stillness.

After we ate our bread, olives, sliced boar meat, and cheese, Lorenzo happily flung himself down on his back and placed his hands under his head, staring upward, where nothing could be seen but an occasional rook and erratic specks of blue that seemed to flake from the sky.

"Oh, look!" I cried, stretching out my arms toward the small butterflies lilting high above us. Everything about them was blue—their wings, their fuzzy bodies. "They're dazzling! See how they open and close the leaflets of their wings."

"And what would they be advertising, signorina?" teased Olmina sleepily.

"The mountains are full of wonderful creatures, eh?" Lorenzo joined in. "One might as well feast upon the vision of these gems as fall from a cliff."

"But beauty is brevity, isn't it?" I mused.

"How do you measure that?" pondered Lorenzo. "A summer's worth of life is long to the butterfly. But we want decades. Yet what are they worth if we're piling loss upon loss? I'd rather count days than years. Each day a year, by butterfly measure." He chuckled at his own philosophizing. "But I've also heard it said that blue butterflies come from the mouths of angels."

"Ah, some shepherd's whim."

"No, signorina, I think there's a whole flock of them above us now. You sense them more easily in mountain places, you know. Forget cathedrals. Here's my divine."

Olmina rolled comfortably onto her side and began to snore lightly. I leaned against a curved stone and began to write about a disease utterly contrary to the pleasant aspect of our resting place.

THE REPUGNANCE OF CLOSED SPACE:

Walls That Bind the Soul

For some sufferers, even the presence of a stone wall in an overgrown garden causes distress. For others, it is a room without windows, a long corridor, or a stairwell. The person may sweat, become chilled, cry out, or contract like charred paper in flame.

A young woman by the name of Esperanza, from Valladolid, clawed the plaster from the walls when she was stricken, as if she were buried alive. Her mother lamented the fact that her daughter had become a vermin and their home a vermin's nest. Even the addition of windows produced no improvement in Esperanza's vexation. Her sister complained that she could hear the terrible sound of Esperanza chewing the walls late at night. For although they tied her hands and her feet upon retiring to sleep, she wriggled up to the head of her bed and rasped the wall with her teeth.

Her father, a man of some wealth and reputation, rarely stayed at home, so great was his frustration with his daughter. One afternoon he appeared covered with brick-red dust, the August wind at his heels. He strode into the house, bearing the look of a man who will not be contradicted, and ordered Esperanza into the courtyard. The servants stood about, wringing their hands, fearful of his mood. He barked out orders: "Bring Esperanza's bed into the garden, and her armoire—put it there beneath the orange trees." As for her mirrors (for she had several more than was befitting a young woman), he ordered them to be arranged in various corners of the courtyard so as to effect the greatest sense of openness. "Now," Don Enrique de la Peña said in a tone of stifled anger, "I want to hear no more about it, no more gnawing the walls like a nest of rats, no more burrowing in this household! I have given you a good life, Daughter, and I will not be shamed by your madness!" Esperanza stood like a dead tree in a salt swamp while her father paced the tiles in a state of chagrin and the servants lifted, rocked, and shoved the dark bulks of oak furniture to the places her father had assigned them. She was the still center of their multiple orbits. At last she spoke in a dulcet voice that outraged her father: "Thank you, Papà, I am glad you've made this decision."

He marched out of the house, fists clenched with an unreasonable sense of defeat. Esperanza began to acquaint herself with her new home. Of course the garden was familiar to her, but now it took on a domestic cast that she must investigate. The sky offered escape from the closed rooms, though it still made her uneasy. The greenery was a true relief, not quite a wall and beautifully impermanent. For that is how Esperanza began to think of it. People didn't understand her and they never had. Her aversion to walls was a horror of permanence. That is why she could never tolerate going to church — all the pronouncements of absolute judgment.

Esperanza never entered the house again. She took her meals out of doors, shat in a hole behind the rosemary, and slept under violent storm (the servants had arranged an oiled cloth tarp over her bed) and stifling sun alike. The maroon bedcurtains faded to a ghastly pink as the weave thinned and shredded. Her four-poster bed, with its headboard carved with putti and grapevines, slowly warped and split. After five or six years the cherubs' heads separated from their bodies and lifted like tiny oracular spheres toward heaven. The bodies, meanwhile, rotted and furred with a livid green mold, took on the luminosity of the damp forest floor as they descended. Esperanza was now in her late twenties, unmarried and an even greater burden to her family. They had patched the walls of their hacienda, but no guest in that immaculate house could ignore the strange woman wandering in the courtyard and her disheveled articles of dress and furniture.

One afternoon a cousin of hers, four or five years of age, said in the sagacious voice of a child, "Esperanza, why don't you come inside? The ceiling is square just like the sky. There's no difference." For he believed that her dismay came from squares and perhaps she had already overcome her discomfort without knowing it. Instead she began to wail with sudden recognition of the courtyard's limits and how the unchanging dimension of the sky confined her. Esperanza yanked open the rusted wrought-iron gate at the back of the garden, which hadn't been opened in years. She stumbled away from the courtyard, from the gleam of her nine mirrors, sunken bed, and dense armoire. She ran into the flooded streets of January and stumbled toward the pine forest at the edge of town, her damp woolen skirts trailing behind her, sprouting phosphorescent orange fungi at the hem. Her loosened bodice harbored small ferns. Her hair supported lichen and club mosses. Her algal skin and above all her stench, like that of a shrunken pond that yields a liquor of decay, emanated for blocks all around. Townspeople swerved away from her, whispering that it must be the green Esperanza, the child who rots at the center of the de la Peña house. She wandered into the forest of Cordera. Though her father searched days and nights with a party of men and lanterns, he never found her. Esperanza's mother believed she had become a tree, perhaps an elm. She left small things—sweets and earrings—for her daughter at the base of a sapling that had begun to grow near the edge of a wet meadow, where it was rumored Esperanza had been glimpsed by a shepherd before she disappeared.

After three more days of riding, we found ourselves late one afternoon on a narrowing track of unrelenting wind. I trusted Lorenzo to find the way, yet it was true that he didn't know these mountains.

When I questioned him, he said, "I'm taking us southwest, always southwest, signorina, just as you asked. I've got a good sense of the sun."

I was reassured; still I felt that we were at the ends of the earth. We couldn't even ride the mules, for the gusts threatened to pitch us off. We held tightly on to ropes that had been fastened to the rock faces with iron rings alongside the path for travelers, and we continued into the evening, for Lorenzo didn't want to be stranded in this place.

"We must stop, take shelter among the rocks," I insisted finally, my legs aching and my eyes straining to find sure footing across the scree that had long ago tumbled down from above. The flat stones appeared to lie all on one plane in the waning light, though they really tilted in jagged heaps, making it a tough scramble.

"I can't go farther," complained Olmina as she abruptly sat

down next to her mule, drawing her woolen cloak and shawl more closely about her.

"No, no, you don't!" cried Lorenzo. "You don't know mountains the way I do. These may not be the Dolomiti, but I can smell the weather coming. With this sharp wind, there'll be a harsh rain, maybe even snow."

"The sky is clear, old goat!" said Olmina, shaking her fist at him. Indeed the stars gleamed above us like holes punched in tin over a fire. The crescent moon descended the western sky like a pale gondola cleaving a black sea.

"Do you see the moon? It holds water—a storm is coming. And there below, see the small cottage in the meadow?"

"Yes, Lorenzo, I see it," I answered, wobbling against the wind, fastening my eyes on the thatched stone hut.

"We can reach it within the hour. Get up on the mule, Olmina, I'll strap you to Fiammetta's back."

"No, no, no!" Olmina fought him away with sudden strength.

"Come on, Nana." I resorted to my childhood name for her, and she relented.

So we slowly progressed, Lorenzo at the front, leading the five mules, Olmina cowering upon the next to the last one, and I following her on foot, preceding the very last mule, all of us buffeted by gusts that increased in force as they whined through every crevice, leaving us stunned, our ears buzzing. All around us the stark peaks loomed like robed hermits come out of their caves to watch us, some of their pates dusted with snow.

When we reached the hut, it turned out to be a low-roofed shed for animals, with four goats huddled inside. Lorenzo, half bent over in the doorway, struck his flint to tinder, and with the small flame he lit a candle stub. He coaxed the terrified animals into one corner, and then Olmina and I settled in another.

Without a word, my dear companion instantly fell asleep on the straw while the goats stared at us and bleated. I noticed a small paper poking out of her pocket. A letter? I would ask her about it later, but I thought it odd, since Olmina didn't correspond with anyone as far as I knew, nor could she even write ... though she'd taught herself to read, sly woman, perhaps she could write as well? Lorenzo pulled in the five mules, closed the door, and made sure the inner latch was firmly fastened. We were all packed inside that stone hut steaming with animal breath, giving each other warmth and comfort.

Lorenzo passed me a hard crust of bread, a bit of cold cooked sausage, and some cherry brandy from Roussillon. "You must fortify yourself, signorina."

The two of us munched our food gratefully while the wind roared down the mountain, shaking the thatch above us. A creature snuffled in the leaves outside the hut, too softly for a bear, I thought—probably a hedgehog. Lorenzo pinched the wick, and we fell into a dense animal darkness. He began to snore loudly. In spite of the noise, I began to nod off . . .

Maurizio whispers, "Gabriella."

His handsome green eyes stray past me. "Gabriella!" He wears the white smock of the sickhouse and his feet are bare. How beautiful they are, strong and arched, the beveled toes, and then above the ankles I see small wings pulsing. He stands in the center of a long room in Santa Caterina's Hospital, sweating profusely. Droplets run down his legs and puddle at his feet. Then I'm near his bedside, where he's lying down. Long rows of vacant beds that fill me with terror line the walls. Perhaps they were emptied by the plague? When I bend to kiss him, he is still and cold. But the pulse in his winged feet contradicts blue skin. I press my lips to his chill forehead, to each dead eye, to the stricken lips. He doesn't stir. I rest my head on his feet, my long hair a shroud. His pulse is in my ear. I'm sure of it and want to bring him back. I stroke the still-beating wings at the ankles, but Maurizio doesn't return.

The animal stench, mules' braying, and icy air creeping through chinks in the stones awakened me. One of the mules shifted his hooves in agitation. The door was slightly ajar; Lorenzo had gone out, perhaps to relieve himself. I got up and peered out upon a changed landscape: the earth was muffled under snow.

The tips of my fingers tingled even within their gloves, and my toes within their boots. I saw the faint pockmarks of Lorenzo's footsteps leading down toward the edge of the stunted pines.

Someone moved there. My spine sharpened. The beasts sheltering with us jerked their heads up and down now in a panic. Olmina slept her blessed sleep, undisturbed. As I watched, the brown figure whipped something side to side. I stood halted by fear. The bear, for that was the thing I beheld, shook Lorenzo like a sack of grain. I couldn't move. Then I jerked into motion, yelled, and stumbled forward, falling halfway to my knees. The massive bear chuffed and dropped Lorenzo. It swung its head back and forth, reading my smell. *Here comes Death,* I thought, my mind honed to a single point of dread.

The bear stood, his russet pelt crackling with frost. His paws were clotted with snow, splotched with blood. I was too far now from the hut to retreat. Then a small gust snapped my cloak out behind me. The bear snorted, then loped downhill into thicker woods.

By the time Olmina appeared at the door of the hut crying our names, I was kneeling beside Lorenzo, clasping his bloody head in my lap, his eyes wide open to nothing. I sobbed, "Don't you leave me, Lorenzo! Stay with me!"

Olmina lurched toward us and crumpled. At first she looked past her husband into the pines as if she didn't believe what she saw. That was some other man. She would search for Lorenzo at the edge of the woods.

I tried to put his viscera back in his body. I put snow in the cavity to stanch the bleeding. I put snow on his throat, which immediately soaked red. I shook his shoulders to wake him up. This couldn't be. Olmina wept, opened her arms to the frozen sky, and bent to Lorenzo. "*Dio mio,* no! Husband, don't go, don't go!" She keened so loudly the mountain itself shook with her cries.

We dragged him up the slope slowly. At last we settled his body in the shed and covered him with a blanket, much to the terror of the animals, who smelled bear on him and clambered up against each other and the back wall. The mules would have bolted if Lorenzo hadn't tied them so well. I took them outside to calm them and secured them to the iron ring set in the stone wall of the shed, all the while looking downhill at the dark red trail in the snow. I didn't want to let the goats loose. The bear was still out there.

Olmina uttered such harsh cries at Lorenzo's feet that I pressed my hands to my ears and dropped down beside his shoulder, sobbing. Then I put my palm to his cheek. He was cold.

After some time—whether one hour or many, I didn't know, for it was impossible to tell the time beyond that daylight still remained—Olmina said, "I must wash him and sit vigil." She turned her face to me, haggard with sorrow and fear. "Could you find some twigs to start a fire? Don't go far."

When I returned with an armful of damp twigs and dead branches, she'd struck a fire, using dry straw, behind stones that had been set in one corner by the shepherds as a crude hearth. A small opening in the thatch drew the smoke away. Olmina lit two candles, one at Lorenzo's head and one at his feet. The four goats crowded up against each other in the farthest corner, bearing quiet if uncomprehending witness. I filled our pot with snow to melt for the final cleansing of the body.

But first we dragged him outside and washed him with snow. There was no other way. We removed his tunic and shirt, his breeches and hose, his leather shoes. We folded up each piece of clothing, even if it was torn. It shocked me to see his leathery, wrinkled body with its terrible wounds. We knelt, each taking one side of him, Olmina his left side, and I his right. We scoured the half-frozen crusts of blood upon his arms, neck, face, making the only sound on the mountain—shhh, shhh, shhh. Snow against cold flesh. But when I reached his legs and feet, the place where the toes were missing, I couldn't go on.

Olmina moaned and lay her head down upon his chest. What would we do without him? We scrubbed and stopped, shivering, then resumed the work, our hands red from his blood, raw from cold. At last we carried him inside the shelter.

The water was warm by now, steam curling from the black pot. I tested it with my finger. Warm water for a dead man.

We laid Lorenzo out upon our best red blanket, a candle beside his shoulder. We each wadded up a piece of his torn shirt, dipped it in water, and wrung it out. I folded the cloth and drew it across his face, down his neck and shoulder, his arm, cleaning between the fingers as if he were a child. We mended him as best we could. I sewed his left arm shut with a strand of my hair. Olmina sewed his neck with a gray thread of her hair.

There were other gashes that we couldn't close. We lay a torn square of linen across his belly, a rough veil to cover the wound.

Olmina looked across at me. "Where, truly, then, is his heart?"

"Here," I said, placing my hand atop hers and setting it on his bristly white chest, slightly closer to her. She lay her other hand on mine.

"There was no priest—he had no priest to bless him." She lifted her head and whispered hoarsely, "He didn't receive his Communion. Signorina, we must say the prayers for him."

"We don't need to say them. The mountain wind will be Vespers for him. The birds will say Matins. The animals Lauds."

She stared at me and shook her head.

We washed his lower body, his hips, legs, feet. He was clean. He was cleaner than he'd ever been. I scraped under his nails with a small twig. Olmina stroked his hair into place. Then she continued to stroke his hair. *There, there.*

At last we dressed him. I brought in the mules, since it was growing dark, and latched the door. We were exhausted and lay down on either side of Lorenzo. Sleep fell like a bludgeon.

When I woke, the whole night had passed. Lorenzo, lifeless and cold, lay next to me. I touched his rigid hand and began to cry like a child.

Olmina was strange, and she wandered in her speech and her body, pacing in and out of the shed. "I must fetch a priest. Otherwise what will become of his soul in purgatory?"

I didn't try to stop her. I let the mules out on a tether so they wouldn't stray far. Some returned and stood at the door or came inside, shuddering with cold. I also tried to urge the goats outside. Two of them refused. They watched me solemnly, and I preferred them to a priest. Olmina trudged back and forth.

After a while we lit new candles at Lorenzo's head and feet and sat beside him. We didn't eat. I spoke some words from *Purgatorio* for his soul.

From the most sacred waters I returned
remade in the way that trees are new,
made new again, when their leaves are new,

pure and ready to ascend to the stars.

Olmina repeated her prayers. Sometimes I heard her, sometimes I wept. But I said nothing more. This was how the two goatherds found us. Astonished, they spoke little, but they knelt, and each placed a hand upon Olmina's shoulders. They removed their black caps as if Lorenzo were one of their own. They came back with shovels and helped us to bury him farther down the mountain in thawed ground. We brought our mules and supplies with us. The herders dug a narrow hole. One of them rolled a large stone upon Lorenzo's chest, to keep wild animals from scavenging him. One of them also brought a simple cross of two pine branches lashed well at the center with leather, which he planted upon the fresh mound. Olmina bent to the cold earth above him and would not be moved. But at last, with dark approaching, the men lifted her and set her upon a mule. They led us down to the village of Xeu Durgel. Lorenzo lay in the mountain. He'd always loved the high places. But it was bitter to leave him in a foreign land, to which we would never return.

CHAPTER 20

❦

Like Cures Like

Olmina didn't speak for a long time. Sometimes at night in the stone farmhouse where we found lodging, she sobbed without cease. The sound undermined time, the round of days, so that I wasn't sure when I had heard it and when I was remembering it or even anticipating the sorrow to come. I slept night and day for long stretches. The distances drawn upon maps were now small compared to the distances between one day and the next, between Olmina and me. We hadn't held each other since his death. Blame was never spoken, but the consequences of my choices harried me like the sharp clicking of her rosary beads. *If only I hadn't chosen the journey. If only my father. If only Lorenzo. The bear. God.*

When I asked the farmer about the town named Santa Engracia, the origin of one of my father's letters, he pointed to the west. I spoke to Olmina about leaving. She nodded wearily in agreement and repeated the old proverb, *La lontananza è madre della dimenticanza. Distance is the mother of forgetting.*

We would never forget, but I was grateful for the lie. I was reminded of that strange malady I'd noted in the book.

LAPSUS:

A Predicament Where a Woman Abruptly Forgets Her Place of Origin and Conceives an Intense Longing for the World at Large, Often a Distant and Exotic Place, of Which She Possesses Extraordinary Knowledge That Can't Be Attributed to Books or Hearsay

Just as the melancholic possesses a greater talent for memory, owing to a dry temperament that retains the impressions of things, so the phlegmatic of watery humor often contracts this disease of concurrent forgetfulness and inexplicable knowledge. Surely the cold flux of the humor predisposes the person to such a state.

In one such case, chronicled by Dr. Menasteri of Treviso, a certain peasant named Giovanna, who worked the radicchio fields renowned for the superb bitterness of their vegetables (relished by Caterina de' Medici), suddenly refused to tend the fields. Her beloved radicchio plants languished. Her husband entreated her, wrung his hands, and finally locked her in their room, one of many peasant dwellings adjoining the large courtyard, because of her bizarre speech and tendency to wander when she left. She no longer knew her home. Giovanna claimed knowledge of a certain place, Akka, where she had never been. There, she said, she was known as Yellow-Wristed Woman. In that village the inhabitants acquired their names from various dyes they concocted to stain their clothing and tents. The dyes derived from the reactions of beetles, plants, moth wings, blood, and urine to sun, moon, and starlight. So Yellow Wrist spread onion skins in the courtyard under the winter stars of the Veneto and arrived at a golden agent, which she walked upon again and again to effect a deeper hue.

Giovanna's husband brought her wilted heads of radicchio and placed them in her lap as gentle remonstrations, but she let them roll to the floor. Soon she began to appear outlandish, sitting bolt upright in her wooden chair by the locked window, her body surrounded by rotting vegetables. On an afternoon of sudden autumn freeze, which clutched at the ankles of women, her husband returned from the baker with a round loaf of hot bread, hoping to please her. The planks of their rude door were split apart. Giovanna had escaped. Trevisan hounds were employed to find her, but the animals moved back and forth confusedly through the fields, unable to locate her scent.

Giovanna was never found, although stories arrived some years later, regarding a foreigner in the Kingdom of Faz, her complexion pale as a slice of apple, who kept a garden of yellow dye plants and vegetable oddities.

Little is known of a possible cure for this malady because the victim usually disappears and therefore cannot be treated.

After leaving the farmhouse, we traveled for a day and came within view of a faraway inn on a fortified jut of rock that resembled nothing so much as the desiccated tongue of San

Antonio, a parched extremity with the village perched like the saint's last dying word on its tip. We were exhausted. Even the four mules—we left one at the farmhouse in payment for their kindness in keeping us—stiffened at the climb and abruptly stopped, beyond ill temperedness. The air was laden with heat.

We dismounted and struggled along the thin track that slanted up the side of the mountain, with its sparse wood of fisted oaks and hissing swaths of dead grasses. The mules finally allowed us to tug them along. Fedele carried the medicine chest and also bore my notes for the book. When the way became too narrow, I stopped and fastened the satchel of papers to my own back. We found a niggardly stream about halfway up and drank a swill of loose clay that barely blunted our thirst. A great number of sulfurous orange and yellow butterflies also sipped from the muddy trace and didn't budge when we knelt there or when the animals disturbed them, slopping and grunting as the turbid water silted their mouths. The butterflies flocked to their bristly lips and nostrils and even to our lips and skin to drink our moisture. Thus strangely embellished with their yellow, we waited and let the mules drink their fill, even though Olmina shook her head and warned against bellyache and bloody flux. For a brief moment I caught a glimpse of her former earthy self, but then she disappeared again into silence. She stood away from the world. She went through the motions. Still, I couldn't help asking her, "What do you think Lorenzo would've made of the butterflies?"

She stared inconsolably at the mention of his name, and then answered, "He would've liked their color—yellow for fire. They're creatures of fire."

When we arrived at the inn, the innkeeper, Cubero, shouted

(with a voice that seemed permanently raised against the world), "Salvador! Salvador! Where are you? We have guests!"

As always, I insisted on carrying the medicine chest myself, wary of the influence of strangers upon the medicaments.

I followed an older man with sleepy, half-lidded eyes who carried my satchels up wide, dark stairs, then turned into a small, uneven stone corridor, finally ascending two narrow steps. Olmina trudged after me with her own bag. Once or twice he turned to chide me. "Wait, señora, wait. I will carry the chest for you. It's not filled with gold pesetas, now, is it?" he scolded good-naturedly. "You should have a good manservant traveling with you to help you with these things."

"I did, but he's gone."

"Ah." He squinted at me as if he were going to ask a question and then, when he saw my face, decided against it. "You have the old chicken coop, but we've made it comfortable and you have the finest outlook, after all."

He waved his thick arms toward a chasm of red stone below us, a saffron-and-brown patchwork of fields, other walled hill towns, and solitary watchtowers that brooded toward the Morisco country, beyond the ranges. He pushed his shirtsleeves up to his elbows and put his hands on his hips as he regarded me in a plain way, head to toe, and remarked, "The beds here are all the same, so servant and lady are equal!" He grinned and then left the room. I bent slowly to sit in the one wooden chair. Lorenzo would have liked this high place. Olmina sat upon her bag and bent her head to her hand. The room, though small, was cleft by silence.

After a while I asked, "What is that letter you carry in your pocket?"

She started. "I didn't want to give it to you, for fear . . . for fear of causing distress." Then because she knew there was no choice, she handed it to me. "I'm sorry, signorina. Dr. Joubert asked me to deliver it to you in Montpellier." Then she went to the bed farthest from the window, as she knew I liked to look out, and turned away from me as she lay down to nap.

The letter was from Hamish.

My dearest doctor, Gabriella,

How clumsy I've been, how remorseful to have caused you misery without mend. If forgiveness is possible, let me dedicate myself to its study. Dear lady, how could you leave without leave-taking? I worry that you endanger yourself and your kind servants with this journey. The road is an incision into the unknown, don't you see? You can't dissect the continent in order to discover your father. I trust that this letter travels straight to your heart and is not miscarried. I trust that this letter precedes me. For I have determined to come and fetch you there in Montpellier. If you don't wish to return with me to Edenburg, then let us voyage back to Venetia. Yes, I will accompany you to your home. And I would woo you if you would permit it. There is no other way. Your father is lost and only he may deliver himself. Dear Gabriella, you have read me—you have translated me unto myself. Let me also peruse the words of the volume hidden within your chest, the library of your distractions, passions, virtues, and reflections. I found two of your coppery hairs upon my doublet and now keep them coiled in my pocket. Your image ever before me, I commend myself to your service,

Edenburg
This 24th of April 1591
Dr. Hamish Urquhart

I placed the letter within the pages of my book. *Now he'll never find us,* I thought. Yet his words clung to me.

While Olmina slept, I began ordering the pages of diseases and cures, and that settled my mind. There were more than I'd thought. In spite of the heat, I asked Salvador to bring a pot of hot water, for I wanted a cup of mint tea for its calming properties. I opened the chest and removed the bottle of crushed Corsican mint, and though I felt slightly ashamed, I used the last few leaves for a decoction for myself.

Olmina remained asleep in our room while the night pressed upon Santa Engracia like the lid of an iron cauldron. As for me, after bread, tough mutton, salty cheese, and a wine thick with sediment, I retired to the terrace, where I spread out my maps upon a thick oak table by the light of an oil lantern, placing stones at the ends to keep them from rolling back in on themselves.

The innkeeper, Cubero, curious, stood nearby straining to see. I waved him over and, explaining the purpose of my journey, inquired if he'd seen or heard anything about a man who fit the description of my father. He had no recollection of a doctor but suggested that I question the apothecary in Tremp. I traced our journey with my finger, as I had nearly every night since we left Venetia, so that the names of the places we'd passed through began to wear thin, especially those at the beginning, which had been touched most often. As I studied the pages of the book, they too were worn in places as if they'd been touched with an iron.

THE BUBOES OF MORPHEUS

These carbuncles, unlike the Black Death, do not originate in Sicily's evil vapors or the Goths' pestilential camps. They come from the realm of sleep; thus many declare them incurable. The patient dreams that her limbs are covered with large, swollen wheals that have not yet broken the surface. Dire weather threatens downbursts, whirlwinds, and storm cauldrons. When the patient awakes, much to her dismay, she finds an ugly bubo behind her knee or protruding from her calf, and then it begins. What lodges in the body during sleep erupts in the daylight.

I was summoned to Orguégra to treat a young noblewoman renowned for her beautiful pallor who experienced this vision in sleep: Great clouds turned like millstones in the sky, black at the center as if they had dark, oily axles, and then frothed white at the edges. Objects were drawn up into the churn: chairs, Morisco carpets, damask linens, lapdogs, fire irons, legs of lamb, entire libraries, and astrolabes, but no persons were taken. Her buboes bloomed yellow and developed poisonous vortices. I could only hasten their eruption in order to relieve her discomfort more rapidly by applying leaves of mandragora (gathered at night before the dew diffused their healing properties), white Pyrenean clay, and salt with a soft cloth soaked in wine. The wrappings were changed three times daily. She suffered greatly from having her hands bound so that she wouldn't scratch herself. Her unsightly brown scars threw her into such a rage that she refused to pay me for her hideous survival. Later I heard that while most of her suitors abandoned her, one remained, a certain gentleman of Napoli, who won her vows with the gift of a small collapsible telescope made of brass. Now she could see far away.

At the apothecary's shop, when I inquired whether anyone had encountered an Italian doctor, a man of moderate height with a slight paunch (though I began to wonder—perhaps my father would be considered tall here or would have grown thin), the apothecary, Alonso Gonzalez, a bony man who twitched, appeared eager to be helpful.

"Yes, I was acquainted with your father, a fine doctor but sullen. Dr. Monatti."

"His name is Dr. Mondini," I corrected him.

"Ah yes, of course. The doctor often went on lone walks in the mountains and once spent the night at a watchtower near the gorge of Lamia." Here the apothecary lowered his voice and nervously tapped his discolored fingers upon the stained pine counter, where many healing powders and secret theriacs had spilled, giving a motley color to the wood. His demeanor resembled that of a priest divulging something in confidence. "The place is stricken, you know—bad waters. But your father wouldn't believe it, insisted on 'like cures like.' Dr. Mondini wanted to cure melancholia with a melancholy place, oh yes. We warned him, my wife and I." I could see his wife standing motionless behind the half-open door, listening. "The waters are dead there, you know. The color is wrong—chalky blue, can't see a thing under the surface, no. It's unnatural. Kills the trees that grow along its banks, and nothing grows in the gorge. It's one of the few clear passages between Moorish and Christian lands. Many soldiers from both sides were trapped and killed there, but that's not the evil of the place, no, no."

Gonzalez's small black eyes switched nervously from Olmina to me. His pale head seemed modeled of ivory, so opaque was the skin, especially where his black hairline drew an *M* on the top of his skull.

"The fields of Don Trujillo also saw many dead, but the furrows have come back to life and yielded crops. The river was dead long before the soldiers came. My grandmother told me the waters were confounded by a crime too old for memory, and they curdled at the bottom like bad milk. Imagine a river of clotted souls held between the steep walls of the gorge—clotted souls!" His blotchy hands, studded with dark hairs, worked the air before him in the manner of a conjurer's.

I jerked my head back slightly, startled, but the narrow little man ran on as if he couldn't stop himself now. "Padre Pablo of Sevilla the Benedictine was well acquainted with such gorges, having clung to one, living like a vulture, for ten years in the north. He wanted to banish the curse of the waters of Lamia. The good man made exorcisms for days, alone on a ledge with only Padre Bautista as visitor, bringing his bread, water, and wine once a day. But one noon, Padre Pablo lowered his bucket to the river and drew the water against all warnings. When he returned to the village, his brow was knotted and black. They say he tasted the water. During Mass on Sunday, he faltered and sputtered an unknown language. We were all terrified of him. He grimaced from the pulpit. That night he departed with only a small bag of his things and—we think—a candle-stick that was missing from the church altar after that night, oh yes. No one ever received word of him again."

I wasn't sure what to make of this tale. I stared at the rows of ceramic jars, the cobalt-blue Latin names on white glaze, the yolk-yellow and blue-leafed vines that twisted around the lips of those jars where the darker clay spoke through the chipped places. They were less lovely than the majolica jars found in Venetian apothecaries. The least used jars of substances like black hellebore (employed for leprosy) sat coated with a fine umber dust.

Señor Gonzalez continued, "I warned your father not to drink the water, but he committed a worse folly, he bathed in it. If it weren't for the tower watchman, who was shirking his duties that day and hunting fallow deer near the gorge, your father would have vanished in the dense blue clay, you know. He stood waist-deep in some kind of stupor and had to be roped and hauled out with the help of some horsemen nearby. No one wanted to touch the water, and they burned the ropes after, a loss of good cordage, if you ask me."

The apothecary peered at me intently, as if it were now my turn to speak of my father. But I was still standing in the opaque water, gently trying to guide him, like a heavy log, to shore. He was wedged there; he wasn't moving. And I was frightened.

"Did my father, then, succumb to the madness of the waters too?"

"I cannot tell, good señora, for to my mind he was a little peculiar before. He departed hastily, as if the very devil were at his heels. And so you've heard nothing from him?"

I wasn't going to tell Alonso Gonzalez anything, for I knew that I might just as well trumpet it throughout the village as tell such a chin-wagger. I simply shook my head, thanked him, and purchased a few medicinals: adder's-tongue for drawing out the foulness of wounds, orpine with honey for soothing all manner of lesions and burns, and fennel seeds for their general salutary effect. At least he received the benefit of my purchases for his trouble, though his disappointed face twitched on the left side as I gave him my coins. I glanced up at the half-open door and noticed that the woman was gone. A slim crack of light stood in her place.

"And when exactly was my father here, then?" I asked, feigning a casual tone while fingering the gathers of my brown skirt. "And where did he say he was going?"

"Oh, señora, he left for the north, Venasque. Or the south, I don't know, maybe Miquinenza or Lérida?"

"Or Almodóvar del Rio!" A woman's voice came in flowing tones from the other room.

"Please excuse my wife, señora, for her rudeness—just because she is from Andaluzia, she thinks that everyone wants to go there! But your other question, yes, he was here at the end of threshing season, July, three years ago now."

We thanked him and left with our medicinals. We were barely two houses away from the apothecary shop when his wife ran up to us, a basket slung over her arm.

"I'm on my way to the baker's, but I have something for you," she said in a low voice. "Your father exchanged this once for some medicament. I believe his purse was growing thin. Don't tell my husband!" And she slipped a small calipers into my hand. "I never knew my father," she added, "so I envy your sadness." Then she stepped quickly ahead of us, for we were, after all, strangers.

Still I called out my thanks to her, but she didn't turn her head.

"Quiet, Signorina!" Olmina spoke for the first time that morning. "She has already risked suspicion by speaking to us. Her husband stands peering at the door."

We left Santa Engracia to explore neighboring villages for traces of the Italian, il Dottor. Sometimes when I conversed with other travelers or villagers, aristocrats or commoners, I wasn't sure we were speaking of the same man. In one village, il Dottor exhibited habits so unlike my father's that I suspected I was following the trail of some renegade or madman posing as a doctor. They spoke of il Dottor as a somber man who grunted enigmatic or incoherent comments, administered medicaments, and then took his leave. Some angrily demanded recompense from me. One fellow spoke of il Dottor as a saint, a man of unfathomable kindness who saw all the wounded as equal and would assist an afflicted brigand at the side of the road as soon as a gangrened knight in a chill castle bed.

Olmina wearied of this pursuit and attempted to change my course toward home.

On an afternoon of tremendous wind, we visited Encantat, where wild asphodel grew. My father always mentioned the extraordinary properties of these roots, which relieve spasms of all sorts and increase the flow of urine, purifying the body. Hippocrates also noted that the roots could be roasted in ashes and eaten by women to restore the monthly flow (a treatment that I hoped to test, for my own flow had ceased, just as it had once before in Venetia, when I fell into grief after my beloved's death). The ancients planted them near the tombs, since asphodel was said to be the favorite food of the dead. I was certain my father wouldn't have passed up the chance to see them firsthand and gather the bulbs.

We attained entrance to a high pine-forested valley between two stark ridges, directed there by a stout shepherd, who told me the finest white-spears grew there, though most of the flowers were spent by now. My hair blew ragged beneath my straw hat, and Olmina began to dote upon me as one would upon a child or the village fool.

"We really should start back, Gabriellina. A storm is coming. I'll make you a tasty cheese pie," she coaxed.

"Since when do you call me Gabriellina? I'm a grown woman," I shouted at her above the wind. "I want you to help me dig for bulbs!"

Olmina pressed her chapped lips together and frowned at the unforgiving rocky soil, then brusquely turned from me and walked away. I remained among the tall spears, which furiously shook their long leaves, exhausted flowers, and multiplying pods, until I managed to unearth several spindle-shaped bulbs. I stowed them in my bag.

Food for my dead, I thought, though their hunger seemed unending.

After spading the wild asphodel, we returned to Santa Engracia and I fell ill. I felt such a chill that it reached backward into other months and years. I heard Lorenzo sitting there at my side, carving wood with the crisp strokes of a knife. I saw the back of my father at the window and then I didn't. Messalina appeared, dripping with ocean.

Olmina tended to me. She brought me black radish soup and bread for supper and stroked my forehead with a damp cloth, even though her sighs told me that she was restless and sometimes resentful.

On the third morning, Salvador brought my chamomile tea, strained of flowers, and I felt better. How odd that sometimes a small thing can effect a large reversal. Healing, finally, is invisible.

"I've asked too much of you on this journey, Olmina," I began hoarsely. "And Lorenzo. He never would have died if . . ."

Olmina began to weep softly and patted my hair. "He loved you very much, Signorina Gabriella, as a man loves a daughter." She pressed a small pillbox into my palm. I observed Olmina's age in her mottled, wrinkled hands. "This is yours — your mother was going to throw them out!" The box contained the lost teeth of my childhood. They resembled little shells. "But he kept them in his shirt pocket always, for good fortune, he said, because they once belonged to our little doctor."

My fist closed over the box, and I pressed my head against Olmina, crying. Lorenzo had carried my teeth like seed pearls as he watched me grow into a woman. And still I wanted to travel to the far ends of the earth — to Barbaria, now — for the father who'd abandoned me.

CHAPTER 21

A Border Between
Continents

The evening before we departed for the port town of Algezer, I pulled out one of my father's letters, marked Taradante, from the bottom of the packet of letters. I'd read it only once before, unlike others that were frequent companions to my night thoughts. Now it struck me why, for I'd forgotten or refused to see most of what it said.

Dear Gabriella,

I grow weary. Watching the full moon rise over the braided sand of the wadi, I feel that I'm on her white surface. Some say that she is utterly smooth. Others argue that she is composed of seas. Aristotle thought she marked the beginning of the imperishable ether stars and the end of the mutable spheres — earth, air, water, and fire. I am only too mutable here in the desert, my watery brain drawn to her pull like those shellfish that multiply exuberantly in her light. But I am also at a border. This life is my changing element, the sand beyond, my imperishable mind. I am too small for myself. All my life I've wrestled with increase, decrease, the gravity of rage and sorrow, the almost weightlessness of forgetting. Cures, panaceas, palliatives. Now I believe the moon is sand, the disk-shaped top of an hourglass draining into the ether away from us. Every month she seeps away and then is turned by some steady, intimate hand. Her own, perhaps. She turns herself. You must turn yourself, Daughter. We can never see it, but we can feel it. My body confines me. I want to live forever. Still I am large enough to rest my head upon her gritty bosom. Be let go. I am nothing more than a mote. But the moon is the wife I have never kissed! She waits for me, she abandons me. She lies in all things moist, the sea and its tributaries, the heart and its vessels, the brain and its damp thoughts, the kidney and its flow, the uterus and its watery longings, the past and its surgent concussions. I wander, I drift, Gabriella, forgive me. I grow weary and must take my rest in the desert. Dreams too partake of the moon. They linger at the gate. If I can sleep, I will tell you my dream. I'll no longer be thirsty. If only I could trick dry Death once more. There is so little water here and so few cisterns to decoy the moon, though the sea still laps at the edge of the continent. Return, return, you say to me, and I wonder, return where? Shall I retrace my journey to find home?

1589
Your father

We traveled several days from Santa Engracia toward and then through the Andaluzian mountains, to the southwest of Hispania, and arrived at the ancient port town of Algezer. The air was rich with the stink of fish and sea snails.

"Is there an inn nearby?" I asked, after we'd greeted the leathery old man who sat cross-legged, mending a net.

"Keep going west till you get to the fallen wall. You'll find it just beyond the rubble." He waved a deeply creased hand with stubby fingers, holding needle and thick thread, toward the far verge of land and then resumed his deft knotted stitches.

But just as we began to follow the track west, he called out, "If you've any interest in selling a mule or two, I'd like to know."

I turned round in the saddle. "Come to the inn tomorrow and we'll discuss it."

"And I've the good fortune to address . . . ?"

"Dr. Mondini."

"Ah. Tomorrow, then." He grinned after us, or rather, I should say, after the mules, which he appeared to be sizing up for a good price.

We settled into plain, whitewashed rooms at the modest inn. From our window on the edge of Andaluzia, we looked across the dusty sea at the Rock of Gibraltar, looming like a watchful white lion. We could also make out the faintest line of the purple Rif Mountains.

I turned to Olmina, to take up a conversation that we'd begun in fits and starts all the way back in Santa Engracia and that even now I half wanted to delay. But at last I asked quietly, "Can you imagine Venetia empty of Lorenzo?"

"It will never be empty of him. That was our home," said Olmina. She paused. "Gabriellina—I can't convince you, then, to come with me?"

And I returned a question: "Won't you come with me to Barbaria?"

"My stubborn Dottoressa." She laughed hoarsely, and her body shuddered next to mine at the thick sill. "You must follow this through to the end, but how will you recognize the end?"

"I'll know, somehow, I'll know," I answered. "I'll make the arrangements, then," I said, leaving her to watch the enormous sea.

Señor Romanesco, our innkeeper, assured me that he would book passage for us. Luckily we had to wait only a couple of days for our ships. Olmina would board the merchant ship *Hyperion* to Venetia early in the morning. I would leave soon after her on the *Charon* to Tanger.

"But why are you traveling alone, señora?" he asked. His mouth, surrounded by a trim black beard, hardened in disapproval. He called me señora, assuming that I was a widow, I suppose.

"I intend to search for my father. One of his letters mentioned a town there, Taradante. Could you tell me if there are any other reputable travelers staying here who seek passage to Tanger? I'm in need of trustworthy companions."

He leaned forward, placing both hands upon the dizzying geometric mosaics of the counter between us, warning, "You'll invite thieves and swindlers into your company if you remain a lady dressed as you are. The desert will swallow you!"

I lowered my voice and said, "I will go as a man."

"Ah. But how will you bear the desert of Barbaria?"

"You know the desert, then? You are Moorish?"

"Ah, the señora is curious," he said, narrowing his eyes. "But let me say that you've come to a border between continents, and as at any border, you'll find that no one here is quite what they seem. The Morisco is a devoted Spaniard. The Jew is now a *converso*. Even the doctor may be the afflicted, if you take my meaning. But an honest innkeeper is an honest innkeeper." He clasped his hands and said, "You'll grow accustomed to the heat and the winds of Barbaria. Learn where the deep wells are, señora. Even the most humble *dar* has its garden, even the most humble soul."

"And what is a *dar?*" I asked.

"The *dar* in Barbaria is the dwelling place, the house with its rooms around a courtyard, as we have even here." He waved at the small patio within, with its octagonal blue and green tiled fountain, which cast a cool, unsteady light on the pale walls.

"Truly, I thank you for your help," I said, turning from him to the submerged shadows of the courtyard, filled with sudden disquiet as I considered the lonely journey ahead.

That evening, Señor Romanesco knocked at our door and announced, "The fisherman has come to look at your animals. I'll accompany you to the stable."

I nodded. Olmina also joined us.

I'd decided to keep Fedele and Fiametta, so only the other two were for sale. These would purchase our ship's passage, so I could still keep a good reserve of ducats.

When I named my price, the man balked. "I can only buy one of them, then."

"Then it is done," I concluded.

"Now, just a moment. Let me have a look at them." He walked around each mule, felt each leg, and tapped the hoofs while they regarded him with mild suspicion, the whites of their eyes widening.

We haggled back and forth. I quietly drove a firm bargain, while Olmina stood nearby, hands on hips, fastening a good hard look at him that would've unnerved me in an instant. We were tougher than the old man had anticipated, and Señor Romanesco stood to one side watching the transaction silently without expression.

I stroked the mules' gray faces, their soft sail-shaped ears, which twitched one way, then another, independently of each other. How far they had borne our supplies with resolute labor! I was sad to let them go, but at least they wouldn't have to travel aboard a ship again.

In the end, the fisherman purchased both, paying us with silver from a wrinkled, oil-stained leather purse. As he left, I overheard him talking to the departing mules about his catch for the day as he patted their backs, well pleased.

Before we returned to our room, Señor Romanesco called me aside in the dusk-lit courtyard and said, "I see that you know how to handle a customer, señora. You're tougher than you appear." He beamed at me, black eyes flashing. "I wish I could recommend suitable traveling companions for you, but there is no one. However, my brother who lives in Tanger and sells spices in the souk is a shrewd man, a good man who would understand your request."

"How will I find him?"

"Ask for him by name and trade in the morning and you'll

find him. Never go out late in the day. And take a manservant with you. They're for hire and plentiful at the port landing. Choose an older man—they understand that true profit rests on constancy."

"Thank you for your kindness—though I've always heard, never trust anyone in a port, and never trust an innkeeper, for that matter." He grinned. "Remember that nothing is what you expect at the edge of the continents." He handed me a slim sheet of paper folded over and sealed with yellow wax, addressed in Arabic. "Here is a letter of introduction."

The night before departure, I asked Olmina a special favor. "Will you cut my hair again?"

"Of course, signorina." She drew the knife and comb from her satchel. "There will be no one else to trust, will there?"

"No one." I clasped her hand where it rested on my shoulder. Then she gathered my hair tightly, close to the nape of my neck, lifted it, and slashed quickly. She finished with small sewing shears, clipping here and there, stepping around me to check her handiwork.

The day arrived. Olmina's ship would set sail just before dawn. The small white houses of Algezer were still stained blue with night behind us when we left the inn. Olmina seemed a shadow in the ashen black garments of a widow, while I wore a brown doublet and breeches, Lorenzo's clothes, recently refitted to my form by an adept tailor. Olmina had insisted I keep them.

We walked in silence down to the seafront, where one other passenger, a middle-aged man attired in the rich velvet garments of a merchant, stood at the end of a narrow dock. Here we awaited the arrival of the small boat that would take them to the ship.

As we stood together, I murmured softly, "So at last you are going home, dear Nana," and I put my arms around her.

Olmina cupped my sun-darkened face in her hands the way a loving mother would hold the face of a cherished daughter. Her callused hands scratched me and I loved them. The faint blue veins I would commit to memory.

We held each other. We were bound by the same presence and absence, as if the world were pillared by two women at the gateway between sea and ocean, Europe and Africa, home and *la parte incognita*. I gave Olmina two leather purses of gold pesetas.

"Only one, Dottoressa, that is fair. You'll need the other." She returned one of the purses to the pocket of my jerkin. She grabbed my shoulder and said in a fierce, low voice, "Won't you come home with me, then?"

I shook my head, staring down at the dock planks.

She picked up her satchel and shuffled toward the small boat and two rowers that had just fastened the lines. The violet sea slapped the pilings. "Good-bye, Olmina, *buona fortuna!*" I cried. But she didn't look back. She walked away in her labored manner and descended the gangplank, steadied by the kindly merchant.

"It must be very difficult to part with your son there," I heard him say.

I turned away and felt the land jolt beneath my feet, as if I'd been falling for a very long time and just now struck the earth. Something broke in me, yet I still walked back to our room at the inn, where I bent to the window and wept. I watched the listless ship slowly gather wind, snapping her sails, then round Gibraltar eastward toward the serene city that shimmered in my mind like a place that no longer existed.

CHAPTER 22

❦

My Father's Keeper

"A man has been asking for you," Señor Romanesco says. I follow him downstairs, to discover Hamish and his servant. He's found me!

He's dressed all in black in the Spanish fashion. His voice rings fluid and deep as if he were a well mender calling from the bottom of a cistern. "Surely you can't go on alone? You'll perish!"

I stare at him, dumbfounded. Finally the words escape: "I miss you." He has come so far. I press my hands to his chest. I remember his body, where the bones lift against the skin, the white span of the ribs, the collar-bone. "I must go to Taradante. My mind and heart are bent upon this."

"Your mind has gone askew. No father would impose such a fate upon his daughter!"

"It is not imposed. I am my father's keeper."
Hamish parts his lips to reply, when—

The innkeeper knocked, and I awoke with a start.

I sat up, looking around the room in desperation. I believed for a moment that Hamish would still be there.

I left on the *Charon* at midafternoon, alone, under the glowering sun. The breeze blew steadily, raking the sea into choppy white crests. The mules shuffled and brayed belowdecks, poor beasts. I sat with the medicine chest behind me near a coil of rope on the forecastle of the ship and held on to a wooden rail, not caring whether I took spray. I welcomed the deafening wind of the straits, the creaking of spars and masts, and the dull thuds of sea against prow. The crew let me be. My face ran with salt.

My eyes were still fixed on Barbaria, as they'd been since we departed, to keep from retching, when I heard a cry from one of the sailors. "Look to starboard, look!" he shouted. "Here come the ladies of Villaderota!"

Another sailor closer to me whooped like a child. Then I saw them coming from the northwest, hundreds of them flinging open the surface of the sea—glistening arcs of light, some in pairs or singly casting sleeves of spray behind them. I'd never seen such a multitude of dolphins before in my life. Roused from numbness, I stood near the bowsprit, hanging on to one of the shrouds, and called out in surprise as they swam directly toward the ship, their numbers parting around it.

"I'm going in!" yelled the young sailor who had dubbed them the "ladies" as he tore off his shirt.

"No, you're not!" chimed a couple of the crew, grabbing his

arms. "We'll not be coming about to pick up a crazy sailor love-struck with dolphins!"

"Maybe the good doctor up there has something to cure you," called out the captain in jest.

His words barely reached me, for at that moment I saw a dolphin just below me roll on her side, still shearing through the prow wave, and glance up, her singular eye a black lens that held and then let me go. Nothing came between us until she swiveled back, and I saw the quick clasp and expulsion of her breath from a hole in the top of her body as she swerved off to the right and joined her companions, gleaming like freshly polished pewter as they leapt in and out of the sea, sewing sky to water. A few minutes later they disappeared to the south, and the ocean sealed itself after them.

So many years had passed since I'd felt that kind of awe. My body shook as I sat back down on the deck, pulling my cape about me like someone who's been delivered a stunning clout to the head. The deckhands were still bantering among themselves when the captain gave the order to reset the sails. We rounded Cape Malabata, and after a journey of three or four hours the bay lay just ahead, with Tanger in full view, looking like the closed fist of a king, encrusted with dusky sapphires.

We disembarked, and a turbaned porter with a short white beard, clad in a blue tunic and pantaloons, immediately attached himself to me. Though I bartered with one or two others, he finally won out. His name was Yousef, and while he spoke little Italian, we shared a broken Spanish between us. I liked the lattice of his brown-toothed smile (for he was missing several teeth) and the way he immediately spoke to the mules and calmed them. I also recalled Señor Romanesco's caution, "Choose an older man."

Drawing a large striped blanket about him, Yousef led me to a fonduk within the medina, where the animals were lodged in fine arched stalls on the ground floor, while the visitors, mostly foreign merchants, were lodged above on the first and second floors.

I was so exhausted I didn't want to leave my small room, didn't want to encounter anything strange or exotic. What a peculiar traveler I'd become, a lonely ascetic bereft of my natural curiosity. What if Hamish had truly come along? I couldn't think of him. My heart was a coffer filled with ghosts.

Yousef brought me a small plate of goat cheese, figs, almonds, honeyed pastries in the shape of little horns, and a bottle of red wine. When I moved to pay him, he shook his head and gave me to understand that he would return the next day and that I should pay him after I had slept.

The room contained two rush mats and in the arched sleeping niche a coarse wool mattress. The window was protected by a surprisingly intricate wooden grille of carved vines and leaves. I quickly closed the shutters and withdrew to my sleeping niche, bringing the leather satchel containing the loose leafs of *The Book of Diseases* and my maps as well as the medicine chest, close to the wall and my body. For a while the conflicting odors of honey and animal urine from the stables below kept me awake, until I wrapped my entire head round with a portion of the blanket.

The next morning, with the help of Yousef, I sought out Sidi Abdullah Romanesco, the brother of the innkeeper in Algezer.

Yousef waved me ahead and followed close behind, touching my left elbow to steer me left, my right to steer me right, as we navigated the way to the quarter of spices. I was grateful. If I'd gone behind him I might have been set upon by those with ill intention. When I'd first mentioned my errand, he shook his head and made the swift gesture of someone picking a pocket.

As we moved through the dried vine- and reed-covered passageways of the medina, only a few unveiled Berber women balancing jars of water on their heads stared at me sharply. Most of the populace, now under the Spanish crown, had grown accustomed to Europeans and paid them little mind. Perhaps the women sensed I was a woman, even in my manly garb. Maybe even Yousef suspected that I wasn't the man I seemed, though he went along without question.

At last we came to the narrow spice souk owned by Sidi Romanesco, off a little courtyard where a large fig tree had fallen over and continued to grow in a different direction, filling the space almost entirely. Passersby simply bent in avoidance of certain branches or perhaps in esteem and walked around it. Sidi, an ample balding man clad in a tan caftan and scuffed leather slippers, stood busy with a customer, an elderly man with a thick goiter. The merchant paused momentarily when he noticed us, directing me to a small red stool on one side of the shop. His opulent ground spices were displayed in conical hills upon flat baskets, in shades of crimson, orange, ocher, umber, green, and black, with various clumps of herbs laid out neatly in baskets to one side.

I recognized henna, absinthe, cinnamon, pepper, and chunks of amber, but many other spices were unknown to me. Their various sweet, pungent, and hot scents laced the warm air, pleasantly stinging my nostrils. Some of these spices must have been medicinal, I decided, for the old man repeatedly pointed to the swelling at his throat and shook his head as Sidi Romanesco offered various herbs. At last the right plant was agreed upon. The spice merchant wrapped a clump of leaves (sweet cicely?) in a small bit of dried palm leaf and sent the man on his way.

"And what is your wish, signor?" he asked me in Italian, correctly assessing my Venetian dress, though it didn't differ that much from the style of Andaluzian men.

I handed him my letter of introduction from the innkeeper.

After reading it, he glanced at me cautiously and asked, "But why is an Italian doctor dressed as a commoner?"

"I believed it would provide safer passage," I replied.

He stared at me in disbelief. "We must get you some Maroccan clothes now, especially if you're traveling into the south, where there can be much danger."

Then he was silent, examining the letter, as if weighing the information there. At last he called out toward the back of the surprisingly deep shop. A nimble young boy appeared.

"Bring us some tea, Hassan, and hurry up, we have guests!" The boy scurried behind a thin blue curtain.

"So"—I addressed the spice merchant—"may I ask, what did you give the man with the swelling?"

"Ah, sweet myrrh to use as a compress," he replied diffidently, seating himself upon a stool behind the spices, rubbing his large paunch with one hand. He folded the letter up and tucked it into a pocket in his robe. Then he said, "There are two mathematicians, I believe, or geometers from Barçalona, staying at my friend's fonduk, traveling to the court of Ahmad al-Mansour in Marruecos. They would be proper companions."

Hassan brought a tray with fragrant honey-mint tea, set it upon a small brass table, and served me first, pouring the tea into a small thick glass from the dented brass pot. He smiled at me as if we were sharing a joke, and the fresh transparency of his good nature startled me. I thought, *Things may change for the better,* a possibility that hadn't entered my heart for a while. Then he served Sidi Romanesco and also poured a glass each for Yousef and himself, the two of them settling cross-legged upon the edge of the woven straw mat to partake of their tea. We sipped it slowly in a silence that seemed courtesy rather than the uneasiness of strangers. I didn't have to explain myself further to the spice merchant. This small respect shone like a coin in my day. Customers who approached understood that they must patiently wait. Sidi Romanesco was taking his tea.

Before leaving, I requested a bit of costly cinnamon from the spice merchant, who, when I drew my purse from my breeches to pay, waved my money away from him as if he were brushing away flies. He wrapped the slivers of bark neatly in palm leaf and gave me the packet. Then he took Yousef aside and spoke to him about our arrangements.

Later that very afternoon he sent the boy to bring word that I might change lodgings to the more commodious fonduk of the mathematicians. And so we transferred my simple effects to a room that possessed a balcony with keyhole-shaped arches opening onto the sea.

The next day, Sidi Romanesco's boy delivered a fine blue caftan, a headscarf, a sand-yellow djellaba, and red leather slippers, for which I was very grateful. These clothes turned out to be the most comfortable I'd ever worn. With consistent generosity, the spice merchant again refused to accept reimbursement (though I'd dispatched a small purse of silver along with Yousef to the souk). Later I sent a note of thanks (translated by one of the scribes in the passageways), not wishing to press payment and offend him.

I would spend the next two days in the cool shadows of my room, reading and writing as I waited for the departure of the caravan. Yousef explained that the traders had already arrived at the outskirts of Tanger but the camels needed to rest before setting out once more for Marruecos and Taradante and then traveling on to Segelmesse, following the salt route.

That first evening I met my Catalonian companions, two middle-aged gentlemen. Antonio Montcada was a thin man, fair as a Hollanter, with large blue eyes and straw-colored hair. Martin Requesne was a swarthy loose-limbed man with amber eyes and curly black hair flecked with gray. They invited me to a light supper of *succussu* and capon in the courtyard, and I accepted reluctantly, uneasy with my guise as a man.

I needn't have worried. For soon Señor Montcada (his tongue loosened by wine) began talking nonstop, regaling us with an account of his previous journey to al-Badi, the palace of Sultan al-Mansour, as well as the general state of affairs in the known world. He paid little attention to me, other than as a handy ear for his tales.

"You may have heard that the sultan dislikes Spaniards for their piracy and the treatment of Moriscos within their borders and is seeking alliance with the English. Of course he ignores his own kidnappings of the Spaniards and the Portuguese!"

"Ha!" interjected Señor Requesne, flinging his hand into the air.

"And at the same time he's gathering handsome sums for their ransoms."

"So you may well wonder why he welcomes us to his court. One of his poets, al-Fishtali, told me that his master always desires news of distant lands and likes to be fully apprised of both ally and enemy. He is a man of great intellectual curiosity. His court includes mathematicians who are poets, diplomats who are generals, physicians who are astronomers, scholars who—"

"Physicians? I am a doctor myself, collecting notes on diseases and cures as I travel," I interrupted, immediately regretting that I'd said anything at all.

"Ah." He paused and scrutinized me for a brief moment, then remarked, "A physician at the court warned me of the most extraordinary disease that plagues foreigners . . ."

He went on to describe an uncanny miasma that afflicts natives of this land and travelers alike, though the latter more gravely. Soon after this intriguing account, I excused myself in order to return to my room so that I might copy it down in full.

Señor Requesne, however, bade me wait a moment and said, "I have something that may interest you, Dottor."

When he returned, wide-striding like a horseman in a hurry, as if he feared I'd be gone (perhaps he'd already experienced guests eager to escape his garrulous friend), he presented me with a sky map of odd constellations, a map drawn by an elder Fadola woman who'd contracted the fever.

"I don't recall all the old desert names for the constellations," he explained. "But the main ones there are Camel's Eye"—here he snuffed all candles on our outdoor table but one and pointed to the map and then the sky, searching for each pattern above us—"the Yellow Djinn . . . Hoofprints of the Moon."

For a few moments, even Señor Montcada kept quiet as we observed the close shimmering stars flung across the night sky, far more numerous than I'd ever seen them before.

"This is a wonderful thing," I exclaimed. "How can I repay you?"

"Hmm, I need a little something for my arthritis. Perhaps you could . . . ?"

"Of course. Where do you suffer?"

He held out his thick hands, swollen at the knuckles. "Please wait, I'll be only a short while."

I walked back to my room, found what was needed in my medicine chest, and then returned with strips of linen wrapped around a small cloth bag of mustard seed powder. "Tomorrow," I advised Señor Requesne, "make a paste of the powder and spread it on the cloth, then press it to the back of your hand and wrap it round. The heat caused thereby will soothe your aching. Only be careful, don't leave it on too long or you may suffer blisters. Then wash your hands well of the paste. Do this every day for a week and your hands should improve. Then repeat the treatment every month."

"Thank you," said Señor Requesne, bowing slightly.

"If there's anything else you require, let me know. This is small payment for the map."

"Oh, you're not obliged. In truth I was given the map and now it pleases me to give it to you, sir."

I nodded and then gladly retired to my room.

ZAARAN MIASMA:

An Archaic Fever Carried by Desert Vapors

The victim contracts the fever that originates in the wasteland of the Zaara from the invisible breath of the sands surrounding the oasis in the season of the khamsin, a southeasterly that blows in winter. The inhabitants there say that if one places a hand near the surface of the desert at dusk, one can feel the exhalations of the ancestors. If a person breaks into fever, then the old ones have come to inhabit him. Because water must be drawn daily from the oasis, the villagers are constantly exposed during winter, though very few die. Foreigners are far more susceptible to the contagion. Unwittingly they carry the voices away from their home. The fever has appeared in Lisboa, Valentia, and Tucca, transmitted not only by the afflicted but also by sand transported in large jars to these ports for construction. So the fever is also called the miasma of masons.

An elderly healer of Marruecos by the name of Fatma, who suffered the fever three times in her sixty years of life, warns that since foreigners do not keep their own ancestors well, they become possessed of others'. Empty jars call the river.

One must know the language of stars to appease them. That is why, according to Fatma, one must learn the sky map as protection, for the names themselves are amulets.

The day before departure, while exploring the city with Yousef as vigilant companion, I came upon the Church of Santa Barbara, patroness of gunsmiths and artillerymen, the saint governing explosions of all sorts, whose name is also evoked against thunderstorms.

Yousef waited outside as I entered to pray, something I hadn't done in a long while. When I stepped inside, my eyes momentarily eclipsed by a cool darkness, I gradually took in a strange row of apparitions. Noble Spanish patriarchs, patrons of the church (I assumed, for I'd seen this once before in Sicilia), were hung after death along the walls beneath archways on either side of the nave, or, to speak precisely, they were mummified and dressed in their favored clothing—hose and shoes, gusseted slit pants, shirts and waistcoats, jackets and broad hats. They dangled from the white church walls so that each supplicant had to run a gauntlet of death grimaces and finery. I couldn't decide whether arrogance or irony was the greater sin here. Some of the patriarchs hung by hooks piercing their lace collars, others by ropes around their necks, which gave them the appearance of being eternally garroted. Some were held by crudely sculpted arms that emerged from the walls behind.

A comely young nun approached from the transept, her eyes fixed upon the floor, though I still greeted her and asked, "What is this display, these arms constantly holding up the dead?"

She answered so quietly I could barely hear her. "The daughters, granddaughters, and great-granddaughters commissioned the arms for their beloved kin."

"And is this not overly prideful?" I ventured.

The nun looked away anxiously toward the altar, as if she awaited a priest, and whispered, "And let the fathers fall?"

"No," I remarked, "but why not use coffins?"

"Ah," she said, nodding, "but there is a lesson here, good sir, for all those who pass. Humility and filial devotion." Still she gazed at the floor, and only then I remembered my appearance. A nun most certainly must never speak to a man alone. Yet she went on, "We must pity those who have no arms to hold them. Those poor devils have no daughters, and eventually they'll crumble in the sand. Do you not have a daughter, sir?"

"No, I don't," I said, barely restraining a dry laugh.

"May you be fortunate, then, in the future to beget one." She scurried away, her robes rustling, hushing.

"Ah yes, may I be fortunate."

Later in my sea-lit room, certain words came to me. *Forgive the fathers. The daughters. I fear for my own father. Help me, Santa Barbara, to find him. Or help me to give him up.*

CHAPTER 23

❧

We Are Housed by the Past

The caravan departed in the blue hour before the hot sun climbed the horizon. It would take five days to reach Taradante. Yousef fitted my mule Fedele as a pack animal, then straddled the other mule, while I engaged a camel for the journey. We rode at the end of the caravan, since camels don't suffer mules easily in front of them (they don't suffer humans well upon them either, to be honest), with one heedful camel driver at some distance behind us.

The two Catalonian gentlemen rode ahead of us, having employed three camels just to carry the tomes of their library. Other travelers included Berber traders and a blue-veiled Arab woman of some distinction flanked by two men with scimitars.

We proceeded with a lot of commotion at the outset, the camels snorting, belching, and grunting like dyspeptic old men, while the three drivers shouted brisk commands up and down the line. The camels' rope bridles and harnesses shook with indigo tassels, as if they still carried bits of night and sleep with them, rendering them cantankerous in the transition. But as soon as the city disappeared behind us, all animals and humans alike settled into an undulant rhythm.

Sitting high on the camel's hump in a saddle that was no more than folded blankets with a forked wood pommel, I lurched and dropped and lurched. There were no stirrups. I had never ridden anything so uncomfortable in my life, but I hoped, with patience, to learn to fall in with the motion. At least the nausea I'd felt off and on for weeks after leaving the northern lands had passed.

As we rode away from the boundaries of Tanger, we passed the tanners, their goat hides soaking in stone vats of crushed sumac bark, giving off a pungent stench. Next to them, some of the softened hides rested in red cochineal dye, looking like the flayed skins of unnamed martyrs. From these bloodred baths came the beautiful maroquin leather covers of many of our books at home. I hadn't fully considered it before, but I would never touch those books again without the knowledge of what underlay the art of their bindings.

As we rode across the stark desert plain, with the Atlas Mountains beyond, Cousin Lavinia's words returned to me from a long-ago letter in which she described painting San Paolo the Hermit. *I begin with burnt sienna and lead white but avoid pure white as a ground. It's too harsh and unforgiving. Even the desert can't be this absolute in its absence of color.* But she'd

326

never seen the Mauritanian earth, its vacant glare nearly stripping one of sight. I could barely look out through the blue-black gauze of my wrapped headscarf, a woven net like the grid of a drawing screen plotting the landscape, the foreshortening, the vanishing point.

By midmorning the faint smoldering curves that marked the wadis snaking out of the mountains were barely distinguishable. Far behind us I observed another caravan dimly, with all the travelers wearing light blue robes. Sweat stung my eyes. The inescapable heat emptied me. There was no perspective, all things were equal: foreground, background, the line of camels, mules, men, and women leveled by the impartial sun, a confounding demon . . .

It was like the devil in the wall at the Benedictine chapel in Subiaco that I had visited as a child.

My father and I had met a hunched priest with strings of yellow-gray hair like rigging dangling around his face. "There are two walls here," he warned us, and he pointed his forefinger toward the small crumbling hole in the wall left of the nave. I stepped back, frightened, as he lowered his voice to a whisper. "You must not look there!"

My father directed a question to the priest about the painting of the raven in a niche on the opposite wall. As they walked away, their backs turned to me, I crept up to the hole and peered in. The gap was dark, but gradually I could make out a twisted profile. Then a hand like a rooster's spur seized me from behind and I leapt back.

"See, see," hissed the priest, as he released my shoulder. "The devil lives between the walls. He is trapped there forever. But don't worry, he won't harm you as long as you don't let him out."

The old monk grinned and my father gave a dry laugh like a cough. The painted devil I'd glimpsed between the walls, between the old plain church and the new embellished one, was a leering demon with sharp nails and lurid eyes. It sat crushed between a history forgotten and one reinvented. The whole chapel nested inside the hewn cave of its older form, the way we are housed by the past when we think we are creating something new.

We stopped at a small mudhole to rest until the intense heat of midday passed. As my camel slowly folded his front legs to sit upon the ground, I thought surely I'd plunge forward. All around me the sounds of beasts eagerly lapping water, travelers conversing in parched tongues, and palm fronds crackling in the wind flattened to a dull pitch. Yousef urged me to drink and I did.

As I rested against a palm trunk in a narrow strip of shade, the camel drivers suddenly began waving their arms, yelling, and drawing the animals closer together. Yousef pulled the mules close and quickly wrapped their muzzles with shreds of torn scarf, no small task, as they jerked their heads away from him. Señor Montcada shouted, "The red sharki is coming. Cover up!"

"What's the red sharki?"

"A hot southeasterly that will scour your skin."

"How long does it last?"

But he didn't hear me, for he'd turned and rushed back to his companion, both of them kneeling against one of the camels that bore their books. A thin red haze began to sift through the palm fronds, and then farther out I saw it, a rolling wall of sand that broke across the desert, scuffling and roaring down upon us.

Taut with fear, I squeezed my eyes shut and crouched against the musky camel, whose stink I almost welcomed, for the world returned to three dimensions through scent. As the sand pelted us and I struggled to breathe through my dark scarf in the shifting body of the desert, something stirred within.

I felt it jump—oh!—like a small fish in my belly.

It jumped again! My body had given me signs for months. The nausea, the cease of my cycles, which I'd read as grief, the heaviness I had blamed on my indulgence in sweets—these were all something more. A child swam in my womb.

The mathematicians left us on the fourth day to pursue their calculations in Marruecos. On the fifth day we mounted stark ridges through scant juniper and pine forests. At dusk we approached a walled village, all squares and rectangles and pointed arches, assembled at the base of brick-red mountains. The cool night air returned to me what the heat of day had drained. The pleasing geometry of human dwellings set against the disorders of the desert secured me once more in the world.

At last we had reached Taradante.

After Yousef made a few inquiries of the gatekeepers, we found lodging with the only person who offered beds to foreigners, a middle-aged woman of indigo skin by the name of Malina. Tall, lean, and wrapped in colorful robes and a blue half veil (covering only the lower part of her face), she ushered us into her cool courtyard. The veil, embroidered with small red triangles and dangling tiny silver coins, jangled lightly and glittered as she moved, drawing attention to the gleam of her good eye. The other resembled a dried fig embedded with an opaque marble. She provided me a plain room across the courtyard, separated from her own by a thin stick fence to keep the goats in. It was one of several rooms in the square cluster of red mud rooms and a granary tower that formed her dwelling.

Malina gave Yousef a smaller room to one side of the court-yard, beneath a single great date palm that shaded the animal stalls. Three goats lay in the straw, watching us pensively as they slowly chewed. She also pointed out a slightly larger stall where we could keep our mules. Luckily she spoke some Italian. I wondered, though I didn't ask, about her kin, who must once have occupied these rooms—whether they died in a plague or war or were lost one by one. For it seemed strange that a woman would live alone in such a compound. There were no other guests.

The next morning I took Malina aside and explained, "I am in need of a woman's garments, for I am only a man by the clothing I put on to travel in safety." I didn't mention that those clothes were growing more uncomfortable around my belly day by day.

"Mmm," she murmured, and she stared at me. "I noticed your face was beardless and oddly smooth, but then I'm not always sure how to judge foreigners." Then she smiled as she stroked my cheek. "Don't worry. I have ample clothing for you."

I put away my man's garb and adopted the loose linen and wool robes of the Susa women. Malina kindly offered me these second-hand garments from among her own and gladly accepted payment.

Yousef was not alarmed. "I knew, Dottoressa, I knew," he informed me quietly, nodding and looking down at his rough feet as he squatted in the courtyard, cleaning a bridle, the first morning I stepped to the well as a woman. "By your scent of salt and sweet. No man, not even a youth, has the smell of a woman."

"But you acted kindly to shield me . . . Weren't you worried about the trouble I'd cause?"

"You pay me well, Dottoressa. There will be no trouble while I serve you." The old man spoke in a plain tone and continued brushing the bridle clean.

"Thank you, then." I sat at the edge of the well, a round mud wall surrounding a cistern, capped by a chipped clay jug to prevent evaporation. Nearby, a simple pail tied to a coil of rope could be used to draw water.

"God, who speaks in the beehive, has many riddles, and why shouldn't we be one of them?" added Yousef, still considering my changing guise.

Malina, who'd probably overheard our conversation, peered at me from her window. Then she entered the courtyard and handed me a small sheathed blade. "Keep this in your belt for the future," she instructed me. "For though Yousef bears respect, others may not. And you must take the room next to mine." She directed Yousef to move my things.

My new room, which opened onto the courtyard, was larger and possessed a narrow window and a crude wooden bed frame with a neatly folded pile of *hendira* blankets, woolens that women wove in pomegranate red, saffron yellow, and night blue, which could be worn as garments or used for sleeping.

A faded wine-red carpet patterned with flocks of triangular

birds lay upon the packed earthen floor. In the darkest corner of the room a large cobalt-glazed jar of water with a snug ceramic lid stood like a watchful young child. When I filled my brass cup and drank, I tasted ancient minerals as if the water had passed through the veins of mountains, like those celebrated waters in Umbria, which I still remembered from former journeys with my father.

Later I spoke to her in the courtyard as she fanned herself under the palm. "Malina, I must ask you . . . I must tell you the reason I am here." I touched her sleeve.

She regarded me cautiously. "It is not necessary. You may take time."

"I've already traveled a long time to get here."

Her look softened. "Come inside, my daughter, and I'll prepare us a cup of tea and something to eat."

She led me into a room just off her sleeping room and knelt to put wood in the curved mud hearth, which resembled a tall, thick-sided pot, with a wide slit along one side for stoking the fire. After it was well lit, she set a kettle there at the top. Numerous herbs hung drying from the log beams of the ceiling. Several jars lined the base of three walls, and it occurred to me that there were many more than were needed for cooking. We sat upon a large red, ocher, and indigo carpet woven with a great geometric tree and all manner of animals scattered here and there among its branches. It shone dully in worn places where people had sat year after year. When the water boiled she tossed a handful of fresh mint leaves into the small pot, then took a piece of flatbread from a covered basket, spread it with cold, stiff honey from a jar, and passed it to me. A blade of light crept slowly along the wall as the sun sank lower.

"I'm searching for my father, an Italian doctor. His name, like mine, is Dr. Mondini."

"Hmm." She poured our tea into earthenware cups.

"He mentioned this place, Taradante, in one of his letters."

"I've heard of an Italian man . . ."

"Yes?"

"Who stubbornly dressed in blue cape, hose, and plumed hat in the blazing midday."

I shook my head and frowned.

"I've heard of a Venetian swindler with burnt skin. He was lost in the pillars of a sandstorm, or some say he joined the blue people on the salt route. He owes my cousin money." She narrowed her eye at me.

"That is not my father," I said heatedly. "He is a doctor!"

"Il Dottor, yes," she murmured at last. "I know a man who has become a recluse." Malina put her hand on mine. "Daughter." She sighed as if reluctant to speak. "He lived here for a time. We worked with the bezoar, the green ones and the stars of antimony. I am a healer of women; he was a healer of men. When his medicines finished, I taught him the smokes, the proverbs, the sand cures. He left almost a year ago." She sighed. "Sometimes the desert calls us to another dream."

No, this wasn't true!

"Stay awhile," she coaxed, seeing the expression on my face. "You are a doctor too. I will teach you the healings that come from the growing things, the silent ones, and the well spirits. I will tell you the ways we sicken and the ways we recover ourselves again."

But I couldn't take in her words. "I can't believe my father was here, and I've missed him!" I sobbed, bringing my hands to my face. Malina let me be.

At dusk, spent and groggy from sadness, I brought Malina the sky map given me by Señor Requesne and unrolled it upon the rug. "I recognize these stars," she said, lifting an oil lamp. "They were spoken by my grandfather when he seethed with fever."

"Oh — you must give me their names so I can fill them in." I wanted to engage myself, to keep going with work. "Yes, later when the night sky is fully dark."

"Tell me about another one," I said.

"Another what?"

"Another malady. I'm writing them down."

"Ah, Daughter, may I see?" Malina kept up the odd habit of calling me Daughter, though we were nearly the same age. I accepted it, even liked it. She went on, "Your father mentioned a book and it caused him distress. Sometimes he cried out for it: 'My book, my maladies, my cures!' "

So it was truly lost . . .

"But don't you have your own papers, Daughter?"

I brought out the satchel with my own large folio of notes. As I straightened the pages to show Malina, I felt an unexpected urge to see them bound. They'd grown into a thing of solid heft and size. Malina ran her dark fingers over the many pages with admiration. Then she began to tell me about the blue worms. Sometimes I stopped her and asked questions, but mostly I just sat upon the rug before the hearth, which she fed now and then with splits of juniper wood as evening crept upon us.

BLUE EAR WORMS:

Desert Parasites That Feed upon Human Utterance

They live in the sand dunes and salt marches of Mauritania, where they hibernate for long periods of time at depths of three to seven arm lengths underground. The adults spend their entire lives in subterranean darkness. Thirty years may pass (and in the village of Melilla in Barbaria, it is said that a century elapses) before the worms appear. For reasons unknown, the young emerge all at once at the surface of the desert or shore as bright cerulean-blue worms, the length of a child's smallest finger. In Mozema, where their brilliance is identical to that of the minaret roof tiles, they are called the little fingers of God. They issue from the sand on nights of the new moon, but only to seek darkness of a different kind, in the warm, moist ear of a woman. No other body crevice will suffice. The blue worms enter the sleepers and reside in the small labyrinths of resonance, grazing upon sounds that drift into the auricle. Some elders say they consume only human speech and howls but are greatly affected by certain languages, which can slow or agitate their activity. Berber and Bedouin words calm, while Portuguese and Ottoman Arabic make them wriggle, causing great distress to the victim. Instruments like the oud and santir generate a low humming among the earworms, a maddening or soothing effect for the person in whom they dwell. The symptoms include muddled hearing; auditory visions brought on by scraping, rustling, and thumping movements; and voluntary muteness in the person who wishes to avoid exciting them.

In certain years, nearly every woman in the village of

Alganziza on the coast below Messa falls victim to the blue ear-worm. The population fluctuates greatly from season to season because of the nomadic peoples who pass through. However, when the earworms begin to emerge, the people paint the white stone walls, houses, and rooftops blue to warn away travelers. The village goes silent. No dogs or other animals are allowed, except for snakes, which are highly prized for their noiseless companionship and consumption of rats. Birds are driven away with long-handled brooms and flailing sticks, though they seldom appear in the town anyway, preferring the river Sus to the north and the date palms along its banks. The inhabitants converse in signs or writings if at all, the men respectful of the women's silence. If there are secrets, now is the time they will fester.

The blue worms consume more at night, feasting, it is said in this village, on the conversations in dreams as well as on those spoken beneath archways or around the supper mat spread upon the floor. The family eats everything with their fingers and in their contentment sometimes forgets the necessity of silence. Then the worms capture the words before the women can hear them. The villagers also suffer insomnia, existing in a listless world for months, enduring the many ailments that arise from a cold, wet humor.

Finally the worm completes its cycle and emerges from the ear of its own accord, well fattened and seeking its original host. It burrows back into the desert to finish its hidden life there. Malina told me that there is even a constellation called the Blue Worm, in the southeastern quarter of the sky, perhaps that same constellation that we call Serpens.

I wasn't certain I would go on looking for my father. I was weary. Even with all my care to retrace his journey, to seek out his peers, I had missed him. I wanted to remain in one place for a while. Yet what about the man who had disappeared in the sandstorm? And Malina appeared to know far more than she revealed. Perhaps it was her way to wait to know me, as she suggested I do before disclosing my purpose to her. Even as I was about to give up, I found another kind of patience, like a coin sewn into my hem. Besides, I knew how to wait. And now I was two.

I watched Malina come and go, visiting the well, milking or feeding the goats, fetching grain from the granary once or twice a day with her basket, to make flatbread. I allowed her to blacken my eyes with kohl to keep the flies away, and to cut strands of my coppery hair to share out with the village women, for the color gleamed as something marvelous to them.

I watched the women and children come and go, visiting Malina's kitchen, where they consulted her about their ailments, leaving little gifts of dates, eggs, or even firewood. A few times I observed a thin tress of my own, woven into a child's hair as an adornment.

I satisfied my growing hunger with eggs, goat cheese, flat-bread, dried fruits, and honey during the day, and with cuscusu, flatbread, occasional goat meat, walnuts, raisins, olives, and oranges from the port of Messa in the evening when I shared a meal with Malina and Yousef. I didn't know if I would ever return to Venetia. This land of desert and mountains suited me now.

Malina instructed me in the ways of the djnoun. "Those small spirits," she said one afternoon as we sat before the hearth, "inhabit all things from the tiniest grain to the largest mountain."

"But the small ones, why do they matter to us?"

"They live with us. We live with them. It is custom. We bear them respect."

"Is there a fire djinn, a hearth djinn?"

"Yes, but they love water more. That is why you must sing when you draw from the well, or the djinn who lives there may taint our water!" She taught me a simple chant for drawing water. I murmured the strange words before I dropped the bucket facedown into the well, before the rope unwound from the bricks.

The monks and nuns of Venetia chanted their prayers early in the morning. That sound always made me stand still, no matter what age I was, no matter where I was going. I stood on the damp stones and breathed the chant, tasted the plain harmonies on my tongue. But this music of Taradante didn't come from within the high cloister walls; it didn't come from the plague churches dedicated to healing. It came from everywhere, from small red mud courtyards, drifting downward from narrow windows, echoing up from wells, granaries, stables, fields, oases, and wadis where shepherds grazed the animals. Children sang to soothe the djnoun in little stones, water, arjun trees, palms. The women sang, the men. Those who believe the desert is soundless, motionless, are mistaken. Malina told me that the desert herself hums. Nothing stands still. Not even sorrow.

Sometimes I walked alone, feeling safe as the outsider everyone in the village knew, to the oasis near the center of town, where exhalations were particularly strong at dawn and dusk. I knew that Yousef followed me, watched me as if I were a stray. So truly I was not alone. I listened for the indecipherable words that rose and fell from the slow-moving boundaries of stone and sand, beneath the calls of birds shrilling to their kind. Perhaps I wanted to hear the voices of which the old ones spoke, though I really wanted to hear my own ancestors, Venetian and Ciprian, who didn't inhabit this place.

But I heard only the slippage of time, the seepage of water, and the murmur of conversations in and around the travelers' tents pitched on the far side of the oasis. Sometimes that was enough. Once, I saw Yousef speaking to a tall foreigner, who stood with his back turned to me outside his tent. He moved his pale hands back and forth as he spoke, a vaguely familiar motion that made my heart leap. I asked Yousef about it.

"That man? He was just asking directions to the souk," he answered.

"Does the man have red hair?" For his head had been covered by a hood.

"I don't know."

I turned away. I didn't want him to see the expectation on my face—for I still kept the secret hope of Hamish, like another gold coin jangling against the coin of patience in my hem.

CHAPTER 24

❦

The Basin of the Dead

Just before sundown in midsummer, Malina came to my room and began stopping up any openings, including chinks in the ceiling between the thuja beams. She cautioned me, "Tonight the moon withdraws and covers herself. A time of danger. She veils the mirror, passes through the basin of the dead. Extinguish your lamp, Daughter, and pray that your soul may pass safely through the dark." *And that of my unborn,* I thought.

After she left, I understood that I was not to leave my room. But filled with insatiable curiosity, I stepped quietly into the small courtyard, fully cloaked. Shutters were latched, carpets hung against the carved wooden doors and windows, whether to protect those within from seeing that other lightless world, or to prevent the disorder of that world from entering the house, I wasn't sure. I was a shadow among other shadows.

A man shouted once in the medina, in fear or exhilaration, and then the town went mute. The light hairs on my arms rose in apprehension. I climbed a ladder on the north side of my room and sat upon the flat roof of the dwelling. The moon had just risen. The lunar cast upon the listless body of the Sus valley and the surrounding desert mountains slowly wore thin, like an old garment, as a dark curved blade fell across the moon's face. I watched the slow scything of her light.

An hour passed, and I didn't move from my place against the wall, knees drawn up to my chest as I sat shivering, on vigil. The moon's covered disk finally glowed like the clotted stump of an amputated leg or arm (for I had seen several such horrors on men returning from one war or another when they came to be treated by my father) or the bloodied head of an infant emerging from her mother. The stars jumped forward. I placed my hands on my belly. I, who had never given birth, considered the child who quickened there at the center of me. *How should I prepare the way?*

Little by little the moon slid into cold radiance once more. The stars receded. A small seep that emerged from an underground spring near the rubble of the outer wall gleamed briefly, then vanished in the sand. An unlikely knot of ferns grew there, and I suddenly craved the young shoots. But as I descended the ladder to gather them, someone moaned without words, a sound like that of a large animal. A smell of old, damp wood rose from the night. I listened for footfalls. Had something come down from the mountains? After a while I heard nothing more, but it so unnerved me I fled indoors. Recalling that ferns offered a cure for fever, I searched for the entry I'd written many months ago for *The Book of Diseases*.

CARTHUSIAN SPLEEN:

Form of Ague Where a Solitary Falls into Trembling and Sullen Aspect

The disease is named after an order of contemplatives who distill the elixir of life, a rare liquor composed of over a hundred herbs and spices, prepared under the breath of prayer. Unfortunately an outbreak of spleen among the usually kind and peaceful nuns caused their order's name to be attached to this affliction, when even their elixir could not effect a cure.

The fever acts like a quick fire on the victim and then scorches all those around her. For the mean of spirit exude a certain burnt odor. Some will say that the reek is fiendish, but I'm not sure that evil is so predictable. Sometimes evil gives off a fragrance.

Once, in Udine, an amiable woman scalded by the ague spat insults at her children. A cobbler's wife in Mainz flung shoes at every customer who spoke the words, "I need . . ." A young classics teacher in Florentia, noted for patience with her girls, began to lecture upon the necessity of the rod and the cage. "Let punishment instruct the frail body, break the will. Let suffering . . ." The ague, however, doesn't affect vengeful souls with the inverse humor, a fact that led my father to say, "Though disease often calls its opposite to table, spleen dines alone."

Carthusian spleen courts death, mingles bitterness with roar. Yet the fever bows to a fern. I've never treated it myself, but my father recommended the gentle and wise spleenwort. This fern grows profusely near freshets and reduces the rancorous fever, chills, and edema of the troubling organ. Spleenwort clenches just as the disease binds, and then the fern uncurls, loosening the bile of a thousand days.

The subsequent night I heard a muffled voice cry out from time to time and then subside. When I questioned Malina, she shrugged evasively and murmured that perhaps one of the neighbors suffered a private grief.

Unable to endure it any longer, I lit an oil lamp and followed the sound of the voice across the red dirt courtyard until I reached the granary. *There, it came from within the storeroom!* The tall tower, with its narrow windows at the top, sent the sound in all directions, making it difficult to mark the source unless you were at the entry. I thought I heard someone call my name, *Gabi, Gabi,* but then the voice fell away into babbling. I unlatched and opened the sagging door. The voice ceased and the dim room appeared empty except for a large mound of barley sloping from the wall to my right.

Old bits of grain and straw crackled beneath my feet as I entered. I lifted the lamp. My stomach tightened when I saw someone huddled in the far corner. A stable stench leapt to my nose from the floor as I stepped forward.

A man in a rough tunic with his back to me crouched there, a torn piece of blue turban cloth tied around his mouth, his arms flung forward on a pile of hay. He seemed a supplicant or a prisoner. His hands were tied at the wrist, and shadows pooled around him. He turned his face a little so I could see the matted gray beard, the faint splinters of light that shone from yellow teeth, the caked blood on his brow where he'd bent his head to raw wrists, arms where dried red rivulets made a crude brocade of his flesh.

My skin prickled.

"Papà?" I whispered fiercely.

His eyes, almost recognizable in the half light, scanned the shadowy room and passed over me as if I were another mud wall. He turned his face away and muttered a rapid string of senseless Latinate words as a dribble of urine ran down his thigh. He clenched and unclenched his hands. He struggled against the long brown cord that bound him to a metal ring in the wall, a ring meant for tying up animals.

"Papà, Papà!" I cried, and he began to bellow through his gag as he butted his head into the straw. Terrified, I dropped the lamp, spilling oil that flashed at my hem and set off his bellowing all the more as I flailed at the flames that tongued my skirts.

Malina came running and threw a blanket on me, choking the fire. Then the air went dark but for the ashen squares of moonlight at the top of the granary. I strained for breath. My father—or the man who seemed my father—thrashed on his meager patch of earth.

Malina pulled me out into the courtyard. "You must not go in there!"

"Who is that man? Why is he bound to the wall like a beast?" My body shook.

"Because he *is* one. Your father went into the desert and he never returned. This creature is bound so that he doesn't hurt himself."

"Why didn't you tell me? Did you think I wouldn't find out?" I cried, clutching her arms.

She shoved me away and lifted the lamp that she'd set on the well, pushing back her sleeve to show a broken scar on her forearm. "This is where your father sank his teeth. I didn't want you to get hurt! Forget him. Mourn him, Daughter. He is like this many months, dead but not dead. Since it is our custom to tend strangers who have no one, I keep him. I bathe him once a week and feed him morning and night. Yet every day, he threatens me."

I couldn't accept what she told me. "Give me the lamp."

She didn't resist as I took it from her hand and stepped back inside the granary toward the man. I touched his shoulder. He jerked back and grunted.

Malina followed me and said, "He was already ailing when he came to me. I tried all my herbs and smokes and the red stones that will stop an inflamed mind, but he must have carried this with him his whole life. We each bear a hidden malady. The seeds lie within until fever, exile, or—"

"Leave me with him," I interrupted. "I need a sponge, a stool, and a basin."

Malina observed me coolly and did not move.

"I must do this," I said. If I could wash him, I would know him. Could the stranger truly be my father?

He watched me with the canny prescience of an animal. I spoke to him in low tones, mumbling whatever came into my head. Lucretius, for instance, which my father sometimes read to me: "All these wandering images still bear the likeness of the things from which they're shed."

Science was a puny balm, but still my words calmed us both.

Malina left and quickly returned with the things I'd requested. She set them near me with grave regard. I began to wash him.

He stared at me walleyed. I sat on the stool and gently cleansed his mangy hands, extended and bound as they were, though he flinched. I washed the crusted blood and pus from his bristly white arms, the way I might sponge the clotted afterbirth from a new-born. The way I might wash the carbuncles of a plague victim or the gashes of someone wounded in battle. I leaned from the stool and washed his speckled brow, the swollen eyes that rolled in fear at my touch, the foolish wedge of the nose that he shoved into my hand in order to smell me, the lips buckled like dried mud around the gag, the sorry flaps of the neck, and the slumped, furry chest. I untied the gag and he howled once and then quieted.

I lifted his tunic, mopped his wretched, corded back, the sad buttocks, the deflated belly. How sorrowful the body becomes. The feet and toenails rude as hooves. I knelt to his feet and then I knew. For my own feet carried the design of my father's feet, the second toe a little longer, the others tapered, the fugitive little toe curled into the next toe, hiding its nail.

I scrubbed each one, as if they were the buds on an infant's foot. I wept, full of bitterness, and then I rinsed the dirtied sea sponge, squeezing slowly with both hands over the basin.

I removed my cloak and dried his body, his feet, with a tenderness that came from old, speechless love. When I finished I looked at his face again, a face that resembled and then no longer resembled my father's, the uncomprehending eyes, the spittle at the corner of his mouth, and I felt no end to desolation.

Malina stood silently against the opposite wall, watching me.

If this world were joined to the underworld like a city to its image in the sea, I thought, then we might walk upon our lost ones, inverted, footfall to footfall, and know their wanderings as our own. For truly, what had happened to him? I glanced upward toward the ceiling of the tower of the granary and saw nothing but ascending darkness now. I untied my father and he lay in the straw against the wall, fitting himself to its curve to sleep. I placed a blanket over him and rested my hand on his ragged head. Maybe he would dream that he had a daughter somewhere in this world. "Good night, Papà."

Malina took my arm and drew me outside into the courtyard. The hunchback moon, said to bring good fortune, shed her faithless light upon us.

"What will you do now?" Malina asked in a low voice.

"I don't know." I mouthed the words with difficulty, my tongue dry as a parched flake of mud. "I could take my father back to Venetia and care for him there."

But as soon as I spoke, I knew I couldn't leave. I had more than my father to consider. And he would never recognize the glistening city he had once called home.

~❦~

CHAPTER 25

A Secret Accord

I fed my father twice daily in the granary and bathed him once a day. We tied him up to prevent harm. He gnawed himself, even through the cloth. He lunged at us and shook his matted gray hair like a wounded lion. Yousef was wary and wouldn't go near him. "That man is no one's father," he told me one morning in the courtyard. "No, no," he said, thoughtfully stroking his bristly white beard. "When a man loses himself but remains, we must leave him to the desert. Let the white vultures take him to God."

"I don't know what to do," I muttered, half to him, half to myself, as I cradled my round belly (mostly hidden by loose robes) with my arms.

"Ask the woman, she will help you."

"No, I must decide, and while I can't, there'll be no decision."

When the moon waned thin as a fingernail, my father grew calmer. I brought him outside for a few days and fastened his rope to the well ring, where from time to time Malina tied up the goats. He ranged the courtyard like a leashed animal and sniffed the air as if he caught the scent of something familiar in this foreign place. Sometimes I brought him a small bowl of figs or olives, but mostly he just scattered them in the dirt, chewing the figs later with the grit stuck to them. He swallowed the olives whole with their pits. I had to take him back into the granary again as the moon waxed full.

I believe he knew me briefly at times.

One hot evening just after the sun had set and the air had begun to cool, he grew quiet and touched my face with his fingers, the way he once touched his books, with tender strokes smoothing the pages. We sat on the rounded edge of the well, and the water below us trembled as if in secret accord with our movements and words.

"Read me, Father . . . What do you see?"

He moved his lips as if searching for some word.

"It doesn't matter. I am here. Gabi. I won't leave you."

Yousef watched us from his narrow window nervously. Then he called out, "Careful, Dottoressa, don't let your guard down!"

Though I knew the danger, I held apprehension at bay, sensing a shift in my father as if the madness had momentarily loosened its grip. As I brought my hands to his ravaged face, he jerked back a little, but his dull eyes brightened and held mine with odd amusement. He laughed and I laughed with him at some unknown delight. He patted my cheek. We laughed until tears welled up, and then the luster in his eyes went out. He'd once told me that my first syllables as a baby were not words but little grunts of laughter. Now his sounds toward the end were the same. But then he fidgeted with his hands, turned away from me, inspected the surrounding area, and plucked a dusty black olive from the ground, swiftly popping it into his mouth. I sat at the well, soundlessly weeping, as my father fell to all fours and scavenged the earth.

I now agreed with Dr. Cardano that my father had suffered this malady in some form since I was a child. My mother must have known and borne the burden with confusion and shame, anger and impatience, patience. I recalled a night when I couldn't sleep, went to my window, and observed my father, visible under the moon, prowling the courtyard, crunching the gravel pathway loudly beneath his trudging feet, pacing around and around our garden. I didn't know what he was doing there, but it made my stomach twist. Then I saw my mother's face dimly at their bedroom window, also watching. Then she withdrew. Later I thought that I'd dreamt it. But how had my father worsened to this point? I'd never know. The moon had hollowed him out.

After our meal on the day that my father and I had laughed together, Malina took me aside, removed her veil, and observed, "Daughter, I notice you do not bleed with the moon." She waited for me to respond. Her mouth, rarely exposed, was set in a solemn expression.

"I will bear a child in a few months," I said shyly, staring down at the rug.

"Ah, I thought so!" She broke into a large smile and clapped her hands. "Blessings on this house!"

Heartened by her response, I looked up. "Will you act as my midwife, then?"

"I would be glad," she declared. "But may I ask, who is the father?"

"I believe he is here in Taradante."

Now she frowned, puzzled. "Who is it, then?"

"He has been following me and yet keeping his distance." I stopped, overcome by a sense of his loyalty.

"And does this bring sorrow?" she asked, mistaking my tears.

"No, it brings me joy I never thought I'd know."

"Ah." She leaned back as if to take in a broader view.

"His name is Hamish. He's from the north."

"But why doesn't he come to you?"

"Because he discerns that I haven't wanted him to approach me yet."

"He is constant, then."

"He is constant."

"You must call him to you!"

"I will." And my heart trembled like an instrument, an aeolian harp shaken by wind, its sound traveling all the way to the oasis and far into the open desert. "But he doesn't know yet about the child, and I want to tell him myself," I cautioned her, knowing how easily the village women conversed. The words I spoke at dusk would be in his tent just after night-fall—though the same good news would never reach my father a few feet away.

CHAPTER 26

❦

Make His Entrance Wide

In the dim morning light, as I pushed open the granary door, I found my motionless father on his side upon the straw — an infant curled in sleep. Then, as I looked more closely, he was a lion, teeth bared, arrested midstride while running, front legs (his arms) drawn back to meet hind legs in readiness for the next bound. *Oh, Papà! You've leapt into the other world.*

Were you waiting for me in the wilderness of memory, so you could finally go? Yesterday we laughed together.

I could touch him now without fear.

I placed my hand on his cold body. An impenetrable chill, dense as iron. My father, dead in this hot clime, lay colder than Lorenzo had been in the mountains. I didn't cry. I numbly washed him, then put on his spectacles, which I'd carried from Tübingen, and his fine shoes, which I'd brought from Leiden. (I kept his calipers from Tremp, for wasn't he a measure of my life?) My father lay strangely restored by his things in death.

I must have been sitting there for a long time, for Malina entered and asked, "Where have you been? I've . . ." And then she saw my blue father in the corner, his livid skin the color of a guttered flame. "Oh!"

"He's gone," I said.

"Oh, Daughter," she murmured, kneeling beside me. "He suffers no more."

Yousef stood in the entry, drawn by her cry. "The man has left us, then?"

"Yes."

"Oh Allah, forgive our living and our dead," he recited in prayer.

"Have mercy on him," Malina continued as I sat with my hand on my father's hand. "Keep him safe and sound and forgive him, honor the place where he settles and make his entrance wide; wash him with water and snow and hail and cleanse him as a white garment is cleansed of dirt. Make his grave large and fill it with light." Then she rose and left me, closing the door.

I didn't know if an hour or three had passed, for the cool interior of the dark granary registered no lapse of time, but Malina and Yousef returned with a bolt of linen cloth. "This is our custom. Do you wish to wrap him?" she asked quietly.

I paused a moment, seeing my father as he would have been in Venetia, encoffined on a black gondola draped with mourning swags, as two men rowed us to the cemetery island. The sound of the oars rose and fell like rhythmic gusts of wind slapping the palm fronds. "Yes, let us wrap him."

But I did nothing and only watched my two companions deftly binding my father. Malina knelt and held the linen bolt with her arms folded into it like a spool. Yousef, no longer afraid of him, unwound a portion of cloth, tucked it neatly at the feet, then wound it around my father, enshrouding him all the way to the head, then back again to the feet, then once more to the head, shearing the cloth there neatly with the knife I lent him from the sheath at my waist and tying it off.

In the early evening we put him on a cedar cart to carry him out into the desert. Yousef hitched one of the mules and tossed two shovels next to the corpse, and along with the village gravedigger we wended our way through the narrow streets toward the main gate. Townsfolk hurried inside their dwellings and latched their shutters when they saw us approach. Some murmured prayers. The lopsided wooden wheels of the cart clattered round and round and no one spoke. As we passed beyond the red town walls of Taradante, the sands moaned with a low gray wind. We moved toward an isolated rise above the spreading fingers of a wadi.

"Before he disappeared, he liked that place," Malina explained.

I liked it too, for one could sit there and view the whole river valley, the red mud villages, the mountains and the sea in the distance.

Malina insisted that we bury my father quickly or his soul would linger in the granary and cause trouble. "We return the dead to their mother as soon as we can so they can find peace."

"It is not our way, but this is not our place," I said.

She touched my shoulder. "I am sorry, Daughter."

When we reached the rise, I observed, "He will like this sky." The darkening violet expanse overhead met the blur of colorless sand. Dark red mountains presided.

The men dug.

We were all silent, but the shovels chucked sand and rang loudly against the stones. I didn't cry. I'd been releasing my father strand by strand from the dense weave of my heart for a long time. But the final cut was at once so severe and so small that it seemed impossible he could slip away from me as he did.

A man with red hair in a pale blue djellaba sat watching us from some distance. The child within kicked hard. I felt my father leave, and I was free.

CHAPTER 27

⁓❦⁓

Stitching Sky to Mountain

A few days later he came to the door. Malina called me from my rough table, where I sat arranging the loose pages of *The Book of Diseases*. I planned to have the sections sewn into signatures for binding. She returned to her room to leave us alone.

He stood like a tree lit by sun in the afternoon doorway.

"Yousef brought me your note, Gabriella."

"Hamish." I tasted the sound of his name, sweet and pungent, precious as cinnamon bark. "Come into the courtyard, where it's cooler."

We were shy, our unspoken words like water brimming between us.

Then sand on the tongue, insoluble minerals of love.

Sand crunched beneath our leather slippers. We moved to the date palm and sat beneath its long fans on a freshly swept rug where grains sifted back again. Three goats gazed at us solemnly.

Yousef had gone to the vegetable souk to buy onions.

We leaned together in silence for a long while.

At last Hamish said, "I'm sorry about the death of your father."

"Oh! But you know, he left long ago."

"Ah."

I began to cry and he held me. After a while we looked to the swifts high above us as they caught the invisible life of the air in their quick beaks. I took his hand, placed it upon my full belly, and said, "I will bear your child in two months."

"Oh!" he cried, startled, briefly pulling his hand away. And then he set it back happily. "I'm going to be a father." And he wept.

The desert day faded. Malina lit a lantern in her room. The moonless blue-black sky hummed with stars that cast their silver through the shadowy palm tree, upon our shoulders, over the courtyard, and across the vast dark earth.

❧

Braiding the Tides

Venetia, 1600

Our Damiana was born on December 21, 1591, in the deep of the Maroccan night. Malina attended by candlelight as I gave birth, akin to animals that bear their young in darkness, when such a grace calls for mystery. And Damiana possessed grace as well as wayward will from the beginning, opening her dusky eyes and clasping me with a keen ferocity for life. Hamish was overjoyed to hold her after the months of feeling her move within me, unseen. The fuzz of her fine copper hair shone all around her scalp, and still shone now in Venetia, almost nine years later, though a little darker, much thicker, and longer.

It was braided down her back by my beloved Olmina, whose crooked hands still bound hair and home, though we'd freed her from all chores. She spent most of her days braiding the tides, as she called it, meaning she sat where Lorenzo had once sat on warm days outside our door, recalling the past, mending the present, dreaming the future, as she alternately watched the sea and napped in a chair with her mouth wide open. Sometimes Damiana mischievously tickled her palate with a straw, prompting a sneeze, or dropped a knob of honey on her tongue, rousing her to sweetness.

The tides withdrew and returned and twisted at her feet. And I had my own strands in hand as doctor, wife, and mother. Mea, a girl from the mountains, helped us now with the household and the herbs. She taught Damiana the ways of the mountain women, and my daughter proved her talent with the sick animals on which she helped Mea practice her healing.

The Book of Diseases was finished at last and published this year. While my father could not hold it in his hands, I held it for him, with all the wisdom he had imparted to me and the good measure I had gained on my own. There would also be the pleasure of passing it on to Damiana.

My mother went to live in Padua with a cousin, for the damp vapors of Venetia brought her many aches in old age and she told me that she'd tired of living on the water. "The earth under my feet will be changeable enough, now that I grow ever closer to it!" she liked to say.

Hamish taught at university and, though a foreigner, thrived in our serene city. His sentences grew marvelously complete. The guild had finally come to their senses regarding my own art of physick and grudgingly accepted me. There would always be some contention, of course, peppering the air. But it came and went.

I possessed a jar of healing stones that I'd carried from the deserts of Barbaria, and sometimes I brought out one bezoar or another to heal a patient. Malina had taught me the distinct virtues of snake, goat, and tree bezoars. I'd also purchased from her a rare gray oval bezoar, which she recommended for all distempers of the mind and body, for it came from the belly of a dolphin found on the beach at Messa. Malina believed that all thoughts, having their source as water, could be purified by this concretion. Once, Damiana helped me in this wise, when I visited a young woman incoherent of speech on a hot September afternoon. I didn't often allow my daughter to come along, for I feared that she might contract some miasma such as occasionally rises in our city and passes in imperceptible particles from one to another. Yet so far she'd been remarkably vigorous as a child, with few ailments.

Mea also convinced me that my girl was ready after treating various sick cats, lapdogs, hens, and parrots that had fallen ill within our city. She'd even gained something of a reputation. One member of the Council of Ten had called her the Little Animal Doctor and paid her handsomely after she treated his small dog (one of those creatures that have broad ears like the sails of caravels), who appeared to be suffering a palsy of his legs. Her prescription then was simple: "Put him outside, and not in a litter either!" She spoke with all the blunt frankness of her age, which we did not censor. The outcome was good, for the little dog regained his strength and in fact led the distinguished councilor on many a chase across the piazza, which was salutary for the man as well.

To return to the hot September afternoon, then, and my daughter's first observance of a human patient: The three of us, Mea, Damiana, and I, took the long ride in the gondola that had been sent for us, to the island of Torcello, where the sufferer, Margarita, lived. I bore the medicine chest and allowed my daughter to carry the bezoars in a strong hempen pouch, the snakestone the size of a black hazelnut, the goatstone a chalky acorn, the tree stone an amber nugget, and the dolphin stone a blue-gray egg. They knocked against each other in conversant tones, which she improvised as we walked up the small dock toward the rather run-down house at the edge of the marsh. "The bezoars say they like it out here, Mamma, because there are more souls in the air! Goat says he's hungry. Dolphin wants me to wash him in the sea . . ." And she went on like this. The slanted shutters of the house rattled in the breeze, and I noticed that several windows bore no shutters at all, nor were there any windowpanes.

When we encountered the young woman at the house, she was so restless she couldn't sit still and chattered constantly. I was able to stop her for a moment and determined she had a low fever.

I asked the servant of the elderly aunt (for the young woman's mother had died several years earlier) to brew the inner white willow bark I removed from the chest. Then Mea showed Damiana how to fold a cloth for the young woman's forehead, for I planned to administer the beneficial tea as both drink and compress. But we had to stop her pacing first.

Damiana said to her, "Do you want to see my stones, which were got from the bellies of animals and a tree?"

This stopped Margarita in her tracks. "But you must sit in

your chair," I added, picking up the cue from my smart daughter.

"There are too many streams in my head that run on and on, rivulets that run down the mountains—but no, now they are stopped by the snow, the incorrigible teeth of ice won't let them pass . . . they strangle . . ."

"Sit down here." I led her to the window. "Close the shutters," I directed the aunt.

"There's too much draft in this house—you must fix the shutters and put in windowpanes." For though glass was expensive, I knew that the aunt was prosperous (from the friend who'd recommended me to her), but she kept a strict purse, as women without men often did needfully. Then I nodded at Damiana, who came forward with her pouch and set each stone out upon the young woman's lap, though Margarita's legs were jumping nervously. Yet again she held still.

"Hold each stone, then press the one you like against your forehead," I instructed her. She chose the blue-gray one and pressed its dense shape first to her eyes, then to her temples and forehead.

"You do it," she said to me. And so I did, also palming her eyes, head, and shoulders while she cupped the heavy bezoar in her hands.

"Now drink your tea."

But she didn't want to let go the bezoar, so we just waited with her for a while, Damiana sitting on one side of her and I on the other. At last she passed it to Damiana.

"Will you come back again?"

"Yes, we will," I answered, smiling at my daughter.

Acknowledgments

I wholeheartedly want to thank my husband, Bill O'Melveny, who has supported my writing with constancy and love for many years, and my daughter, Adrienne O'Melveny Jaffe, who kept nudging me, saying, "I want to read that story!" I'm grateful to my extraordinary mentors, Jim Krusoe for his boundless generosity and perceptive eye, and Deena Metzger for her abundant encouragement from the very beginning. I'm thankful for the writing group where several of these sections were first written. The following women offered critique and camaraderie: Bronwyn Jones, Elinor Aurthur, Katya Williamson, Bairbre Dowling, Ruth Bochner, and Doris Koenig. Many people have given their support along the way and I thank them—my sister Lisa O'Connor, Cathy Colman, Catherine Halcrow, assistant curator of Biosciences at the National Museum of Science and Industry in London, Rachel Careau, Michelle Latiolais, Carla and Bruce Burman, Joyce Waterman, Irene Rafael, Jill Bonart, Margit Bassler, Jurgen Ladenburger, Jane Alexander Stewart, Jeannette Rasker, Mary Ellen Dorin, Anne Spadone Jacobson, Loretta Sparks, Betty Calame, Alma Luz Villanueva, Brad Kessler, Kate Haake, Eloise Klein Healy, and the community of writers at Antioch University Los Angeles, as well as the remarkable writers in Jim Krusoe's Wednesday night writing class at Santa Monica College, in particular Dylan Landis, Monona Wali, and Zen Chang.

My deepest appreciation goes out to my brilliant agent, Dan Lazar, and to my dedicated first editor, Allison McCabe. Many thanks to all at Little, Brown and Company, in particular my wonderful editor Judy Clain, and also Michael Pietsch, Nathan Rostron, Amanda Tobier, Carolyn O'Keefe, Pamela Marshall, Morgan Moroney, Heather Fain, Amanda Brown, Nicole Dewey, Peggy Freudenthal, and Keith Hayes.